Roommates

April Gaisford

To my bestie from another teste. Thanks for taking me to Spiderman all those
years ago.
I love you, bitch.

There are 356 days in a year. May all 365 of your dreams come true.

Chinese fortune cookie

1

Contents

Chapter One

"Can I get a blowjob?"

Bruiser has ordered this shot four times tonight. I look at him, plaster on my biggest fake smile, and reply, "Anything for you, sweetie." He sits on the stool, snickering. His large body shakes in his riding vest. He rides his motorcycle out to my bar several times a week. His favorite pastime is ordering drinks with obscene names, then having one of the servers deliver them to someone in the bar. It is homophobic, but business is business. Most of the patrons don't mind.

The Drunken Moose is not officially a biker bar. Located on the edge of town, a little west of the Twin Cities in Minnesota, many bikers use it as a resting place before returning home. The dive bar attracts people for the laid-back vibe, variety of drinks, and cheap, greasy food. A small dance floor sits near the updated electronic jukebox. Several high-top tables are scattered around a few family-style tables, with booths lining three walls and a long bar on the fourth wall. The floors aren't always sticky, but they quickly get that way with the right crowd. The crowd varies from night to night. Tonight, being a Thursday, is primarily bikers. A few younger adults are at a booth, grabbing a drink after work. There are some stragglers around too. And one single guy at the end of the bar.

I finish mixing the shot for Bruiser. I am just about to hand it to him when another regular sits down one seat over. Antony is an older gay man who loves to flirt with all the bikers. Most know him by now, and several will even flirt back with him. He looks extra suave tonight with his beige chinos, loose-fitting striped button-up shirt, and dark hair slicked back. The idea hits me as soon as I spot him. I make eye contact with him as he is about to order and give him a sly wink. He grins at me and leans back in his chair, waiting to see what mischief I will create.

Bruiser has been coming to my bar for years. Even though I've never seen him outside these four walls, I get to know my regulars well. I suspect that Bruiser is gay, just so closeted from being in an unforgiving community. Even if I am wrong, with the amount of trouble he has caused in my bar tonight, I don't really feel bad about what I'm about to do. People are not very accepting of his jokes tonight. We had to kick one guy out earlier and have the bouncer step in another time. If Bruiser can stir up some trouble for me, I can dish out a little payback.

"Bruiser," I say, much louder than necessary. I pause as most of the patrons turn their attention to me. The timing is exquisite. The song on the jukebox just ended, and a new one hasn't been selected. Bruiser looks at me with delight, but it quickly fades when he realizes I'm speaking too loud and still holding his shot in my hand. "Would like to give you a blow job, Antony."

I place the shot in front of Antony. There are a couple of gasps around the room, everyone waiting to see the reaction. Bruiser looks terrified, but Antony seems elated. He turns towards Bruiser, moving a hand to rest on Bruiser's beefy arm, and says, just as loudly as I did, "Well, honey, all you had to do was ask."

The entire bar erupts in laughter as Antony grabs and downs the shot. He licks his lips, glancing upward and moaning loudly. The laughter continues. Bruiser has turned a startling shade of red all over his face, neck, ears, and even his arms. While the laughter continues, Antony removes his hand, and I lean in close to Bruiser, who is still frozen in place. I'm not even sure he is breathing at this point. I speak to him in a voice that only he can hear.

"If you continue ordering these drinks to wreak havoc in my bar, I will force them down you, glass and all." I give him a pointed stare, but he exhales and nods. "Now, I believe you should buy Mr. Antony here a regular drink and how about another for yourself, hm?"

Still stunned by everything, Bruiser simply nods. I pour a couple of beers for the two. Antony slides over a seat to sit next to Bruiser and begins chatting with him in a friendly manner. The tension soon falls, and everyone returns to normal, maybe a little happier for the wear.

The night continues on. Antony eventually leaves his spot next to Bruiser to mingle with others. Bruiser stays, running up his tab on beers instead of obscenely named shots. The only thing that makes this night different from most other nights is the guy sitting at the end of the bar. He came in early in the afternoon, seeming to arrive after work. He wears jeans, a band t-shirt, and a rugged grey jacket. His light brown hair is messy, showing he either slept in it or spent too much time styling it. My guess is the first. His light blue eyes always look tired, and he has a perpetual five o'clock shadow. He ordered a beer when he first arrived, but he only ordered water after finishing it.

He first showed up a couple of weeks ago. This is the third day in a row he has been here, which says a lot since we are closed on Monday. Even my most dedicated regulars don't show up every day. He always does the same thing. Orders a beer, pays with cash and drinks water until closing. This week, I noticed him sneaking out the back into the alley shortly before closing. He is friendly when I speak to him but never shares much and doesn't ask any questions. As I watch, he runs his hands through his hair before leaning against the wall. I type an order into our computer system and return to serving drinks.

Several minutes later, I leave the kitchen carrying a plate of chicken tenders and fries. Our small kitchen doesn't serve excellent quality food, but it keeps our patrons happy and is easy to make. I walk over to the guy at the end and place the plate in front of him. "Hey, this order was messed up, and we can't serve it to a paying customer. Since you've been here for several hours without eating, I thought you'd like it," I lie. Pity is the driving emotion, but there is more to it. I want to know his story. I want to know him. I need to know why he looks so sad. Who hurt him so badly that he spends his evenings in a dive bar alone?

He glances at me with a weak smile and says, "Oh, no thanks." I push the plate towards him, "If you don't eat it, I'll have to throw it away. Here, I'll help." I smile at him, grab a fry, and pop it in my mouth. Before he can respond, I grab a ketchup bottle and a few napkins. I hand the bottle to him but pause. "Here, or are you a ranch guy?" I raise my eyebrows as he still hasn't moved towards the food. "Don't tell me you're a 'eat fries with a fork' kind of guy? I'll get you a fork, but I'm gonna judge you." He gives a halfhearted grunt that is supposed to be a laugh and takes the ketchup.

"No need for a fork," he says in a smooth voice. He slides the plate closer and offers a weak "Thank you" as he puts ketchup on the plate. I grab a glass and ask what kind of beer he wants, adding on the house. When he hesitates again, I give him a stern look. Sitting further away but still close enough to overhear, Bruiser says, "Man, don't test her. It's not worth it." Bruiser shakes his head, taking a long swig from his drink. I smile and turn back to the man at the end of the bar as he tells me what he wants to drink. I slide him the drink and walk away, leaving him to eat in peace.

I've been working at Drunken Moose since before I was legally old enough to. I started as a helping hand. Stocking, cleaning, entertaining guest, and attracting a younger crowd. Even though there isn't a dress code, I've always worn tight pants with a too-small top. My breasts usually spill out of the top, but the tips are worth it. I don't mind showing what I have and bringing in extra money. I am rarely harassed for it, but when I am, the bouncers and owner, when present, are quick to jump in and escort the offender off the property. The owner never escorts Bruiser out when he orders his obscenely named drinks. I suspect some favoritism regarding Bruiser, but I never asked. He's mostly harmless, and after my threat earlier, I doubt he'll cause any more problems. When I turned 21, I started bartending. Then a few years later, I was promoted to manager. Now, I sit in the office, looking through schedules and inventory. I've been putting money away, hoping to buy this bar when the owner finally sells. Most people don't grow up wanting to own a bar, but I'm not most people. This place has been a second home to me for nearly a decade. I'm not going to let it go.

A noise sounds in the hallway, and I glance at the clock. A quarter until closing time. I wonder if it's the cook, one of the servers shutting down, or maybe the guy from the end of the bar sneaking out. I stop with the books I'm working on, planning to finish them tomorrow anyway. In the bar, I find it empty. The kitchen is dark. I see Mark, the cook, coming out of the walk-in. He nods, and I tell him I'll see him tomorrow. Candy walks by one of our younger servers. I ask if she's heading out, and she says she is. We say goodbye as she makes her way towards the door. I walk to the back, thinking it probably wouldn't have been Mark or Candy I heard moments ago. Stepping out the door, I peek out into the alley. There's a light at the dead end, with several trash cans scattered around. It's not terribly dirty or creepy for an alley behind a bar. It is still an alley, though.

A movement at the end of the alley catches my attention, and I notice a large blue tarp shifting around. I first think it's a cat but notice a familiar gym bag, then a foot poking out. I move towards the tarp, pausing for a minute. A long sigh comes from it. I nudge the foot poking out, and the tarp stops moving. I nudge it again.

"You can stay under there, but I'm not leaving until I get some answers." I wait for a moment, then hear the smooth voice from before. "I'm just waiting on my ride. I thought it might rain." He says this as perfectly logical, and I should have already known. The night is clear, though, with no chance of rain. I think for a minute, glancing down the alleyway. It doesn't make sense that he would wait at the end of the alley for a ride. No one can see him unless the driver is looking for him specifically. There is a bus stop at the end of the block, but it doesn't run overnight.

"Is your ride by chance the red line that runs at 6:15 in the morning?" He doesn't reply or move.

"What's your name?" I ask softly.

"James"

"Hi, James. I'm Addy."

I pause for a second, considering the situation. Then decide to go with my gut. I grab James's bag and tell him to come with me. I start walking back towards the bar door. He rustles under the tarp, but I don't look back to see if he follows.

"Hey! Don't take my bag!"

I walk into the bar and check all the locks to ensure everything is shut down. He enters the bar and follows me. I toss his bag over my shoulder and grab my own things. I make my way towards the front door without speaking to James. He follows me cautiously as I turn off the lights, set the alarm, and lead him to the parking lot. We walk quietly to my car. I drop his bag in the back seat and tell him to get in, motioning towards the front while climbing into the driver's seat. He opens the passenger door but hesitates.

"Look, if I were going to kill you or hurt you, I would've done it in the empty, mostly dark alley. I'm offering you a warm place to sleep. There's a bus stop in front of my apartment building. I'd offer to give you a ride to a hotel or a friend's house, but I'm guessing those aren't options if you're sleeping in the alley. I'm putting my faith in you that you aren't a murderer or anything."

I wait, watching him. His face is more tired than earlier; his hair is more tousled than usual. He looks sad but is clearly considering the offer. I start the car, "Even Flow" by Pearl Jam, blaring out of the radio. I quickly turn it down and offer a small apology for it being so loud. He smiles and climbs into the car. He says, "If you are going to kill me or do other unspeakable things to me, could you turn the music back up?" I laugh at him but turn the music to a loud but comfortable level.

I shoot off a text to my roommates before driving, letting them know I am bringing someone back. I don't typically bring people back with me. I'm pretty happy with the arrangement I have now. I drive into the city, heading towards the apartment I share with two others. Rosie and Megs have been my best friends since school. I grew up a few houses down from Rosie and have known her my whole life. Megs came into our lives in high school. We immediately accepted them. We've all lived together since graduation. Kendra used to live with us, but a couple of years ago, she left us to marry Edwin, her college sweetheart. We gave her a hard time, but Edwin is a good man and treats her well. So we allow it. Kendra still comes over regularly and stays in her old room. It has been converted into a spare now.

I park in the underground garage and grab James' bag. I hand it back to him as we head up to my apartment. Rosie and Megs have gone to bed already. The apartment appears empty when we walk in. Walking into the apartment, we enter the open kitchen and living room space. The kitchen area to the left is clean. The island has a few dishes in the sink, but the bar behind it is clear. Beyond that is an oversized modular grey couch, currently shaped like a horseshoe, facing the tv on the side wall. A few colorful chairs and end tables with dozens of plants fill the space in front of the glass wall at the end of the room. On the other side of the window is our small balcony, with more chairs, tables, and plants. The left wall has two bedrooms, Megs's and the spare. On the right wall is a door in the back, closer to the balcony, which leads to Rosie's room. Next to us, on the right of the entryway, is a hallway that leads to my room, a bathroom, and the laundry room. I lead James into my room.

"I'll change the sheets, and you can sleep in here. Megs, one of my roommates, wakes up early. Sleeping in here will give you more privacy. There's a bathroom down the hall, and here," I point to the door across from my room, "is a laundry room if you want to wash any clothes or anything."

He's taking it all in but isn't showing any emotions. I'm not really sure what to do anymore. The confidence I felt when I grabbed his bag in the alley has faded. I'm generally not shy, but I also don't normally invite people I don't know into our home like this. I take a deep breath, trying to muster that bit of confidence again. "Why don't you head to the bathroom while I change the sheets?" He nods and starts walking that way. I watch momentarily, then walk into my room.

JAMES

I stand in the bathroom. It's spacious and clean. It's immaculate, not like the bathrooms at the rest stops. The ones you know were cleaned at some point but only offer the knowledge that somebody probably carried in a spray bottle. No, this bathroom is actually clean. The white tiles are pristine. The glass around the shower doesn't even have soap scum on it. Even the counter doesn't have many personal items. Is this Addy's bathroom or a guest room that is never used?

I lock the door and start the shower. As I turn on the water, the thought occurs to me that I could stay in here as long as I want. I won't, but I probably could. I have only known Addy for technically less than an hour. I've watched her at the Drunken Moose for weeks, though. She's the reason I keep going back there. Something is comforting and appealing about her. I fish out my few toiletries from my gym bag, strip down and climb into the shower.

The hot water hits my body, and an overwhelming emotion consumes me. I can't remember the last time someone has shown me so much kindness in a single evening. From the meal and beer to the ride, now the shower, and the clean sheets in the bedroom Addy is giving up. I don't know what possessed her to show me such kindness, but I am grateful at this moment. The last few weeks have been the worst of my life. I still don't know how I will bounce back from this. It is a mess. I am thankful I still have a job, but how long would they let me keep it if they knew what was happening?

I wash away the grime of several days and put on the cleanest clothes in my bag. I finally walk out of the warmth of the bathroom. I pad down the hallway, pausing in front of the bedroom door. She changed the sheets from a pale yellow set to a dark grey color. They look warm and clean. Her room is dark, with grey walls and dark wood floors running through the apartment. I debate the offer to wash my clothes when she gets my attention. She's standing in the kitchen, digging through the fridge.

"Come sit with me," she motions to several chairs at the high-top bar on the island.

I drop my gym bag inside her room and walk to the kitchen. I sit in the middle, watching her move things around. "Beer or wine? Or something harder?" She is holding a can of beer in one hand and grabs a bottle of wine with the other. "Beer is fine." She replaces the bottle of wine and grabs a second can.

"This is my favorite import. A lager we get at the bar. I can't find it in any stores. It's not a top seller at the bar, but I keep ordering it for myself. Don't tell," she says with a smirk as she slides the can over to me. "Want a glass?" she pauses before grabbing one. I shake my head, popping the can open. I take a sip, smiling and nodding at her. "It's good." She smiles again, gliding around the kitchen.

She's not a classically beautiful woman, but something is appealing about her. It's one of the reasons I keep going back to Drunken Moose. That and they don't kick me out when I've only ordered one beer over several hours. Her dark blonde hair is pulled back into a ponytail. She's changed into an oversized t-shirt and black sweatpants. Her sharp features look more friendly now than before. She must maintain an edge to keep some authority in the bar. She walks around and sits down next to me. At this angle, I can tell she's nearly as tall as I am. She looks strong but not athletic, like the duties of her job keep her in shape instead of a gym.

She slides a plate in front of me. She places one in front of her and grabs her beer. Both plates have a slice of dark loaf on them. I look up at her, and she supplies, "My roommate Megs likes to bake. They're a health nut, so there is definitely some kind of vegetable in there." She frowns, then adds, "You probably wouldn't have known that if I didn't tell you. You won't notice, though. It's super good. Megs is a great cook."

I nod and break a piece off, popping it in my mouth. It's chocolatey and so moist. Addy was right; I can't tell there are vegetables in it. I would've eaten it either way. The vegetables are an added bonus for me. While I occasionally grab a salad, protein bars and candy bars don't provide much nutrition when I can't afford the salad.

We sit quietly, eating the food. She wants to ask me more questions but doesn't say anything. When I finish my loaf, I look over at her. "Thank you," I say softly. Then add, "For all of it. The food, shower, the room. It's ..." I pause, searching for the right word. "Great." My gaze slips down to the can in my hands, picking at the tab. I want to tell her more, but I don't know where to start, what to say. I don't want her to kick me out tonight. I also don't really want to vocalize my story. She finally speaks up.

"You don't have to tell me anything. I usually sleep late. Megs gets up in a couple of hours, and Rosie, my other roommate, shortly after her." She stops as if she's unsure of what else to say.

"I'm getting a divorce," I blurt out, awkward and loud.

"I'm getting a divorce," I start again, more softly this time. "She's really fucked me over. I don't have access to my savings. She changed the locks on the house and had my car repossessed." I look up at her, meeting her eyes. She is processing what I said. "I have a job. And have opened a new bank account, but there are still several bills in my name I have to pay and just haven't been able to save enough for an apartment."

Addy nods, but it makes me feel self-conscious. What my ex is doing has destroyed my confidence. I usually feel safe in the corner of the bar where no one bothers me. Speaking my problems out loud to someone I barely know is fucking scary. She finally asks, "What do you do for work?" I sigh, releasing so much tension I had been holding in.

"I'm a journalist."

"Do you like it?" Addy asks.

"I love it. It's my dream job. I've been working for a magazine for 8 years now."

Addy smiles at me. Her smile loosens something in my chest. The stress and desperation I have felt the past few weeks since I first filed for divorce have been so consuming. Her smile breaks through that. Her kindness allows me to breathe.

"Do you want to wash some clothes?" I nod to her.

She gets up and grabs our plates, placing them in the sink. She finishes her beer and tosses it in a bin, and I do the same. Then I follow her to the laundry room. I grab my bag from her room and walk into the room across the hall. She already has the washer open and is grabbing some detergent. I add in my clothes, and she starts it.

"I'll switch it over for you when it's done. Go get some sleep." Again, I nod.

I hesitate for a moment, then finally turn, and walk to the bedroom. I stop and glance back to say something, but she has already turned off the lights. I walk into the bedroom and shut the door. Once in the bed, I sigh at the comfort of the bed and pillows. Before I can even recap the events of the past few hours, I fall into a deep sleep.

Chapter Two

I wake several hours later. The smell of coffee and quiet chatter creep into the bedroom. It's still dark and warm, and for a few minutes, I forget everything else. As I blink my eyes open, my situation comes crashing back. I sigh as the all-encompassing depression of my situation takes hold again. At least there were a few moments of bliss.

I sneak down the hallway to relieve myself, trying not to focus on the halting chatter that comes when I leave the room. I peek in the mirror, noticing how tired I still look despite my first good night of rest in weeks. I take a deep breath, standing up straighter, trying to garner the will to begin the day. I run my fingers through my hair and decide to stop dilly-dallying. I walk out of the bedroom and head towards the kitchen. A woman is standing near the sink with a mug of coffee raised to her lips. She's absolutely stunning. Her shoulder-length hair is warm brown and curly, falling softly over a knit cardigan. Her loose pants drag the floor, highlighting her short stature. She looks at me and smiles, making my heart skip a beat. I didn't even know it could still react after such devastation from my last relationship. Her face is soft and round. Never in my life have I so badly wanted to kiss someone's nose as I do hers. I force myself to keep breathing and walking normally to not give myself away.

Addy is sitting at the bar where we sat last night. She looks surprisingly rested for likely having less sleep than I did. She also has a mug in front of her, still in the loose t-shirt and black sweats I saw her in last night. When she notices me, she gives a warm smile.

"Good morning. James, this is Rosie. Rosie, James," Addy says, motioning between us.

"Hi, James! Thanks for not stealing all our stuff last night. I've grown fond of my plants." Rosie says to me. The smirk on her face is my new favorite thing in the world. "Want some coffee?" She adds as I realize I'm making this situation awkward by not saying anything. I'll blame it on being half awake. I nod and move over to sit next to Addy.

After handing me a mug of coffee, Rosie asks if I want anything to eat. I shake my head no. My stomach is in knots, unsure how to process my current situation. Despite being a journalist, I'm not sure what to say next. If I should ask anything. Or tell them things. So instead, I sip my coffee, trying and failing to suppress a moan at the smooth flavor and heat of the drink. Addy chuckles next to me while Rosie seems to ignore the noise. I try to make the situation better by stating, "The coffee is delicious," but my brain misfires at the last minute, and what actually comes out of my mouth is, "The coffee is very yummy." This time, Addy turns her head away from me, trying to hide her laugh. Rosie turns to me, looking at me with both intrigue and confusion.

"Delicious," I say, my voice deeper than I mean it to be. "The coffee is delicious." I keep my eyes down, accepting the fate of weirdo that will soon be in the alley again.

"Thanks," Rosie replies to my surprise. "Addy tells me you are a journalist. Are you working on any juicy stories right now?" I look up at her, seeing hope in her eyes for getting a good scoop. I shrug and offer, "Not at the moment, but I hear there is a big story they're going to have us start working on today." Rosie nods, sipping on her coffee.

Addy looks at me, "So James. Jim? Is it Jimothy?" I laugh as she recreates one of my favorite scenes from The Office. I give my best Jim impression and say, "Jimothy is fine." Then I look at Rosie the way Jim looks at the cameras in the popular TV show. She bursts out laughing, followed by Addy and me. As the laughter dies down, Addy says, "I was going to ask if you wanted to come back tonight, but knowing you're a fan of The Office, I think we're going to make you stay." Rosie nods enthusiastically.

"Is that all it takes to get a room around here? A few Office quotes? Because I have lots of them." I smile, looking between the two of them. I realize I'm still waiting for the ground to drop out and send me spiraling down again. The weight of the last few weeks has been heavy, and I don't know how to live without it.

Rosie gives me a curious look. "I know we just met, and you don't know us, but maybe you could get to." I glance over to Addy, who nods in agreement. I say, "Well, if the offer stands, then I'd like to come back. No offense to the Drunken Moose, but this place is a lot nicer." Addy nods before speaking. "I work the midday shift today. If you meet me there, I can bring you back here. And you can leave your gym bag here." I smile at her, again feeling overwhelmed with emotions swirling around.

An alarm goes off, and we look towards Rosie, who is picking up her phone. "Time to get ready." She chugs her coffee, places her mug in her sink then rushes off to her room. I watch her go, then look over at Addy, who is also watching her. Am I mistaken that there is heat in her eyes? Are they a couple? They don't share a room. Addy looks over at me, noticing my gaze in her direction. Without acknowledging anything, she asks, "Do you need a ride to work?" I shake my head, clearing it as much as answering her question. "No, I can take the bus." She grabs her phone and shoves it in my direction.

"Okay, well, why don't you give me your number? I'll text you so you can have mine in case you do need anything."

I take her phone, enter my number, then hand it back. She types out a few things, then I hear my phone ding in my pocket. Pulling it out, I realize she messaged me and included a link and what looks to be login information.

"That's the bus schedule and our Wi-Fi login. Feel free to use it."

I log into the Wi-Fi and check the bus schedule, realizing I have about a half-hour before the next bus runs. That'll be the one I need to get on to make it to work on time. When I look up, Addy has already left the room. I type out thanks in the messages and then get ready for the day.

I arrive at work a little while later. Addy and Rosie were speaking in her bedroom while I was getting ready. They spoke softly enough that I couldn't make out anything they were saying. They were still in Rosie's room when I left. I took out what I would need for work from my gym bag, stuffing my clean clothes inside, then left it in the laundry room. There wasn't much in it, and I didn't care if they did dig through it. I probably would in their situation, but I didn't want to leave it in the way either.

At work, I'm greeted in the usual manner. A few hellos, a few nods, a few ignoring me altogether. At least that part has stayed the same. Work is the only place my ex hasn't been able to dig her claws into. I get to my desk, ready to boot up my laptop, when the intern walks over and hands me a note. He is a young kid who started as an intern last summer and stayed on through the school year. He comes in before school during the week to help when he can. I take the note from him and offer him thanks as he rushes off to the next person. The message simply states *Conference room. 9 AM,* I glance at the clock. I have enough time to grab a coffee and get in there.

I sit at the conference table, letting my laptop wake up while blowing on the hot coffee. Several other journalists are in the room. Finally, the editor comes in.

"Okay. Big Scoop Friday," he announces like this is a regular thing. We rarely start big scoops on Fridays because we don't want to deal with it over the weekend if we can avoid it, but it'll give me something to keep busy.

"Apparently, there is a group of land owners with some questionable practices. I've only gotten a couple of hints, so you'll need to do more legwork than usual on this story," he proclaims. He puffs his chest out like this is something to be proud of. I don't particularly care for him. I love my job, and he doesn't typically interfere with my process. A few folders are passed around. I get mine and open it, seeing a brief about a businessman with properties outside of town. "There are accusations of money laundering, worker's rights violations, and more. You each have a separate business to start with but keep me in the loop with where it goes. I want preliminary reports by next week."

I read over the man I have been assigned. It's a surprisingly large business for the area. I head back to my desk and start basic research about the man. After a few hours, my stomach grumbles, and I realize I need to eat something. I check my wallet to see how much cash I have. Not much, but enough to get a sandwich from the café downstairs. I grab my phone and make my way there. I check my messages and see a few new ones, which is surprising. I haven't had new messages in a while. I open the app and check them. They are all from messages I don't recognize.

> Addy gave me your number. This is Megs. I'm planning dinner tonight. Any allergies? I need to know so I don't kill you.

I chuckle, realizing each of them have now mentioned something sinister regarding my presence, despite still allowing me in. I reply, letting Megs know I have no allergies, will eat anything given to me, then update the contact in my phone. I check the rest of the messages.

> Hi, this is Rosie!

> Addy gave me your number.

> Hope that's okay.

> I enjoyed chatting with you this morning.

> Hope you come back tonight.

So, Rosie likes to send a lot of messages. Usually, that would irritate me, but I don't mind it at all from her. I reply and let her know I'm glad she has my number and that I'll be there tonight. Then I update her contact too. The last message is from Addy.

> I get off work at 4. If you can't be at the Drunken Moose by then, I can come to get you.

For as many messages as Rosie sends, Addy is direct. Apparently, I enjoy both styles from these women. I text her back to let her know I'll be there by 4. I grab a sandwich from the café and head back to my desk to eat, realizing there are only a few hours left, and I'm actually excited to leave and go to the bar.

After finishing my meal, I continue digging up past stories about the business owner, not finding anything nefarious, but I didn't expect to in my preliminary search. My phone begins to ring, and I answer it immediately, forgetting to screen it. I instantly regret it when I hear, "Well, it's about time you took my phone call." Whitney. My ex. The reason I screen my calls. The bane of my existence.

"What do you want?" I ask with a bit of ice in my voice. I don't want to worsen this situation, but I don't want to talk to her either.

"I want you to come home, baby. I miss you. I need to know you're safe. Come home, and I'll make your favorite dinner." I close my eyes, placing my fingers on the bridge of my nose and massaging. I really don't want to deal with her. Ever.

"What is my favorite meal, Whitney?" She hesitates, knowing she was caught in a lie. "Chicken Alfredo." She responds confidently.

"I hate chicken alfredo. That's your favorite meal." It's not true. I don't hate the meal, but it's not my favorite.

"Fine. We can order in. Just please come home, baby. I want you here."

I sigh loudly. "You changed the locks, had my car repo'ed, and froze my bank accounts. I think if you actually wanted me, none of that would've happened. What's the deal, Whitney? Did your Daddy find out about me?" I learned last week she had been seeing another man for the better part of our marriage. As if everything else she had done wasn't bad enough, she had been cheating on me with a man she calls Daddy. I'm not upset about the kink part of it, but it was never something she told me she was into.

"No, he...." She huffed a breath, clearly upset at how this conversation was going. "Look, I'm just trying to save you the cost of the divorce. Come home, and I'll set everything back the way it was."

I didn't know if it was the confidence that I had somewhere to go tonight or just genuinely being tired of her shit.

"No thanks," I say and hang up. Then turn my phone off and get back to work. I should check in with the lawyer, but I don't want to deal with that now. It's Friday afternoon, and I have plans with people I want to get to know. I'm not going to waste energy on her anymore.

Megs

Looking around the kitchen, I mentally list everything I need for dinner. We all take turns cooking, and this week it is mine. Of course, the week Addy brings some random guy home is the week I have to cook. Despite the messages this morning, I'm still unsure what to prepare. I'll stick with my original plan and make a bit extra. He said he would eat anything. Guess I'll put that to the test.

Cooking always sends me to a magical realm where my mind wanders, and I don't have to think about the day-to-day drivel. I forget about the programs I offer at the gym. The nutrition. The exercises. The people that pay exorbitant amounts to not listen to what I say. I forget who I am and who I'm not and just get to be. Today, my mind doesn't want to let go. I'm overcome with worry about this new guy. Rosie and Addy are both smitten with him. I love my girls, but it's always awkward having someone else around. Even when Kendra started bringing Edwin around, I was nervous. I've warmed up to him now but miss having Kendra here all the time. Will James steal one of them away? Will he take both? Will I be left out? I sigh as I turn the chicken over in the skillet. I glance around our apartment, wanting to keep it as it is. I turn the volume up on the music, hoping to silence these uncertainties.

After a while, Rosie comes out and sits at the bar. "It smells so good." I decided to make her favorite, chicken alfredo. Hope the new guy likes it. "Addy just texted and said they'll be here in 15," Rosie adds, stealing a cucumber slice from my salad. I give her an evil eye but don't care. She chuckles at me, keeping an eye on me. She knows all of my insecurities. It's one of the reasons I clicked with them so well in high school. They aren't as overcome with them as I am, but they still accept me for who I am. We remain silent until the door opens, and Addy walks in with the stranger behind her.

Both are smiling like something funny happened in the hallway. James shuts the door and turns to face me. His face is gorgeous. His light blue eyes are the color of the sky. The five o'clock shadow on his face reminds me of a rugged cabin, or maybe it's because he's also wearing an unbuttoned flannel shirt with a t-shirt underneath. His broad shoulders and tall stature fill out the clothes nicely. I've never experienced instant attraction to a person, but this man makes me understand how people could feel that. I suddenly find myself wanting to see him with less clothing. I shoot Rosie a look, trying to convey a *what the fuck, why didn't you warn me a flipping god was walking in here*. Rosie smirks at me, and I notice him stepping closer to me.

"Hi, I'm James," he says with a smooth voice; I want to bottle it to cook with later. What the hell has come over me?? I never have thoughts like this! I notice his hand is stretched out towards me. I clear my throat, hoping it'll clear my mind too. I wipe my hands quickly on my pants, wiping off sweat and juices from the salad I was preparing, and stretch my hand to meet his. Despite his rugged appearance, his hands are smooth. I'm guessing he's never handled an ax before.

"Megs," I say, my voice dropping an octave lower than normal. What is happening to me?

Addy moves over to the seat next to Rosie. She places a kiss on Rosie's cheek, their customary greeting. James watches them. Maybe he doesn't know how our relationships work. Perhaps if he's only been around since last night, no one has explained anything to him. As she reaches into my salad to steal a cherry tomato, Addy says, "Megs is non-binary. They prefer they/them pronouns. We'll remind you if you forget." She pops the tomato in her mouth, waiting for James to react. He looks back at me, giving a soft smile.

I unwittingly hold my breath, watching him for a reaction. It's always nerve-wracking to admit that to someone else. I've been out about being non-binary since after high school, but I never know how someone new will react.

"Thanks for letting me know. I've never been around anyone that's non-binary. I'll do my best with the pronouns, but I hope you won't hold it against me if I get them wrong sometimes." I smile at his acceptance, releasing a heavy breath.

"I won't hold it against you if you don't hold my cooking against me." I look over to my girls and ask where they want to sit. The three of us usually sit at the high top, but with four, the conversation can get tricky. Rosie suggests moving to the couch, and everyone agrees. We had a full dinner table before Kendra left, but we replaced it with chairs and a bookshelf once she was gone. It made more sense for the three of us. "I hope you like chicken alfredo," I announce as I slide the dishes onto the counter for everyone to serve themselves.

JAMES

As soon as Megs says chicken alfredo, my eyes widen, and I don't know how to react. Does she know Whitney? Is this a prank? Sensing my discomfort, Megs adds, "It's Rosie's favorite." I glance at Rosie, who already has a huge serving on her plate and is adding more. Her hair is pulled back in a loose bun at the bottom of her head today, and she is wearing a flowy shirt with leggings. She glances up slowly as she plops more food onto her plate.

"It's true. I love this stuff!! Megs makes the best chicken alfredo!" Rosie adds salad and bread to her plate and approaches the couch. Addy holds a plate out to me, "Everything okay?"

"Yeah, um..." I scratch the back of my neck with one hand while reaching for the plate with the other. "Déjà vu, I guess."

I shrug and offer an apologetic smile to Addy and Megs, then put food on my plate. I grab silverware and a napkin and head towards the couch. Megs comes over with wine and wine glasses and pours some for everyone. I sit next to Rosie, who has already dug into her food. Megs comes to sit on my other side while Addy sits on the end of the U, next to Rosie. I take a bite of the chicken alfredo. The creamy sauce evenly coats the perfectly cooked pasta. The chicken is moist and well-seasoned. I glance at Rosie, who is eating like she's never had a proper meal in her life. Then look over to Megs.

"I think chicken alfredo may be my new favorite too." Their smile beams at the compliment.

We sit quietly for a few minutes, everyone eating their food. As most of it disappears, I decide to ask some questions. "How did you meet?" I say to no one in particular.

Addy is the one to respond. "Rosie grew up down the street from me. Her family moved in after mine. We officially met in school and were pretty much inseparable after that point. Megs moved in high school. They were quiet and shy and so freaking awkward. It was the best. Rosie invited Megs to the movies with us the first week they showed up at school. It took Megs a little longer to come around, but we've all been together since high school." She pauses, taking a sip of her wine. "What about you? Did you grow up around here?"

I smile at her, glancing at Rosie and Megs. They are just finishing up their food. My plate is empty now. I leave it on the end table and prop my elbows on my knees with my wine glass in both hands. "I grew up about 30 minutes north of here," I answer. "I always thought I would leave the area, and I did for college, but when I got the job offer for the magazine, I knew I had to come back for it. It's not fancy and won't make me famous, but I love the magazine and what they do." Rosie finishes her drink, leaning back next to me.

"What magazine is it?" She is sitting close enough to me that I can smell a sweet lemon scent.

"It's called Under. The goal is to expose the story underneath popular business-es or groups, but even if we investigate a story and find there is nothing under it, we'll run that too. Occasionally we have feel-good articles that don't have a hidden agenda."

Megs looks at me with wide eyes. "Oh, I love that magazine! I buy it when a new issue comes out! Are you J. Witler?" they ask, using the initial I put on my articles.

"Yep, that's me," I respond.

"Oh my god!" Megs says enthusiastically.

I offer them an appreciative glance. People don't normally recognize me, and I'm unsure how to react. The only people that know it's me are either in the business or my family. It's fun to meet someone outside of that group.

"Do you have boyfriends? Or girlfriends? Or what would you call them?" I glance around at Rosie and Addy, then return to Megs. This question has been bugging me since I saw Addy kiss Rosie's cheek earlier. I've waited as long as possible to ask and need to know now.

Addy replies, "I'll call them whatever they want to be called, depending on who it is. As for the three of us, we're in a loose, non-committal, unrestrictive relationship. We frequently fuck and go on dates together and with others, but we're also not committed to a specific relationship style. It's worked for us for a while." I notice Rosie squirm next to me. Maybe she's uncomfortable with the vulgarity of Addy's reply. I hope it's that and not that I've made her uncomfortable. I give a small grunt, processing what has been said.

"What about you?" Rosie asks. "Addy mentioned divorce but didn't go into specifics." I look towards Rosie. She looks so sweet and innocent. Soft where Addy is hard. Open where Megs is closed off. In this moment, I can see how the three work together and complement each other.

"I met Whitney in college. We hit it off instantly. After a year, I proposed. Married the year after that. It's been six years since we got married. We've been in counseling for the past four years. I filed for divorce three weeks ago. When she got the papers, she froze all of our bank accounts, had my car repossessed because her father had given it to me earlier this year but hadn't transferred the title, and changed the locks on the house. That's when I realized all of my friends were actually her friends, and I had no one left. So, I've been staying in bars and alleys, showering at truck stops, and working late just to stay somewhere dry." I stop talking, fidgeting with the empty wine glass in my hand. The ease of the evening suddenly feels heavy again.

Megs's hand moves to my knee as I feel Rosie's hand touch my shoulder. It is Megs who speaks first. "You can stay here. We have a spare room we can put you in." Before I can refuse or accept, Rosie adds, "You don't need to decide now. Stay tonight and see how you feel in the morning. Who knows? Maybe you'll be sick of Addy in another hour." Rosie and Megs snicker while Addy makes a face at her.

"Hardy har har. Keep it up, Rosie, and I'll water all your damn succulents." Rosie gasps loudly.

"You wouldn't dare!"

Despite the threats, Rosie and Addy work together to clear all the dishes, carrying them to the sink to rinse and load the dishwasher. I watch with awe and longing at the ease they have together. I have always wanted it in my relationship but never quite managed it.

Chapter Three

While Addy and Rosie clean up, Megs speaks up. "We're gonna smoke cannabis on the balcony. Want to join us?" My eyes go wide at her bluntness. I'm not opposed to smoking. I'm just surprised at the candid questions.

"Yeah, I..." I stutter over my shock, trying to regain my composure. "If you'll share, I'll join you."

They nod and walk to their room to gather the items they need. Watching the three of them move around so effortlessly leaves me with a feeling of loneliness. I almost had that with Whitney. It was great in the beginning. We would laugh and talk and cuddle every day. I've spent months trying to figure out what went wrong. I know I didn't do everything right. Despite all the changes we tried to implement, our relationship never felt easy for more than a few hours. Something always took us back to fighting and arguing.

Megs comes back through the living room. They walk directly in front of me, grabbing my arm and dragging me with them. I follow them to the balcony, where they plop on the worn couch. Their apartment is located on a hill overlooking the city with a large lake behind it. Several other buildings are around, but they don't obstruct the view. It is gorgeous. The sun is setting, leaving behind several vibrant colors. The buildings blend into the cityscape with the water and forest in the distance. I sit staring for several minutes. I was totally unaware the city had such beautiful views. I always assumed it was just a regular area, like every other city.

"This is my favorite place," Megs said, also staring out at the view. "Rosie found the apartment for us. We didn't think we'd be able to afford it. It seems most people don't know about this view. Rosie seems to have a sixth sense about finding things that work. That are right."

As Megs looks at me, it feels like they are assessing me. Before I can react, Addy and Rosie come out. Addy squeezes in between Megs and me, handing a beer to them. Rosie sits on my other side, giving me a beer too. I nod thanks and lean back on the couch, looking at the view as the sun continues its descent. Rosie pulls her legs up to her chest, inching closer to me. Megs flicks a lighter and takes a hit. Looking back at Rosie, she appears cold. It is a warm spring day that quickly fades into a chilly night. I am still warm, so I slip off my flannel shirt and wrap it around her legs. She grins, pulling it tighter to wrap around. It doesn't go unnoticed that she also moves closer, her legs pressed against mine now. We sit, smoking in silence for a few minutes. I put my arm around Rosie, keeping her close. Someone turns on some music through a speaker, but the volume stays low.

After putting the joint out, I lean back on the couch, keeping my gaze on the darkening sky. Everyone is quiet. I don't know if this is normal for them. I sigh as the weight of the cannabis presses down on my body. My mind begins to wander, and I speak before I know what is happening.

"There were signs, you know," I speak gently. I can feel the others listening. Or I am just really high. The sounds are spinning brightly through the sky.

"There were signs. On the second date, she wanted to go to this expensive restaurant in the Cities. Black tie. Reservations months in advance. She said she had them. I told her I couldn't afford it, but she told me to put it on a credit card. I was young and naïve, so I did. Took months to pay off." I feel Rosie rest her head against my shoulder. The touch stirs something in my gut, driving me to keep speaking.

"She wanted me to spend my entire savings on the wedding. By that time, I had grown a pair and told her no. I gave her my budget and said anything over that amount would have to come from her. I never saw a final total, but I'm pretty sure it was more than what I gave." The cannabis has opened a secret door to my feelings, and I can't stop speaking.

"After we had been married a year or so, I started working at Under. I finally wrote and published my first article for them. I was ecstatic. I went out with coworkers to celebrate. I invited her, told her to invite our friends. She never showed up. I eventually left the party before almost everyone else. When I got out of the cab, she met me on the front lawn, yelling about how horrible I was. Being drunk, I started yelling about how horrible she was. We moved the argument inside, and it kept getting worse. All the little things started coming out. The trash that wasn't taken out on time. The gas bill that was paid a week late. The empty milk carton that hadn't been replaced. Those all snowballed into big issues. I work too much. I don't love her. I don't shower her with attention every waking moment of the day. After an hour or so of yelling, I tried to go to bed. My buzz was gone, and I had a headache. She stopped me. She shoved me out of our bedroom, then locked the door." I grunted a laugh at the situation. "I should've known then how bad it would get. But I didn't. I didn't know."

I lean forward and put my hands on my knees, cradling my face in my palms. I rub my eyes with my fingers, trying to remove the memories of my ex from my life. Realization hits me; that night was the first indicator that she had highjacked all our friends. She convinced them all to stay away from my celebration. I can feel my eyes stinging. There were other times when friends didn't show up. Other times, she locked me out of various rooms in the house, bedroom, bathroom, and office space. Anything to keep my attention on her and stay under her thumb. Taking a deep breath, I just want to calm down enough that the tears disappear. Then Rosie moves. She shifts from my side to wrap her arm across my shoulder, her other hand resting on my forearm. The feeling of her holding me, offering me comfort, and not judging me for my situation or emotions breaks the dam inside me. My chest heaves as the swirling emotions are unleashed. Rosie moves her hand from my forearm to wrap around my head. Her cradling me sends another heaving sob through my body. I know how weak this makes me look. My brokenness is on full display for strangers that have taken me in.

As Rosie squeezes her small arms around my head and shoulders, another hand strokes my back. Long, soothing strokes. The tears stream down my face as everything else fades away. The hand on my back continues to soothe me while Rosie's arms, engulfing me in her sweet lemon scent, provide safety and warmth. I calm enough to take a few deep breaths. Wiping my face off with my hands, I realize this is all I really need. Comfort and safety. People around to care for me, help me through difficult times and celebrate with me.

I finally sit back and apologize for ruining the evening. I look up at Rosie, who also has tear-stained cheeks. I reach out with my hand and wipe her tears away with my thumb. "I'm a sympathetic crier. I can't help it." She says, offering a small smile. I chuckle softly as Megs passes over a box of tissue. I take one and wipe Rosie's face, then my own.

"I'm guessing you don't normally sit out here smoking and sobbing?" I ask with a smirk, trying to lighten the mood. Megs is the one to respond. "Not normally, but it is cathartic. And may or may not have happened more than once."

They're not wrong. They grab a large blanket and hand a corner to me. I sit back, wrapping the blanket around Rosie and pulling her back to my side. Addy and Megs straighten the blanket over themselves. One of them changes the music to something more upbeat. I'm thankful for the change. I'm also grateful they didn't push or shame me for breaking down. I don't know how I lucked into their kindness, but I'll do anything to keep it.

Rosie

I'm the only one in our group that has pursued relationships with men. Addy, despite being bisexual, has always preferred women. Megs never tries to find a relationship. Megs said they're asexual and like what the three of us have going on and don't want anything else. So that leaves me alone in the men department.

I've never seen a man break down the way James just did. It was surprisingly refreshing. The men I've been with before were all macho and bottled their feelings up. Even after the breakups, they never showed many emotions. Clearly, I've been going after the wrong men.

Megs is chatting idly with Addy. James is trying to pay attention, but I don't bother. We have returned to our earlier position, me leaning into his side, stealing his warmth. The evening has cooled off more than I anticipated, leaving my clothes ineffective against the chill. The flannel he gave me is still wrapped around my body, along with the blanket Megs grabbed. With these extra layers and his body heat, I am content and don't care to stay involved in the conversation.

I let out a long sigh, staring out at the view. James places a small kiss on the top of my head. I snake my arm around his middle, holding onto him. Cannabis usually makes me cuddlier, even more so than usual. I love cuddling. James is an excellent cuddler. At the least, he's cuddling well with me. I've never been shy about cuddling with someone, no matter how soon after I've met them. If they are okay with cuddling, then I'm turning them into a burrito, with me being the tortilla. I giggle against James, enjoying the high from smoking and the thought of being a burrito shell. After a few minutes, the warmth of his body and the extra layers consumes me. I close my eyes, listening to his steady breathing, my friends' light chatter and laughter, and sounds from the city beyond. I drift off, the feeling of bliss overpowering my ability to stay awake and in the present. As my consciousness fades into slumber, I have a strong sense that James belongs with us. It's the same feeling I had when Megs moved to town and when I found this apartment. I don't know what the future will bring, but I'm confident it will include James.

Addy

The sun is down entirely. Megs and I stopped talking a few minutes ago. Rosie is asleep on James, who seems spaced out but content. He probably feels better after letting out his emotions earlier. Megs really hit the nail on the head when they said sobbing after smoking is cathartic. I haven't cried like that in a long time, but I do remember how good it can feel after a difficult period.

It's time to head inside. It's getting colder, and I still have to work tomorrow. I stand up, pulling the blanket with me to fold. James and Megs blink their eyes several times, returning to the present. I sit the blanket down and move to Rosie, waking her up. James is still confused by my sudden movements and shakes Rosie more.

"Nooooooo. I'll just stay here." Rosie grumbles sleepily.

"I can help you," James states, shifting like he might pick her up.

"Hm, I need to stretch first."

Rosie stands, raising her arms over her hand. Despite the loose shirt she's wearing, it's short and shows off her stomach's soft, flat planes. Her belly button pokes out just above her leggings. My core is flooded with heat, and I want to kiss it. My eyes slide up her petite body, intending to look at her face but pause at her breasts. She ditched the bra after work. The shirt covers her hard nipples, leaving little to the imagination. Knowing how they look, it isn't hard for me to remember what exactly is under the shirt. Another wave of heat crashes through my body. Before I can look at Rosie's face, I notice James staring at her with the same intensity. It's no surprise that he is attracted to Rosie. She's fucking adorable and kind, to boot. What's not to want? I glance at Megs, who looks exasperated.

"Okay, horn dogs. Let's get inside. This bitch is cold." They state, pointing at themselves. Rosie and I chuckle while Megs flaps their hands in a shooing motion to get us to move.

"I'm not....It wasn't....I...no" James looks terrified that he was caught staring.

"It's okay. We all know Rosie is the attractive one." I offer. Rosie smiles and shrugs at him, handing his shirt back.

We all finally get inside. Megs offers to show James to the spare room with the Jack and Jill bathroom. I follow Rosie past my room to the bathroom that we share. I shut the bathroom door, expecting her to start brushing her teeth or washing her face. When I turn back towards her, she has her hair down and is rubbing her fingers through it. Her face is lifted towards the ceiling, pushing her breasts out. Her nipples are still stiff from the cold outside. I groan loudly at her.

"Fuck, Rosie. What are you doing?"

I glide towards her and place my hands on her hips. My hands slide up her sides, dragging her shirt up. A small gasp escapes her lips as my thumbs slide under her breast. I glance at her soft mouth, rubbing my thumbs over her nipples. Despite knowing her for nearly two decades and fucking her regularly, I never tire of being with Rosie. I lean down, placing my lips over her nipple. I lick my tongue across it, then suck it as I pull away, stretching her breast. Her hands drop down to my shoulders. Her fingers slip into my hair as I move to the other nipple. Instead of licking this one, I nibble on it, causing her to moan and press her body into me.

"My dirty little minx."

I whisper my nickname for her as I kiss her neck, moving up to her jaw. My hands slide down, cupping her ass. I hold her close to my body as my lips finally reach hers. I don't kiss her right away. My lips hover just above hers. I can feel her soft flesh brush against mine occasionally. Our breath mingles together. I sway my lips against hers, teasing her, not giving her what she wants. Her fingers are still in my hair. She presses them against my head, trying to bring me closer. The height difference between us gives me the advantage in this situation. I leave one hand firmly cupped on her ass, the other slides up her back, across her shoulders, and firmly grasp the back of her neck.

"Tell me, little minx, did cuddling with him get you all riled up?" I whisper against her lips. She closes her eyes and nods.

"Do you need a release? Do you want me to fuck you?" I squeeze her ass to emphasize my question.

"Yes, Addy. Yes, please," she begs breathily.

I crash my lips into her, giving her the kiss she desperately desires. I love when she begs me. I kiss her firmly but keep my lips together. I pull back from the kiss, tightening my grip on the back of her neck. She lets out a small gasp as I lean back and look at her. Her deep brown eyes move up to mine. Her tongue slides over her slightly swollen lips. Heat sinks into my core, causing my pussy to clench in anticipation. She's waiting for me to give her instructions. She's so good at following rules. She can occasionally be bratty, but she's entirely submissive right now.

"Go to your room. Take off your clothes. And wait for me."

She nods and runs off to her room. I know she'll be waiting for me once I get into her room. I step into my room, changing out of my clothes. I grab my strap-on harness. Normally, I prefer to focus on her when she's this submissive, but I'm also very worked up and want to handle both of us simultaneously. I grab the double-ended dildo, ensuring I have the proper attachment for the strap-on. I grab a long kimono to wrap around me, knowing we have company not familiar with our bedroom activities. I walk down to Rosie's room, checking to see if James or Megs are around. Both bedroom doors are shut, and the lights are off. I sneak into Rosie's room, closing the door behind me.

She's sitting on the edge of her bed, completely naked for me. Her brown curls fall softly across her shoulders, stretched out from her long day. I walk over and stand in front of her. I slide my fingers through her hair on the back of her head and grab it tightly as she gasps up at me.

"You're such a good girl, aren't you?" I can feel her try to nod in my hand, but I tighten my grasp, not letting her move.

"Let me reward you now."

I push her back onto the bed, swatting her ass cheek closest to me to encourage her to move further. She slides back, leaving her legs spread apart for me. I slide between her legs, placing my hands on her knees. "Oh, little minx. I can see from here how wet you are." I lean in, placing my mouth on the inside of one knee. I gently kiss down the inside of her thigh while my other hand stays on her other knee. She keeps her eyes on me as I glance between her eyes and the next spot I will kiss. Just before I reach her pussy, I pull back and move to the other leg. She watches intently, her fingers gently stroking her stomach. This time, I kiss her thigh from her knee in, but I keep eye contact with her. When I reach the middle, I lean in close, so she can feel me breathing against her clit. Slowly, I stretch my legs back to lie on my stomach. I lick my lips, still staring into her eyes, not touching her.

"Addy," she whines. "Please."

I'm not going to deny my girl any longer. I stick my tongue out, sliding straight up the middle, pressing against her clit. I suck it into my mouth, swirling my tongue around it. She moans, arching her chest up. I wrap one arm around her thigh and squeeze her breast. I lick her lips, slipping my tongue past them as I press my nose against her clit. She tastes divine. I lick up and down her core. I suck on her clit, massaging my hands on her inner thighs. My fingers move dangerously close to her vulva but never touch her there. I dart my tongue in and out of her opening. I press several kisses over her labia and then her clit. I flick my tongue against her until I can feel her clenching around my tongue.

"Rosie, grab the lube. I want you to come while I fuck you like he would."

She nods, quickly shuffling to her end table to grab the bottle of lube. I squirt out some, dropping it to the side. I stroke the dildo, get it in place, securing the harness. I lean back over her and press my lips against hers. Her arms wrap around me, stroking my back. Her breasts rub against mine. I slide my tongue along her lips, encouraging her to open her mouth for me. She does, and our tongues swirl together.

Desire drives our actions as I lower my body so we are pressed together. Rosie's soft skin presses against my own. I'm not athletic the way Megs is, but Rosie is softer. I love squeezing her sides in my hand, rubbing my fingers along her thighs. I pull away from her mouth, kissing down her jaw, under her chin. I inhale her sugary lemon scent. I place more kisses down her neck, then nibble along her collarbone. She lets out a small giggle. I lean back to look at her face. She's always beautiful, but she's drop dead gorgeous in the throes of passion. I slide one hand down to her pussy. I spread her apart and slip my fingers in. I know she's ready; I just want to feel it for myself. I pump my fingers several times, then position the dildo at her entrance. I make sure everything is lined up, then slide in slowly. Just an inch. She moans because I am moving so slowly. She is desperate and frustrated because I won't push faster.

I bring my fingers up to my lips, licking her fluids off. This seems to drive her insane. "Fuck" she whispers, "Fuck fuck fuck." She wraps her legs around my back, forcing the dildo into her. She thrusts against me, getting deeper as she thrusts wildly. "Oh, my little minx wants it bad," I whisper. I shift around, forcing her back down so I can take over. I thrust inside her, rough strokes. The other end of the dildo is rubbing against my G-spot. I can feel my orgasm growing, the pleasure building with each thrust. Her hands grab my breast, squeezing hard and twisting in a manner that has my own pussy clenching hard. I cry out at the sudden movement. Her hands stay on my breasts, squeezing my nipples. I slam into her harder. My forearm rests flat beside her head, grabbing her hair with my hand, and pulling her face towards mine. I kiss her mouth again, shoving my tongue against hers. She moans into my mouth, deepening the kiss. My hand glides between our bodies, flicking my fingers against her clit. She arches her chest into me, her head still held in place with my hands. The door opens just as I am about to tell her to come for me.

"Shit, you two already started? Let me in!" Megs says. They enter the room, going to Rosie's drawer with her sex toys.

"We broke the other harness last time," Rosie says between ragged breaths. Megs curses under their breath.

"I don't want to get pegged." I look back at Megs, still on top of Rosie, and she beams up at me.

"I do. I'll make you a rope harness. But I don't have a double-ended dildo." Rosie says.

"That's fine. I just want to play with you two." Megs replies.

Rosie shuffles out from under me and over to Megs. I plop down on my back, watching the two of them. Rosie got into ropes several years back. She is an excellent rigger. She likes to be tied up too, which works well for me. Megs is usually down for anything which is suitable for all of us. Megs strips their clothes down to a beige binder that almost matches their skin and a pair of black briefs. Rosie is already grabbing different links of ropes. She looks back to Megs. "Briefs staying on?" Megs thinks for a moment, then steps out of the briefs, tossing them to the side. Rosie grabs a white rope and wraps it around Megs's athletic body.

"New binder?" I ask, nodding at Megs. They nod back at me. "Looks good," Megs smirks at me, then turns their attention back to Rosie, who is still kneeling at their feet, twisting the rope. Rosie looks fantastic in that position. Even though Megs interrupted us, I think I can forgive them for giving me this view.

Rosie finally puts the extra rope aside. She hesitantly grabs the dildo. We learned a while back that we need to check in with Megs more frequently. We try our best to make them feel comfortable and find the best way to do it is to be vocal, narrating our intentions. Rosie isn't as vocal during sex as I am. I see what she is thinking and sit up to take a more authoritative position.

"Megs," they look at me, "Rosie has been such a good girl today. Will you reward her with a taste?"

Megs looks down at Rosie and gives a slight nod. Rosie inches closer on her knees. Megs steps out, widening their stance. Rosie keeps her eyes locked on Megs. This is as much for Rosie so she can watch Megs's reaction as it is for Megs to feel in control. Megs places their hand on the back of Rosie's head. Rosie keeps her hands resting on her thigh as she finally leans in, her tongue reaching out to lick Megs's clit. Megs releases a tight breath, their eyes never breaking contact. Rosie continues to work Megs with her tongue. She licks, sucks, and nibbles on them as they watch. I let out a breathy curse, caressing my own clit. Megs glances over at me and nods.

"Get over here, little minx."

Rosie rolls back on her heels, walking over to me. She crawls across the bed until she reaches me. She throws one leg over so she is straddling me. She positions herself over my lower abdomen, knowing to wait for Megs to join us. Megs grabs the dildo Rosie had taken out and positions it in the harness Rosie rigged. Megs makes some adjustments, then moves over behind Rosie. Megs places their hands on Rosie's arms, stroking her. They place small kisses on her shoulders. Rosie leans back against Megs, loving the attention. We've done this before, both of us penetrating Rosie simultaneously. It's not something we often do, but it's always fun.

"Megs, get our girl ready."

I grab the lube, handing the bottle over to Megs. They take it, squirt a bit out on one finger, then press that finger against Rosie. She folds over to lean against my chest. I wrap my arms around her, stroking her back. Megs presses their finger further into Rosie as she groans at the sensation. While Megs works their finger in Rosie's ass, I continue rubbing her arms and back to comfort and distract her.

"You're being such a good girl." I coo into her ear. "And in a minute, we're both going to be inside you, showing you what a good girl you are. I'm going to give my little minx exactly what she wants."

Rosie is already panting as Megs slides a second finger in. I squeeze one arm between Rosie's body and my own. I find her clit with my fingers and gently swirl. Her breathing becomes more erratic when Megs adds another finger to Rosie's ass. Rosie is writhing between us. I love everything that is happening. Her body moving against mine. Her soft moans. Megs's fingers are deep inside Rosie's ass. I look up to Megs, "She ready?" I'm getting impatient myself now. Megs nods, pulling their fingers out of Rosie. Megs leans back to get more lube for the strap-on. I put my arms on Rosie's shoulder, guiding her up. She lifts her body, positions the dildo I have directly into her core, then lowers her body slowly, sighing the whole way down. Once she's flush against me, she bends forwards, planting her lips against mine. I kiss her deeply, tangling my hands in her curls.

Megs shifts, straddling my thighs, getting into position behind Rosie. Even though I can't feel or see them enter Rosie, I know they have. Rosie's body tenses. We pause, waiting for Rosie to signal she's okay. Megs's hands move over Rosie's hips, mine rub along her sides. Rosie drops her head onto my shoulder. I cradle her head with one hand while the other continues to stroke her back. Megs pushes again, shifting deeper into Rosie. "Fuck" she whispers against my shoulder. I look up at Megs and smile, knowing Rosie loves this. Megs thrusts again, this time sinking completely in Rosie. We pause again, letting her adjust to the feeling of two dildos inside her, two bodies wrapped around her. After a moment, Rosie pushes up just a bit, shifting so I can see her face.

"What a good girl my little minx is." I stroke her face with my thumb. "I'm going to start moving now."

I speak to Rosie loud enough that Megs can hear me. I begin sliding my hips up and down. Rosie moans loudly. James can hear us by now if he hasn't been able to. I'm not that concerned. This feels too good to worry about anything else. I continue to thrusts slowly, in and out of Rosie. The end of my dildo slowly brushes against my G-spot. My orgasm begins to build again. I maintain my slow pace, enjoying the buildup. Megs's hands move around to Rosie's breast. Megs squeezes her breasts, then takes Rosie's nipples between their fingers, pinching them playfully. "Fuck, Megs." Rosie groans at the touch. Rosie moves one hand to my breast, rubbing, caressing, mimicking Megs's movements.

Finally, Megs begins to move also. It takes a moment or two for us to sync up. Once we get in the same rhythm, the pleasure builds even faster. We're pumping in and out of Rosie. My dildo is rubbing my G-spot quickly, driving my orgasm closer by the minute. Megs's hands are on Rosie's breast, squeezing, pinching. The site of her breasts being used is causing my pussy to clench. Megs moves one hand up to wrap around Rosie's neck. They aren't choking her, just placing their hand against her throat. Rosie leans her body back against Megs. They're rocking together. Rosie's breathing quickens, and I know she's close. I bite my lip, knowing my own orgasm is at hand. Megs shifts their weight, thrusting harder inside Rosie. Their hand drops to where Rosie and I meet. With a deft movement I can't comprehend now, they rub both of our clits at the same time. As my own orgasm reaches its climax, I see Megs's fingers tighten just enough to press into the skin on Rosie's neck. Then Rosie grabs my breast in a firm grasp that borders on pain. These two motions send my orgasm flying over the edge. My hips thrust wildly as I yell out. Stars explode in my vision while my whole body escapes into some distant land of pure pleasure. Above me, Rosie is shaking with her own orgasm. Her head tipped towards the ceiling in a silent scream, her hands still clenched tight around my breast.

As we both come back to our bodies, back to reality, away from the land of euphoria, she settles on top of me. Megs slowly pulls out, climbing off the bed to remove the harness. I wrap my arms around Rosie's tiny body, keeping her flush against me. Megs unlatches the clasps of my harness, then removing the dildo from me, then slowly from Rosie. Rosie gasps, then sighs as her body is left empty. Megs returns to bed moments later. I shift Rosie to the side so Megs and I can sandwich her in between us. We soothingly rub her body, all snuggling close, needing connection to return fully to real life. We stay like this for several minutes.

"I think he's one of us," Rosie says sleepily.

I shift and look down at her, then up to Megs. Megs looks slightly worried about what Rosie said but tries to hide it. I store that bit of information away to consider later. At this moment, I'm not concerned about anything but what I can touch, which is Rosie and Megs.

Chapter Four

MEGS

Addy and Rosie fall asleep almost as soon as Rosie speaks. I can't sleep. Rosie has a sixth sense about these things. She said James is one of us, but does that mean he's like Edwin? Is he going to break up what we have? Kendra was one of my best friends. Now I barely see her once a week. I don't want James to come in and take them away. Addy isn't usually interested in men, but it's obvious he is having some effect on her. Rosie is more open and accepting of people. Though she doesn't just let anyone into our group. She never said anything about Kendra's husband when we first met him. Edwin is a nice enough guy but isn't one of us.

My thoughts eventually chase me from the bed. As much as I love being around my girls, I prefer to sleep alone. I stop by the kitchen to grab a drink. My mind is still wandering through our situation. James has been here just over a day and is already a thorn in my side. Clearly, Rosie knows what she's talking about if he's consuming my thoughts too. I roll my eyes, even though no one is around to see it. I make my way to the bedroom. The lights in the bathroom switch off, then footsteps pad into the next room. Guess we weren't very quiet at all.

I manage a few hours of fitful sleep. I couldn't calm my mind down enough to sleep soundly. I finally get out of bed and go make coffee and breakfast. In the kitchen, I start the water for the French press and then crack some eggs. I try to catch the kettle before it whistles, but I'm lost in my thoughts. The kettle screams for several seconds before I realize it. I cringe, hoping I didn't wake anyone up.

Then I remember I'm making breakfast for everyone, so they probably should wake up. I shrug to myself again, without anyone around to see it.

Addy and Rosie come out of the room a few minutes later. Addy rushes through to her room to put on clothes, only wrapped up in her kimono. A smile crosses my face, remembering why she was in Rosie's room with only a kimono. I greet Rosie as she sits at the high top. I slide a mug of coffee in front of her, then a plate of eggs. Addy returns in her sweats, sitting next to Rosie. I greet her with breakfast, then take my own coffee. I lean against the counter, watching them eat while sipping my drink. It's hot and flavorful. I always try to intercept the coffee-making process. Addy has no respect and would live on instant coffee. Rosie is just impatient and can't wait for it to properly brew. But not me. I cherish each sip of the coffee.

As they finish eating, I ask the question that has been bugging me all night. "What are we doing with James?"

Rosie and Addy look at each other. Neither have an actual answer to this question. I want a plan in place before we continue to let him stay here. I want to know where this is going. I want to know that his presence won't cause a rift in our relationship. I need more information.

Addy finally speaks up. "I don't honestly know. I just know when I saw him trying to hide in the alley, I couldn't let him stay there."

"We should ask what he thinks. Get a feel for his goals. What if he doesn't even want to be here?" Rosie asks. I find comfort in her anxiety this morning. Addy gives her a quizzical look.

"Okay, we ask what he wants. Do we want to offer the room to him if he wants to stay?" Addy raises her eyebrows at both Rosie and me while taking a sip of her coffee.

Rosie appears to be deep in thought. I nervously bite my lip. My stomach is in knots. I don't have any answers to this situation. I just want them. Rosie comes to a conclusion. "Why don't we offer the room rent-free for a couple of weeks until he can get back on his feet. Then we can reassess. Maybe we won't like him. Maybe he'll fit in so perfectly we will decide not to let him go and keep him captive."

I groan, "Rosie, we've been through this. We can't take hostages!" I say this jokingly. This isn't the first time Rosie has suggested kidnapping someone she likes. It's always in jest, but this time, James walks out of his room as I say this. He looks a bit stunned at my declaration. I raise my eyebrows at him to convey I am, in fact, referring to him. Addy and Rosie laugh at the face he makes. He shakes his head and sits next to Rosie at the counter. I slide him coffee and eggs, not allowing him to refuse. He's still a guest. I will still treat him well, even if it makes me nervous. He sips his coffee.

"Mmm, do you have some secret coffee magic spells that you use to create this stuff? It tastes divine. I've never had coffee this good. Seriously, " James cranes his head as if looking for something hidden around the kitchen, "Is it drugs? Are there drugs in here that make it so good?"

I'm glad he likes the coffee so much. I heard about his comment when Rosie made coffee for him. I'm also happy to hear she made a cup of coffee equally good to my own by a stranger's standards. Maybe she has been listening to some of my tips. James starts to eat his food. I stare pointedly at Addy, trying to coax her silently into talking to James about his plans. I'm pretty sure my anxiety will settle down once we talk about it, but I don't want to be the one that starts the conversation. That doesn't sound like something I want to do.

"James, what are your plans?" Addy asks bluntly. Well, that's one way of starting the conversation.

"Um, well," he coughs, sitting his fork down. "I don't really know. Do you mean today? On weekends, I've been going into the office to fuck around and kill time. I can get out of your hair if you need me to."

"No, James," Rosie says more gently than Addy. "We want to know if you want to stay here. If you need to or even want to." She sips her coffee as all of us look at James. He seems a bit stunned. After such a late, emotional evening, we hit him with an intense conversation for early Saturday.

He takes a sip of his coffee, thinking about his answer. "I understand that you don't know me well. And I can figure out a way to pay rent. I would like to stay with you if that's an option. I can leave if you don't want me here." Hearing

James's response makes me feel a bit guilty. He clearly hasn't had the easiest time. I probably didn't need to force this conversation so early. Although, it is best to get it out of the way.

"Why don't you stay in the room for a couple of weeks? Don't worry about rent. You can help with chores and groceries. We're not going to kick you to the street, but maybe we don't need to make any permanent decisions right away." Addy finally offers a solution I can live with. Rosie nods, adding, "We can get to know each other. And if things don't work out, it won't be a big deal." She gives him such a sweet smile. I love that about her so much. She's always so kind and gentle. He looks at each of us. I nod when he looks at me. I don't want to say any words, but I like this idea. It's non-committal and will be easy to change the situation if needed.

"I think that will be a good idea." He grins, clearly happy to have a warm place to stay. "What are everyone's plans today?"

Addy explains, "I have to go to work in a bit. Rosie said she's working on grading and lesson plans, or something equally boring." Rosie shoves her arm playfully, but Addy continues. "Megs is going on a hike. What about you, James? You much of a hiker?"

I choke on my coffee as she asks James. It's not that I don't like company when I hike. Addy is just always much more straightforward than I prefer.

"I didn't have any plans, but I would like to go hiking with you if that's okay," James says, looking over at me. He is assessing me, and his look makes me feel uncomfortable but, at the same time, intrigued. I take a deep breath, trying to return to my regular breathing pattern after choking.

"Are you much of a hiker?" I ask him.

"Well, no. And I only have sneakers. Is that a problem?" He looks almost bashful with his answer. I think for a moment. The hike I had planned for myself wouldn't be good for a beginner or someone with only sneakers. I could easily switch trails, though. There isn't a reason I have to do that hike today. Fine, I decide. I'll go on an easier hike and take him along. Maybe I can get to know him better. Maybe I'll be able to tell if there's something concerning about him while we are out.

"We can go to Lyn's Peak," I add a nod to solidify my response. Yes, this will work.

JAMES

Megs names a trail I've heard of once or twice but know nothing about. They finish their coffee and instruct me to get dressed and grab water. I finish my coffee and do what I'm told. Their line of questioning this morning made me feel anxious about this situation. I want to stay here and get to know them all better. I don't want to go back to the alley or fuck around the office; just trying to keep dry and warm. I'll need to contact my lawyer this week to see what I can do to move the divorce along and sort out my finances.

I come out of my room several minutes later. I'm wearing my sneakers, a pair of jeans and a t-shirt, with my grey jacket. I didn't grab many clothes when I left my house because I wasn't expecting to be locked out. Megs made the hike seem like something I could manage. I hope that's true. I'm not a gym rat. Not even a work-out-at-home kind of guy. Hopefully, Megs won't hold it against me. They finally come out of their room, ready to go.

When they walk out, I stare for several moments. Megs was attractive in their lounge clothes last night, but it was toned down and hidden. Now, they're wearing leggings that show off their muscled legs. A top with the sleeves ripped off shows their tight stomach and chest smoothed down with a bra. Megs's hair is shaved on the sides and longer, strawberry blonde on the top. They have a bandana wrapped around the shaved parts. The top part is wavy, stunningly hanging over the bandana. Their skin is a smooth golden color that appears natural. Maybe the hikes have tanned their skin. They grab a light jacket and their water bottle, asking if I'm ready to go. I'm jolted back to reality but unable to speak. I nod my head and follow them out the door.

Megs leads us to the garage, unlocking a small white sedan. I climb into the passenger seat. Their car is clean, without much inside. They start the radio and pull out of the garage. Once in the open air, they roll down the windows. I keep my eyes on the side of the road, watching everything pass by. Occasionally I glance back to Megs. They are content to ignore me for now. I have nothing worth saying over the radio and wind, so I stay quiet.

After a short drive, Megs pulls into a parking lot in a forest. They climb out, grabbing their water and jacket.

"It's not a long trail. It is on a hill, but it's not a steep incline. This is where I bring Rosie and Addy when they come with me." Megs offers as they move to the trailhead. A sign indicates Lyn's Peak is 1.3 miles from the trail. I can do that. Shouldn't be too bad, right?

For the first few minutes, we chat idly. I ask about their hiking. They answer the questions, sometimes asking the same of me. The sun is rising higher into the sky. It will be a nice day. The trees grow denser around the trail. Green leaves and plants are everywhere, showing the arrival of spring. Little critters flit around in the wilderness surrounding the path. There aren't any other people that we've seen. It's surprisingly peaceful. I've never been one to go on hikes, but being here makes me think I should. Without being fully aware, I say the last part out loud when Megs lets out a breath. I begin to offer an apology, but Megs speaks first.

"Our last roommate, Kendra, said the same thing to me once. I've hiked for a long time. I started around 17 when I was old enough to drive. It was a way for me to clear my head. For the most part, I went alone. Sometimes Addy and Rosie joined me." Megs pauses to toss a stick off the trail. "In college, a group of students would hike near the campus. I joined them, and that was where I met Kendra. She said the same thing during the first hike. We stuck together on the hikes, then started going on our own. Then Addy and Rosie joined. Then we started hanging out around town. One thing led to another, and then one day, she was part of the group.

"I was enamored with Kendra. She really seemed to understand me. It was so easy to be with her all the time. She let me be me. She encouraged me to figure out who I am. I wouldn't be who I am now without her." Megs is lost in thought as they move through the trail. They are at ease in nature. This is their safe space. I stay quiet, listening to their words. "While I was with her, I realized I was asexual. As much as I loved her, I didn't want to have sex. But that was where Rosie and Addy came in. They did, well, do, like having sex. So, the three of them would play together, and I got an emotional connection with them. It was perfect for me. I thought it was that way for the others, but I guess I was wrong." Megs sighs, stepping over a large rock. They glance back to make sure I step over it. With a nod, they carry on.

"We were together for about a year. We'd been in the apartment for about six months. I thought everything was great. We never had a conversation to define our relationship or expectations. I assumed we didn't need one. Then Kendra said she was going on a date. My heart was broken. I spent the night in my room with Rosie trying to console me. Addy even came home early. They convinced me everything would be okay, and Kendra wasn't leaving us. And she didn't. Not for a while anyway." Megs doesn't stop to look at me as they speak. They continue walking through the forest, sharing their story with me. I only listen and watch where my next step should be. It is as if I'm not even here; they are just sharing their truth with the forest. "After a few months, Kendra began to see Edwin more. He came over a time or two, but mostly she went to him. Every weekend, then some weeknights, then she just didn't come back one day. They came and moved her stuff a few weeks later. We got a call one evening that they were engaged. I was so happy and heartbroken." Megs pauses, glancing around the forest. They take a deep breath, then look at me. I wait, matching their look. I don't know what to say, so I say nothing.

"Anyways, I know Edwin didn't steal her. I know she chose to leave and is happy now. We still see her occasionally. But she was my first love. She was the only other person we've let into our lives." They start walking again. The trail is inclining more. It's not difficult, but my breathing is becoming more labored. I try to take deep breaths to keep it level. Megs doesn't have the same issues I am. They are silent for a few more minutes.

We finally reach the peak. The trees break, and the trail ends at the top of a cliff. A log fence around the cliff's edge has a bench opposite it. We walk over to the fence, taking in the view. It's a fantastic view. I can see for miles. Bright green trees and several more lakes fill the land before us. Birds soar through the sky. The sky is mostly clear, with a few clouds dancing amongst the blue sky. The sun is high now. A light wind caresses my skin as I look around. In one direction, I can see the city where we live, the flat expanse of civilization beyond it. The lakes bloom with trees growing new leaves, swaying lightly in the breeze.

"I know Addy and Rosie are prettier and better choices than me, but I can't lose them the way I did Kendra."

I look to Megs, taking them in. The weight of their admission sinks into me, dropping like a rock through the water. At first, I feel the pain they are trying to convey. The self-doubt and anxiety they are admitting to. As the words settle, though, the realization that they don't understand their own worth hits me. Before I speak, I look Megs up and down, searching for any indication of why they don't see their own beauty and value.

"You don't see it, do you?" I ask softly.

Megs gives me a confused look. "What?"

"You are beautiful, Megs." They scrunch their face, showing they don't believe me. "I don't know why you don't think you are." I place my hand on their arm, turning them to look at me. "I don't know who made you feel less than beautiful like you have no value. But it's a lie." I pause, then add, "And I'm going to need their names."

"Shut up," Megs says, shoving my hand off their arm, but a small smile creeps over their face.

"Nope. I'm serious. I need names." I give them a pointed look, holding my hand out as if waiting for a physical list. They swat my hand away, but I grab theirs. "Megs, you are beautiful." They shake their head. "No."

"You are strong." They take a step away from me. "That's..." they start, but I take another step towards them.

"You are kind." They take a few more steps away from me, but I keep walking towards them, my grin growing.

"You are caring."

"No!" Megs shouts as they turn and run. Well, this won't do. I chase them around the overlook.

"You are attractive," I shout.

"Stop!" They keep running, laughing as their steps lead them away from me.

"You make delicious food."

"You love your friends."

"And they love you too!"

"You are beautiful, Megs!" I shout as I finally grab them. I'm out of breath from running but have finally caught up. They are giggling as I pull them close to me. I place my hands on either side of their face, keeping them next to me and their eyes on me.

"Megs, you are beautiful." I say seriously. "Just as beautiful as Rosie and Addy. And you are worthy. I know I haven't known you long, but I can see that much in how you treat them and me."

We stand like that for a moment, letting our breathing settle. Megs searches my face as if trying to find the lie. It's not a lie. They are beautiful, and I can see their value. "I'm not here to steal away Addy, Rosie, or even you." My thumbs lightly stroke their cheeks. They place their hands on my elbows, and I smile. "You are beautiful," I repeat, more softly than before.

"Fine," they finally say. "But don't try to kiss me."

I laugh and drop my hands from their face. I take one of their hands, dragging them to the bench to sit down. I sip some water. "I'm definitely not a runner." I chuckle, nudging them lightly. They shrug, drinking their own water. They lean back against the bench, looking out over the fence.

"Can I ask you something?" They nod at me.

"So, being asexual, does that mean you never have sex?" They shake their head.

"No, I have sex and play with the girls sometimes. I just don't really want it and tend to forget it's a thing people do." I nod, considering the answer. I know nothing about being asexual, but now is an excellent time to learn.

"Is that why you didn't want me to kiss you?" I inquire, smirking, "Or is it because boys have cooties? Because I can assure you, I'm cootie free."

They let out a deep laugh, and it causes me to laugh along. I watch them as they laugh, though. Megs really is beautiful, and it's a shame they don't see it.

As they calm down from laughing, they say, "No, it's not cooties, but thanks for sharing that information. I'll be sure to pass that along. I'm not a big kisser." They say with a shrug. They look down at their bottle in their lap, fidgeting with the grip. "Thank you for saying that. I appreciate it."

"It's true." I offer with a shrug, hoping to convey it's not a big deal because it is true. We sit for a few more minutes before they ask if I'm ready to return. We get back on the trail. This time our conversation is lighter, and we get to know each other on a surface level. Now that both of us have had deeply emotional confessions, we keep things more trivial, just enjoying the company and space. It's a wonderful morning, and I'm delighted I went hiking with them.

Chapter Five

After Megs and James leave, I begin working on my schoolwork. Being an elementary teacher is demanding, but I love my kids. I work quietly at the table in the main living area. I sit in my comfy chair, wearing sweatpants, fuzzy socks, and a huge shirt. It's my favorite lounging attire. My hair is in a high bun, and I put on glasses. I don't need them to see but wear them when working on the computer. They help block the blue light, and it's just better when I wear them. I have soft music playing in the background, and the sun is shining through our wall of windows, warm on my face.

I am so focused on my work; I don't notice Addy walk up behind me. She wraps her arms around my waist, resting her chin on my shoulder. I lean back, pressing the side of my face against hers. She whispers hello and presses a kiss on my cheek. I can tell she's reading over my lesson plan. She's always curious about what I'm doing at school. I sigh and wrap my arms around her. We've never tried to commit to a regular relationship. I once thought it was just us being contrary. The truth is that neither of us wants a traditional relationship. We don't need the marriage or house or 'until death do us part.' We won't leave each other, but we're not buying into what society tells us we need either.

"I'm leaving for work." She sighs into my neck again. Sometimes I hate that she works at the bar because she works weekends. With my teaching schedule, we rarely have the same days off. The benefit to Addy being a manager now is that she can schedule some days off. Not every weekend, but she can take one off frequently enough that we can still have fun. I tighten my arms around her shoulders, holding her close. I lean my head away from her, exposing my neck. She presses her lips against my neck, placing several kisses there.

"Ugh," she groans, pulling away from me.

"Aww," I pout at her.

"I have to go." She pulls away from me, not wanting to start something she doesn't have the time to finish. "Text me and let me know how Megs and James are when they get back," she points at me as she walks towards the door. I give her a thumbs-up as I turn back to my work.

Once she's out the door, I turn the music up a bit louder since there's no one else here. I continue working on my lesson plan, thinking about my students. I make sure my plan accounts for each one, adding in certain activities this week, while other activities can wait until a later time. I've always wanted kids of my own. Although, being a teacher, I think one kid is probably okay. Some kids are downright scary. I can't actually conceive with Megs or Addy. They would support me if I said I wanted to have kids. Neither of them really cares if they do or not. We've never expressly talked about that, either. As much as we talk, we skip over things that would traditionally be important. Whatever we are doing, though, works for us, and that's all that matters.

I finish my work, glad to finish it this early on a Saturday. I walk over to the couch, turning on the tv. With no one else here, I watch some of my romcoms. Addy prefers horror flicks, while Megs likes a lot of sci-fi. I like those too, but sometimes I want a funny love story with a happy ending. I start up one of my favorites, snuggling into the couch. I grab a pillow and a blanket, wrapping up like a burrito and stuffing pillows around for extra fluff. As the show plays, my eyes begin to droop. The warmth from the sun, the exhaustion from staying up late and finishing my school work, in addition to just sitting, lead to me dozing off.

After some time, I'm startled awake by the door opening. James and Megs walk in, talking animatedly. They seem to be in some argument, but a friendly one.

They are laughing loudly, trying to drive home their points. I sit up, rubbing my face, realizing I left my glasses on. I push them up on my head to rub my eyes again.

"Holy shit," James says before quickly walking to his room. "I'm taking a shower." He announces to no one in particular as he rushes through the living room. I look back at Megs, perplexed about what just happened, and they look back at me and burst out laughing.

"What? Why are you laughing?" I try to stand, but the blanket and pillows are all twisted, as are my clothes. I look down to see what James reacted to. My breast is hanging out of the collar of my shirt. Apparently, I got too comfortable in my pillow and blanket burrito. I tug my shirt collar, adjusting it to cover everything back up.

"I guess he'll be taking a cold shower now." Megs laughs at me more, wiping their face. I roll my eyes, asking how their trip was. They tell me about the hike and the conversation they had about Kendra. I'm relieved that Megs was able to share their story with James. Maybe that will help him understand some of their fears and anxiety. Hopefully, James knowing Megs's story will make the next couple of weeks easier while we work out what things are with him. There is an attraction between us, all of us. Even Megs seems to be affected positively by his presence. Maybe they aren't physically attracted to him the way Addy and I are, but Megs definitely has something happening.

I walk to the bedroom, planning to change into a shirt that won't showcase my breasts. I send a text to Addy while I'm at it.

> *Megs and James just got back. They were play fighting when they walked in. Seems like a good sign.*

> *Also, James saw my left breast.*

> *Have a great night!*

> *Loooove youuuuu.*

I giggle, knowing it will drive her nuts if I don't reply for a while. I leave my phone on my nightstand, grabbing a shirt from my dresser to put on. Before I even have the new shirt on, I hear my phone chime, then chime again. And several more times. I grab it, already smiling, knowing what Addy will say.

> *Your left breast?!?!*

> *Just the left one?!?!*

> *What about the right? Because that one's bigger.*

> *How?*

> *Rosie!!*

> *Rose Lucille Stewart! Tell me now!!*

> *Dammit*

I toss the phone back on the nightstand. I walk back towards the living room to plop down on the couch. Megs already disappeared to their room. I'm sure Addy will text them to get details of what happened. They won't be able to answer with Megs getting in the shower. Addy will stew at work trying to figure out why James saw my breast. Serves her right for kissing my neck and then leaving for work. I giggle at myself, starting my romcom over. I don't turn myself into a pillow burrito but cover up, getting comfortable on the couch.

Addy

I cannot believe Rosie sent those texts to me then ghosted me. Oh, I am going to get her back for that. Megs too. They never responded when I asked them about it. I don't know what happened, but I really want to. I'm not concerned at all. I know Rosie is a big girl. Megs would absolutely beat James if he stepped out of line. But Rosie just sent those messages to mess with me. Unfortunately, it's working. I need to know how he saw her breasts. Now, I will be stuck thinking about her breasts all night. I guess there are worse things to think about for several hours.

I pass around the bar area, checking in on guests. It's relatively busy tonight. I always prefer busier nights. Time passes faster on those nights. Many of the regulars are here. It doesn't escape me that the seat at the end of the bar remains empty. I'm glad he's at our apartment and won't be sleeping in the alley tonight. There is rain in the forecast. That information doesn't keep me from missing him, though. We need to find a way for him to get into the apartment. We can ensure his schedule will allow us to be there when he needs to be. I remind myself to bring it up later, even though I'll likely forget. At that moment, I'm flagged by a customer a few seats down. I walk down to where Bruiser is sitting, asking what he wants. He hasn't ordered any obscenely named drinks since the other night. I'm delighted about that.

Bruiser orders another beer. "I noticed that guy that's been sitting at the end hasn't been around lately." He nods in the direction of the seat I am observing.

"Oh yeah?" I respond as I pour his drink.

"Yep. It's almost like he found somewhere better to be." Bruiser raises his eyebrows at me. I assess him for a minute before slowly sliding his beer to him. Could he know the guy at the end of the bar is at my apartment right now? No, he's just speculating, looking for gossip.

"What?" I say, "You trying to say there's somewhere better than Drunken Moose, Bruiser?" I throw an accusing look his way.

"No, no!" He stutters through his response. "That's not... you know what. Aw man. Addy. Get out of here." He finally answers as I start laughing at him.

"I'm just giving you a hard time Bruiser. We know this is your favorite place." We both smile at each other before I move to serve another customer.

The night goes more slowly than I would like it to. I really want to be at home with my family and James. Neither Rosie nor Megs have responded to me. I'm still trying to figure out how James saw her left breast. Now I'm trying to figure out how I can see her left breast. I love seeing Rosie naked. We both slept with boys first before we messed around with each other. Around middle school, I knew I was bisexual, being more attracted to girls than boys. I think Rosie figured it out later, but she's never shown much preference for any gender.

The first time she and I messed around was after prom in high school. We had both taken boys, emphasis on the boy part. It was not a good time. After our dates went home, we went back to my place. My mom was at her latest boyfriend's. Rosie and I had the place to ourselves. Instead of taking the dresses off, we ordered pizza and tapped into my mom's alcohol cabinet. She kept so much that she never noticed if some went missing. We drank and commiserated about our terrible dates. We laughed and ate. Well after the point we should have gone to bed, she looked at me and spoke the words I'll never forget. "Addy, please kiss me." She said it in such a sweet, gentle way, the way she always speaks, but also with so much fire and passion. I could never deny Rosie anything. I gave her what she asked for. We touched each other, unsure and nervous. We cuddled until the sun was up, and she had to go home. I was positive I had ruined everything. That, or she wouldn't acknowledge it. The next time I saw her, she kissed my cheek and thanked me for a great night. That was when I knew I was in love with Rosie and would never let her leave.

I turn away from serving customers at the bar. I walk around the tables, checking in with customers, trying to clear my head. I'm primarily successful for a while on the floor, but the bartender calls out and says one of the kegs needs to be replaced. I tell him I'll take care of it and walk towards the back to make the swap. As I'm walking, I begin to think of Megs. They were so shy when they first came to our school. Rosie was positive they needed to be with us. In hindsight, she was right. I was hesitant to add another person, especially what we thought was another girl, to our group. The summer after we all graduated from high school, we were together constantly. That was when Megs told us they were nonbinary. When I realized they had felt safe enough to share their truth with us, I knew I loved them, too. They told us they were nonbinary and wanted us to use they/them pronouns. Rosie agreed enthusiastically. I looked at them far more seriously than I meant to. I could tell I threw Megs off with my look alone, but

I couldn't help it. I said, "I love you." Rosie gasped, and Megs just stared at me. That summer was the first time I slept with Megs, and a few weeks later, all three of us played together. Since then, we've been fine-tuning our process, learning what each other likes.

I get the keg replaced and finish out my shift. I manage to stay focused, for the most part. Rosie's left titty continues to plague my thoughts. When my shift ends and everything is cleaned, I get in my car to leave. Again, Rosie's breast is all that is in my mind. After what the three of us did last night, one would think I wouldn't be this obsessed. Rosie does have really great tits, though.

My favorite time is when she ties them up. In the last few years, we've begun to explore our kinks. With Megs being asexual, they tend to help with ours. It's a mutually beneficial situation. They get to participate in our playtime, and we get the benefit of a person that's not all worked up. I realized my kinks are primal and dominating. I love to be in charge and control things. Rosie likes to be tied up and to tie others up. I don't like being tied, which is where Megs comes in. Rosie is very good at being submissive. The three of us have found an excellent pattern to make the experience pleasurable for all of us.

I park my car in the garage and realize I was zoned out for the entire drive, daydreaming about our kinks. I need to go take a cold shower. An icy shower. I shove out of the car with a sigh, heading towards the apartment. I'm unsure if I'm nervous or excited to see what everyone is doing when I get in, but I'm definitely worked up. I unlock the door and move in slowly. All the lights are off. There is a soft glow over the main living area from the tv. Whatever show they were watching ended. The tv is on the home page of the streaming service they were using. I pad towards the couch, realizing they are still there. James is in the middle. His legs are propped up on the coffee table, his head tipped over Rosie's. Rosie has her head on his shoulder, curled up around his side, much like she was last night. Her blanket is also wrapped across his chest. I'm surprised to see Megs is still on the couch too. They are lying on the long side of the sofa beside James. While they aren't cuddled next to him, their hand is on James's. I wonder if they did that after he fell asleep. I move around the end, pulling a blanket over Megs.

I grab the remote and turn the tv off. I don't want to disturb any of them. They seem peaceful. I take a quick, freezing shower, then go to bed myself. It's been a long day, but I feel good about how it went.

Chapter Six

Four large cardboard boxes have been staring at me in my workspace all day.

This Thursday is not going the way I had planned.

The weekend was terrific. After the hike, Rosie, Megs, and I watched movies all afternoon. We watched Rosie's romcom. Then Megs had a new indie Sci-Fi film they wanted to watch. The movie wasn't my favorite, but the company was. I convinced them to end the night with Die Hard. I know it's a Christmas movie, but I could watch it every day. It's one of my favorites. We fell asleep like that.

Sunday was similar. We talked. We ate. They read for a bit while I did some research. I helped with some chores. Surprisingly because I wanted to. They didn't ask for help. I wanted to. I wanted to not only show my appreciation for letting me stay there but also to make things easier for them. I wanted to lessen their burdens. I had once felt that way for Whitney. She took advantage of me. I ended up doing most of the chores, much to her chagrin. I never did them right. Nothing was ever enough for her. It's not the same with Rosie, Megs, and Addy. They were thankful for my help. Even though I don't know them well, they will always be grateful for the support.

We've even managed to fall into a seamless routine during the week. My schedule fits in well with their established one. I'm not in the way while they are getting ready. In the evenings, dinner and clean-up go smoothly. Sometimes we would sit around chatting; other times, we would watch tv. Whatever we did, it always felt natural, like this is supposed to be happening. Thinking about it drags up so many emotions. I'm sad that I never felt anything like this with my parents, Whitney, or any other roommates. I'm angry that I didn't know this was real. I didn't know I could find this when it's been here the whole time. I'm elated that I get this now. Even if it doesn't last, at least I get to enjoy this bliss for a bit. I'm also terrified of losing it. With my divorce so messy, I don't want to drag my new friends into it, but I don't want to give them up for anything.

And now there are boxes. In my workspace.

The four boxes were dropped off this morning. I was out of the office, researching the landowner story the magazine is preparing to run. When I got back, they were waiting at the front desk. They sent me up with the boxes loaded on a dolly. There wasn't a note or message. They just told me they were from Whitney. I don't know what she put in them. I'm honestly nervous about opening them and don't want to know what is inside them.

On Monday, I called my lawyer. I asked for any updates on the divorce. He hadn't heard anything from her. I filed for a fair divorce. I keep the house since it's in my name; we split what is in our names and leave it at that. We shared a bank account, but there wasn't much in it after the bills. I assume she changed the locks on the house because she wanted to keep it. So, on Monday, I had the lawyer revise it. I offered to let Whitney take over the loan, not even the house's value, just the amount still owed, and everything else stayed the same. I asked when I could come to retrieve more of my things. Staring at these large boxes, I guess this is more of my items. I haven't heard anything else from the lawyer.

I text our group chat to ask if any of them could give me a ride. It gives me a warm fuzzy feeling to think about being included in the group chat when I open it. I've been in group chats before, but there's something special about this one. Megs says they can come get me. They get off work about the same time I do. I glance at the clock, seeing it's almost time to meet them. I load them on the dolly and walk down to the sidewalk. I only wait for a few minutes when Megs pulls up. They get out to help me load the boxes. I'm concerned they won't fit, but Megs gets them all in their tiny car. I return the dolly, then climb into their vehicle. We start the drive in silence.

"What do you think is in them?" Megs asks after several minutes.

"I hope it's just my clothes and a few valuables still intact."

"Do you think your ex would break them?"

"Yes," I stare out the window, unwilling to think about the large boxes taking up the rest of the car.

We finally arrive at the apartment. Megs and I make two trips, carrying one box at a time due to the size. We take them back to the room I have been staying in. Unlike Addy's room, this room is bright. Windows face the same direction as the main room window. Large curtains block the sun, but they are open now. The dark floors match the rest of the apartment, along with the bare white walls. There are a couple of faded spots where pictures or decorations used to hang. The bed has a modern, light-colored wood frame and currently has white sheets. There is a small desk that looks like it's from Ikea between the bed and the door to the bathroom. A small closet is next to the bathroom. The wall opposite the bed is bare. Once, a tv was mounted, but all the hardware has been removed. Even with minimal decorations, I feel comfortable in this space.

I stand in the room, staring at the boxes stacked against the end of the bed. Megs walks in, handing me a pair of scissors. They ask if I want any help, but I decline. Being uncertain about what I will find, I don't want to expose them to anything Whitney might have put in them. One box sounds as if it contains broken glass. My hopes are not high that my things have been packed properly. Megs squeezes my shoulder, letting me know they'll be in the kitchen if I need help. Rosie comes into the apartment. Megs leaves, then they start speaking softly. They are too far away to discern what is being said. I imagine Megs is telling Rosie how moody I am and to give me space.

With a deep sigh, I step to the closest box and cut it open. I have chosen the right one to start with because this one has a note on top. I recognize Whitney's handwriting on the outside. I open the envelope to find three small words on it.

Fuck your stuff

Yep, this isn't going to be good. I pull the first items out, realizing it's my clothes. Just before I release a sigh of relief, I grab a shirt, but I am holding the wrong part in my hand. I shift it around, lifting it up. I curse out loud. The shirt has been shredded. It wouldn't be so bad if I were into fringe and things with holes. But I'm not. I toss it to the side and grab another garment. Shredded. I grab some pants. They aren't shredded, but the crotch has been cut out. I go through the rest of the clothes, cursing and tossing pieces to the side. My anger is rising. At least half of my wardrobe was still at the house. Several thousand dollars of clothes, ruined by my ex.

I'm breathing heavily, cursing, and throwing shredded clothes around the room. I notice movement out of the corner of my eye. Megs is standing in the doorway, but Rosie is already in the room, moving towards me. Before I can react, her arms are wrapped around my middle, her body pressed against my back. I hang my head, tossing the last garment in my hand to the floor. Rosie tightens her grip around my stomach. I place my hands on top of her arms. The clothes are scattered around the room. It's a startling display of rage. I try to take a deep breath, but it's stuttered by my rage and hurt. Rosie's hands move across my chest, covering more of my body.

"I'm sorry," she whispers.

I struggle to think of something to say. It's not Rosie's fault. She shouldn't be apologizing to me. She didn't ruin my clothes. Then it hits me that there are still three more boxes to go through. If Whitney did this to my clothes, what did she do to the rest of my things? My mind starts racing through all the valuables I had left in the house, imagining what those things look like now. I'm frozen in place. I can't move. I can't face those boxes. This may be a mistake. Maybe things with Whitney weren't that bad. Maybe it isn't better to leave her. Maybe I should go back. My mind is racing. My breathing is quick and shallow. My body is numb. My vision is fading away. All I can see is what my mind imagines is in those boxes. My photographs of my parents. My grandparents. My awards from writing. My favorite collectibles. The rest of my clothes. It's all shattered, torn, ruined, and spinning. Everything surrounds me. Its... It's broken. It's all broken. I'm broken. Everything is ruined. I'm ruined.

James.

I can hear the soft voice speaking to me. Calling me from far away. The images of my broken and damaged belongings still race through my vision.

James, can you hear me?

It's not Whitney. This one is soft and gentle, warm. This voice is happy and not spinning. Not ruined.

"Hey, you still with me?" Rosie. Her face comes into view. Her soft, delicate face. She looks worried. Why is Rosie so worried?

The room begins to come into focus. I can hear the noises of the apartment again. The dishwasher is running. Feet are shuffling into the room. I can feel Rosie's hands on my arms. She's standing in front of me now. I open my mouth to speak to her, but my mouth is parched. Suddenly, Megs appears, handing me a bottle of water. They grab the chair from the desk and slide it behind me. Rosie gently pulls me until I collapse in the chair. My body hurts. My head is still spinning. I blink several times, looking up at Rosie. She takes the bottle from me, opens it, then hands it back to me.

"You spaced out on us there," Rosie says gently.

I take a sip of the water as she kneels before me. The water coats my mouth, forcing away the dryness and bringing me back to reality with the cool temperature. I take a large gulp this time. Megs appears with some medicine, handing me some small round pills. They tell me it's ibuprofen. I take them with another large drink. I try to say sorry, but my voice is hoarse. Both Rosie and Megs nod. I don't know if they have ever been in my shoes, but they understand my feelings. Rosie's hand is gently rubbing my thigh. Megs begins to grab all the clothes, stuffing them back in the box. They work quickly and then carry the box out of the room. I'm unsure what I shouted in my rage or if they saw enough to know everything was destroyed. I don't stop Megs. I'm thankful for their willingness to remove the clothes.

"Guess I need to go shopping," I say with a huff that sounds more like a sob than I want it to. My voice is rough and scratchy.

Rosie leans up on her knees, wrapping her arms around my shoulders. This position has an awkward height difference, but I appreciate the movement. I place my head on her shoulder. She squeezes me tightly, her fingers rubbing small circles on my back. Her sweet lemon scent is calming. So soothing and sweet. I don't know how long she holds me. I don't know that I would stop her. At this moment, I feel safe. Still numb, but safe. Megs finally comes in, "Dinner will be here in five. I ordered delivery."

I lift my head to look at her. Rosie's arms loosen around my shoulders. She rises, taking my hand and pulling me up with her. She places her hands on either side of my face. "You are safe." I offer a weak smile. Her statement forces something to settle in my gut. It feels like her statement is grabbing hold of the rage and hurt and reeling them in. Those emotions aren't gone, but they aren't so strong anymore, either. Has anyone ever told me I am safe before?

She lets go slowly, watching to see if I'll break again. When she's confident I'm not going to fall into pieces on the floor like the clothes that were just there, she leaves the room, the door left open. I stare after her for a moment, my brain still working on functioning skills. My feet begin moving. I walk into the bathroom to clean up and prepare to be part of civilization again. Or at least part of dinner. I splash water on my face. As I walk back into the apartment, the scent of Chinese food hits me.

Megs swears Chinese food is vital to recovering from emotional breakdowns. I question their sources during dinner but can't deny that I feel better after eating the food. Megs and Rosie offer to take the rest of the boxes out of my room. I decline the offer. Despite still feeling off from my earlier episode, I prefer to deal with the boxes tonight. I want to be done with them. I don't want them looming for a future date. They understand but insist I open them in the living room with them present. I concede to their demand. Maybe having company will make it easier to process.

I grab one box, and Megs grabs the other. Rosie grabs beer for all of us. As I sit on the couch, Megs brings out the last box, and Rosie hands me the scissors. I take a large swig of my beer, then another for good measure. I start with the package that sounds like broken glass. I look up to Megs and Rosie. Both have neutral looks, but I know they will support whatever happens. I open the box. It contains several framed photographs. All splintered and broken. Several of my journalism awards are here. Those are only chipped or slightly cracked since they are thicker glass. I pull the pictures out. I consider sitting them in a pile next to me but change my mind and hand them over to Rosie. She takes them in, smiling at each one.

"Your parents?" She asks, looking at the photo, then passing it to Megs.

I nod as she looks at the next one. "That's my dad's parents. I was really close to them when I was young."

There are many photos of my family, but I notice none of Whitney and me together. I pull out the awards, seeing which can be saved or aren't worth the effort. After a few minutes, I have a small stack of mementos on the coffee table in the middle of the couch. I push the box to the side, sliding another to open. I cut open the top, seeing it's all clothes. I only lift the first shirt to confirm it is shredded like the other. I slide that box over, not bothering to remove any more of the contents, moving the final one in front of me.

I hesitate, taking a deep breath. I feel Rosie's hand stroking my back. I glance back at her. She offers a kind, encouraging smile. Pulling strength I cannot manage on my own from her, I turn back and cut the box. I lift the flaps, and a noise escapes my lips. It's something between a gasp, a sob, and a laugh. I had a collection of action figures from my favorite books, movies, and series. Some were collectibles, still in their box. Others were just figures that I liked. All the boxes are empty. All the toys have been taken apart. Arms and legs and heads are floating in the box. I pull pieces out, sitting them on the table. Most of these can be snapped back into place. The monetary value of the items was never as important to me as the sentimental value. These things made me happy, not rich. I toss the packaging the figures came in into the large box with the glass. They're trash now. Megs and

Rosie move closer to the box. They see what I am doing and mimic my actions, separating the bits and pieces into piles.

Then Rosie lifts up a small bit of torn paper with a part of a fancy border on it. She asks if it's important, but I don't immediately recognize what it's from. Megs finds another piece with words on it. Now I know what this is.

"It's my marriage certificate," I say, grabbing the pieces from them. Megs turns back to the box, sorting through the pieces. Rosie places her hand on my forearm, letting me know she's there. I take a deep breath, releasing it slowly.

"If only it were this easy to end it." I give a weak smile to Megs and Rosie. Rosie looks concerned, and Megs seems uncomfortable.

I toss the bits of the certificate into the box with the trash. I have copies saved on my hard drive, and I can always get more copies from the courthouse should I need one. I return to the bits and pieces, putting some together and separating others. I ask how their day went, trying to make idle chatter. We talk uncomfortably for a bit. Megs eventually turns on some music. We get more beers and finally settle into a comfortable mood. Chatting, drinking, restoring my bits and pieces. All of the pieces are in the box. By the night's end, all figures are back to their original state or as close as we can get them. I'm feeling better, and Megs and Rosie aren't looking at me like I'll break anymore. She wasn't entirely successful for as much damage as Whitney tried to do.

Addy

I'm at work tonight. It's as busy as usual. The weather is finally starting to warm up. I'm sure most of our regular bikers are still out riding. I'm bored tonight, wishing I could be anywhere else. Nick, the owner, is hanging around tonight. It's not common for him to be here. He tends to stick to daytime shifts now. He insists he's put in enough evening shifts that he deserves to not work them anymore. I don't really care. The evening shift is where all the regulars are. Morning shifts are weird to me. I like the nighttime hours anyways. I'd much rather be in my apartment for the sunrise than nighttime.

Earlier in the afternoon, Rosie sent me a text telling me to call her on break. I asked if everything was okay. Her response was, "Not really. It's not urgent. Just call on break." At least that gave me something to think about for a couple of hours. What could be significant enough to warrant a phone call but not for a few hours? I start coming up with ideas that make sense. Rosie had a student do something ridiculous but didn't want to text. Megs had a client do something stupid but doesn't want to text. James told them a new joke that didn't translate into text. Then I start thinking up crazier ideas. There's probably an alligator in the bathroom. We will let it live there, and all share one bathroom now. Our government has been overthrown by aliens, but they only told a few people who are now required to share this information through conversation instead of text. At this point, it becomes a game to think of crazier scenarios. This really makes my evening fly by.

I finally decide that Megs has become an all-powerful sorcerer. James is now a jellyfish. Rosie has spoons for fingers and, therefore, cannot text. This is the most acceptable answer for why Rosie needs me to call her. I chuckle as I clock out and grab the food I ordered for dinner. I head back to the break room and settle in with my dinner. I grab my phone and call Rosie. As soon as she picks up, I start speaking.

"Okay. Don't worry. I've already figured it out. Megs finally mastered wizardry. James is a jellyfish in the bathroom, and you have spoons for fingers."

"What in the actual fuck, Addy?" Rosie sounds confused, but I'm sure it's just because she's so impressed with my deduction skills.

"The reason you wanted me to call instead of texting to tell me the problem. You have spoon fingers. Spoongers? Fingoons? What are we calling them?" I know she can't see me, but I'm still smiling. I hear her laughing on the other end of the phone.

"Addy," she pauses as if unsure what to say. "If I didn't know you so well, I'd send you to the psych ward. Why would James be a jellyfish?"

"Really, Rosie? I figure out that Megs has superpowers, and you have spoongers, and THAT is what you want to know? I don't know. I didn't turn him into a jellyfish! Ask Megs!"

Rosie chuckles into the phone. "You are something special, Addy."

"Aww, I love you too." I croon, taking a bite of my food. "So, what's up for real? Am I right?" I ask, shoving more food in my mouth.

"Don't talk with food in your mouth," Rosie instructs. "No, you weren't right, doofus. You know those boxes James asked for help bringing home? Don't answer that. I can hear you chewing already. He opened them when he got home." Rosie keeps talking, not giving me a chance to say anything. Fine by me; I'll keep eating my chicken tenders.

"His ex packed up a bunch of his shit and delivered it today so he wouldn't have to return to his house. She ruined all of his stuff, Addy. It was bad. The clothes were cut and ripped. She cut the crotch out of every pair of pants. She smashed some photos and shoved them in a box with some awards he had. There was broken glass and wood from the frames all over in the box." I don't really know how to process all of this information. It sounds like it was pretty bad, based on Rosie's tone describing the situation. I listen as she continues, unsure how it could actually get worse. "He had all of these action figures from movies and stuff. His ex opened every box and ripped the arms and heads, and legs off every single one. If it had a part that could come off, she took it off and threw it in the box. We've been working on piecing them back together but aren't finished yet."

She pauses, taking a drink. I let what she has just told me sink in. "So she ruined all of his stuff?"

"Yep, all of it," Rosie confirms. "But Addy, that's not even the worst part. He had an emotional breakdown after opening the first box. He was yelling and screaming at all of his clothes. Then he just froze. I tried to comfort him, but he didn't move. Didn't respond. His eyes were glazed over. I don't think he could hear me." This news is concerning.

"Are you okay, Rosie?" I can hear the concern in my own voice.

"Yeah, I'm okay." She replies more softly. "It was just scary and sad to see him like that."

"How is he now?"

"He seems better. We ate and are putting his figures back together. Maybe he'll be okay now. I just wanted you to know about it. It was too much to type."

Well, that reason wasn't as enjoyable as my spoongers for a phone call, but I can accept that. I chat with Rosie for the rest of my break. We formulate a plan to help him feel better. I don't know if it will work, but Rosie is on board. She'll get Megs on board later. Now, I just need to finish my shift and get back home.

Inside my apartment, it's dark, but James's light is still on. Rosie and Megs have already gone to bed. The door to James's room is cracked. Did he fall asleep with the light on? I grab a bottle of whiskey I keep for a lousy day and grab a tumbler too. I carry both with me as I walk to his room. I push the door back just enough to see where he is. He sits in the chair facing his desk, his back to me. Little action figures are placed around the surface, along with a box that looks to have more sitting to the side. I knock gently before moving in any further.

"James," I say softly in case he is asleep.

He turns to look at me. His eyes are glossy with bags under them. His shoulders could be carrying the weight of the world. Without him speaking, I move into the room. I hand him the glass tumbler, remove the lid from the bottle, and pour about two shots worth into the glass. I sit back on the edge of his bed, taking a long drink straight from the bottle. He stares at his tumbler for a moment, then takes a sip. I look at his figures, waiting to see if he will say anything. When he doesn't, I speak.

"Rosie told me what happened." I motion towards the figures, taking another drink. He nods at me, looking at them. "Why are you still awake?"

"Can't sleep." He answers, pointing a finger at his head. "My mind is racing."

"Then drink up." I clink the bottle with his tumbler. This time we both drink together. I stand and move behind him. I take in the different figures he has on the shelf. Some I recognize, some I don't. One catches my eye.

"Holy shit!" I exclaim, grabbing the figure. "Where did you get Master Rick?"

He has a figure of Rick from the tv show Rick and Morty. He's wearing a BDSM harness and has a riding crop in his hand. I turn it over in my hand, taking in all the details. James's smile is weak, but a light in his eyes shows he is happy about my interest.

"I have an enamel pin of Master Rick," I offer.

James reaches up and takes the figure from my hand. His fingers are smooth against my own. "I got it in a special deal from a figure maker. He has a 3-D printer and makes custom orders every now and then. This is one of my favorites." He holds it in his hands, staring at it, looking so very lost.

"Can you take a day off work tomorrow?" I ask abruptly. Megs always cringes at my bluntness. Rosie is much better at conversing like a well-adjusted human, but she's not here. I am. I look down at him, waiting for his answer. His brow creases in confusion, but he shakes it off to answer.

"I...um, yeah, I guess."

"Good. You should take the day off. I'm off. Rosie has a half-day and will be home early. Megs still has work, but they don't like what I have planned anyway. They'll join us later." I place my hand on his drink, guiding it towards his mouth. "Finish that, get in bed, and I'll be back in a minute," I command.

I take another swig from my bottle. He shakes his head at me but puts the figure down. "You really like bossing people around, huh?" He asks before sipping on his drink. "I'm the alpha around here." I wink at him before leaving the room. I walk towards my room, getting ready for bed. I put on a t-shirt and shorts to sleep in. Usually, I'd sleep in underwear, but I don't want to give him the wrong idea right now. While the idea of doing dirty things with James is absolutely one I want to explore, now isn't the time. He needs comfort and companionship. He's not ready for my brand of sex. Once I'm ready, I head back to his room. He's standing next to the bed in pajama pants and a shirt.

"Get in the bed," I instruct. I stand by the lights, waiting for him to get in before I turn them off.

"Why? Are you going to tuck me in? Read me a bedtime story?" He asks sarcastically.

"No, but if you keep up that attitude, I will spank you." I glare at him teasingly, stepping closer and pushing him towards the bed. "I'm going to cuddle with you. Now get in." He doesn't hesitate again. He crawls under the covers as I turn the lights off. He holds the sheets up so I can crawl in front of him. "Oh, no, hun. I'm the big spoon." He looks confused but drops the sheets. He watches as I move through the dark to the other side. He has rolled onto his back, eyes staying on me. I crawl next to him, shoving his shoulder to get him to roll over. He finally relents and rolls onto his side. I wrap my body around him. I slip my arm under his head while the other wraps around his chest. He lets me get situated, pulling him close to me. I curl my legs against his, then adjust the blankets before slipping my arm around his chest again.

"I've never been the little spoon before," he says softly.

"It's nice, isn't it? I think you'll like being little spoon." He nods his head against mine. My fingers make little circles against his chest. I stretch my hand back to his head, rubbing my fingers through his hair. He slides both hands on top of my arm on his chest. He finally releases a deep breath. I can feel his body settle in against mine.

"What are we doing tomorrow?" His voice is barely above a whisper. He sounds almost childlike. I tighten my grip around him.

"We're going to buy you new clothes. You're going to need something nice to wear when we all go out to dinner."

"Dinner?" He shifts as if trying to turn to look at me. I tighten my grip, not letting him move.

"Yes, the four of us are going to dinner. Now, go to sleep. You need rest, so you don't look out of place with three hotties."

He laughs softly but doesn't move or try to speak again. I continue to rub his chest and head, keeping my body pressed against his. His grip on my forearm eventually loosens as his breathing deepens. I hadn't planned on sleeping in his room when Rosie and I came up with the plan to go out. Seeing him sitting in the chair made me realize he needed someone to comfort him. I've done that enough for Rosie and Megs; I knew what I needed to do when I saw him. I stay close to him all night, eventually drifting into a peaceful sleep. I enjoy cuddling with him, feeling his warmth against my body, holding him in my arms. It's too early to say what this is or if it will last, but it sure is nice. I don't want to let go of him.

Chapter Seven

JAMES

I've never had anyone hold me like Rosie and Addy did last night. I always thought being the little spoon while cuddling would be emasculating. My first instinct when she wrapped her body around me was to push her away. Her arms tightened, and suddenly I couldn't figure out why I had never done this before. Addy knew what I needed when I didn't. She knew how to make me accept what I needed without question. Part of me wants to say the alcohol made me give in to her, but that's not true. How she has treated me in the past week differs from anything I've ever experienced. I want to give her what she wants without question. I want to make her happy in all aspects.

I slept better than I have in months if not years. Addy stayed with me all night. I was warm and didn't feel alone. As I wake up, I inhale her scent of almonds. I don't move initially. Addy is still tangled in the sheets with me. Her breathing is deep and slow, informing me she is still asleep. Not wanting to disturb her, I blink my eyes open slowly. We've shifted during the night. I now face her, my chin on the top of her breasts. Her chin is leaning against my forehead. Our arms are wrapped around each other, and our legs are tangled with the blankets. An emotion stirs in my chest that I haven't felt in a while. I can't develop feelings for her. I'm in the midst of what is going to be a nasty divorce. Now isn't the time for me to fall for someone.

But...

Her tits are amazing.

They are full, matching the frame of her body. They aren't too big or too small. I rub my hands along her back, pulling her closer, simultaneously realizing she isn't wearing a bra. My cock awakens at that. As it hardens, I push my hips away from her while tipping my face down. That seems like a logical move to make. Totally inconspicuous. Suddenly, my face is surrounded by her glorious breasts, still covered by her shirt. I take a deep breath as her tits move close to my mouth, only fabric keeping them from me. Did I move again? I am trying not to move much so I don't wake her. Then I hear her exhale slowly as her breasts shift slightly away from my face. I know it's not heartbreak, but it almost feels like it as she pulls away. The morning air hits my face again, and I want to be buried in her breasts. She chuckles, and I'm frozen into place. She said last night she was just here to cuddle. Is she going to be angry? I don't move at all, waiting for her reaction.

Her arm wraps around my head, pulling me closer to her breasts. I sigh a relief, and she says, "You can stay there for a bit." I smush my face into the fabric of her shirt as much as I can. It physically hurts me how much I want it gone. My cock jolts as I rub my face against her breasts again. My hands press against her back. I silently pray to whatever gods are listening; just kill me now. I could die here, spending eternity remembering my face being buried in her chest.

She pulls her arm away from my head, sliding her fingers down my arm. She grabs my elbow, pulling my arm around to the front. When it's close enough, she holds my hand. I look up at her as she presses a kiss to my palm. The same palm is then pressed against her breast.

"I'm not going to fuck you now, but you can have this before we get up."

I silently vow to give this woman everything I have and ever will have. My thumb caresses her breast, not daring to move to the nipple. I look back at her face. She's shifted her face up, eyes closed. She doesn't seem uncomfortable. My thumb strokes her breast, daring to move lower. The fabric of her shirt is soft, leaving me to wonder what the skin underneath feels like. I caress her nipple gently; a smooth exhale escapes her lips. Since she's always bold with me, I decide to be bold too. I shift until my mouth settles over her nipple. Addy gasps but doesn't stop me.

My tongue licks her nipple over her shirt, soaking the material. Her hand settles on my head, tangling in my hair. I take this as encouragement to keep going. My teeth close down gently around the hard bud on her breast. I pull back with my teeth still clamped around her nipple. She moans, but it changes to a laugh as she pulls back. She crawls away out of the bed.

"Aww, no. Come back," I whine, reaching for Addy as she stands up.

Her laughs tell me she's feigning being unimpressed. "No. Save some for later. Go shower and take care of that," she points at my waist, where we both know my cock is at full mast. "Rosie will be back soon."

Addy is out of the room, heading to her own shower. I groan, rubbing my hands across my face. If only the gods had worked fast, I could've made that moment last for eternity. Hopefully, something better is in store for me than just one t-shirt-covered breast. I go to the shower, thinking about turning it cold. Instead, I turn it to a comfortable temperature.

After getting undressed, I step into the water, letting the warm jets hit my body. My cock is still rock hard, phantom tits on my face. I wrap my fingers around the base, pulling softly to the end. It twitches in my hand, pre cum already leaking from the tip. I stroke myself softly, letting Addy's breast and that moan fill my head. Suddenly, Rosie appears in my mind. Her arms around me. Her breast, which was exposed when she was wrapped in the blankets on the couch, pops into my head. Her soft lips and cheeks. I stroke my member, increasing the speed. The orgasm builds low, ready to burst. Then Megs is standing in my vision. They kneel in front of me and part their lips. Their lips wrap around the tip of my penis as my fingers slide from the tip to the base. I imagine Megs taking all of me in. Then I explode. Warm jets of cum fly through the shower, landing on the floor. I keep stroking myself, pulling every bit of the orgasm out.

Megs is still kneeling in front of me. Rosie's hands are all over my chest. Addy is behind me, rubbing my back, speaking softly. "Look what a good job you did for me," Addy praises. My hips jolt as the last bit leaks from the tip of my penis. My eyes open as the vision of the three roommates fades away. I'm standing alone in the shower, relieved but slightly confused. I don't know if Addy is the kind to give praise. I also didn't know I was into it. I'll think about that at a different time.

Rosie

The school is scheduled for a half-day, with teacher planning in the afternoon. With all my planning done and everything graded, I convince the principal to let me leave earlier. I would have told him I had explosive diarrhea if I needed to. Thankfully, it didn't come to that. I kick my shoes off as I enter the apartment. Addy and James are on the balcony. It's such a gorgeous day that I don't blame them. I drop my stuff in my room then step onto the balcony. Addy is in jeans and a loose crop top. The tiniest sliver of her toned stomach peaks through when she moves. James is also wearing jeans and a shirt. Not a crop top, to my dismay. I wouldn't mind seeing more of his body. I'm betting it's a good one.

"Come on," I whine at them. "I'm starving. I put off lunch to meet up with you. You have about," I glance down at my watch, "fifteen minutes to feed me before I turn into a monster."

Without waiting, I turn to get my shoes and leave. I am not kidding about being hangry. I need to be fed very soon. I can hear Addy moving quickly, and James follows suit. I insist we take my Jeep out. I tell them the reason is we need more room for bags. James insists he isn't buying that much. The truth is I don't like Addy's driving. I love her, but she scares me when she's behind the wheel.

At the mall, I make a beeline to the food court. James and Addy keep just a few steps behind me. I don't know if I'm actually that fast or if they are scared of me. Either way, a girl's got to eat. Once we have our food, we sit and chat casually while eating. The food fills my belly, pushing away the hangry monster about to take over. We joke, talk about which stores to hit, what we need. James grows more pensive as we speak, participating less in our conversation. I keep an eye on him but don't say anything. He's had a rough week. The weekdays went well. The weekends have been rough for him.

We finish our food and head for the stores. Since we're here for James, we let him take the lead. We offer advice, help him find deals, and pick out colors that look good on him. Addy is enjoying herself. James seems removed now. He'll nod or offer a few words occasionally, but nothing significant. I watch him, making sure this shift doesn't get worse. We have lovely plans tonight, and I don't want him to miss them or feel bad during them. He's picked out several suitable outfits, including one that will be perfect for tonight.

While walking down one of the hallways, I step up to his side and slip my hand through his arm. He looks at my hand, then gives a smile that doesn't reach his eyes but doesn't react beyond that. He doesn't push me away, but I can't help but wonder if he doesn't want me to touch him. We walk in silence for a few minutes. Addy is ahead of us, going to a shop she wants to stop in. When she finally finds it, I tell her James and I will wait outside and pull him over to a bench with several large flower pots on either side. I sit next to him, positioning my body to face him. I keep my hands to myself this time.

"What's up, James?" I ask gently. "You seem really distracted."

He shrugs, and I think he won't answer. His eyes lift to mine. He looks sad but also full of longing. He seems very confused. There are lots of emotions he's dealing with. I struggle to keep my hands to myself. Touch is my preferred method of comfort. It comes easily to me.

"I..." he stops, searching for the right words.

"I like you. And Addy. And Megs." He looks down at his hands. Now I'm the confused one.

"We like you too, James."

"No, I..." he shakes his head, then changes the direction of the conversation. "Addy said we're going out tonight. Where are we going?"

I purse my lips at the shifting topic. "We're going to that new chic restaurant downtown. We've only been once but really enjoyed it. It's got a great atmosphere, and the food is good. Megs said they've gotten two new clients this week and want to celebrate."

He looks back at his hands, letting the conversation drop. What was he going to say before he changed topics? Addy is still moving around the store. I watch her for a couple of minutes. She is not someone I would call graceful. In the short time I watch her, she bumps into two signs and nearly knocks over a mannequin. Shaking my head, I look back at James. He's still lost in thought, staring down at his hands. I've really enjoyed having him here this week. He blends in surprisingly well with our group. Even though he's only been here a week. The lightbulb goes off in my head. He's ONLY been here a week. He just said he likes us. He meant more than just roommates or friends. A small burst of happiness explodes, realizing he said Megs too. They're always worried about being left out or separated.

Without thinking through my actions, I grab his hand, pulling it towards me. He looks up, not quite startled, not quite sure what to do. "James," I should have thought this through more. I pause, letting the words float around in my head. "We like you too," I say softly, squeezing his hand. I hope this conveys we feel the same way about him. His brows crease together as he shakes his head. Before he can say anything, I speak up again. "You fit with us so well. I know we're all still getting to know each other. I know you are going through a nasty divorce. I don't want to rush this, but I don't want you to think you're alone in this."

He thinks for several moments. I don't say anything else. I keep his hand in mine, not letting him go. Not knowing what he is thinking is hard. He needs space to work it out. I can't rush that. I can't tell him how to feel. He finally speaks.

"It's been a long time since my relationship with Whitney began, but I worry it started the same way. I want to give you all everything. I want to be everything for you. But I couldn't even do that for one woman. I can't do that for three people. You've been so kind to me. You deserve better." He tries to pull his hand away, but I tighten my grip. I think for a moment, processing what he just said.

"You're really in your head," I say with a small smile. He doesn't look at me, but he does nod his head. I grab his chin, turning him to look at me. "I don't know what things were like in your last relationship. I can assure you none of us would ruin your belongings like that. We're not asking you to move in and get married.

We're not even looking for sex. We just want you the way you are. You belong with us, James. We're here for you, no matter how that looks. You're our friend now."

His eyes are searching mine. I realize this is one of those moments in movies and books where we would kiss. For a second, I wish he would. I imagine his lips are soft and gentle while also being desperate. The reality is that it wouldn't actually help right now. He's going through stuff, and the last thing we need to do is complicate that with sex. He smiles at me. It's the best thing I've seen all day. His smile is gorgeous. He still seems pensive, but hopefully, he'll feel better soon. I pat his cheek, trying to tone down the intimacy. He nods at me.

"Friend." He says, his smile finally growing. "I can do friend."

JAMES

Rosie's chat lifts my mood. I was spiraling into a dark place that has become familiar. She pulled me out so quickly. She's very intuitive. Fear of losing them the way I have Whitney is still on the cusp of every thought. Whitney was my everything for so long. Even though she hasn't filled that spot in several months, lingering emotions remain around her. I'm not entirely over her. I don't necessarily love her anymore, but she's still a significant part of my life. Rosie's declaration that we can be friends pushed the fear back enough for the darkness to fade. It's not gone, but I can enjoy my time now. Not that I particularly enjoy shopping, but I do have good company.

We decide to rest before heading out to dinner. I'm grateful because I am exhausted from staying awake late and the ever-swirling emotions. I'm pretty sure I loved Whitney too hard. There are still feelings for her. I don't feel good thinking I've abandoned her. She's mentioned that a few times since I filed the divorce papers. I should have left her a long time ago. There never seemed to be a right moment to do it. It's evident that I waited too long to leave her, though.

I pull on the new outfit the girls helped me pick out today. It's been a long time since I wore nice clothes. The outfit isn't black tie or anything, but it is nice. The jeans are dark and not ripped or shredded, like most of my others. I have a blue button-down that Rosie swore would make my eyes pop. I don't see it, but if she says so, it must be true. The new loafers are brown, completing the outfit. I style my shaggy hair as best I can. It really needs to be cut. I make a mental note to do that soon. I roll up my sleeves, making my way into the living room. I take a deep breath, reminding myself we're only going out as friends. I step into the room, looking up at the three of them.

My cock didn't get the memo.

Rosie looks beautiful. She is in a loose yellow dress that stops at mid-thigh. The top is more fitted, perfectly accentuating her round breasts. Half of her hair is pulled back away from her face. Big brown curls fall across her shoulders. Her makeup is soft and looks natural. She wears pumps that match the dress and make her calves look amazing. The dress is cotton and looks soft.

Addy is wearing a tight pencil skirt. Her ass looks fantastic in it. She's wearing boots with a slight heel on them. She's taller than I am. She has an oversized button-up shirt tucked into the skirt. It's the kind of workplace outfit that would have men drooling. Probably women too. Her hair is pulled into a tight ponytail at the top of her head. It falls down her back in a smooth shape. Her long neck is exposed behind the collar of the shirt. Her lips are a deep red that sends my thoughts straight to the gutter.

Megs looks absolutely stunning. Megs is wearing pants, not in a dress or skirt like their friends. The jeans look similar to my own, dark, solid, but also hug the right parts of their legs. I can still tell how muscular they are in the jeans. They have on a long sleeve Henley shirt, with the sleeves pushed up their forearms. Their hair is pushed back, not finished with gel, but still out of their face.

We said friends, but they didn't have to look this stunning tonight.

"We must look magnificent if he can't move or speak," Addy chimes. Rosie groans. Megs keeps their eyes on me.

"You...ah," I cough. My throat is suddenly dry. "Yes. You all look exquisite." Addy smiles while Rosie beams at me. I return my gaze to Megs, who still has a neutral look on their face. My feet finally begin working, and I shuffle to the door. "Ready?"

The restaurant is bright, with plants, exposed bricks, and Edison lights through-out. It has a hipster vibe I wasn't expecting but still enjoy. Despite being crowded, the noise isn't unbearable. We can still have a decent conversation between the four of us. We are at a half booth, half table near the back of the restaurant. Addy and Rosie sit across from Megs and me. The conversation has been pleasant, and I feel good. We all look great. I feel comfortable and happy with the three of them here.

We are all sipping wine as the server brings over our appetizers. Megs is telling us about their new clients. The gym they work in recently had a few very affluent couples join. They sound pretty eccentric. The evening is going so smoothly. The food is excellent. The wine is good. Even the conversation is interesting.

"James?"

The hair on the back of my neck stands up. I tense my body as I look around, searching for the sound of the devil in a female body.

"What are you doing here?"

I finally spot Whitney. She's standing a few feet behind Addy. Her platinum blonde hair falls straight over her shoulders. She is wearing a corset and mini skirt that feels indecent in this setting. Her breasts, which are not naturally as large as they appear, are shoved up high on her chest. Behind her are a few of her girlfriends in similar attire. This is pretty typical attire for her to wear on a Monday. I really don't want to interact with her now.

"I'm having dinner," I reply in a calm tone. Rosie is looking between Whitney and me. Addy has turned to look at her, taking in her friends at the same time. Next to me, Megs is throwing death glares at her. I hope to never be on the receiving end of that look, but at this moment, I love it. Apparently, they have figured out who Whitney is. I offer nothing else to Whitney. I don't want to know what she is doing here. I don't want to introduce my friends. I want her to leave.

She huffs, crossing her arms under her breasts, trying but failing to push them up more. "Did you get the boxes I sent? I dropped them off at your office. Since you asked for your stuff, I wanted to help you out." She takes in the other three, then focuses her stare on me.

"I got them."

She flings her hands to her sides in exasperation. She isn't happy that I am not biting and fighting with her anymore. She doesn't seem to grasp how done I am with this relationship. I can see her shifting tactics. Her face softens; she tilts her head sideways with a soft smile. Her hands ease at her side and drop in front of her. She tries to step towards me, but Addy turns in her chair. Her legs stick out, blocking Whitney's path to me. Whitney shoots her a hateful glance but quickly returns her attention to me.

"James, baby. Why don't you come with me tonight? We can go get you new clothes. I'm so sorry about that. I was so sad and angry when you left. I was hurting and shouldn't have done that. I won't do it again. Let's start over. Let's go home." She puts extra emphasis on 'home.' "I can even do that thing you like. I'll make you feel good, baby." She winks at me, holding her hands out, hoping I'll go with her. This tactic worked on me so many times. I never wanted to upset her. I tried to keep the peace. Everything would be fine if we could start over. Just get back to our normal. That was never reality, though. It was just a vicious cycle of gaslighting and fighting.

Before I even say anything, Addy lets out a loud laugh. "You can't do 'that thing he likes,'" the words are laced with mockery and sarcasm; I struggle to hide my laughter, "if you are starting over. You wouldn't know what he likes." Addy pauses for dramatic effect. Then in her deep, commanding voice, she adds, "You don't know what he likes."

This sets Whitney off. Whitney never did know what I liked. She always claimed she did, but she never asked if I liked it. She did things other men liked. The acts were acceptable but never mind-blowing for me. It wasn't actually what

I liked. Whitney is now throwing her hands in the air, yelling, causing a massive scene in the restaurant. Everyone around us is staring. Addy is in fight mode. Rosie seems frozen, unsure how to handle a grown adult acting this way. Megs also appears to be in fight mode.

"So, what, you're just going to leave me for three whores? Is that what this is? You're so stupid, James. I can't believe I ever wanted to be with you." I let her yell, staring at her with a blank expression. The maître d has walked up with a man in black pants and a black shirt resembling a bouncer. I'm momentarily impressed that they have a bouncer in this restaurant. Whitney continues her verbal assault on my friends and me.

"You think you can just fuck anything with legs? Ha, and look what you have now. A slut, an immature little girl, and a fucking wannabe dude." Before Whitney can get another syllable out, Megs shoots up, bumping the table, causing the dishes to rattle.

"That's enough" is the only thing Megs seethes. Their voice is low and demanding. It seems to startle Whitney. She jumps back directly into the bouncer's arms. He proceeds to escort her out of the restaurant. Her friends follow along. There is a mix of proud and embarrassed women as they all leave. I reach up and take Megs's hand in mine. Theirs is balled in a fist, so I hold my hand over theirs. Megs watches until they are all out of the restaurant. They never take their eyes off the group. Addy has turned back to the table, her eyes on Megs. Rosie is watching Megs and me, waiting for a reaction. I gently tug on Megs's hand, pulling them down beside me.

Without letting go of Megs's hand, I wrap my other arm around their shoulders, pulling them into a hug. They bury their face in my neck, taking deep breaths. I whisper in their ear, "I'm so sorry." I repeat that several times. Megs's breathing returns to normal. They try to pull away, but I catch the back of their neck, holding them close. This time, I whisper something different. "You are beautiful the way you are. Thank you." I let their neck go, meeting their eyes as they sit back. They look on the verge of tears, but none fall. They give a subtle nod, turning towards Rosie and Addy. They immediately start asking questions.

Are we okay? Do we want to leave? Do we need anything? I keep Megs's hand in mine, not letting go. They don't seem to mind. They don't make a move to pull away. Their fist loosens, wrapping their fingers around my own. The contact is comforting and encouraging in so many different ways.

"I'm good, but I don't want to go. I don't want to let her ruin another night. We still have our main dishes coming." I offer. Megs nods as a man in a suit walks up to the table.

"I am so sorry for that altercation. We do not allow guests to cause a scene or yell such horrible things at other guests. That woman has been removed and will not be allowed to return. We will also be comping your meal tonight. It's on us. We are very sorry this has happened." The man seems genuinely upset over what just happened. I wish this didn't feel like an ordinary Tuesday for me.

"Well, there you have it. We can't leave now." I say to my friends, and I look back at the man. "And you don't need to comp our meal. It wasn't your fault."

"We allowed that guest to remain for too long. I apologize again. Ah! Here comes your food now. Please let me know what else you need." He grabs the plates from the server walking up, handing them to us. "Get them another bottle of wine! We will make this better!" He shouts as he walks off, tending to other business. The food smells delicious. The rest of the patrons return to their tables, returning to their own meals. Rosie looks shell-shocked. Addy is still laser-focused on Megs, who stares down at their food as if they've never seen a plate before. I squeeze their hand in mine. They look up at me, and I smile. "You alright?" I ask softly. My thumb glides up and down their wrist. They take a deep breath, then nod at me. Their other hand moves to the table, grabbing their fork to take a bite.

"We just got free food. We should enjoy it." They smirk at us. I give a small laugh. Before letting go of their hand to eat, I squeeze it one more time. They squeeze back.

The evening passes, and we return to good spirits. We all pitched in to leave a massive tip on the table. At least what the meal would've cost. We didn't feel right leaving nothing. On the drive back, I sit with Megs, holding their hand the whole way. Friends hold each other's hands, right? The action really is meant to be a platonic show of support. I can't deny strong feelings for these three. However, it's just friendship. That's all. There's definitely nothing more than friendship going on. Definitely just platonic feelings. That occasionally involves dirty thoughts. That's all.

When the door closes at the apartment, Megs announces, "We're going to smoke, and no one is going to cry. Not even you, James!"

"Oh, come on! Can't we forget about that?" I complain dramatically as Rosie drags me out back.

We all pile on the couch on the balcony. We smoke, talk, and laugh together. The night doesn't get serious like it did the last time. We joke and cuddle, teasing each other but staying close. It's the perfect ending to what could have been a terrible day. I feel lighter than I have in weeks. The feeling isn't just from the blunt, either. At one point, Addy tells us about her idea where Megs gains superpowers, and I become a jellyfish. I have no idea what she is talking about, but Rosie is cuddling with me; Megs's legs are propped on mine, and Addy is animatedly describing Rosie with spoons for fingers. I pray to the gods again, asking them to keep this moment for eternity. This feels better than one cloth-covered breast.

Chapter Eight

JAMES

The past three weeks have been great. After the incident with Whitney at the restaurant, they gave me a key to the apartment. They told me not to worry about rent. I can afford rent, but I am glad they didn't let me. Several debts need to be paid off. The sooner I can pay those off, the better. I found a cheap old car that still runs. It's ugly, but I no longer have to take the bus. I haven't heard anything else from Whitney or her lawyer. I check in with mine weekly, but there hasn't been anything new. I thought for sure she would've done something after her outburst. There hasn't been a single peep.

Life in the apartment is fantastic. I love spending my evenings with Megs and Rosie, and Addy when she isn't at the bar. Sometimes I'll drive to Addy's bar after work to spend time with her. The weekends are spent relaxing together. Megs dragged all of us on a hike once. That was quite an adventure. Addy loudly complained the whole time. Rosie managed to stop every few feet to look at something, flowers, bugs, leaves. Megs walked off without us several times. I was secretly googling plants I saw and spouting off the Latin name. Rosie found it very interesting that I knew so much. Addy just complained louder. I still don't know how that was possible. Megs eventually called me out for using the phone. They swore they were never doing this again. I have a feeling it will happen again, though. It was a fun morning.

Even work has been going well. Our editor said he wants the landowner story run by the end of summer. Some of the other journalists are making great strides in their stories. Mine isn't going as quickly, but still developing well. The lands are owned by a man named Martin Stewart. He owns quite a few businesses but even more land. I have maps of all of his property on my desk, along with his financial reports. I've just started digging into them, but some severe discrepancies exist. There are a few suspicious names on his employee roster. I haven't pinpointed the cause of these discrepancies, but I know I'm close to it. I plan to do surveillance of the lands and see what comes from that. I doubt I'll learn much, but it's a start. There's definitely a story here, and I still have time to work it out.

It's Tuesday afternoon. I finally head back to the apartment, ready for a nice evening. Maybe a beer, something good for dinner. Perhaps I'll even be able to convince them to watch some of my shows. I don't usually ask to watch what I want. I'm just happy to be with them. It would be nice to pick something tonight. I walk into the apartment, basking in the soft light from the sunset. Before I can shut the door, Addy is wrapped around my body, pushing me towards my room.

"Get dressed! You're coming out with me."

I stumble, trying to regain my footing. Addy pushes me, yelling at me to move. We finally reach my room, and I sit my stuff down. She lets me go, standing in the doorway, egging me on. She's wearing a black dress with spaghetti straps and ends mid-thigh. Her hair is down. Her makeup is done; her favorite red lipstick and a smokey eye. She looks amazing. I look down at my watch. It's only 5 pm.

"And where are we going?"

Addy starts bouncing between each foot. Did she eat a bag of sugar? Why is Addy so hyper? She moves her body towards me, dancing to music only she can hear. "I wanna dance. I wanna move. It's been so long since I've been dancing, and no one will go with me tonight. Megs has to get up really early for her new clients. Rosie is just being a turd. Those kids don't need her all well-rested tomorrow." Addy turns her head back towards Rosie's room on the other side of the apartment and sticks her tongue out.

"I heard that!" Rosie yells from her room.

Addy looks back at me with a cringe on her face. "Eesh, see? I need you to go with me. Please?" She begs, dragging out the last syllable. Even though I wanted a relaxing evening, spending time with her does sound enticing. I haven't been out with just Addy much. We usually travel in threes if all of us aren't available. That has helped with some of the sexual tension. Some, not all. I still need to get laid. The thought crosses my mind that I could pick someone up at the club. I'm not sure how Addy would feel about that. Either way, I decide to go with Addy.

"Alright, let me get ready."

Addy

When we were younger, Megs, Rosie, and I went to a club nearly every weekend. I loved going. Being able to move my body to the music was so freeing. It was never about picking up lovers or hooking up. I just liked to lose myself in the music. That's not to say I didn't hook up. I've had my fair share of lovers. Outside of my roommates, my favorite experiences come from backrooms and dark alleys behind bars and clubs. A good quickie can be just as enjoyable as dancing.

We pull up to my favorite club. It's one of the few that's open on a Tuesday night. It's never packed, but it does seem pretty crowded tonight. Must be a party happening. Bridesmaids usually love this spot too. The music is loud and perfect for dancing. The dance floor is vast and dim but not so dark you can't see. The drinks are reasonably priced, usually well made too. That bit depends on the bartender. There's no fee to get in tonight, another perk of coming on a Tuesday.

James walks towards the bar first. While it wouldn't be my first stop, I follow him. He sits on a stool while I stand close, swaying with the music. My body is pretty wound up, needing a good release. Rosie and I have been playing more than usual recently. I love it, but now I want more. More movement. More release. Instead of bogging Rosie down with my demands, I came here tonight. With James. Not that I plan to fuck him, but I won't say no, either. He orders two beers, but I slide the bartender my card before he can pay and tell them to open the tab. I dragged him out; I can at least pay.

He takes a drink of his beer and turns towards me, placing his hand on my hips. I change my movement from swaying to an up-down motion. His hand will be more comfortable that way. Then I get to enjoy his touch longer. He leans in close, asking if I come here often. I laugh at the standard pick-up line. That's not what he asked, but I still chuckle at him. I explain how we used to go a lot, but I haven't been in a while. I tell him how the dancing makes me feel. I ask if he goes dancing much.

"I went with Whitney when we first started dating. But she went too much for me. I haven't been in a long time. I'm probably not a good partner." I raise my eyebrows at him.

"No, I... I'm not a good dance partner. I'm a perfectly adequate partner."

"Oh, perfectly adequate, huh?" I tease.

He groans, taking another drink of his beer. I finish mine off, pushing his towards his mouth to get him to do the same. The music changes to a popular upbeat song. I sashay towards the dance floor, dragging him along with me. I've been couped up for a while. I'm ready to dance. He follows me out to the floor. There are many people out, but it isn't overly crowded. We pick a spot off to the side. I shake my hips in rhythm to the music, my hands waving above my head. He stands awkwardly next to me, stepping from foot to foot. I laugh at him, taking a step closer. I press my front to him, draping one arm over his shoulder while the other floats through the air around us. His hands drop on my hips, matching my rhythm. Our bodies sync to the sound of the music. I close my eyes, pushing against him. His hands slide up and down my back. I lose myself to the music, to his touch. This feels so good, so right.

The song changes, and he pushes me away. I think he will leave, but he spins me around, holding my hands above my head. I turn a couple of times, feeling my dress lift slightly off my body. It's not a loose dress, but the fabric peels away all the same. He wraps his arms around my waist, pulling me into him. My back crashes into his chest. Our bodies mesh together, moving in sync effortlessly. His hands are stroking my stomach and my hips, holding me close. He leans his head against my neck. My hand wraps around his head, fingers tangling in his hair.

We dance like this for several minutes. Our bodies pressed back to front, swaying to the song. His hands explore my body, my hand caressing his head. I drop my head back on his shoulder. His mouth is instantly on my neck. It's a weak spot of mine. I groan, knowing he can feel the vibrations in my neck. His hands suddenly tighten against my body, and he stops moving. I turn to look at him. I give him a quizzical look.

"Sorry," he whispers against my neck. He begins dancing again but slower, more subdued. "I got carried away."

The song ends, leading straight into another. I step away from him and pull him towards the bar. It's even more crowded now than it was. We find one seat, and I motion for him to take it. I flag down the bartender and order a couple more beers for us. I stand next to James, my hand resting on his shoulder. I keep thinking of what Rosie would say in this situation. I know what I want to ask James, but my brain only functions in awkward, indelicate settings. I'm sure Rosie would have some polite way to ask, but I don't. Our drinks arrive, and he lifts his. Then I ask my question in proper Addy form, bluntly and ill-timed.

"When was the last time you had sex?"

He spits his drink, coughing through the shock of my question. I laugh, grabbing some napkins to soak up the mess.

"Fuck" he says, wiping his mouth with the back of his hand. "Give me some warning next time. Shit." He offers an apology to the bartender, who is eyeing him sourly. My hand is still on James's back, rubbing him even though he has stopped coughing.

"I don't know. It's been a long time. When was the last time you had sex?" He says facetiously.

"Sunday." He groans at me, taking a long drink from his beer. I do the same.

"My point is you don't have to apologize for that." I watch him for a minute before adding my following blunt and ill-timed comment. I ensure his drink is down so he doesn't spit again. "I'm willing to fuck you."

His eyes go wide. He doesn't respond for several moments. I know he's processing what I just said. I meant it too. He's attractive. I really like him. I've been interested since he first showed up in my bar. I didn't think I'd hidden that fact well. I've tried to tone it down since Rosie mentioned he has conflicting feelings about us. He deserves to feel safe and welcome without sexual advances. We've all made inappropriate jokes since he started staying with us. Even Megs has popped off a few zingers. I take another sip of my beer and lean into him.

"I don't expect anything from you, but the advances aren't unwelcome. Finish your beer, and let's go back to dancing. This time, don't hold back." I command.

"Yes, Ma'am." This time, my eyes go wide. I lift my hand, stroking his hair.

"Good boy," I whisper into his ear. His smile grows, and I know I've tapped into something he would enjoy.

He wraps his arm around my waist. I sway to the music again as we finish our beers. Finally, he stands and shoves towards me. His hands stay on my waist, his eyes focused on mine. Pushing me backward, he forces me back to the dance floor. His gaze is intense as we begin swaying to the rhythm. My hands drag up his arms, fingers clenching behind his head. His hands shift, one on my lower back, the other on my ass. I take a step into him, pressing my body against his. His arms wrap around me tightly. His broad shoulders cover my body in a tight embrace. For several minutes, we move to the music, bound tightly together. His warmth encompasses me. I begin to sweat due to his body heat, the dancing, and my body temperature rising at our closeness.

When the song changes again, he spins me out, pulling me back just as quickly, my back to his front. We resume the position from earlier. This time, I start with my head on his shoulder, neck exposed to him. I fully understand that going further could make things awkward around the apartment. With his difficult divorce, fucking him now wouldn't be the best decision. I know all of this. But I also know his body feels so good against my own. I know I want him more than I've ever wanted any other man. I know whatever this is between us isn't going away anytime soon. I know I want James badly.

My hand is tangled in his hair. He has one arm stretched across my belly, the other resting on my hipbone. His lips finally settle on my neck, placing small kisses in a column leading to my jaw. My other hand lands on his, guiding him up just enough his fingers can graze the bottom of my breast. I intentionally didn't wear a bra with this dress. He groans against my neck. "Fuck, Addy." I switch my hips from a swaying motion to a grinding one. I press back against him as hard as I can. He's already stiff against my ass.

In a fluid motion, I spin so I am facing him. Both of my arms drape over his shoulders. One of his hands rests on my ass. The other is on my back. This dress has a reasonably open back. I can feel the smooth skin of his hand against my spine. Without hesitating, I press my lips against his. It's gentler than I would like, but I don't want to force this. If he wants to stop, he gets to decide that. He hesitates at first but quickly kisses me back, wrapping his arms tighter around me. My lips move against his, kissing him passionately. I slide my tongue along the seam of his lips, asking for permission, begging to take more. I want more of his taste, more of him.

He parts his lips, allowing my tongue in. As our tongues swirl together in his mouth, I push my hands to the back of his neck. I rub the sides of his neck, keeping him close to me. His hand tightens on my ass. I press my hips into him more, feeling his stiff cock shove against my front. I feel more erratic. I want more of him. I want to take him and don't want to wait any longer. I don't want to deny the feelings I have for him. I want him inside me.

I slide one hand from his neck down his chest, across his stomach, pausing at his waistband. My tongue pulls out of his mouth. "James," I say softly against him. My hand drops lower. I step back just enough to slide my hand between our bodies, then I cup his rigid member in my hand through his jeans. He drops his forehead against mine, breathing heavily. We're still moving together but are entirely out of sync with the music. "Let's go to the bathroom." His eyes go wide. Before he responds, he crashes his lips into mine. His tongue darts into my mouth. I press mine against his, taking in his taste. I tighten my fingers around his cock, squeezing it firmly. He breaks the kiss. His hands grab my hips. He pushes me around to lead the way in a fluid motion but keeps me close to hide his enormous erection.

He keeps his hands on my hips, my hands on his as I guide him to the bathroom. It's occupied, and there is a line. What the hell? This is a Tuesday night. Why are there so many people here? James leans against my back. He curses against my neck, lips kissing me again. James is too worked up to stop. His hands squeeze my hips as he thrusts his hard member against my ass. I don't want to wait in this line, and already people are getting in line behind us. I debate leading him out to the alley. I've been to this spot enough to know it's lit well. Then I remember I've been here before. I turn in his arms, looking at him,

"Do you trust me?"

He seems to consider this for a second, then nods his head. I grab his hand and pull him down the hallway. The end is dark, and people don't go back there. The exit at the end of the hallway leads to the alley. Only the office is down here, and it appears empty tonight. There's a turn at the end, so it's mostly blocked from site. Once around the bend, I push him against the wall. My lips are against his, kissing him deeply. My hands are on his neck, holding him close. He has one hand on my neck, the other on my ass. I press my tongue into his mouth, breaking through his lips. He opens his mouth for me, deepening the kiss. His hand squeezes against my ass, and I moan into the kiss. At the sound, both of his hands grab my ass, lifting me up against him. I wrap my legs around his waist, then he turns and slams my body against the wall. I growl at him satisfactorily, attacking his neck with kisses and nips. He grinds his hips against me. My thin panties are already soaked. I move one hand to his shirt, pulling it away from his body to slide underneath. I want to touch his skin. I want to feel him. I finally touch his lower back, and he presses into me harder.

He drags one hand from my ass to my shoulder. He pulls the strap down, exposing my breast. His hand covers it as he kisses me again. He grips my breast in his hand tightly. His thumb strokes the nipple. As quickly as he kissed me, his mouth leaves only to land on my breast. I arch back, pressing my breast closer to his mouth. He tongues the bud, and I writhe under him. I can't wait. I need him inside me now.

"James," I moan.

His upper body presses me against the wall. With one hand still cupped on my ass, my legs around his waist, he shifts his hips back just enough to get his hand between us. My short dress is already bunched around my hips. His lips plant small kisses along my jaw. His fingers graze the outside of my underwear lightly enough that I can feel it against my entrance.

"Ugh, you're so wet." He says against my jaw.

"Fuck me, James. Get a condom and fuck me."

He freezes. I shift my head to look at him, confused about why he stopped.

"Shit. I don't have a condom."

I give him a confused look, unsure why anyone would go out without condoms these days. But it doesn't matter because I'm always prepared. Girl Scouts honor or what the fuck ever. I grab my small wristlet, open it, and pull out a condom. I hold it up to him with my eyebrows raised.

"Why is that so hot?" he asks.

"Put it on and fuck me. Now," I command. James smirks at me, "Yes, ma'am."

I drop one leg, holding my weight while he unzips his pants. His hard cock springs out, and I can't resist. I wrap my fingers around it, squeezing it in my hand. It feels even better in my hand than in his jeans. It's long and girthy. His penis is so large. My mouth is watering as my pussy clenches, ready for it. I let go to step out of my underwear, slipping them into the pocket of his jeans. He slips the condom on, lining himself up with my entrance. The tip barely pushes in. His hands are on my ass. He lifts me up, my legs wrapping around his waist again. Without hesitation, he thrusts inside me. He fills me so fantastically I nearly yell out.

"Oh fuck. James. Fuck, you're so big."

He pauses, letting me adjust. I'm honestly impressed with his patience. I wouldn't have the same reaction in his place. His lips find mine, instantly pressing his tongue in my mouth. He pulls back his hips, then thrusts inside me quickly. I tip my head back, breaking the kiss. I drop my head on his shoulder. I can't focus on kissing him while he fills me so thoroughly. He begins thrusting steadily, jamming his hips inside me deeply. We're breathing heavily against each other.

I can feel my orgasm growing closer with each thrust. His jeans are pressing against my clit in the most enjoyable way. My pussy clenches in anticipation of the orgasm.

"Fuck Addy, I'm about to come."

"Do it. Come inside of me, James. Come for me," I whisper against his neck. His movements become more erratic. He's thrusting inside me deeply. I gasp as my own climax finally hits. I close my eyes tight, wrapping my arms around him tighter. Lights explode behind my closed eyes as my pussy clenches firmly around his thrusting cock. He curses against my neck as he thrusts deep once again. He stills against me, seated deep inside. His hips and cock jolt inside me with his orgasm. We stay pressed tightly against each other as we slowly come back down from our orgasms. My fingers press against his neck, pushing his head back. My lips meet his in a tender kiss, not the rough passionate one from before. He kisses me back, his tongue slips into my mouth, caressing my own. We stay locked together for another moment. He breaks the kiss, pressing several around my cheeks and jaw. He finally pulls back and looks me in the eye. We smile at each other, laughing softly at what we just did. He eventually takes a step back, pulling out of me. I groan at the emptiness. He tucks himself back in. I take the condom from him, telling him I need to go to the bathroom. I instruct him to go to the bar and grab us drinks. He winks at me and responds, "Yes, ma'am." Then walks off. I watch his ass as he walks towards the bar.

I clean up in the bathroom, disposing of the condom. I can't wipe the smile off my face, remembering my lacy panties are still in James's pocket. I find him at the bar with a couple of drinks. The club is still surprisingly crowded, but now there is a woman in a white dress with a tiara and sash that reads 'Bride.' That explains the crowd. I walk up to his side again, and he instantly wraps his arm around my waist. As I grab the beer, he presses a kiss on my forehead. We stay silent for a few minutes, just drinking, basking in our post-coital bliss. Then he asks if I want to go get something to eat. I nod and close out my tab. He leads me to a little hole-in-the-wall restaurant just a few blocks down. While I could drive, the cool evening air is nice. And I don't have to worry about parking. We eat dinner, giggling and chatting about nothing for a while. I was worried about him being awkward. Or me being awkward, to be honest. Things are good, though. We're happy, and this feels right. Like this is what was supposed to be.

Chapter Nine

"Addy and James are having sex."

"What?? How do you know that?"

Megs called me from work. They are staying later than expected and wanted to let me know. Addy is working tonight, and James will be home soon. I take the time to catch up with Megs, but now they've dropped this bomb on me. I knew one of us would end up having sex with James eventually. I thought it wouldn't happen until his divorce was finalized. Though, there's no telling when that will happen at this rate. It isn't surprising Addy had sex with him first. She's always been hypersexual and more aggressive with what she wants than Megs or me. I'm concerned about how James will handle this, though. Will he have a problem with Addy not being monogamous with him? We haven't discussed the potential for any relationship, let alone a sexual polyamorous one.

"Addy was still awake when I got up this morning. But she was cleaning! And singing! Cleaning the bathroom, Rosie!!"

I consider this information. Addy isn't a fan of cleaning and will usually do anything to avoid what she has to do. The bathroom is usually my chore. It's easier for me to do it and give Addy a task she's more willing to do. The bathroom was surprisingly clean this morning; I just assumed I needed coffee. The singing pretty much confirms Addy was in a good mood. She never sings. She can be in a good mood without singing, but she won't sing without being in a good mood. This is common for her after sex, especially the dirtier it is. She loves doing some kinky things. She gets a high from deviant sexual acts. So that information adds up. She went out with James, but that doesn't necessarily mean she did something with him. Addy has no limit to people that want to be with her or whom she is willing to be with.

"Okay....but how do you know it's James?"

"So Addy went to bed before he got up, but he was still out of bed before I left. He could not stop grinning. He would space out, staring at the wall, then start giggling. Rosie, obviously, he was giggling about Addy."

Okay, that makes sense. There is still a chance they hooked up with other people, but it seems less likely. They went out dancing with each other. I discuss the probability of Addy and James having sex with Megs over the phone. We discuss how it happened, debating the most logical scenarios. We carry on like this for several minutes. I'm moving around the kitchen, getting things ready for dinner. There is still time before I need to prep anything, but I like having something to do with my body while chatting with Megs. Then, a knock sounds on the door.

"Huh, someone is at the door. Maybe James forgot his keys."

I walk to the door. Megs is quiet, listening to see who is knocking at our home. We don't have many unexpected visitors. We invite people over and know they are coming. That's what we all prefer. I open the door, trying to stop myself from gasping.

"Oh, hi, my little baby! Oh, I've missed you so much." My mother barrels into the apartment, wrapping her large arms around me.

"Mom, I didn't know you were coming."

"Oh shit," Megs says into the phone, still against my face. "Text me when she leaves. I'll stay away until then. Good luck." With that, the phone disconnects, and I place it down. Megs doesn't like my mother, for good reasons. She's a religious conservative. She refuses to acknowledge Megs's pronouns. She also makes many slanderous terms about the three of us. She's convinced this is just a phase for me, and soon I'll settle down, get married, and have lots of babies for her to spoil.

She's tried to set me up with almost every guy my age attending her church. I went on dates with a couple of them when I was younger. They were easily the most boring dates I have ever been on. I don't spend a lot of time with my mother. I call her frequently, but I limit interactions. She insists on visiting, though.

Today, she is wearing jeans and a flowery shirt. After she had me, she gained a lot of weight. She is a large woman now. She has a giant bag on her shoulder. Her hair was recently dyed again to look red. I never understood why she always chose red, but that is the color she has always died her hair. She insists it's natural, but no one believes that. She grew up in the South but hasn't lived there since she met my father. Despite the time away, her accent is still thick.

"I know we didn't have any plans. But I missed you. I wanted to come visit you. So. Where are your roommates? Did they finally move out? Is Addy still working at that bar? Are you dating anyone?"

She does this all the time. Fires off a series of questions I don't get time to respond to. I pick and respond to one or two questions I'm comfortable answering. Before I can say anything else, the front door opens again. James walks through. My mother takes a long inhale, taking in James. His eyebrows shoot up, seeing someone else in the kitchen unexpectedly. He looks between her and me, trying to piece together who she might be.

"Are you the new boyfriend? Did that queer girl finally move out? Oh, Rosie, I like him. Do a little spin for me." She flaps her hands at James while he stands there, wide-eyed and stunned.

"No, Mom." I rub my face, exasperated at her comments. "Megs still lives here. Still not a girl. This is James. James, this is my mother, Marge." I motion between the two. I intentionally leave the boyfriend comments alone, hoping she'll drop that subject. James smiles, catching up to the situation. He holds his hand out. "Nice to meet you, ma'am. I can see where Rosie gets her gorgeous looks." I roll my eyes at him. I didn't realize he could be such a ham. I'll have to give him hell about that another time.

My mom giggles, actually giggles. "Oh, Rosie, let's keep this one." She shakes his hand, speaking to me but still ogling James.

I groan loudly. "Mom, he's a person. Not a dog."

"Are you staying for dinner, Marge?" James asks. I know he's being kind, but he didn't need to go that far. I give him a horrified look, but before I can say anything, Mom is already gushing about how she would love to and how I never invite her over. Realizing I won't be able to change her mind now, I walk over to James and wrap my arms around his shoulders. The only way to talk to him now will be by whispering.

"You really didn't need to do that. I can still get her to leave."

He wraps his arms around me, hugging me back. His arms are large and consuming. Suddenly I'm sad I don't hug him every time he walks in the door. His face is buried in my hair, next to my ear. "Don't worry," he whispers to me. "I'll make dinner. You let her talk, and I'll be here for moral support. I can pretend to be the boyfriend. Most mothers love me anyways." I chuckle softly in his ear, squeezing him tightly before pulling away. It's surprising that he has already picked up enough to realize how difficult she can be to deal with. Maybe it's not that difficult. Maybe I have it all written on my face. I should check my reactions, but I won't.

"Marge, come over here and sit at the counter. I'm going to go clean up, then I'll make dinner. Come chat with our Rosie for a bit." He walks into the kitchen effortlessly; I can't help but be impressed. I try not to focus on the fact that he said *our* Rosie and why I don't hate it. He pulls out a couple of glasses and eyes my mother, considering something. "Let me guess, you like a good red wine?"

"Oh! Of course! How did you know?" My mother swoons at him. She's so easily impressed.

"Just a hunch." He pours two glasses and slides them over. He walks towards the end of the counter, where I'm still frozen, watching this interaction. His hand touches my hips while his lips lightly graze my face, then turn towards my ear. "Sit, drink; I'll be right back. I've got you." His hand tightens on my hip in emphasis. My throat is suddenly parched. Has he always been this enchanting? I didn't realize he could play the boyfriend role so well. I have to remind myself that he isn't, in fact, my boyfriend. My body finally starts moving, and I sit next to my mother.

She's already talking about melodrama in her church group. She stayed home to raise me and never went back into the workforce. She had a few odd jobs around town. She did work at her church and occasionally volunteered at the school. She was also involved in nearly every adult activity around town. Book club, yoga, knitting.

She isn't a bad mother. I know she loves me, but she really only loves the version of me she has in her head. She's never accepted that I'm not straight and don't want to be in a traditional relationship. She always has backhanded comments about living with Addy and Megs or working at the school. She thought she would raise a mini version of herself, and I couldn't be further from that. I love her all the same, though. She's still my family, and I won't let that go. I nod, offering a gasp or "You don't say" occasionally, frequently sipping on my wine. This woman could talk to a wall and never run out of things to say.

James comes out of his room and heads into the kitchen. He picks up where I left off, gathering ingredients and prepping them for dinner. Without asking, he grabs the bottle of wine, tops my glass, and pours one for himself.

"Good job, Rosie. You've already got this one trained. Oh, he's a keeper for sure."

I cringe, grabbing my glass to take a large drink. I hope we have more wine because this night will not go smoothly without it. At least Megs and Addy won't be around. They hate my mother and don't put up with her comments the way I do. Things always end in yelling and name-calling when they are together. James eyes me for a moment but doesn't say anything. He starts cutting the meat to cook.

"So, James. Rosie doesn't tell me anything. Tell me how you met. Where do you work? Do you go to church? Oh, Rosie needs to go to a good church. That will get her back on the path she needs to be on. I'm sure a good boy like you could get her to do that."

I groan out her name. He responds before I can tell James he doesn't need to answer any of that. I hold my breath while he talks.

"Well, Marge, I'm a journalist for a small magazine in town. I do actually go to church. I've been asking Rosie to go with me. I think she will finally go this week." I give him an odd look as my mom questions him about his church.

"I go to the Church of the Seraphim Morningstar. It's a new church downtown, but they are so serious about the lifestyle." I try to hide my laugh at James's response. He doesn't attend church, but my mother seems to buy it.

"I've never heard of that one. Are they strict? Rosie needs some guidance to make better choices."

Without missing a beat, James responds to her. "Oh, they are very strict. They are so serious; most services are held on Saturday nights, so members are less tempted to stray out into the temptations around town."

My mother basically starts cheering at this information. "Now that is a good idea. I've been telling my pastor we need more weekend services to keep young people from straying. Oh, you must take her, James." He winks at me and promises to. My mother finally turns her attention back to me. She starts asking me if I've been in touch with any of my classmates from high school, but before I can even think of an answer, she begins telling me all the gossip. I vaguely listen, keeping my eye on James. He moves through the kitchen effortlessly. He makes this whole situation feel like it's totally normal, like my mother's presence isn't something to cower from. Once the food is ready, he plates a dish for each of us, placing them in front of us. He tops off our wine then walks around the high top to sit beside me. He leans against me, placing his lips in my hair just above my ear. It looks like a kiss, but he gently whispers, "You're doing well. You've got this." His hand rubs my shoulders then he begins eating. His encouragement sends butterflies flitting around my stomach.

Somehow my mother manages to devour her food and still not stop talking. She moves from the small-town drama to talk about the drama in her book group. Who knew a bunch of old ladies talking about books could be so dramatic? When dinner is finished, James places all the dishes in the sink. I worry he'll offer some dessert, but Mom stands and thanks him for the food.

"That was delicious, but I need to get back to your father. He'll be all worried about me. You know how he gets." I know how Mom likes to pretend he gets. While my mother can talk for hours, my father is more distant. He probably wouldn't notice if she didn't come home for a week. I hug her and tell her goodbye. She walks towards the door. James holds his hand out and opens his mouth to speak. Mom grabs his hand and pulls him into her chest for a hug. "Now, you take care of my baby girl. She's special. My husband owns lots of land, and we aren't scared to hide a body there."

"MOM!" James chuckles, seeing the empty threat for what it is. She smiles at him.

"You get her to that church of yours. Get her away from those gay friends she has. She doesn't need roommates like that. She deserves better than some confused girls leading her away from our Lord."

I start to correct her, but James pats her shoulder, guiding her towards the door. "Sure thing Marge." She finally walks out the door, and I sigh. James looks at me with a big goofy smile on his face. It's infectious, and I start laughing. "Thank you. You're a lifesaver." He raises his voice to mimic hers, "Anything for my precious baby girl." I laugh harder at him. He steps towards me and wraps his arms around me. I sigh and relax against his body. His hug is comforting. He gives me space to calm my body down after interacting with her. I step back and look up at him. "What is the Church of Seraphim Morningstar?"

He laughs, "Oh, that. Well, don't tell her, but I took the Morningstar name from the series Lucifer. It's his last name on the show. Seraphim is a type of angel." I burst out laughing again.

"Oh my god. You told my mother you're going to take me to a church of Lucifer!" I start laughing so hard I have to bend over. He grabs onto my waist to keep me upright. We both laugh together hysterically. I finally calm down, wiping the tears away from my eyes.

"She is right. You are a keeper." I smile at him. He looks like he wants to say something else, but I speak up before he gets the chance. "I'm going to change into some pj's, then I'll do the dishes." I head towards the bedroom without waiting for his response.

When I return to the kitchen a few minutes later, he's almost done with the dishes. "You didn't have to do that," I say to him. I don't want him to do an unfair share of chores around the place. He cooked and saved me from my mother. I can do the dishes. "I know," he says as he puts the last few plates in. He adds detergent and starts it. "There wasn't much. Now we can sit and finish this bottle of wine together." I smile and nod to him. That sound perfect to me. He may be a keeper.

Addy

Rosie told Megs and me about the situation with James and her mom. She was so bubbly and happy when she spoke of him. I've never seen her recount an incident with her mom the way she did this one. She is catching feelings for him. I want to tell her about the club the other night, but I don't want to take away her happiness. I'll let her know soon. Probably. Eventually. We didn't talk about what would happen after. If this would be a regular thing or not. I'm fine with whatever happens. I don't typically like to have those conversations. With this situation, though, I almost want to have that conversation.

It's Friday night at the bar. I came in the early afternoon to prepare for the evening rush. Nick, the owner, is here tonight. He stays when the evening rush comes in. The bar starts to fill up with our regulars, a few others, and a bridal party. They look similar to the group I saw at the club on Tuesday, but honestly, I don't know what a bridal party would look like. Would they really look that different? I move about, serving customers, helping in the kitchen, filling my regular duties. A little after 6 pm, Nick calls me back into the office.

"You need to clock out and get out of here." I'm stunned. I stare at him for a minute.

"What? What are you talking about?"

"I'm talking about you fucking some guy in my hallway while you were working. That's what."

"What in the fuck, Nick? What are you talking about?" I am so confused right now.

"I'm talking about this!" He flips his phone up to me. It's a dark image that takes me a moment to realize what I'm looking at. It's James and me in the hallway at the club. My breath catches as my mind processes this.

"Where did you get that?" I ask more calmly than I thought I could.

"One of the customers out there showed me. Imagine my horror at seeing one of my managers getting fucked in my hallway while on the clock. It's despicable."

"First of all, Nick, that isn't even your hallway. Look!" I point to the phone. "That's an exit. Your hallway doesn't look like that. Second, this was taken Tuesday night when I was off. Third, where the fuck did you get that photo?" I can't control my anger anymore. I need to know who took that picture and how it made its way to my boss. Does James know about this? I'm not upset about being caught. This isn't my first time, and won't be my last. I am angry that someone took a photo without me knowing and is now sharing that photo.

"So you don't deny fucking this guy in the hallway?"

Is Nick serious right now? He is trying to fire me and is concerned about what I do in my own time. I roll my eyes at him. "No, I'm not denying I fucked him. The evidence is in your hand. But you have no fucking right to fire me for what I do on my own time." He seems to consider this, looking at his phone for another minute. He's really looking at the photo too long. Nothing is visible; James's body covers mine, but it's still apparent what we were doing.

"Look, I think you should go home tonight. Let me think about this. Come back in the morning, and we'll talk about it when we've both calmed down."

"Look at it or masturbate to it?" I seethe. He may be onto something about taking time to cool down, but I am beyond livid about this situation. "Watch it." He casts me an angry glare.

"Fine. But I'm supposed to close tomorrow. Are you changing the schedule?" He looks up at me as if I have some audacity to ask such a thing.

"No, I'm not changing the schedule. You can work a double for leaving me short tonight. Now get out before I change my mind and fire you."

"Fuck," I shout as I storm out of the office. This is not how I planned for this night to go. I need to go calm down before I lose my job. I need to find out where he got that photo. I also need to get Nick to delete his copy. I storm into the bar area, heading to the computer to clock out.

"Addy! Psst, Addy, come here."

I turn and see Bruiser trying to get my attention. "I can't, Bruiser. I'm going home. NICK," I say much more loudly than necessary, "can come out and serve you." I slam my fingers against the computer, pushing most of the correct buttons to leave.

"No, Addy. Come here." I sigh heavily and walk over to Bruiser once I'm done on the computer.

"What?" I seethe, unable to control my anger.

"I saw that woman over there talking to Nick earlier." He points over his shoulders at the bridal party. I take a quick glance as he continues talking. "I couldn't hear what she said, but she showed her his phone and pointed in your direction." Now I glare at the group, searching for who might have been at the club and ratted me out. Then I spot her. She turns her head in my direction. She looks at me but quickly looks away. There's no doubt about it. Whitney was at the club and is now at my bar, trying to get me fired. She turns back to her group and starts laughing. I fume while staring at her, my vision turning red. Without looking away, I grab a tumbler and the first liquor I can get my hands on. I pour a large drink and slide it in front of Bruiser. "Thank you," I mumble to Bruiser. I'm not going to put that on his tab. That oversized drink is on Nick tonight.

I debate how to handle this situation. If I march over there and try to pick a fight, Nick will fire me and ban me from the bar, assuming he doesn't call the cops and have me arrested. Even though at least half of my anger is directed at him, I go home and calm down. Talk to James and Rosie and Megs. One of them will know what to do. Then I remember Rosie is going out with coworkers tonight, and Megs is having a night out with Kendra. Fine. James can help me with this situation.

The drive to the apartment does nothing to quell my anger. In fact, when I pull into the garage for the apartment, I'm even angrier than when I left the bar. His ex, the invasion of privacy, Nick's stupidity, nearly losing my job and bar. And somehow, Bruiser helped me, another point that angers me for some unexplainable reason. I storm into the apartment.

"JAMES!"

He comes out of his room, looking confused and nervous. My breathing is heavy, and I need to work out this anger. Suddenly an idea hits me. I can't take my frustration out on him physically or emotionally, but I can sexually. He's been teasing me with honorifics lately. Let's see if he can live up to that.

"Come with me."

He follows me into my room, and I slam the door behind him. He stands quietly near the bed. I'm pacing back and forth on the side. I finally stop, inhale deeply, then blow it out forcefully. I look at him. I know my face is still angry, but I'm using most of my concentration on calming my body. I continue breathing deeply, letting my mind settle. I need to be in a better head space if I am going to dominate him. He waits calmly, but I can tell he's anxious about my arrival and mood.

"It seems we weren't alone on Tuesday night." He opens his mouth to speak, but I lift my hand, placing it over his mouth. I step closer to him, leveling my voice, keeping my gaze on his. "A certain bitch" I say more callously than I intend, "took a picture of the hallway while you were balls deep in my cunt." His eyes are wide as he looks at me. To his credit, he doesn't try to speak again. I drop my hand from his mouth to his chest. "That same bitch showed up at my bar tonight. Do you know what she did?" He shakes his head.

"Use your words, James."

"No."

"No, what?" He thinks for a moment, looking at me. Even though we haven't talked about this before, he catches onto what I mean.

"No, ma'am."

"Good." I walk around him, dragging my fingers across his shoulders and back. He has nice, broad shoulders that I want to bite, want to scratch. "That bitch," I trail both hands down his spine as I talk to him, speaking with less spite than before, "gave that picture to my perverted boss, who threatened to fire me." He turns his head to speak but thinks better of it. My fingers pause at the hem of his shirt, waiting to see if he'll speak. When he doesn't, I lift his shirt over his head as I continue. "That bitch nearly cost me my job. My bar. And I am beyond angry." My voice is still level. Even though the anger is still there, I'm more settled in my actions than I was earlier. Once his shirt is off, I toss it on the floor as I step before him. He's only a couple of inches taller than me. He's currently barefoot, and I'm still in my work shoes. I'm looking him straight in the eye. "Now, I know this isn't your fault. I chose to fuck you in that hallway. Your ex chose to be a pervert. But I'm going to work off my frustration on you. Understand?" Again, he nods.

"Words! James."

"Yes, yes, ma'am."

"I'm not going to hurt you, but I want you to pick a safe word." He thinks for a moment, then answers, "Cactus." I give a small laugh. "Cactus, not normal, but ok."

"Well, you're being kind of prickly," he sasses at me.

I grab onto his jaw, holding him tight as I step close. "There will be no talking. I don't need a brat right now." His eyes widen, but he nods, then quickly adds, "Yes, ma'am." I loosen my grip, stroking his jaw kindly.

"Good. I'm not going to hit you or do any kind of impact. I'm not in a good head space for that. But you will do as you're told without question or comment. Understand?"

"Yes, ma'am."

I step back and smile at him. I finally get to look at his bare chest. His muscles are defined but not ripped. His skin is smooth. He has a large tattoo on his ribs. It looks like a mermaid, but not a sweet innocent one. I make a note to ask him about it later. My mind has finally settled, and I know what I want to do to him.

"Have you ever had a ruined orgasm?"

"No."

"What's your safe word?"

"Cactus."

"Use it when you need it. I won't stop for 'no.'" I turn my back to him. "Unzip my top."

He steps up and begins working on the zipper. He pulls the zipper down smoothly, his fingers avoiding my skin. Once the top is unconnected, I turn towards him, letting it slip down. I toss it into a pile with his shirt. I caress my hand over my breast, keeping my eyes on his. His gaze drops to my hand, watching my fingers pinch and pull my nipple. He licks his lips. He is wearing sweatpants, the outline of his cock visible in them. "Do you want a turn?" He nods, taking a step towards me. I shake my head, taking a step back. "No. Words, James."

"Yes, ma'am." I nod at him, placing his hand on my breast. He gently massages it. Taking his other hand, I put it on my other breast. He looks up at me, analyzing my reaction. I don't give him one. He turns his attention back to his hands on my breast. With my eyes on his face, I focus on the feeling of his hands on me. His hands are smooth and warm. His fingers are gentle on my breasts and nipples. He pinches one. I let my eyes flutter shut. His touch spreads warmth through my body, pooling in my center. I want to remain in charge during this scene. I don't need my desire to take over during this first part. This is his punishment for having a bitch of an ex that tried to get me fired.

I step back, pulling away from his touch. My breasts are hit with cool air in the absence of his hands. His gaze returns to mine.

"Pants off."

"Yes, ma'am," he steps out, kicking them to the side. He now stands naked before me.

"Flat on your back." I nod my head towards the bed. He hesitates for a moment, then climbs on the bed. I can tell he hasn't been a sub before. Not that it matters to me. This isn't a serious scene. I plan to watch him for signs of distress and check in with him if needed. I don't know how comfortable he is using a safe word, but I don't want to find out he won't use it. His ex probably bossed him around during their relationship. I want him to know he has power in this room. Even though I'm leading and commanding him, he still has power here. He can stop this at any moment.

James is lying on the bed, watching me. He seems uncertain about what to do with his hands. He places them behind his head, then drops them to his side. He puts them on his chest then back to his sides. His uncertainty makes me smile. I'll deal with those hands in a moment. I take in his naked body entirely again. His chest is smooth. His legs are firm, with sandy blonde hair. He is groomed around his enormous cock, which is now mostly erect. There is a tattoo of an octopus on his thigh. I know I still have my jeans on, but it's not time for him to see me. I climb onto the bed next to him. I grab one wrist, pulling it above his head. "What's your safe word?" I ask again to keep it fresh on his mind.

"Cactus," he answers hoarsely. I lift his hand towards my headboard. Since Rosie and I like to play frequently, I have a set of straps that stay connected to my bed. Makes things more manageable when we get carried away. Rosie likes being restrained. I'm very interested in seeing how James responds to it. I make sure the strap is secure, then grab his other wrist. I straddle his chest, place the other wrist in the other strap, and tighten it. He's watching my every move, taking in everything I do. I shift my legs down, bringing my face close to his. "You're being so good for me. Now I'm going to give you a little reward."

He bites his lip, trying to hide the smile. I feel his cock jump against my thigh. I'm not directly over him, but close enough to feel him. His positive response encourages me to keep going. I would change directions if he wasn't responding well. I'm delighted that isn't the case. I press my breasts against his chest, putting my lips against his. He meets mine, and I instantly shove my tongue in his mouth. I swirl my tongue around his, showing him exactly what I plan to do to his dick in a minute. He lifts his head towards mine, trying to deepen the kiss.

I pull back, smiling at him. He looks sad over the kiss ending, but I'm sure he won't mind for long. I place my hand on his chin, lifting his face to a position I want it in. Then I press kisses down his jaw, over his neck, and down his chest. I pause at the center of his chest, releasing his jaw. I suck one nipple into my mouth. Then I scrape my teeth along it. He lets out a small breath, so I press my lips down in a gentle kiss. I repeat the motions on the other nipple. This time he doesn't gasp. He is watching me with his chin tucked down as far as it will go.

I sit up, reaching behind his head to grab the pillows. I lift his head with one hand, adjusting the pillows with the other. At this angle, his face is right against my breast. He begins pressing kisses on them. I think he's reaching for my nipple but can't quite reach. Once the pillows are in place, I push his head back, sitting straight on his stomach. Time to give him some instructions.

"Keep your eyes on me. Tell me before you come. There will be a punishment if you don't."

"Yes, ma'am."

I don't have a punishment planned if he comes without telling me, but I'm sure I can come up with something. I don't have many punishments for men who come without informing me since I mostly play with Rosie. I lift my hips off him. I crawl back, kissing down his chest again. His cock is rock hard now. Before I reach it with my kisses, I veer off to one side, kissing his hips, then his thigh, and down to his knee. I kiss back up but again avoid his cock. I press my lips lightly against his balls. He groans at the light touch. I look up at him. His eyes are still on me, so I continue. I press kisses to his other thigh, traveling down to his knee and back up to his hip. I kiss over to the base of his member, then lick my way to the tip. He hisses a breath out at the touch. I wrap my lips around the tip, swirling my lip against the very end of his cock, the way I had just been swirling his tongue.

I lick my lips, ensuring they are wet enough before sliding his cock into my mouth. It has been a while since I've sucked dick. At first, I worry I won't be able to take it all in. After I get halfway down, I slide back. I gather more spit, wetting my lips and sliding down further. He curses, and I pause at the bottom to glance at him. The angle is awkward, but it's enough to see his eyes still on me. I pull back, taking my lips off his member. I lick from the base to the tip, adding extra moisture to his member.

One hand rubs his balls. I grip them gently, squeezing and caressing them in my palm. Keeping my hand there, I place my lips over his cock, swallowing him again. I take all of him in. I feel the tip of his penis poking the back of my throat. I can't fit his whole cock in my mouth. It's too long. I use my free hand to grip the base. I lay flat on my stomach so my hands can hold him while my mouth is over his cock. I slide back then down again smoothly. I keep sliding up and down his cock, increasing my speed.

"Fuck, Addy"

I wrap my lips around him tightly, sucking hard as I slide back. I let go of the base, propping myself up a bit. I keep his balls pressed into my palm. My middle finger presses against his perineum, working the tendons in that area. I won't go lower today, but one day I might explore other parts of his body. He groans under my touch. While my fingers keep massaging, I place kisses along his cock. I swirl my tongue over the tip, then take his cock into my mouth. I bob up and down his length. My tongue presses against the bottom as I pull up, my upper lip tucking under my teeth on my descent.

"Please don't stop that," he begs.

I consider making him be specific but decide to let him off the hook this time. I don't want to stop what I am doing right now. Another time, I'll make him say exactly what he wants. For now, I'm giving him what he wants for being good. I keep bobbing in the same way. It only takes another minute before his balls tighten in my palm.

"Oh god. I'm going to come...I'm... fuck. I'm coming," he says breathily.

I can feel his cock flinch. I look up at him, seeing his eyes are closed. I take my hands and mouth off.

"Eyes open," I command.

His eyes shoot up as the first jet of come flies out of the tip and lands on his stomach. More spurts, but he groans with the denial of his actual orgasm. I reach up and gently wrap my fingers around his member, and I stroke up and down gently. He whimpers as the rest of his penis continues releasing jizz on itself. I said I would give him a ruined orgasm, not torture him. I stroke him until he stops, his member going partially soft. I lay it down on his stomach, not moving to clean the cum off him. I lean up, placing a kiss on his cheek.

"You did so well for me. You're being so good."

He is breathing heavily, but his eyes are closed. He leans his cheek against mine. I'm not nearly done with him, but I give soft touches and gentle kisses. As his breathing calms down, I sit back and look at him. I ask if he's okay, and he nods.

"Good. Because it's my turn now."

JAMES

My eyebrows shoot up when Addy speaks to me. I'm not sure if I can go another round right away. I need some time to recover. Unless she wants me to eat her out. That I can definitely manage. I lick my lips in anticipation. I want to know what she tastes and feels like against my tongue. I was so swept up in the club that I didn't even think of putting my fingers in my mouth after I felt how wet she was. I'm still kicking myself for that oversight. I could have tasted her on my fingers then, but my cock was in charge. It's not now, and I want to savor every bit of her.

She climbs off the bed, moving away from me. The lack of her body leaves me feeling chilled, but my eyes stay trained on her. I've never had a ruined orgasm before. It was a different experience. I really thought I was going to orgasm. When she looked up at me and spoke, my orgasm sank into a deep part of my brain while the jizz spurted across my stomach and penis. I've never felt such a small amount of release and such a desire to continue fucking before. I'm not ready to process my emotional response to a ruined orgasm.

Addy reaches into her drawers, taking something out. She takes off her pants and lacy underwear, tossing them aside. My tongue can't stop rubbing my lips. I want her to come sit on my face so badly. It doesn't even register that she has pulled something out of her drawer. She places the device by my side and releases one wrist from the straps. She rubs my wrist, telling me to sit up. I immediately slide back against the headboard. Maybe she'll stand over me while I eat her pussy.

"I'm going to touch myself while you watch. You are not to touch until I tell you to. Then you do exactly as I say. Understand?"

I stare, stunned by what she has said. Whitney would never touch herself in front of me. She was always embarrassed. I never understood why. I would have loved watching her, but she was never comfortable doing it. I've never been with a partner before in a situation to touch themselves. I pretty much always had penetrative sex with partners. I'm excited and enthralled by Addy's words. Of course, Addy would be comfortable masturbating in front of me. I can't help but wonder if there is anything Addy isn't comfortable with. I'm so distracted by my thoughts; I almost forget to answer her.

"Yes, ma'am"

I'm back against the headboard, sitting on her pillows. One hand is still strapped down. The other hand is resting on the bed next to my hip. The device she took out of her drawer finally registers. It's a blue curved wand with two ball shapes on either end. One is larger than the other. My brain also notes that she is now completely naked in front of me. She's sitting on the bed, getting into a relaxed position.

I've been so wrapped up in tasting her I didn't realize she's completely naked. I take in her body. It's smooth with gently defined muscles on her stomach. Her legs look strong, smooth, and so soft. My fingers jump, wanting to reach out and touch her. One day, I'll do things to earn a punishment, but today, right now, at this moment, I don't want to lose what she is offering me. Her breasts are perfectly round, with a peaked nipple. I want to wrap my mouth around her breasts again.

"Eyes stay on me. That hand stays on the bed." She nods her head at my hand by my hip. I nod but quickly add, "yes, ma'am."

She leans back on one hand. Her breasts are pushed out towards me in this position. They look so round and soft. My fingers flinch to touch them. This is going to be more challenging than I expected. She grabs the blue wand, pressing a button on it. It jumps to life, humming softly. So it vibrates too. I watch intently as she places it against the apex of her core. She rubs it around for a moment, then settles on the perfect spot. Her eyes stay focused on mine. Her breathing becomes shallower. She adjusts the wand's position, biting her lip as it hits the right place. I can tell her orgasm is growing. The fluids are glistening in her core. Her breasts are heaving up and down with her quickening breath. She is absolutely stunning. I can't take my eyes off her. While my hand is itching to touch her, I'm frozen in place by her movements. She shifts her hips closer to my hand. She lays down on her back as one leg stretches over my hips, resting her foot on the pillows behind me.

Addy presses a button on the wand, and the humming grows louder. Her head is laid back against the bed. My fingers flinch again. Her ass is so close to my hand. A slight lift of my index finger and I could stroke her thigh, but I don't. I stare at her pussy. The blue toy vibrates fast against her clit. It stands out against the pink of her lips. She moves her hand to her breast. She starts by caressing it, then squeezes it hard. I can see the indents of her fingers in the tender flesh. She releases her skin, marks from her fingers fading quickly. She grabs her nipple with her fingers and twists it painfully. She cries out as she does. Her breathing is loud. Her body is clenching. The lips of her vulva twitch, moisture building with the orgasm.

She lifts her head and meets my eyes. Hers are glazed over, another indicator of her approaching orgasm, and I imagine my own are too. "Fuck me with two fingers."

"Yes, ma'am." She doesn't have to tell me twice.

I slip two fingers inside her, glad she finally allowed me to touch her. She's so tight and wet. I pump my fingers in and out, her pussy sporadically clenching around my fingers. She presses the button on the wand for the third time. The sound of the vibrator increases again. I can feel the vibrations inside her pussy. It must be strong against her. She moans loudly, arching her back off the bed. Her free hand fell onto the bed, and she gripped the bedsheet.

"Harder!"

She yells at me. I comply, slamming my fingers in and out of her quickly. She twists her body again, angling her breast towards my leg. Instinctually, my hand, which is still bound, jerks to interact. There's a soft clanging against the bed as my wrist meets resistance. Right, the straps. I look back at her as she cries out. Her pussy clenches around her fingers. I continue thrusting them deep inside her. My free hand keeps jerking against the headboard. I want to touch her breast, her throat, take the toy from her and control it myself. I thought being allowed to touch her with one hand would be enough, but I want more. I want to touch her with both hands.

Her body settles down, and she turns the toy off. She didn't say to stop or remove my fingers. I don't want to hurt her by still slamming into her when she's sensitive after an orgasm. I slow my fingers, letting them rest inside her warm cunt. Her eyes finally meet mine.

"You can release your other hand now."

I pull my fingers out of her slowly. She lets out a small gasp as they completely leave her body. She's still watching me as I bring my hands from her pussy straight to my mouth. I don't know what she will do next, but I'm not passing up this chance to taste her again. With her eyes on me, I place my fingers in my mouth, sucking her taste off. Sweet, with a hint of almond. I wonder if her body wash is almond-scented. Her bottom lip is sucked in between her teeth. I suck and lick all the taste I can get off my fingers before reaching over to undo the other strap. I rub my wrist with my wet fingers, looking back at her. She holds her arm out, implying I should lie next to her.

"Come here."

She speaks gently. She adjusts her leg off my hips as I shift up. I lay down next to her. She turns on her side, wrapping her legs and arms around me. Her lips are on mine as soon as I am close enough. My tongue is instantly in her mouth. I wrap my arms around her back, bringing her close to me. I squeeze her tight, feeling something wet and sticky squish between our bodies. I laugh, remembering the jizz on my stomach that was never cleaned up. I keep my lips against her, kissing her deeply. My hands stroke her breast. I dare to squeeze her breast in my hand. I don't squeeze nearly as hard as she did. My cock jumps against her hips, ready for a real orgasm. She pulls back from my kiss. Her hands go to either side of my face, stroking my hair, my cheeks.

"You did so well for me. You're so good."

I preen under her praise. I've never willingly been submissive before. I've never considered myself submissive, and I don't know if I would be for anyone else. But I will do anything for Addy's praise. I lean down, kissing her gently this time. It's hard to not thrust my hips against her. I use the last bit of my own willpower to stop from humping her and busting in her belly button.

"I've got one more instruction for you, love. Think you're up for it?"

I don't know what she's got in store for me next. Mentally, I'm pretty much up for anything. Physically might be a different story. My cock is gunning for her warm cunt, and I want nothing but to sink deep inside her. But like the obedient submissive I'm trying to be, I say, "Yes, ma'am."

"How good are you at pulling out?"

I raise my eyebrows, a bit surprised at her question. It's not something I do regularly, but at this point in my life, I know when to pull out. I can always pull out early to be on the safe side. I shrug at her and reply, "I can do it."

"Good. I want you to fuck me, but I want you to come on my tits."

My cock jumps at her words. "Fuck." I breathe, dropping my head by her shoulder. Yes, she owns me now. I am her's forever. No one can replace what she has given me here. Her hands move to my shoulders, running her fingers across my muscles. I press my lips against her neck, her ear, her jaw, her collarbone. Her hands travel down my chest, across my stomach. One hand slides down, wrapping around my hard cock. It's almost painful. From the ruined orgasm, then watching her masturbate while I can't touch, I'm concerned I won't last more than three pumps. At least she has already had one orgasm.

Her fingers gently stroke my member and position her legs underneath me. Her hand lines the tip of my cock with her entrance. Her head moves close to mine, her lips against my ear. "Fuck me, love." She whispers against my ear, her breath hot against my skin.

"Wait."

This is quite possibly the stupidest thing I have ever said. But I can't, in good conscience, continue this. "I don't want to fuck you without a condom." Her fingers are still stroking me but slower. I don't think I have any STIs, but I don't know. It occurs to me that she just had her mouth around me. I probably should've said something then. Before I feel entirely like a shit bag, she responds.

"That's probably a good call. Fuck me with the condom, then pull it off."

She points to a box on the nightstand with condoms in it. I grab one, putting it on fast. I shift back into position over her and slam inside her. I don't wait any longer. I don't think my cock can wait. Being inside her is glorious. She's warm and encompassing. I reach over to the footboard, holding on so I don't collapse from pleasure. She groans as I pull back out. This is the second time I have slammed into her instead of easing in. The desire to be buried deep inside her is strong, unlike anything I have ever felt. As I slam down again, her arms wrap around my shoulders, pulling me to her. I continue thrusting hard and fast. My lips collide with hers in a deep, passionate kiss. My orgasm is right on the edge, already close to the build-up earlier. I groan as my balls tense, remembering what I am supposed to do. I pull out of her, ripping the condom off and tossing it on the bed. She grabs the toy and turns it on, pressing it against her clit. I adjust my legs closer to her chest so my cock is aimed at her breasts.

"Come on me. Coat me in your cum."

With her words, my penis jolts, spraying semen across her breasts. As the first jets land on her, she twists and contorts again, crying out with her orgasm. She turns her head, mouth hitting my thigh. She bites down on my thigh, just above my knee, as her orgasm spasms. The sensation of her teeth on my flesh stirs deep in my groin, forcing the last dregs from the tip of my dick. She turns off the vibrator, tossing it to the side. It bounces and hits the floor, but she doesn't react. Our breathing is heavy. I look down at her. Her blonde hair is splayed out around her head. Her cheeks are flushed, eyes still glazed over. Her chest is covered with my semen. There are light teeth marks on my thigh, fading quickly. My hand is still clenched around my cock, frozen from the ecstasy. She slides her hands up to my shoulders, pulling me down. I shift my legs back, then collapse, half on her, half on the bed. She pulls me tight, her chest pressing to mine, the sticky fluid rubbing between us. She glances down with a smirk.

"We'll clean that up in a bit. Just hold me for now."

I do. I have no desire to move. With my face beside Addy's neck, I gently kiss her skin. Her hands hold onto my back, not letting me go. I haven't experienced post-orgasmic bliss like this before. Our breathing settles into a regular pace. Her eyes are closed. I'm not sure if she's going to sleep or not. I ask quietly, "Are you still mad?" She peeks one eye open, then chuckles at me.

"No, love. I'm not angry anymore. You did well." Her hand slides to my head, running her nails against my scalp. "You did well." A shiver runs down my spine. I don't know if it's from her scratching me or her praise, but it feels like heaven.

Chapter Ten

We cuddle for a while, coming down from our orgasm high. I love having Addy's body under mine. She eventually coaxes me out of bed, stating we need to shower. Given that both of us were covered in several bodily fluids, she has a point. I grab my clothes, leave her bedroom, and head for mine.

"No, come with me," she speaks gently, not in her dominating, alpha voice.

I turn and follow her to her bathroom. She starts the water, letting it warm up for us. Her shower is bigger than the one I share with Megs. While we wait, her eyes roam over my body, taking me in. I want to do the same to her, but I'm mesmerized, watching her stare at me. She steps towards me. Her fingers lift to my stomach. She traces around the stains from my release. It isn't a sexual touch. It's searching, feeling, learning. Her hands slide to my ribs, then over the mermaid. She raises my arm to get a better view. I hold my arm up, letting her look. Her eyes finally move up to mine.

"Tell me about this."

Her voice is still soft. She pulls away and steps into the shower. She motions for me to follow. We step into the water together. I begin to speak. "The first year I was with Whitney, she dressed as a mermaid for Halloween. I don't think she remembers that because she never said anything. I wanted to get a tattoo of her, but the real her. This is that tattoo. It seems like it should be pretty, but it isn't. A siren more than a mermaid."

Addy takes in my words. She's standing in the water but lets enough through to hit my skin. She turns sideways, dragging my arm more into the stream. I step in with her. Her fingers begin to rub my body, cleaning the fluids off. She grabs her loofa, adds soap, then washes my body. It's not sexual. There is something deeply intimate about her movements. She cleans my entire body slowly. When she finishes, I take the loofa and do the same to her. As we're washing, she asks what I thought about what we just did. At first, the conversation feels awkward. I'm not used to sharing my thoughts and feelings about sexual acts. It's just not something I've ever done, but Addy is sharing her thoughts. That gives me more confidence to share my own. I tell her what I liked. There wasn't anything that I genuinely didn't like. I wanted to be able to touch, but I also enjoyed not being able to.

The conversation with Addy, the shower, the intimacy of everything we have done this afternoon consumes my thoughts. I forget about the reason she was angry. This is something I need to address soon. There isn't anything I can do now. My mind is racing with thoughts of Addy and Rosie and Megs. Nothing else really matters at the moment. I want to be with them. As uncomfortable as I am with the concept, I need to have a conversation with all of them. Megs has concerns about me breaking the group up. This is absolutely something I do not want to happen. I can't say it would be easy to leave them, but I would rather do that than endanger their relationship. Rosie genuinely cares about me. I've never had another person be as concerned with my emotional well-being as she is. Her thoughts beyond that remain unknown to me. I need to talk with all three of them together, whether it is comfortable or not.

Megs

I arrive at the apartment shortly after Rosie does. Both of us were out later than expected. I went out with Kendra to catch up and have drinks. I don't typically drink much, especially if I am driving. It's so bittersweet to see Kendra. I still have feelings for her. As much as I hate to say it, I sometimes wish things would end with Edwin so she could come back to us. I don't really want that for her. I am happy that she is happy.

When I walk into the apartment, I'm surprised to see Addy at home and in a good mood. She's supposed to be at work. Before I can ask what happened, James speaks up and says he wants to talk to all of us. I look to Rosie and Addy, but they don't know what this is about. He saunters over to the couch and sits in the middle. So we follow suit. Addy sits on one side of him, Rosie on Addy's other side. I take the seat next to James, turning towards him. He's fidgeting with his fingers. His nervousness increases my own.

"Addy and I had sex." Well, duh.

I nod at him. I already knew that. Rosie tries to act surprised but can't pull it off. She laughs, "We already know. You two didn't hide it very well." A slight blush appears on his cheeks. Addy shrugs, leaning back on the couch. Her body is still close to James's. Just another indicator that there has been a change in their relationship. He pauses for a moment. Our lack of shock has thrown him off. When he starts speaking, he's looking at his hands but quickly meets our eyes, shifting between the three of us.

"I know I'm still married legally. My relationship with Whitney has been over for a long time, though. Things are complicated with her since she won't let that go." He takes a deep breath. "I have feelings for you three. All of you." He looks at me when he says the last bit. This does surprise me.

"What..." I'm not positive what I want to say. "What are you saying?"

He shrugs. His hands move through the air, his elbows leaning on his thighs as he leans forward. "I don't know how this thing you three have works, but I want to be part of it. I want to be with you. I..." He looks up to the ceiling as if the right words will fall from the sky.

"I only know how to be monogamous, but I want all three of you."

I stare at him. I don't know what to say, what to do with my hands. Addy is rubbing his back. She seems undisturbed by what he is saying. Rosie is processing everything. She's staring off into space. I have been feeling something for James. I enjoy being around him. He's fun and gentle and accepting of me. Most people still try to force me into some box. He does slip up with pronouns or some awkward touch, but he's always quick to apologize and adjust.

I've never had a typical relationship. In high school, I didn't date anyone. I was happy alone or with Rosie and Addy. I loosely dated Kendra in college, but she never considered what we were doing to be dating. It's why it was so easy for her to leave when Edwin came along. I've all but resigned myself to being single forever. I plan to live with Rosie and Addy for as long as possible. Then when I'm old enough, I'll move into a retirement home, watch the birds, complain about the weather, take up knitting and bridge, or whatever the current card game for old people is. I haven't considered any other reality. James is offering one to me. A different reality, where I have a family. One that I choose and has chosen me. I can't let myself hope for that.

"Do you want to be exclusive with the three of us? Just the four of us together, no one else." Rosie asks, finally coming back to reality.

'Yes, if that's okay with everyone else." He looks at Rosie and Addy. Rosie nods at him. Addy gives a half-shrug that is somehow both committal and carefree. I don't know how she manages to be serious and light simultaneously. James looks at me, waiting for my response.

Exclusiveness is easy. I don't hook up with other people anyways. Rosie and Addy do, and that has never bothered me. They've always come home to sleep, and that's really all I can ask for. I stare at James, his light blue eyes searching my own, waiting patiently. I don't know how to process what I'm being told. What they are offering me. I'm terrified to even think about it. How can I let myself have it? Without taking his eyes off me, he slides his fingers over mine, taking my hand in his. I look down at our hands. This feels so natural, so right. My heart is telling me to say yes, to accept this invitation. My brain is screeching warning lights, throwing red flags around. But all of the red flags are blank. There aren't any reasons for red flags.

"What..." I close my eyes, breaking contact with him. I swallow, trying to clear my throat. My mouth is so dry. I open my eyes again. He is still just patiently waiting. He rivals Rosie in her patience with my feelings. Is that not worth pursuing?

"What are you wanting? A dating relationship? Is this a long-term thing?" I express a few of my doubts. He squeezes my hand gently.

"Honestly, I'm not sure what the future will bring. I just know I have feelings for all of you, and I don't want to hide them. If I have overstepped, I apologize and will step back."

I shake my head. He hasn't overstepped. The feelings are there, and I can see it in all of us. Before I can think of anything else, he speaks again.

"I want to take you on dates. I want to show you off to people." He's looking between all three of us as he tells us this. "I want to have sex with you and not worry about ostracizing the others. I want to do relationship stuff like watch movies, go to Ikea, and argue over the dishes." Rosie chuckles, and Addy pats his back. I stare at him. "I want to call you mine and to be yours." He leans back on the couch, letting us process his words.

My heart seems to vibrate in my chest. I can go to Ikea and argue over chores. He's speaking things I've never allowed in my thoughts but have always known were there. To have acceptance and love and be treated like everyone else. My mind is suddenly heavy. I lean back, resting my cheek against his shoulder.

"Okay," I say, barely above a whisper. James's hand squeezes mine, bringing it to his lips. Addy and Rosie are staring at me. Both are sitting up with stunned looks on their faces. They understand the weight of what I have just agreed to. Rosie and Addy accept my answer, then repeat it. I close my eyes. My emotions are heavy and make me feel sleepy. His skin is warm against mine. I feel safe and accepted and loved.

Rosie

I can't believe Megs just agreed to be in a committed relationship. After Kendra, I thought they'd stay with us for a while. I've been so worried they couldn't move on from Kendra. Megs has always been reserved, but they were worse after Kendra left. Kendra asked Megs to be in her wedding party. Megs turned it down. They went to the wedding; we all did. I don't think Megs would have emotionally handled being in the wedding well. We were all there to support both Kendra and Megs. Megs is happy for Kendra; I didn't think they would recover from their heartbreak after she left.

The idea of officially being with James intrigues me. We've shared partners in the past, primarily other women. There have been a few men, but they were always temporary. I get the impression that James doesn't want this to be temporary. Especially considering he brought up the idea first. We obviously can't get married, but who needs that anyway? There are other ways we could commit to each other. I love the idea of not having a traditional relationship. My mother would hate it, but she doesn't need to know. James could go home with me for the holidays while Megs and Addy....Woah. That's moving a bit fast. We still haven't even reached the summer. I should probably stop that train of thought and derail that train.

We sit in silence for several minutes. Everyone is contemplating the reality of what we just spoke about. Addy finally gets up and goes to the kitchen. She can't stand sitting in silence. She grabs the remote to start music, going to get drinks. With her gone, I slide up next to James, taking her spot. He stretches his arm out, welcoming me into his side. He's such a great cuddler. He plants a small kiss on the top of my head. I squeeze my arms around his middle. My face rests against his shoulder. I take a breath, noticing he smells like Addy's soap. For a moment, I consider why he would smell like her soap but can't pinpoint a logical, non-sexual cause.

"So, what did Addy do to you that made you want to define our relationship?" I ask. He freezes, but Addy quickly provides the answer.

"Oh, I went all pleasure domme to work out my frustrations on him."

My eyes shoot up as I sit to look at her. James is turning a deep shade of red. Even Megs has turned their head and is looking at Addy with suspicion. Even knowing her most of our lives, her bluntness still catches me off guard. Of course, she has some crass comment that seems to explain everything. She walks over with four beers, handing us each one. Then she sits on the coffee table, facing James.

"Ok, I got a lot of bombs to drop all at once." She holds her hand to us, "Please hold all questions until the end." I roll my eyes at her, leaning back into James. I'm sure Addy has an actual reason for her comments. She usually does; she just has terrible delivery.

"First, I fucked James in the hallway at the club earlier this week. Then tonight, Nick had a fucking picture of me wrapped around James in the hallway and wanted to fire me for it. Turns out his bitch ex was at the club, took a photo, then fucking stalked me and tried to get me fired. Nick was ready to fire me, but I talked him out of it. He still sent me home for the night. Naturally, I was livid. So I took it out on James, a la domination."

I'm stunned at all of this new information. His ex caught them? She was nearly fired? Obviously, she would dominate James for it. That is a very Addy thing to do and doesn't surprise me. I can also understand how that would lead James to want to define our relationship. He knows how things are with Megs, their anxiety, and fears about the relationship. I'm still considering what all of this means. James moves his arm around me to take a drink from his bottle. He's still holding Megs's hand, who is also quiet. He isn't making eye contact and intentionally avoiding it. Addy is making eye contact with us, waiting for our reactions.

"You were submissive?" James still won't look at me.

"He was submissive. And so good at it. He did an excellent job." Addy speaks in her alpha voice, rubbing his thigh.

Ah. That makes sense. He's probably embarrassed about being submissive to her. I'm convinced Addy could get a male lion to submit to her. Men, especially those without experience or introduction to kinks, tend to insist they are dominant. It's part of the reason Addy likes girls so much. They will be submissive. I wonder how hard James pushed back against her when she started. Addy can be intimidating when she gets in alpha mode. Probably even worse if she's also angry. I curl around his arm, looking up at him.

"Did you like it?" I speak gently, not wanting to make him uncomfortable.

"Yes," he answers softly.

I grin, snuggling into him more. I bet Addy could dream up some crazy things with two submissive players. Megs will follow Addy's directions, but I wouldn't consider them submissive. Megs won't kneel or crawl. An image of James kneeling pops into my head, and heat pools in my core. The thought of playing with them in those roles excites me. That's definitely something we're putting on a to-do list. We're all lost deep in thought when James speaks up.

"Do you have a lot of kinks?"

I answer him, "I wouldn't say a lot, but there are several between us."

"What are your kinks? What do you want?"

I don't hesitate to answer. I already know, and Megs and Addy know too. I've discussed it several times.

"I want to suspend a partner."

"Suspend?" James asks.

"Yes, with ropes. From the ceiling." He considers for a moment.

"Have you done it before?"

"No. I don't have the equipment here. I've never found someone I would want to rig like that. Megs or Addy have offered, but I don't know. I kind of want to tie up a guy."

James nods, not saying anything else. He turns his head towards Addy and takes a sip, waiting for her answer. She finally looks up and responds.

"I want to chase someone."

James huffs out a laugh, shaking his head. "What...why?" Addy explains her primal kink to him, going into detail about what it means and what she wants from it. It's pretty clear he is new to all of this and hasn't even considered some of these things before. Addy really got into kink in college. She was friends with a guy who introduced her to a kink community. She dragged Megs and me into it. Megs was mainly along for the ride, never committing to anything but always willing to play. Addy and I found our kinks, though. We both fell in love with the lifestyle and learned as much as possible. We didn't stay close to the community but carried everything with us. We occasionally meet up with people we know but mostly stick to ourselves. It's been enough for a while. Once Addy finishes explaining, James stares off, processing everything.

"I...I think I want to watch," he admits.

"Watch what?"

"I... an orgy?" He stutters through his embarrassment.

"James, are you saying you want to watch the three of us? It's okay to admit that. It's pretty fucking hot." I squeeze his arm tighter, looking up at his face. He looks down at me; relief and nervousness are written on his face. The thought occurs to me that I haven't actually kissed him. This isn't the right moment, but I will soon. I'm not going to let Addy have all the fun. He finally nods at me. I sip my beer. There isn't anything else I want to say. For a moment, we're all quiet again. There has been a lot to think about in the last hour. It doesn't escape me that Megs hasn't answered his question. Is James too distracted to have noticed? Megs has always gotten off the hook when questions like that come up.

"Wait, Megs didn't answer. What do you want?" So James did notice.

"Oh, I don't really have any kinks."

"Surely there is something you want to do, though."

Megs bites their lip, clearly trying to decide how much they want to share. I'm sure they know we wouldn't judge them. Maybe they're nervous about James. I can't imagine what they would want that is so embarrassing. James just admitted to being a voyeur. Addy wants to chase someone like prey, and I want to suspend someone from the ceiling. Is Megs into something weirder? What could that be?

"I want to have sex with a man," they all but whisper. I have to stifle my gasp. I never realized they hadn't had sex with a man. I always assumed Megs had slept with other people when we weren't around. They have been with Kendra and us. They've played with Addy and me with other people, but always in a more supportive role, never the one being touched.

"I'm not saying I want to have sex with you. Or that I want to have sex with any man. Or that I will ever do it. It's just... that's just my deepest, darkest desire," they rush out this statement quickly.

Addy and James are as stunned as I am. Addy asks the next question before James and I have time to consider words. Of course, it's Addy.

"How many people have you slept with?"

Megs answers softly, burying their face behind James's arm. "Three."

Me. Addy. Kendra. There's nothing wrong with that. I always assumed they had been with more people. I let their admission settle with me. James moves, pulling his arm away from Megs. For a moment, I can't breathe. What is he doing? Then he settles back, wrapping his arm around Megs's back, pulling them in closer to him. I let out a sigh. I can see Megs visibly relax into his arm.

Addy finishes her beer. Her leg is bouncing. She's clearly uncomfortable, though I'm not sure about what. She probably also didn't realize Megs had only been with us. It's weird seeing Addy worked up and nervous. She slaps her hands on her legs and stands up.

"Well. I'm going to bed now. I have to work a double, so I won't be around tomorrow."

She looks at each of us, her hands twitching by her side. She awkwardly pats each of us on the head before walking quickly to dispose of her beer bottle, then straight into her room. Megs sits up. "Leave it to Addy to make it awkward, but I think I'm going to bed too. What are you two doing tomorrow?"

"I need to do some research for my current story. I'll be gone most of the day and evening."

I look to Megs. "There is a new art exhibit I want to go to. Do you want to go with me?" Megs nods, offering a soft positive response. They stand, then pat James and me on the head before walking to their bedroom laughing. I squeeze my arms around James again before also standing.

"We should probably get to bed too. Thanks for bringing up our relationship. I'm excited to move forward with you." I lean in and press a small kiss on his cheek. His cheek is warm and still red from embarrassment. As much as I want to kiss his lips, I decide to wait. As right as some of the other moments felt, this one doesn't feel like the right moment. I don't need to wait for the perfect moment, but I want it to be a good one. I stand to leave, but he grabs my hand to stop me. I look down at him.

"Can we go on a date Sunday?"

"Yeah, I would like that." I really would.

MEGS

Rosie insists we go out to eat before going to the art exhibit. I prefer to eat at home, but I also like spending time with Rosie. She assures me the restaurant has excellent salads. Not that I particularly care for salads. I'm willing to eat most things, but I do appreciate her thoughts of my diet. Rosie is such a thoughtful person.

She is always thinking of others. That's probably why she brought me along, to see how I'm doing after my evening with Kendra and then James. It has been a long 24 hours, but honestly, I feel better about it than I thought I would. Kendra is doing well. She's settled into a happy life. Now I have the chance to do the same. I still try to restrain my hope. This is new. James could grow tired of it all in a couple of months. It may not work out at all, but I'm going to let myself be happy. And a little hopeful.

The restaurant is bright and colorful. It's not crowded, so they let us choose our table. Rosie picks a booth across from a large window. I slide to one side. Rosie slides in next to me instead of sitting across. I raise my eyebrows at her, wondering why she is sitting next to me instead of across. She shrugs, "If I sit next to you, it's easier to hear. And I just want to be close to you." I nod, grabbing the menu to look it over.

Rosie is wearing a long skirt with a tank top. The two look like they could be a dress, but I've seen her wear them separately enough to know they aren't. I stuck with my preferred jeans and a shirt. I am wearing a plain black shirt. It is comfortable enough but still passable at an art exhibit. We sit in silence until our order is in. Once the server leaves, Rosie starts talking.

"How are you feeling after yesterday?"

"Fine, honestly. Kendra is doing well. She said they may try for a baby soon. Who knows? She's moving on and doing well. Then James gave me the opportunity to do the same. So I took it." I say with a shrug. "How are you feeling?"

She nods her head, then smiles at me. "That's great to hear about Kendra. I'm excited to see where things go with James. I've been interested since Addy first brought him home. I'm glad you are into it too. I think it could be good for all of us."

She starts talking about work and how all her kids are doing. The school year is almost over for her. She took the summer off but is still getting paid through the school. In the past, she's worked over the summer but said she isn't planning to this year. She might offer some tutoring or something if she gets too bored. She's just looking to relax now. I'm sure she'll enjoy it for a week or two, then be bored. As our lunch comes, a thought occurs to me. Rosie and I go out together frequently, but it's not usually this structured. It's more like we run errands and see where the day will take us. Or a hike or something. After our conversation last night, this feels different.

"Rosie, is this a date?"

She doesn't look shocked by my question. That leads me to think she has considered this already. She finally answers. "Not really, I guess. Not that I wouldn't go on a date with you. We've just done this so often that it feels natural. Plus, I think you'll enjoy the art exhibit." She takes a sip of her water and then looks at me. "Do you want it to be a date?"

I haven't considered that option. Would I want it to be a date? I did agree to be in a relationship with all three of them. Does that mean solo dates with all of them? I wouldn't want to go on solo dates with them all regularly. That sounds like a lot of work and planning and organizing. I like things the way they are, where we go when the opportunity arises. That's all this is, right?

"You don't have to answer that," Rosie says, touching my hand gently. Her touch brings me back from my spinning mind. She knows me so well. "I'm happy with this being a date or just something we do. We can call this whatever you want. I just like spending time with you. I love you, and I want to do things with you."

That's an answer I can live with. I smile back at Rosie, nudging her shoulder with mine gently. I turn back to eating. We split the bill and then go to the art exhibit. Rosie loops her arm through mine as we walk the few blocks between the restaurant and the gallery. The art is imaginative. She was right that it is something I like. We spend the afternoon roaming around the exhibits. We discuss different aspects of the pieces, pretending we know anything about art. We laugh and have fun. If this is a date, I can definitely get used to it. This is how I like spending my time.

Chapter Eleven

I have been working on the landowner case for a while now. More details have unfolded about the land owner. There are numerous discrepancies in the use of his lands and the income he reports. I have uncovered links to money laundering, but I am solidifying my sources and ensuring they are soundproof. What I have learned will be life-changing for his family and his employees. We have discussed going to the police but aren't ready yet. I'd like to make some contacts within his business soon. Once we are prepared to publish the article, I'll turn my documents, sans sources' names, to the police for them to sort through. Martin Stewart isn't going to be a businessman for much longer.

While working on my article, Rosie texts me to ask about the date. She has this idea: we pick our two favorite places and take each other there. I love the idea. I get to know her better, and it's not a traditional dinner and movie thing. I have already decided on the two places I will take her. I pack up my office as I finish my work for the day. I want everything to look nice and organized. I don't want things lying around my desk.

I head back to the apartment. I feel terrible that Addy had to pull a double today. I'm not the least bit surprised that Whitney pulled some shit like this. She was always dramatic and keen to find the information she wanted. The concerning part is how quickly she managed to identify Addy. Hopefully, it was just a coincidence. Whitney probably recognized Addy from the restaurant we all went to and had been to her bar before. I've been to Drunken Moose several times before this spring. It's a good bar. It was not my favorite because it wasn't close to my work or home, but I would still venture out occasionally. I probably took Whitney at some point and just forgot about it.

The apartment is quiet. I assume Megs and Rosie aren't back from their exhibit yet. I shower and decide to take a nap. The rest of the evening will be pretty chill. I could use a chill weekend. Things have been so crazy lately. I need to contact my lawyer next week to push things along. I thought I would be more upset about Whitney changing the locks and keeping all my stuff hostage. After she ruined my things and sent them to me, I am rebuilding what I had. I've gotten new clothes and a few trinkets. I've even hung some photos in new frames in my room. Things aren't entirely terrible, and I can't wait for tomorrow.

Rosie told me she wanted to go in the morning. So I wake up early on a Sunday, ready to go on a date with Rosie to our favorite places. I slip on jeans and a nice button-down. I debate grabbing a nice jacket but decide not to. Hopefully, she'll let me know if I need one before we leave. We didn't say how fancy the places we're going are. Mine are casual, but I'm unsure about the places Rosie has picked. Something makes me think they'll be more informal too.

I wait in the kitchen for Rosie. Megs is refusing to give me coffee, and this annoys me. "Just let me have a drink of yours then." I don't know how to function without coffee. Megs rolls their eyes but finally hands me their mug. I inhale the rich scent of the coffee they have. I take a small sip, testing the temperature. The bold flavor hits my tongue. The coffee is hot but not scalding. With my eyes on Megs, I lift the cup, drinking as much as possible.

"Hey!" They shout, reaching to take their drink back. I turn away, trying not to spill any on my clothes. They are still trying to grab the coffee from me but are careful not to spill it. I don't know if that concern is about my clothes or their coffee. I finally hand it back, having drunk about half of it.

"I'm telling Rosie."

I laugh at them, wiping my lips. I stick my tongue out as Rosie finally enters the kitchen.

"JAMES DRANK HALF MY COFFEE. I told him not to."

I groan at Megs for tattling on me. Oh, I'm going to think of something to get them back. Eventually. I stick my tongue out at them again. We both laugh at each. I turn to take Rosie in. She is in a more casual outfit. She's wearing a dress that looks like a long t-shirt. It's a pretty pastel purple that looks stunning against her creamy smooth skin. Her hair is braided to the side and falls over one shoulder. She rolls her eyes at our antics, moving closer to the door. I step up next to her and place my hand on her back. I need to touch her more. She's so soft and warm. I want all of her on me.

I press a kiss against her cheek, "You look gorgeous." She smiles up at me. "You look nice too." She says goodbye to Megs and walks out the door. I follow her to her Jeep and climb in the passenger seat. I typically prefer to drive on dates, but we are going to her stops first, and my car isn't nearly as nice as hers. The AC doesn't work well. It's not a problem in the mornings, but this afternoon will be warm. We will probably want AC if we stay out long enough.

"Where are we going first? Does it have coffee?"

She glances at me, then back at the road. She's such a good driver. The complete opposite of Addy. "It's a coffee shop. They have great coffee and even better breakfast foods. It's a wonderful little shop and my absolute favorite." I can imagine Rosie sitting at a table in a coffee shop, sipping on a latte or something, reading a book, or grading some papers. There's something so traditionally beautiful about Rosie. On the outside, she fits the narrative of the girl next door. She's sweet, gentle, so kind, and quietly beautiful. But in private, she really lets out who she is. She is all those things but so much more.

When we get to the coffee shop, I follow her inside. The sway of her hips as she walks swishes the dress's material. The dress isn't form-fitting, so I don't get a great view of her ass, but I can see it as she steps. Her ass pokes out on the sides. I'm mesmerized by her walk. I want to grab her ass, sink my teeth into it, squeeze my fingers into her flesh...

"Stop staring."

My eyes shoot up to hers. I feel embarrassed that she caught me and offer a shrug and a smirk as an apology. She laughs, taking my arm to lead me to the counter. I'm thrilled she has a great sense of humor. At the register, we both order food and drinks. We find a table near the back when someone calls out to Rosie. She turns and looks in that direction with the biggest grin.

"Mrs. Wallace!"

A dark-skinned woman with grey hair walks out of the kitchen area. She's wiping her hands on her apron, matching Rosie's smile. They greet each other with a warm hug. If this is how Rosie is always welcomed, I can see why this is her favorite spot. I stand back, watching the interaction.

"How are you doing, Mrs. Wallace?"

"Oh, you know me. I'm working all the time. My son was in town last week. He's already gone, but it was so nice to have him for a visit."

The two women chat idly for several minutes. They are catching up on how things are going in their lives with Rosie's students and Mrs. Wallace's store. Our food arrives at the counter, and I grab it so Rosie doesn't have to stop talking. I put the plates and drinks on the table and hear Rosie's voice.

"James, come here! I want you to meet Mrs. Wallace. She owns this store. I came here frequently during college, and she always gave me tips and advice on my studies. I probably wouldn't have graduated if it weren't for her advice. I wouldn't be half the teacher I am without her." The elderly woman flaps her hands at the compliment as if she could shoo the thought away. I step to Rosie's side, placing my hand on her back. I extend my other hand, but Rosie speaks before I can. "Mrs. Wallace, this is James, my boyfriend."

Both Mrs. Wallace and I look surprised at this. I knew what I was asking the other night. It's still shocking to hear it out loud. I turn my gaze from Rosie to her friend, a goofy grin now plastered across my face. Mrs. Wallace finally breaks into a smile. She knocks my hand away and pulls me into a hug. Despite being several inches shorter than me, she grabs my shoulders and pulls me down to her. I wrap my arms around her, hugging her back. I would hug anyone right now with Rosie's words still ringing in my ear.

Mrs. Wallace releases me. She instructs me to take care of Rosie. She tells us to eat our food before it gets cold and returns to the kitchen. I sit at the table, not taking my eyes off Rosie. She sips from her cup, offering me a quizzical look.

"What?"

I shrug. "Nothing. You're just adorable." She laughs at me as she starts eating her food. I'm not only happy that she agreed to the date but thankful that this is where she wanted to go. Emotions are buzzing through me at being welcomed into her life and called her boyfriend. That feels better than I could have imagined.

We eat our breakfast. I have a breakfast burrito while Rosie has a cinnamon roll. She tells me Mrs. Wallace makes most of the pastries, and they are the best. She breaks off a small portion of her cinnamon roll and offers it to me. I open my mouth, taking the food in. I close my lips around her fingers. My eyes are on her, but hers are on my lips. I swipe my tongue across her fingers before leaning back to chew the food. It really is good. It's soft and sweet, the way I imagine Rosie is. Her eyes finally meet mine. I lick my lips, "Perfect." I leave my comment at that, not specifying whether it's her or the cinnamon roll I'm talking about, but it's both.

We leave the coffee shop after saying goodbye to Mrs. Wallace. We both promise to visit again soon. The café is one I will definitely be back to again. Rosie drives for several minutes, taking us to the next stop. We turn off the main road onto a side street. Street parking has trees, flower pots, and benches scattered along the sidewalk. There are small shops on both sides. Restaurants, boutiques, and trinket stores fill the buildings with various signs and paintings on the window. She parks on the street near a small bookstore. We get out of the Jeep and walk towards the bookstore. She takes my hand, lacing her fingers with mine.

"I love this bookstore. I don't come nearly as much as I want to, but it's my favorite."

Inside, shelves stacked throughout the middle are filled with books. Books line the walls, floor to ceiling. A single register stands in the middle. Exposed brick behind the register is covered with posters for different books. Several people are perusing the shelves. Oversized plush chairs are scattered throughout the store. It's not a large building, but it is so full of books it feels magical. Rosie leads me through tables and shelves. She's looking at the titles, but I'm still watching her. She's in her element here. She's on a mission. I'm unsure if it's to find a book she already wants or a random one. She grabs a book, reading the back. She shrugs her shoulders and puts the book back. All of this without even acknowledging me.

I follow along, picking up a couple of books, feigning interest in them. I like reading and will probably buy a book. I'm more interested in Rosie, though. Eventually, she seems to find the book she was looking for. She shows it to me, explaining the story and why she wants that particular book. I take it from her, thumbing through it. I tuck it under my arm, taking her hand back in mine. She gives me a sweet smile that I love so much from her.

"So, I have 2 ideas while we're here."

"Is that so?"

"Yes. First, you have to tell me about your favorite book."

I think for a moment. I haven't considered what my favorite book is in a while, so I need to think through what I've read.

"It is *Things Fall Apart* by Chinua Achebe." She nods, considering my answer. I match the description of the book she is buying, detailing the book I just mentioned. "I read it in high school, and it opened my eyes to other cultures and not having happy endings in stories. I like the writing and really enjoy the story. So that's my favorite book."

"I love it."

She turns, pulling me along to a different area of the store. She hasn't said where we are going or what we are doing. I walk behind her, enjoying the feel of her fingers tangled with mine. She stops at a shelf, looking over all the books, and I notice that a few covers have half-naked men on them. Then I see the sign indicating this is the romance section. Well, that wasn't what I was expecting.

"Aha!"

She grabs a book off the shelf, flipping through the pages. She slows, scanning each page before she finally stops. Her eyes move to mine, and she has a wicked grin on her face. I'm suddenly very nervous about what is going on in her mind.

"The second thing we're going to do is a game." I raise my eyebrows at her, intrigued. "These are all the spicy books, with detailed sex scenes. We'll take turns reading them to each other until we can't stand it anymore."

My eyebrows shoot up at her. My mind is going a mile a minute. We're going to be reading sex scenes. Out loud. In public? This is going to be fun and challenging.

"Ok...what do I get if I win?" She rubs her chin, considering my question.

"What do you want?"

I don't even need time to think. I know exactly what I want from Rosie. "A kiss." She smiles at me, considering this. "And if I win?" I mimic her motion from earlier and rub my chin. "What do you want?

"A kiss. But I choose the time and place."

"Deal."

I stick my hand out, shaking her hand. I'm not positive what I've gotten myself into, but this feels like a win-win situation. Either way, I'm getting a kiss. Unless she decides to torture me and make me wait for it. I decide I just need to win. That's the best option. She steps in front of me, so I can read over her shoulder as she reads the words out loud. I've never read a spicy romance novel before. Skimming the page before she starts reading, I realize I'm in trouble. I had no clue these were so explicit.

Rosie starts reading in a quiet voice. I assume this is so other people don't hear, but I quickly realize she came prepared. Her voice changes to a sultry one. It's not the same as Addy's alpha voice but it has the same effect. She leans into me, her shoulders against my chest, her ass rubbing against my hips. I'm in trouble. I'm definitely not going to win. She starts reading as the scene takes off. The man and woman were touching each other and kissing. Then the woman goes down on the man. Another man joins them and starts going down on the woman. She's reading the words but moaning when the characters moan. She presses her hips against mine. The image of her doing those things to me fills my brain. Her hips swirl over my aching cock, and she moans softly with her story again. I can feel it stirring to life. If she keeps going like this, I'll be standing in the middle of the store with a raging hard-on.

I'm now convinced she did this on purpose. She can't lose. She can be all kinds of horny and still walk out of this store without anyone knowing. As much as I want to win, I don't want to walk through this store with tented pants, knowing I can't fuck her in her parked car. I need to throw in the towel; as much as I don't want her to stop, I reach up and slam the book closed. She looks up at me, surprised at first, but it quickly fades to laughter.

"Do you own this book?" I ask through gritted teeth. She shakes her head no, the smile still on her face. I take the book from her, adding it to the other still in my arm.

"Does this mean I win?"

"Yes," I grit out.

She turns to face me, giggling as she wraps her arms around my neck. I place my free hand on her hip, resting my face against her neck. I press a couple of small kisses against her sensitive skin. I breathe against her ear. "That wasn't a fair game, and you know it." She laughs louder, squeezing before pulling away.

"I know, but you look adorable right now."

"Do you read this a lot?"

She shrugs with a half nod. "I read a lot of it, but I read other things too." I consider her answer. Thankfully my member didn't spring to life, but it's not far from it. I have an idea, but I can't focus on it too much.

"Pick out another one. You can read them to me later to make up for cheating. I'm going to find a book on toe fungus."

She laughs as I turn and walk away. I don't need to find that book, but I must get away from her body. I want her so much. Listening to her read those dirty things was such a tease. I want to do those things to her. I want her to do them to me. I want to touch her, hold her, taste her. Maybe I do need to find that book on toe fungus.

She meets me at the register with another book. I take it, handing all three to the cashier and grabbing my wallet. Rosie tries to protest, but I insist. After I pay, I give her the bag. She places a kiss on my cheek. Her lips are full and soft, leaving me to think of what they would feel like on other parts. Yep, should have bought a toe fungus book.

Rosie

Teasing James is my new favorite activity. I didn't realize he would react so quickly. I thought it would be harder to get him to break. There are butterflies in my stomach thinking about how easy it was. If I just need to rub my ass and say some dirty words to get him that worked up, I can only imagine how he would react if I did more. I had planned to do more while reading, like squeezing his member, rubbing my breast against his chest, speaking against his ear, maybe even licking it. I never intended to play fair, but I also didn't intend to win that quickly. I'm excited to have the kiss to hold over him, and I'm going to tease him with that too.

I let him drive to the next location. That would be easier than me driving. He knows where he's going. He takes us to the business district. He parks near several tall glass buildings. They aren't quite skyscrapers, but there are about a dozen floors to each. We walk into one of the buildings and take the elevator up. There's a small entryway with a sign for Under, the magazine he works for. I follow him in, taking in his office.

There is a small reception area with a window overlooking the city. The view isn't as good as our apartment's, but it's not bad either. A couch and coffee table fill the entry, standard lobby area things. He leads me past all that into an area with cubicles. The walls are about chest high. I can see into most of them while standing but sitting would offer a feeling of privacy. He leads me through the maze of desks, printers, and filing cabinets, stopping at one on the back wall. There is a corner desk in the cubical. This one is more private than some of the others. It has three closed sides, one being the wall. A couple of action figures are around the desk, along with two photos pinned to the wall near the computer. There are no papers or any other items. He keeps his desk tidy.

"This is where you work?"

He's been quiet since he led me in here. His hands are in his pockets, watching me. He nods, looking a bit anxious but also natural. He fits in here nicely, and this is the space he has carved for himself.

"Tell me about it."

He shrugs, seeming to be at a loss for words. "I started working here right after college. Even though I go out and do interviews and gather other information, this has always been my favorite place to write." He rubs the back of his neck with his hand. "It's quiet. I've got decent coworkers, and I like the work. Before Addy took me in, I spent a lot of time here. I didn't really sleep here since there's no room," he waves his hand around to make his point. "But I'd sit and write or research or just daydream sometimes." He shrugs again. A smile forms across my face.

"Okay. Show me. Let me see you at work."

He moves around me and sits in the chair. He leans up to the computer. He pretends to type, but in a wildly exaggerated form, lifting his whole arm with each button he clicks. I laugh at him, stepping closer. I turn him in the chair to face me, then slip into his lap. I wrap my arms around his shoulders. Speaking gently, I say, "Thank you for showing me this." It feels like a big moment for him. I want to ask if he ever brought Whitney here, but I don't want to spoil the moment. He wraps his arm around my lower back, placing his hand on my hip. The other hand rests on my knee.

Sitting here in his office isn't exactly romantic. It's not really something that would be deemed first kiss worthy, but it's what I want. He s shown me something special about him. He met the specifications of our favorite places date. This kiss isn't just a reward for that. It's appreciation, emotion, and yearning, all wrapped in my lips. I don't even care that I planned to tease him with it. I want this now.

I lean closer and ever so gently press my lips against his. My eyes close, feeling his lips against mine. He kisses me back immediately. His hand on my hip glides over my back, pulling me closer to him. The hand on my knee moves to my hip that his other hand just left. I slide one hand to his neck, deepening the kiss. My lips part slightly, and his tongue slips into my mouth. I open my mouth more, kissing him back, meeting his tongue with mine. My thumb caresses his jaw, fingertips sliding back into his hair. So much for teasing him with the kiss I won.

He squeezes my hip. I shift slightly, turning towards him more. As I do, I feel his cock jump to life. I remember how frustrated he was at the bookstore. I drop my free hand to the other side of his neck, then slide my other hand down his chest. I seek the outline of his cock through his pants. He groans at me, breaking the kiss. His forehead presses against mine as he tries to breathe deeply. He's trying not to get an erection, which is the opposite of what I'm trying to do. I flatten my palm against him, rubbing harder to increase the pressure through his pants. He hisses my name at this change. I slide down his body, kneeling on the floor before him.

"Let me give you another reason this is your favorite place."

I keep my eyes on him as I unbuckle his pants. I slide my fingers in, wrapping around his cock. I tug it lightly, letting him shift his position to pull his rigid member out of his pants. His eyes are intently focused on my hand. I wrap my fingers around, stroking up and down slowly. Addy had mentioned he was big, but holding it in my hand still feels surprising. He is definitely significant. I lick my lips, leaning in to press a kiss on the back side of the head. He groans, rolling his head back momentarily. Then his eyes are back on me. It feels like he can't stop watching. I lick my lips again, then slide the head in, swirling my tongue around the tip. He groans again, shifting his hips towards me. I press my tongue on the underside of the head, then take more of his cock in my mouth. I wrap my hand around the base, sliding up and down the top half. I let my mouth adjust to his size before taking him deeper. He grabs the back of my head. His fingers caressing me. The feeling of his fingers against my head causes me to moan against him. His hips thrust up again, his cock jumping in my mouth.

I flatten my hand against his stomach, leaving only my thumb and forefinger to support his rigid member in my mouth. I swirl my tongue around the length as I pull back up, then slide down, taking in as much as possible. When I feel him hit the back of my throat, I pause, holding him in my mouth. He is breathing hard, one hand on my head, the other on my shoulder. He squeezes my shoulder tightly. I suck tightly as I pull back to the tip, then slide down, repeating the process.

"Oh shit, Rosie. Fuck, keep doing that."

I appease him, swallowing as much as possible, pausing, then sucking vigorously as I pull back. My free hand caresses his thigh, squeezing it occasionally. My jaw starts to sting with discomfort. As I'm about to switch techniques, he mutters, "I'm gonna come." I use my free hand to stroke the part of his shaft that isn't in my mouth. I keep sliding down, but I don't pause. I bob up and down, once, twice, then I feel warm squirts hitting the back of my throat. I swallow the first bit, slowing my movements to pull the rest out of him. I suck him once more, then switch to licking. I ensure nothing is left behind, swallowing every bit that hits my tongue. When nothing else comes out, I look up at him. His eyes are on mine with fire in them. His fingers wrap around my jaw, dragging me up to him. He crashes against my lips. I kiss him back, sticking my tongue in his mouth. I'm sure he can taste himself on my tongue. That seems to drive him crazier.

He suddenly flips me around, pressing my chest and stomach against his desk. I glance back to see him putting his cock back in his pants. He flips my dress over my back, his lips instantly on my ass cheeks. He's kissing and nipping all over. His fingers slide up my thighs, pausing at my panty-covered core. I didn't intend on things going this way when we left, but I still have on one of my sexier black lace thongs. His fingers brush against the material as his mouth moves between my ass cheeks.

"James," I moan, placing my head on my arm against the desk.

Then the elevator dings and opens. I freeze, but James quickly stands, dropping my dress back down. A tall man with olive skin and dark hair walks through the office. He's wearing a t-shirt, sweats, and flip-flops. At first, he doesn't seem to notice us, but James calls out to him, giving him a wave. The guy waves back.

"Getting some work done?" The other man asks.

"Yeah, and showing my girlfriend around." James grabs my ass, causing me to squeak in surprise.

I wave my hand, my face burning with embarrassment. The guy nods, offering a soft hi. "Well, I'll leave you alone." He enters an office along the same wall as James's cubicle and closes the door. James is wrapped around me instantly, kissing my cheek, neck, and collarbone. "He'll stay in there for hours. He's divorced too and doesn't want to be at home," he explains. His fingers are slipping under my dress, searching for my core again.

"Are you sure? Shouldn't we leave?"

"I'm not leaving until I'm done with you."

He guides me back against the desk. I lean down. I'm nervous about the guy walking back out, but that also excites me. I've never considered myself an exhibitionist, but the risk of getting caught is exciting. Plus, I won't get alone time with James back at the apartment. Even with Addy at work, Megs is still around. I know they don't want to get involved in sex much, but I don't want to be rude, either. James doesn't waste any time once I'm against the desk. His fingers hook my thong, sliding it down. He instructs me to step out, and I do. I notice he tucks the thong in his pocket. Then his face is buried in my ass.

"Oh fuck," I moan.

"Shhh. You gotta be quiet, baby."

He knocks my foot with his knee, widening my stance for him. His fingers spread me open as his tongue finds my wet core. He groans against me as he licks up my core, flicking his tongue against my clit. I press my hips back against him, wanting more pressure. He licks several more times, then his tongue dives inside me. I struggle to keep the noises inside. I want to cry out at his touch. His tongue moves back against my clit, swirling and sucking it into his mouth. My legs are shaking, so ready to explode. He is really good at working his tongue. He licks down the length the continues back to my other hole. He circles it with his tongue, pressing against it. Chills run through me as a string of curses escapes my lips.

"You like that?" His voice is deep and husky.

"Mmhmm," I groan, nodding my head too.

His tongue slides back to my core, leaving my ass feeling empty and bare. His tongue is dragging through me, lapping up my wetness. Two of his fingers touch my clit, squeezing and massaging it. My pussy clenches tight against his face. His other hand slides up my thigh, over my ass cheek, then a finger presses against my other hole. He's just touching, teasing, not actually entering. He continues this assault on my clit, pussy, and ass for several minutes. My orgasm is growing stronger with each lick, each touch, each press. I'm fighting hard to keep the noises to a minimum. I bite into my forearm to control the noise. As my orgasm grows, I feel a tingling low in my abdomen. It does not happen every time, but I've had this feeling enough to know what it means.

"James, I'm gonna squirt. I'm so close."

He pauses for a second, stunned by my declaration. I know it's not quite as common for women to squirt, but I didn't want him to be surprised or caught off guard. I hold my breath as his mouth pulls back from me just a little. I'm praying he doesn't stop, moaning at the loss of his tongue against my pussy. His finger leaves my ass. I turn to see what he is doing, but before I can move the material from my dress, his mouth is back on my pussy. His tongue is assaulting my core, and his fingers are squeezing my clit. Then his finger slips inside my ass. I cry out at the sudden pressure. There isn't any discomfort since he has been toying with it. He pulled away from me to lick his finger before he inserted it. Right as that light bulb clicks on, my orgasm hits. My vision is covered with fireworks. My body is clenching and jerking against him. I feel more fluid than usual gush out against his face. He keeps licking my pussy, as if trying to taste everything. My orgasm lasts longer than expected. I squeeze my eyes shut, riding the high. His finger slips out of my ass, and my body shivers against him. As I come down, he slowly moves away, cool air hitting my wet, hot skin. He stands quickly, wrapping his arms around me, pressing his lips to mine. I throw my arms around his shoulder, as much for intimacy as for support. I can taste and feel my juices on his face. It's a good thing I went with light makeup. I'll probably need to wash my face to remove the wetness. He pulls back, looking down at me.

"You are fucking amazing," he whispers, pressing kisses to my cheek and neck. I bury my face into his shoulder, a little embarrassed. He chuckles, squeezing my body. "Come on, let's get cleaned up." He leads me to the bathroom. I glance back at the office his coworker went to. I can't see the other man. I don't know if he heard us or is just ignoring us. In the bathroom, I wipe myself clean, wiping off my face too. James is waiting for me when I'm done. I step close to him.

"You didn't give me my panties back."

"I know," he says with a smirk.

"James!"

"What?" He teases but hands them over to me. I glance around quickly, then I slip them on. Once I'm adjusted, he pulls me towards the door. "Come on. I need some food now." I take his hand, following him back to the Jeep.

He drives us to a diner on the outskirts of town. It's a one-story building that looks like it was built in the fifties. There are windows around three-quarters of the building with an overhang above them. I imagine it was red once, but now it's grey. The rest of the building is bricks. A sign in the window indicates this place is called Tina's. He leads me inside, picking a booth near the window.

"My grandparents used to bring me here when I was young," he tells me. "This was the place we always went to celebrate. Birthdays, end of school, after games, competitions, anything. The food is greasy, and the milkshakes are thick." A server walks up, and we both order drinks.

"Were you close to your grandparents?" I ask.

"Yeah, they had a lot to do with my childhood. Both parents worked, and my grandparents filled in when they were gone. A lot of who I am is because of them. They both passed when I was a teen, though." I grab his hand, offering an apology. He shrugs, "It's okay." The server comes back with our drinks and takes our order. Since the menu isn't complicated, it is easy to pick quickly. We sit and chat more about his grandparents. He tells me how he played baseball, and they were at every game. I listen to his stories. I can feel the love he has for them. I ask about his parents, but he isn't as close to them as he was to his grandparents. They are still around, he tells me, but he doesn't talk with them much.

We chat for the rest of the meal. It's easy and comfortable. I'm sure that has to do with the orgasms we both just had, but it's also more. James and I work well together. Things are easy and smooth. I don't have to try to be anything around him. I can be me, not some idea of who I should be. He isn't surprised when I say crass things. Addy has desensitized him a lot. We laugh easily, and the conversation flows smoothly. It's the perfect end to the morning we've had. We split a chocolate milkshake. We argue about what kind. He wants mint chocolate chip, and I want a brownie. We settle on sharing a chocolate milkshake. I suggest we get our own, but he says that isn't a good idea. He is right. The milkshake is big and thick. It's so chocolatey. I moan several times as the creamy chocolate shake hits my lips. He groans at me when I do. When we're done, he pays the check, and we head back to the apartment. The ride back is quiet. We're both happy and content and don't feel the need to fill the silence between us.

Chapter Twelve

JAMES

It's been a week since Rosie was in my office. One glorious week of teasing and cuddling and talking, but no sex. We've fooled around, but my dick is aching to be inside her. Addy has been busy with work. She's been working extra hours to get back on good terms with her boss. I haven't seen her much. When she is around, she's exhausted. She's even fallen asleep on the couch watching movies with us. I've offered to do things for her. I feel terrible about her situation, knowing it's Whitney's fault. There isn't too much I can do for Addy, though. I help with her chores. The rest of the time, I'm lusting after Rosie.

Rosie is such a tease. She's got about a week and a half until school is out, then she'll be home for the summer. I've debated taking time off work to be with her, even if it's only a few days. She's been teasing me more since our date too. She read some of the dirty books I bought her at the bookstore to me. I thought those would lead to something, but it was more teasing.

I've been on edge this past week. I swear I can still smell her in my cubicle. I'll get a whiff of her scent and can feel her on my face again. Her tastes, her scent, her noises were so glorious. Her skin was so soft; she was perfect. Just as I start to daydream about her again, my computer dings. I force myself to look at the message. Three times last week, I caught a whiff of her and started daydreaming. Then I had to go to the restroom quickly, trying to hide my boner. The last time, the secretary gave me a knowing glance. I told her my lunch was probably bad, but I don't think she bought it. Stomach issues don't cause a bulge in the front of my pants.

There is a notification in my email. I have been trying to find a good source for my landowner story. I put out some feelers with contacts I know in the field. The new email is from an anonymous source. It's alphanumeric and doesn't have any logic to it. I read the email. A person who knows my contact has some information they want to give me and need a time and place. Without hesitation, I send the address to Addy's bar and when I can be there after work. I'm not too concerned with safety issues. The bar is public, offering a sense of security. An email comes back almost instantly. It just says, "Okay."

"Can I get a beer and some fries?"

I kiss Addy's cheek then she types in my order. She gets my beer, and I take my usual spot at the end of the bar. She brings my drink to me, then stands, staring at me, lost in thought. I ask what she's thinking. She shrugs, but I call her back before she walks off. She steps close, leaning against the bar. This section of the bar doesn't have a work surface on the other side, just storage below. This means she can lean close to me. I grab her hand, leaning over to kiss her again.

"I've missed you lately."

She wraps her arms around my shoulders, and I do the same. She gives me a quick squeeze, kissing my cheek. "I'm off tomorrow, and I'm not closing tonight. So we can do something fun." She winks at me, wandering off to serve others. Bruiser makes some obscene comment I don't fully catch. Addy does, though.

She grabs an olive and throws it at him. That section of the bar erupts in laughter. I chuckle, shaking my head. Pulling out my laptop, I set up to take notes from whoever shows up.

My order of fries comes, and I finish them all off. The person I'm meeting is about 20 minutes late. It's not unheard of; I hope they haven't backed out. I debate ordering water or leaving when someone walks in the front door. A man in dark jeans, a hoodie, and sunglasses looks around. Not many people notice him. There isn't really anything noteworthy about him. He looks in my direction and starts walking towards me. He sits on the stool beside me, then says, "James?"

"Yeah, that's me."

"Do I gotta introduce myself?" His dialect is thick and not local. Spanish may be his first language.

"No. I won't take any notes on your identity."

He doesn't say anything else. Addy walks towards us, glancing at me. The man looks out of place now. His entrance was typical and didn't draw attention. He has kept his hood and sunglasses on, which is more noticeable in a bar. Addy asks if he wants anything. He shakes his head at her. She asks if I'm okay. I recognize the hint of concern in her voice. Her question works in this setting to ask about my drink and check in on me. I offer her a small smile and reply that I'm fine. She turns to leave. The man pulls a manilla envelope out of his hoodie. He places it on the bar, then stands.

"That should be everything you need."

He turns and leaves. I watch him exit the bar. This must be good information if he is this wary about giving it to me. I can only hope that is the case. Once he leaves the bar, I take the envelope, sliding the contents out. Without entirely removing them, I glance at the first page. The first is an email communication between the landowner and someone else. They discuss how much money needs to be prepared for the next cycle. It confirms my suspicion of money laundering. I glance at the following few pages. They are photocopies of several pages of financial reports. This is all great information, but I am concerned about their legitimacy. Most of these could be created in Microsoft Word. Then I see a thumb drive at the bottom of the envelope. Bingo.

I send out an email to my tech gal. I don't want to plug the thumb drive directly into my laptop. I don't know what's actually on there. I hope these reports are in a verifiable form. My email explains my situation, asking when she can check out the drive for me. She usually replies during business hours. So I pack up all my stuff. I pay Addy, hugging her again before leaving. I'm elated at how things are turning out with this case. It could be huge for the magazine.

Rosie

The last week of school is usually a clusterfuck. Everything is crazy; kids and teachers are ready for summer but need to cram in a few last-minute things. Today was more difficult than expected. A student in my class was placed in summer school. The student struggled all year and needs extra time before the fall. The family is furious and blames me for everything. They insisted on meeting with the principal and me to discuss this topic. However, they spent half the meeting berating and accusing me before the principal dismissed me to deal with them. I know their words aren't true. I did my best for my student; they greatly improved over the year. But that doesn't stop the negative thoughts. My mind is racing with everything I did wrong. Everything I should have done differently.

It takes everything I have not to cry on the way home. Once in the apartment, I drop my stuff in my room, taking a deep breath as I collapse on the bed. Due to my late meeting, everyone else is home now. Addy was off today, and James and Megs are home from their jobs. I sit for a few minutes, breathing as the words swirl through my head. Then it hits me. I can work this out through subspace. Addy and I haven't done a scene in a while; she'll play with me now. I head straight for her room, on a mission.

In Addy's room, it's dark. She has music quietly playing. She's propped up on her bed, playing on her phone. She hears me come in. I drop to my knees, palms up on my thighs, head down, normal submissive position. My eyes are closed as I firmly say, "I need you." She sits up, placing her phone to the side. She walks over, stopping in front of me. Her hand rubs my hair, my face. I lean into her hand ever so slightly.

"Bad day, huh?" She's still using her normal voice, not the alpha voice I desperately want. I nod against her hand. "You sure?" Her fingers scoop my chin, lifting my face up to her. I meet her eyes. Tears threaten to burst out, but I find my voice and steadily reply, "Yes, ma'am." Addy nods, placing a small kiss on my forehead. She releases my face and turns to her dresser, where all her toys are. I drop my eyes to the ground before me, patiently waiting, focusing on breathing, trying to silence my thoughts.

"Impact?" She asks in her alpha voice.

"Yes, ma'am."

"Bondage?"

"Yes, ma'am."

She pauses for a moment. I can't see her with my eyes still down, but I know she is considering something. Given the number of times we have done this, I can't help but wonder what she is thinking. While we change things up, we both agree to only so many options. I'm unsure if I should be nervous, but I focus on my breath. In. Out. Hush my thoughts. Addy will let me know when she sorts it out. For now, I breathe in. I feel my body. I focus on my knees, my ankles, my shoulders, my breath.

"What about degradation and exhibitionism?"

Okay, I wasn't expecting that. I force myself to remain in my position, not turning to look at Addy. Does she mean like a webcam?

"How so?"

"James and Megs."

"Oh." That's an interesting thought. We've never had an audience. Megs has played with us, but never from a purely voyeuristic position.

"They could watch, limited involvement."

"Yes, ma'am."

This will give me something extra to focus on. Removing my negative thoughts further, hopefully. If not, that's what safe words are for. "Good girl." Addy walks next to me. Her fingers lift my chin as she places a kiss against my lips. It's brief, then she releases me and tells me to stay.

"James, Megs!"

I hear shuffling as James and Megs enter the room. Megs curses under their breath. I can't see what is happening, but they are standing in the doorway.

"Rosie has had a hard day, and we're going to do a scene. I'm thinking you two could watch. Not really play, just watch."

"Damn, I just started making scones. I can't, but I'll come in for aftercare." Megs hurries off, clearly in the middle of baking. I missed that when I came into the apartment. That just leaves James. The urge to turn and look at him is intense. I take a deep breath, settling myself again.

"So, like, just sit and watch? No touching?" His voice is deep and husky, as if he is already in play mode. It sends a chill down my spine, pooling as warmth in my core. I love the sound of deep voices.

"Yes. You'll do as I say, but I won't have much for you to do. Watch, maybe speak. You can sit in my chair."

There is a pause. I can't help but wonder what he is thinking. We haven't done anything crazy with him. Addy said she made him a sub, but from my understanding, it was more pleasure and teasing than what she has in store for me now. James has expressed an interest in learning more about what we do together. I wait patiently, trying to silence the little aches from being in this position. I haven't done this in a while, and my body shows that.

"Okay," James speaks softly but clearly.

Addy addresses him again. "This session will be more intense than what you and I did. I need your assurances that you can handle this. If you can't, you can use your safe word or leave. Megs will help you process. Since there are multiple people involved, I will likely stay with Rosie unless I'm at a point I can leave her. Do you understand?" James doesn't say anything out loud, so Addy continues. "I plan to use impact tools and some degradation. You will sit and not touch or speak unless told to. If you are uncomfortable, you will use your safe word or leave to find Megs. You must talk to Megs about it. Are we clear?"

"Yes....er...uh... Yes, ma'am."

"Good," I can hear the smirk in her voice. "Sit." James moves to the chair, sitting down. Addy walks back to her dresser, removing more items and placing them on her bed.

"James, safe word."

"Cactus."

"Good. Rosie?"

"Burrito." James chuckles at my word.

"Good. Let's play."

Her voice is deep. It's the alpha voice I love so much. There's a warmth spreading through my core at her words. My focus remains on my breath, my posture, my space. Addy moves over to the bed, sitting on the edge.

"Rosie, crawl to James and stand facing him."

I do as I'm told. My body is glad for the shift out of the kneeling position. I rise in front of James. My eyes stay down as my hands clasp behind my back. My flowery dress hangs over my body, crumbled slightly from kneeling and the long day at work. James is wearing sweatpants and a t-shirt. I can already see the outlines of his growing erection. We still haven't had sex, something I should rectify soon, but not now. Addy steps up behind me and unbuttons my dress. When the tips of her fingers graze my back, several of the comments from the family today come crashing back. I have been so distracted by James coming in that I almost forgot. Immediately, the negative thoughts take over again.

"Tell me your thoughts."

Addy knows I struggle with negative thoughts. She knows about my self-doubt, my low confidence, my struggles to feel worthy. Addy knows all of that. James doesn't. He hasn't seen me break down because I thought I was stupid and wrong. This may be a mistake. I don't want him to know that side of me yet. Tears spring to my eyes as Addy finishes unbuttoning my dress. She brushes it off my shoulders, leaving me in a lime green bralette and a lacy purple thong. My arms flinch, wanting to cover myself from James. Addy stops me, gripping my arms behind me, keeping them against my lower back. I take a deep breath, trying to breathe in confidence. I remind myself that we've seen James weak. We didn't judge him. We've helped him with his emotions a lot in the past few weeks. I can do the same too.

Before I can speak, I feel a smack against my ass with a paddle. I gasp at the sudden impact. I knew it would happen, though; I took too long to answer. I rush out a response quickly.

"I'm not pretty." James grunts at that comment. Out of the corner of my eye, Addy waves the paddle at him. A gentle reminder that he is to be quiet. I'm almost surprised she didn't pop him too, but this is his first time. Some noises are to be expected.

"What else?"

"I'm not worthy."

"And?"

"I'm not good at my job."

"Do you believe that?"

My head drops lower. I want to say, 'No, I don't believe that,' but that isn't true.

"Yes," I respond softly.

Her fingers are on my bralette. She lifts it over my head, guiding my arms up then back down. My breasts are exposed to James. She places the paddle against one breast, rubbing it across the top. Then she moves to the other, repeating the process.

"Isn't she exquisite, James?" It sounds like he may not be breathing. He offers a breathless, "Yes, Ma'am." The paddle strikes my breast, then the other. It's not a hard hit, just enough to turn the skin slightly red. Now her hands are on my breast, caressing, squeezing, pinching.

"Oh, Rosie, my little minx. We can't let you think you aren't beautiful." She pinches my nipple, twisting it. "That you aren't worthy." Now the paddle strikes that same breast, causing me to groan. Her hand covers the hurt, touching it softly. She takes my other nipple, pinching and twisting it. "We know you are good at your job." Smack. "Now, we're going to show you how wonderful you are." Her hand rubs the breast she just smacked. She moves to the bed, grabbing different items. She walks behind me, wrapping her arms around my stomach. A small metal chain brushes against my skin. There is pressure on my nipple as she places a clamp on one then the other. Her front is pressed against my back; I lean into her, closing my eyes.

"Look at how beautiful she is." I crack my eyes to see James staring at my breasts, with the chain hanging against my stomach. Addy picked a purple one that matches my thong well. I don't know if she did that on purpose, but it has James's attention. His eyes rove my body, taking in every inch. It feels uncomfortable to be this exposed, this open. Addy tugs on the chain, pulling my nipples down. A surge crashes into my core; all thoughts have gone from my mind, replaced with need and desire. Her hands are on my stomach, caressing me softly. One hand moves down to my panties. Her fingers dance along the edge, then slip beneath. They slide all the way down. Her middle finger curves inside me while her other fingers rest on the outside. Her finger glides in slow circles as if she's exploring casually. I remain still, leaning into her. My chest heaves as my breath quickens. As smoothly as she entered, she pulls out and steps away from me. Her body leaves mine, leaving me feeling cold without her warmth. She steps towards James.

"Open," he opens his mouth, and she places her finger on his tongue. His lips wrap around her finger. His eyes are on Addy for a moment, then slide to me. When his eyes meet mine, his cheeks hollow a touch, caused by him sucking my taste off her finger. My embarrassment and negative thoughts fade as I see the heat and desire in his eyes. He still wants me, even knowing my negative thoughts and seeing my mismatched underwear and crumbled dress. My weak moments are still enticing to him. As my confidence rises, the negative thoughts also rise.

He's only turned on because we're in a scene.

It wouldn't be the same if Addy weren't in control.

He wouldn't be interested in a broken me.

Addy is back to my side as if she can hear my thoughts too. "Turn to the bed, place your hands on the frame, bend over." I get into the position she just instructed. My ass is more exposed now. James is off to my side but still has a good view of my ass. Addy slips my thong over my cheeks. She doesn't remove it, just slides it down. With the lacy waist stretching against my thighs, I feel more exposed than before. He isn't really seeing anything new. The thong I wore on our date didn't leave much to the imagination. He has seen this before. His face was buried there just a week and a half ago. Wetness pools against my core at the thought.

On the bed, Addy grabs her phone. She clicks a few things then hands the phone to James. I have an idea of where she is going with this. She informs him to wait a moment, then adjusts a slider bar on her phone. She steps back to the bed, grabbing the lube and a black anal plug. She tells him to adjust it. The plug jumps to life, vibrating with different intensities as he slides the bar on the app. We invested in some app-controlled toys a while ago, and they are some of my favorites. My pussy clenches as he revs up the motion. Addy hands him the toy as she squeezes some lube on her fingers. She steps behind me. Her fingers are against my ass, the cool gel rubbing against my tight hole. I press against her, waiting for her to enter.

"Oh, our little minx is so ready to have that big plug in her ass."

Without warning, she slips two fingers inside me at once. There is a slight burning sensation at the sudden penetration. It's nothing I can't handle. Very slowly, she swirls her fingers around, stretching me out. A soft moan escapes my lips at her touch. She spreads her fingers apart, toying with me more. Then she slides them in and out several times.

"James, are you ready to see that plug in her ass?"

"Yes, ma'am."

Addy steps back, pulling her fingers out of me. I drop my head down at the sudden emptiness. I can hear Addy applying lube to the toy. Then it's pressing against me. I want it deep inside, vibrating, bringing me some pleasure. Addy tells James to set it to a low level. There is a soft hum against my ass as the toy vibrates. Addy presses it against me. Her fingers massage my hole as she pushes the toy in further. The toy goes in smoothly, vibrating my ass pleasurably. Once it's properly in, Addy taps it several times, eliciting a groan from me. She slides my thong back up, covering the toy. Grabbing a wipe, she cleans her fingers off.

"James, it's up to you to pleasure Rosie. I'm going to deal with the negative thoughts."

I feel the toy ramp up suddenly inside me. My body jerks and a loud groan leaves my mouth. Addy grabs the paddle and steps towards James. She swats the side of his knee.

"I said pleasure. Not force an orgasm."

James chuckles, but the toy slows back down. "Good. Rosie, count." She smacks my ass. It was a soft sting, just a beginning tap.

"One."

She smacks the other side a bit harder. "Two."

James increases the vibration the third time as she hits, then brings it back down. That makes the hit more intense, and I moan, pressing my ass out. Her hand is massaging my ass, right where her paddle had just landed.

"Three." Smack, smack, smack. Vibration increases, then slowly returns to normal.

"Four. FiveSix."

My thighs squeeze together, trying to create more friction against my clit. My body is searching for release. I can't think of anything besides the sensations in and on my ass. Addy whispers to James, but I can't make out the words. The vibration in my ass slowly increases. A brutal smack lands against my ass. The paddle's sting and the toy mix's pleasure create a fog of pleasure and pain in my brain.

"Seven."

The vibration increases more. Smack.

"Eight."

The vibration grows, becoming more intense. I can feel my orgasm growing. I don't typically orgasm from anal alone, but with the paddle and James watching, it's intense. Two brutal smacks land on either cheek as the vibration grows again.

"NINE-TEN," I cry in one breath. Addy is wrapped around my body, massaging my ass. She rips my thong down. I step out of it as she turns my body to face James fully. Addy leans back against the footboard of her bed. She pulls me back against her. She grabs one thigh, lifts my leg, and guides my foot to a box she has on the floor. In this position, I am on full display for James. Addy has one arm around my stomach, caressing the underside of my breasts. Her other hand moves down to the apex of my thighs. She moves her fingers, spreading my labia, landing on my clit. She flicks her finger against it. The touch nearly sends me over the edge. My ass presses back against her.

"James, touch yourself. Let Rosie watch you. Let her see what you do to her."

I can hear him shifting around in the chair. I look at him. He is quickly dropping his pants to the floor. His erect cock is leaking at the tip. He strokes it once, twice. His eyes are glued to my body, dancing between Addy's hand, my breasts, my face. He reaches over to Addy's phone, increasing the vibration of the plug in my ass again. It pushes me right to the edge, but Addy's fingers stop against me. I groan at the halting orgasm. I shift my hips, searching for any sensation that will push me over the edge. Addy smacks my throbbing pussy.

"I didn't say you could come yet. Open your mouth."

I part my lips, trying to keep my hips still. It's tough to be still between the vibration and James's intense gaze on me. Addy grabs the chain between the nipple clamps, and she tugs it down gently. James and I both moan at the movement. She lifts the chain to my mouth, placing it between my teeth. Her fingers press on my chin, closing my mouth.

"Both of you will come at the same time. Watch each other. See your reactions to each other."

Addy's fingers are against my clit, expertly working it. I feel my orgasm building again. It's so close. It's almost there and....

"Can I come on her?" Addy's fingers freeze, once again denying my orgasm. I've never had a man come on me before. I don't know how I feel about it, but Addy decides for me.

"I love it. Yes. Rosie, on your knees."

She guides me forward, kneeling on the floor as James stands in front of me. She pulls her hand away from my clit. I groan loudly, just wanting to finally feel the release of my desire. Her hand grabs the back of my hair, pulling my head back. With the chain from the nipple clamps still in my mouth, my breasts are also stretched. The sensations in my body are so intense. The plug is still vibrating fast in my ass. My breasts are stretched tightly. Addy is pulling my hair tightly. James is standing over me, stroking his cock, staring at me like a tall glass of water in the middle of a desert.

Then Addy puts a vibrating wand against my clit.

She is still behind me. It's a good thing she is there because my orgasm is so intense I'm positive I would be on the floor. My back arches as my body erupts with pleasure. Stars explode in my vision, my entire body tenses, clutching against the orgasm. My head falls back, pulling the chain and my breasts as I cry out loudly. Addy and James are cursing as my soul floats back to my body. Before I can settle, Addy increases the vibration. I open my eyes just in time to see James erupt on my breasts. I look down, seeing his semen landing sporadically across me. Addy presses the wand harder into my clit, and I burst again. James is huffing over me, cursing as he comes down from his orgasm. My body is still clenching and spasming with my own. Addy is pressing gentle kisses along my neck.

My body finally begins to settle. Addy removes the wand vibrator, shifting to grab her phone. The plug in my ass stills. Addy is still supporting my weight. My breathing is erratic, my chest heaving. She removes the clips from my nipple, a small groan escaping my lips as she does so. She tells James to hand her a pillow. She lowers me to the floor on my side, hands caressing my arm. She tells James where the wipes are. Her voice is soft and soothing now, not the alpha voice anymore. My eyes close as my head rests against the pillow. I feel exhausted but also on cloud nine. My body is still shaking slightly from the intense orgasms. James kneels in front of me. He presses several kisses to my forehead, whispering how beautiful I am. He wipes my chest, cleaning his mess off me. Addy tells me she's pulling the plug out. I press down as much as I can as she pulls it out. Once out, she tells James to get me in the bed.

He lifts me gently and places me down on her bed. He curls up next to me, wrapping his arms around me, pulling me close to his chest. I take a deep inhale, breathing in his scent. Addy drapes a weighted blanket over James and me. I hear her whispering to James but can't quite decipher the words. My mind is silent, in post-orgasm ecstasy. James continues to rub his hands over my back and sides, kissing my face.

I shiver slightly, my body trying to return to normal. I take a deep breath, snuggling closer to James. His hands have slowed their motion over my body. This is probably my favorite part of any scene. The aftercare is always the best. I love the intimacy offered after an intense session. It's deeper than regular sex, bringing us closer because of the intense, somewhat uncomfortable acts. James and I lay like that for several moments. He speaks softly against my forehead, not looking down at me.

"Do you really believe those things you said?"

"Sometimes." My voice is scratchy and hoarse from the orgasm.

He pauses, thinking about what I just said. As much as I don't want to believe that stuff, it is sometimes hard not to believe it. Most of the time, I know my worth. Just most of the time, though. He presses a slow kiss against my forehead. I close my eyes, savoring the touch of his lips.

"If it's any consolation, I think you are beautiful all the time."

I preen against his words, snuggling tighter against him. I sigh against his chest, pressing several kisses there. I don't trust my voice to work entirely. Addy walks in, bringing along the scent of freshly baked scones.

"Oh, my beautiful little subs. Such good little sluts."

I chuckle, shuffling a bit to look at her. Megs is standing in the doorway, carrying a plate of chocolate scones. They make their way to the bed, sitting down next to me. Addy tosses some clothes at me, and I sit up and grab the shirt. James helps slip it over my arms. I adjust to sit up straighter, but my bare ass hits the bed, and I hiss at the pressure on my raw skin. Addy chuckles.

"Did you forget your ass is raw?"

I nod my head, pouting my lips. They all laugh at me. Addy instructs me to move to the edge of the bed. James holds my arm as I crawl over him. Addy walks to me and begins rubbing my butt and thighs with lotion. James is stroking my face and hair as if he can't keep his hands off me. When Addy finishes, she helps me into some sweatpants. I settle, slowly, back in between James and Megs. Addy hands a bottle of water to James and me. I take a sip, then Megs gives me a scone.

"Finally."

We eat the delicious chocolate scones, cuddling in Addy's bed. We chat for a bit, then Addy starts a movie. As bad as the day was, the evening ended on a much better note. I can't think of a better way to spend the evening. Even with a sore ass, I wouldn't trade it for anything.

Chapter Thirteen

The past few weeks since James joined us have been fun. I am less worried about him being part of our group than I was when he showed up. He's been helpful and fun to have around. Addy and Rosie are always fooling around with him. Which leaves me to do other activities with him. He perfectly evens out our little group. He's been a massive help with dinner and chores. Even going as far as learning some healthy meals I prefer to make. We've started shopping for groceries together. That task has been more enjoyable than I thought it could be. I typically listen to podcasts or audiobooks while I'm out. When James goes, we check out new stores or restaurants and buy groceries. At this point, I'm not upset that he's here. I'm still hesitant to fully trust him for the long haul, but for now, things are good.

Today is Rosie's last day of school. Addy worked an earlier shift and should be home soon. James and I are chilling on the couch. I asked if he wanted to watch this new Sci-Fi Indie film I had heard about. He agreed to watch it but do

esn't seem to enjoy it as much as I do. He's more into older, big production films. We all take turns watching the shows we want. James has been tolerating our choices more to get on our good side. I worry that it may lead to resentment, but I'm glad I have someone to watch my films with. While he may not like the movie, he still seems content to sit with me. I'm beside him, but we aren't cuddling or anything.

Suddenly, the apartment door burst open. Addy explodes into the apartment, louder than one person should be able.

"WE HAVE TO PLAN ROSIE'S BIRTHDAY!!"

James is startled by the sudden burst. He shifts on the couch, using his body to block mine. His arms are out to either side, ready to protect me from danger. Even though Addy technically isn't dangerous, she certainly presents that way. I place my hands on his shoulders, bringing them down to get a better view of Addy. James's face is scrambled. His brain is still trying to process whether there is a threat or not. I rub his arms, trying to calm and bring him back to reality before he attacks Addy. Though I would definitely enjoy watching that.

"What the fuck, Addy? Yes, we need to plan Rosie's birthday, but we can be civil about it. Sheesh."

James looks back at me, dropping his arms to his side. I turn the movie off and walk to the kitchen. No matter what happens at this point, Addy won't let me finish that movie until every detail of Rosie's birthday is planned. Rosie is so good at throwing birthday celebrations. Even if it is just the three of us celebrating. She goes all out, buying decorations, having themed food, and finding the perfect gift. She's always done that. Even in high school, she found ways to make birthdays special for everyone.

The planning gene is something that skipped over Addy and me. We are not good at planning parties. One year, Addy took over for Rosie's birthday, and the theme was supposed to be flowers. It seemed pretty enough, but all Addy did was buy some plants that died before we gave them to her. It was terrible. We always try to make her birthday as special as we can, but it's never as good as what she does for us. Maybe James can help with that this year.

"When is her birthday?" he asks.

"On June 16th," I reply. "Giving us about two weeks to plan it." He thinks for a minute, asking if we have any ideas. I shake my head. I really haven't given her birthday much thought yet.

"Ok, hear me out." Addy holds her hands out for us to wait, "Chuck E Cheese."

James mistakenly sips his drink while Addy is talking. He'll learn one day not to do that. He chokes, turning back towards the sink as he spits his beverage. I laugh loudly, both at her response and at James.

"What? It's fun!"

"Yeah, no, keep going, Addy," James says. "Let's get the terrible ideas out of the way first."

She shoves his arm playfully. He laughs, wiping his face with his sleeve. I wipe my eyes, laughing so hard tears are coming out. As we settle, we all focus on coming up with an idea. Every idea I come up with sounds terrible in my head. James asks what we have done in the past. Addy recounts the last few years. Both James and I cringe at what we'd done. I was involved in planning all these parties and still see how terrible they were.

"This is her 27th birthday. We have to do something special. Something to make up for 20 bad birthdays," Addy whines.

I have no idea what to do. I haven't figured it out in the past ten years; I doubt any good ideas will come now. We should try to ask Rosie how she does it. It would be too obvious to ask now. Maybe I'll set up a random email account and email her. No, she would see through that. James finally speaks up, interrupting my random line of thoughts.

"What if we host a small party here? We can do a burrito theme. Have a burrito bar with toppings and meat and whatever, some drinks. We can move the couch to make room for dancing. Get some balloons. Megs, you can make a cake look like a burrito, right?"

"Fuck, that's brilliant!"

Addy throws her arms around James, squeezing him tight. "She loves burritos. I can get some margaritas mix from the bar. We have her favorite. James, you do decorations; Megs, you do food?" I nod in agreement. This sounds perfect. It's not too overwhelming. Rosie will love it. I knew having James involved would make this easier. Yep, never doubted that.

It is finally the day of Rosie's party. The most challenging part has been keeping it a surprise. We want her to think we were doing another classic Addy and Megs birthday. Rosie doesn't seem to suspect anything else. She has meager expectations. I'm very excited about the party. There is a time before guests start showing up. James is helping me prep the rest of the food. He is currently making meat for the burritos. I am icing some cookies to look like tacos.

Balloons float around the apartment. The couch is against the wall. The living room is open for dancing or mingling. Our sound system is geared up with a great playlist she'll love. Addy prepped the drinks earlier and ensures Rosie stays out of the apartment while we finish setting up. Honestly, that was harder than we expected. Since she has been out of school for the past couple of weeks, she's turned into a total couch potato. She reads or watches movies all day. It's funny seeing her so relaxed. She's not usually content being lazy for that long.

James and I chat idly while we are working. It's nice having James around, especially to help with this. Addy can get so distracted; she's rarely helpful with setting up events. Even when Rosie plans them, she usually sends Addy for ice while she and I prepare everything. Just then, James's phone rings, and he glances back.

"Will you answer that and put it on speaker for me?"

There isn't a name on the contact, just the phone number. I hit the answer button, then tap speaker. I place the phone on the counter as James says 'hello,' and return to my cookies. At first, no one says anything. Then we hear moaning.

"Oh fuck. Fuck me, Daddy. Yeah, fuck me real good. Oh, I've never had it this good before."

I drop my icing, rushing over to end the call. It is his ex, Whitney, calling. It seems like a pocket dial, but it sounded intentional. He seems frozen in place. I leave his phone on the counter after ending the call.

"James?"

He finally blinks a few times, then shakes his head to clear it. I rub his arm to help him focus and let him know he's not alone. He coughs, clearing his throat. His eyes meet mine. A small smile forms on his face, but he still looks sad.

"I knew she was sleeping with him. Probably been fucking him for a year or more. It was never real, though. I was just aware of it."

I wrap my arms around his back. Even though I'm a few inches shorter than him, he buries his face in my neck. I rub his shoulders and feel him take a deep breath against my skin. He pulls back, straightening his body. He rests his cheek on my forehead. My eyes close, squeezing his body a bit more. I'm not really sure what to say at this point. I don't think "Sorry your ex-wife pocket dialed you while fucking another dude" really needs to be said out loud. He huffs, pulling away from me. Picking up the spatula, he returns to the meat he was cooking.

"I really wish that part of my life was over."

"At least it's close to being over," I offer softly.

"Yeah, hopefully. Let's not allow this to ruin Rosie's birthday, though."

I agree, and we get back to work. I change the subject, continuing with the small talk. James chats with me, but the call still gnaws away at him. I'm hoping he can let it go soon. He said she hasn't made any contact with him or his lawyer. Surely, she can't still think he will get back together with her. It seems she is only making things worse for herself.

ROSIE

It's my birthday. I didn't have any big plans or expectations for the day. It's a Saturday, and I had assumed Addy would be at work. Surprisingly, she took the day off. Addy said she wants to spend it with me and me alone. It's not unusual for Addy to want to hang out, but she was a little too insistent. It makes me wonder if they are up to something. I'm nervous about what they would come up with. Addy has really been trying to hype up Chuck E. Cheese lately.

She's had me out all day. We went shopping, had coffee, and went to a bookstore. She even took me to get ice cream then to a park to eat it. At least the weather is nice for something like that. As much as I love being out with Addy, I am ready to get home and relax. I would love to have a simple dinner with my friends. Maybe some cake, but honestly, that's not even necessary. Finally, Addy tells me it's time to go home. Relief washes over me as she drives back. I walk towards the apartment, but Addy is literally skipping. What is with her?

"SURPRISE!!"

Several people are shouting when we enter the apartment. They threw me a surprise party! And kept it a secret! I squeal, taking in the people and the decorations. Several of my coworkers and a few friends from college are here. The apartment isn't crowded, but it doesn't feel empty either. James and Megs come over, taking the bags from my hands.

"You did all of this for me?" I ask, looking between the two. The couch is in a different location. Taco balloons and decorations hang all around. Some sort of food line is set up on the counter. A few people have margaritas. There's even cake and cookies on the counter, next to a pile of presents. I'm so excited I could burst. A huge grin breaks out on my face. Megs tells me they all did it. James offers a quick hug and quiet hello before taking my stuff to my room. Addy walks me through the setup. She tells me the theme is burritos, and I absolutely love it.

When James comes back, we all make our own burritos, stuffing them with whatever we want. Then Megs made a cake that looks like a burrito. I don't know how they did it, but it looks incredible. After cake, the music is turned up, and everyone starts dancing. I take turns dancing with several friends. Some group dances, a few dances with just one other person. My favorite is when James, Addy, and Megs dance with me. The party is lovely. It's not convoluted or complex. The party is perfect and exactly what I want all parties to be like. As the night wears on, people start to leave. They all offer hugs and birthday wishes. Soon, it's just the four of us left.

As soon as the last guest is in the hallway, Addy shouts, "PRESENTS!" She shoves me towards the couch that is still in the wrong spot, then starts bringing all the gifts over. I laugh, sitting down on the couch. She hands them to me to open. I take note of who gave what so I can thank everyone properly. There are several books, some lotions, various body products, and a couple of gift cards. When I'm opening the last gift, James gets up and walks to his room. Addy hands me the most awkwardly wrapped package imaginable. Seriously, I sometimes wonder how she is a fully functional adult.

"Open it! Hurry!"

She shoves the gift closer. I grab it from her, realizing it's heavier than it looks. Tearing the paper off, green leaves start poking through holes. Addy bought me a new plant. It's a green leafy one I'm unfamiliar with but very excited to learn about. Addy starts rambling about what it is and how the person at the nursery insists it is a great gift. I'm sure Addy ate most of the burrito cake because she is too hyper now. I hug her and thank her as Megs walks over with a gift. James returns to the living area with two massive bags. My eyes go wide. He smirks at me but just sits next to me.

Megs's gift is in a clothes box with wrapping paper that has tacos on it. I comment on how adorable it is and start ripping paper. Inside the present is a dress. It's blue and has a wide skirt. The top is fitted with cap sleeves. The dress's fabric is covered in burritos, tacos, avocados, limes, and squiggles. I squeal again. The dress is adorable and funky and absolutely my style. Plus, the material is soft. I hug them, telling them how excited I am to wear it.

Finally, James slides the two bags to me. I open one, pulling tissue paper out of it. There is a flat plastic bag with something folded inside. After unzipping the plastic bag, I pull the material out. It's a soft, fuzzy fleece. I stand up, holding the blanket up. It's a circle and printed to look like a burrito. I wrap it around me. It's warm and snuggly.

"Look! I'm a burrito!"

I giggle, sitting back down with the blanket draped across my shoulders. The second bag has no tissue paper but is taped at the top. James tells me there wasn't enough room to put the tissue paper in. Once the tape breaks, giant stuffed objects come flying out. We all laugh at the sudden eruption. There are two giant squishy pillows in the bag. One looks like an avocado, the other looks like a succulent.

"They didn't have a burrito. But I figured since you can be a burrito now, these would be just fine."

I laugh and throw my arms around his shoulders. I tell him how perfect it all is. I sit back, holding several things in my lap.

"Thank you all so much. This is the perfect birthday."

Addy pumps her arm in the air, letting out a whooping yell. I sigh contently, leaning back, snuggling with my new blanket and pillows. James and Megs are the first to move. Both stand and start picking up things. Addy follows their lead, but she begins by grabbing my gifts and carrying them to my room. I copy her, bringing my pillows, blanket, and plant. I place the plant on my desk, having already decided on the perfect spot. Everything else goes on the bed. I walk towards the door, planning to help clean up. Addy stops me.

"No, this is your birthday. We'll clean up; you just go to bed. You know you're tired anyway."

She kisses my cheek then swats my butt, encouraging me to go to the bathroom. I don't argue with her. She isn't wrong; I am tired. I get ready for bed in the bathroom, then stop in the kitchen. They are nearly done cleaning, and I don't feel so bad leaving them alone. I hug each of them, thanking them again and saying good night. I make my way to my room. Pulling on sleep shorts and a loose shirt, I crawl into bed, happy and exhausted.

I start to drift off but never fully get to sleep. I toss and turn a few times. The living room lights have been turned off. I grab my burrito blanket, wrapping it around my shoulders. The light in James's room is still on, shining under his door. Megs's room is dark, and Addy's seems to be too. I pad silently across the living room. Knocking lightly on his door, I don't wait for him to respond as I step into his room and pull the door shut behind me. He is just walking out of the bathroom.

"Oh, hi." He smiles at me. He has already changed into shorts and a shirt for bed too. He looks comfortable and ready to go to sleep.

"I couldn't sleep," I speak softly. He nods, reaching his arm out towards me. I step closer to him and let him pull me in. He presses his lips against my forehead. "Want to stay in here?" I nod against him. He gently pushes me towards the bed as he turns the lights off. He crawls in, sliding close to me. He wraps his arms around me, holding me tight to his chest.

"Thank you," I say in barely more than a whisper. "For the gifts and the party and everything. This birthday really has been perfect." He rubs his hands on my back, pressing another kiss to my forehead. I close my eyes, enjoying the warmth of his arms wrapped around me and the fuzzy blanket.

"You're welcome. Now sleep, my little burrito." I chuckle at his words but keep my eyes closed. It's only a few moments before I drift off to sleep, feeling safe and secure in his arms.

Chapter Fourteen

The light is bright, causing me to wake. I'm warm, snuggled up to James's chest. I slept soundly in his arms all night. I don't always sleep all night, but I did with him last night. As I wake, I shift to look at him. He is still asleep and looks so calm. I rub my hands over his back. My fingers drag down his shirt to the hem. I caress his skin underneath, then slide my fingers up his bare back, under his shirt. His back is warm and smooth. I can feel ridges from some muscles. When I reach his shoulders, I flatten my hands, pulling him closer.

I feel him shift, then his lips are against my forehead. At this moment, the thought occurs to me that his cock hasn't been inside my pussy. We've done oral and fingered each other, but it hasn't gotten further than that. My pussy clenches at the thought of him being inside me. I want it now. I lift my head, pressing several kisses against his neck. With all our playing around, I've learned a few of his favorite spots. There is one spot on his neck that always gets him going when I suck on it. I kiss his neck in search of the perfect spot. He moans, stretching his neck to give me better access. Found it.

"Mmm, good morning." He mumbles sleepily, but his hands rub my sides and back, inching very close to my ass. I push my ass towards him, silently letting him know I want him to go lower. He takes the hint, and his hands are on my ass, squeezing my cheeks. I drag one hand down his back, caressing the skin above his shorts. He moans my name. I slip my fingers under the band of his shorts. The skin is soft and smooth. My fingers slide to the front, grazing the skin above his hips.

"Fuck, Rosie."

My name on his lips drives me crazy. My pussy clenches again. I can't wait any longer. In one swift move, I pull my hands back, pushing him on his back. Then I'm straddling him. I press my lips against his. I'm so desperate to have him inside me. I need more contact with him. Morning breath doesn't matter at this point. He kisses me back. His member is hard against my core. My fingers move to his neck, his hair, claiming him as mine. I grind against him. He moans into my mouth. His hands slide up my back, under my shirt. He stops on my ribs, his thumbs wrapping around to stroke my breasts. He lightly flicks my nipple.

"I want you inside me."

"I have condoms on the desk."

He nods, and I see a box sitting on the edge. I grab the box, pulling out one. I'm ready for him to fuck me. To slide inside me and fill me up. I grind my hips against him as his hands pull at my shirt, trying to lift it over my head. There is a knock at the door. At first, it doesn't register. My hands are on his chest, the condom still squeezed between my fingers. His hands halt as we hear Addy's voice singing out on the other side of his door.

"Oh, dear sweet Rosie. My beautiful precious lover. Your mother is here."

"Fuck," we both say. I let my shirt slide back down, climbing off James. I groan again. My pussy aches as I move away from him. Nothing like getting cock blocked by my own mother. I let Addy know I'll be out in a minute, then stand beside his bed. His eyes are closed, and he's breathing deeply through his nose. His cock is tenting his pants. I close my eyes, taking a few deep breaths myself. Anything to calm my screaming core. It's not effective, but I can't keep my mother waiting.

"This isn't over," he growls at me.

I look back at him before making my way out of his room. His eyes are laced with desire. His hand moves to his cock. My pussy clenches. I never thought I would be so jealous of a person's hand, but I want nothing more than to do that myself. I have half a mind to hop on him and tell my mother to wait. Instead, I close my eyes, taking another deep breath. I wonder if he ever got that book on toe fungus from our trip to the bookstore. I could stand to read a chapter or three.

I step out, pulling the door shut behind me. Addy asks, "What's going on in there? Does he need some help? Do you need some help?" She wiggles her eyebrows at me suggestively.

"Shut up," I mumble. I'm frustrated but trying not to let it show how angry I am. I want it so bad. My mother is sitting at our bar, eyeing the cup of coffee Addy gave her. Addy's coffee isn't as good as Megs's, but it isn't terrible. Although, there is a chance she poisoned my mother. She's never liked her.

"Good morning, Rosie. It took you long enough to get out here. Happy birthday, my little baby." Her arms are around me, squeezing me tightly. These are not the arms I want around me or the body part I want to be squeezing. I sigh, trying to push those thoughts from my mind. It's not going to happen now. The sooner I accept that the sooner I can stop being angry about it.

"Did you forget we are taking you out for the day? I already told you about it. Your Daddy is in the car waiting. You know he isn't very patient."

"We agreed on 11 am."

"I know, sweetie. What time do you think it is?"

I glance around. I didn't think I had slept that late. My eyes land on the clock in the kitchen. It's 10:15. If Mom had waited until 11, I could have James balls deep inside me. I groan at my mom. "Fine. I'll go get dressed." I head to my room and put on the dress Megs gave me last night. I style my hair and throw on some light makeup. Nothing too fancy. When I come back out, James is talking with my mother. Addy and Megs are nowhere to be found. I walk to stand next to James.

His arm wraps around me. He presses a kiss against my ear, then whispers in an extra soft voice. "Don't you worry, baby. I'm gonna tear that pussy up soon." I clench at his words. Turning to look him in the eyes, my cheeks flush.

"Aw, look at you two love birds. James, you should come with us. Rosie's Daddy would be thrilled to meet you. I'm sure he would love you. We're very excited for Rosie to finally be in a committed relationship with a man."

James flinches slightly when she mentions my father. I remember how James's ex-wife refers to her new partner as Daddy. It must still be a sore spot for him. The dig my mother takes at my relationship status doesn't escape me. While I want to correct her, ultimately, it's just not worth it. She'd never accept anything other than traditional hetero marriage. No matter how many times I've told her I don't want that. I'm about to answer her when James speaks up first.

"As much as I would love that, I already promised Megs I would help them with the shopping today."

My mother's lips thin, clearly unsatisfied with his response. She really doesn't like Megs. She huffs a breath out. "Fine." Her eyes move up and down my outfit. The disgusted look is still on her face. She looks over to James, "I suppose it's nice that you are helping the women with their chores, but don't fall victim to doing everything for them. You should be the man of the house." Her eyes turn back to me. "Is that really what you are wearing?"

"First, gross. Second, yes."

She huffs again, grabbing her bag and walking towards the door. She left the coffee Addy gave her untouched. I kiss James's cheek, apologizing for my mother's behavior loud enough for her to hear. I follow her out the door. I'm annoyed by her comments, annoyed about being cock blocked, annoyed that they showed up early only to insult me. At this point, I don't even try to improve my mood. I'm just going to be angry for a little bit.

JAMES

Rosie's mother really is atrocious today. I'm unsure if Rosie realizes how awful she is or just tolerates it because she is her mother. Thankfully none of that rubbed off on Rosie. She is a beautiful, kind, thoughtful woman. I'm pretty upset that we were interrupted this morning. I vow to make sure I get time alone with her soon.

My cock aches to be inside her. Even with fooling around with her and having sex with Addy, I still want Rosie. The desire to be with all of them is intense.

As much as I didn't want to go out with Rosie's parents today, I am genuinely excited to go out with Megs. We will get groceries when we're done, but I have a few other plans before that. After Rosie and her mother leave, Megs and Addy come out of their rooms.

"Is she gone?"

"Yeah, the coast is clear," I answer.

Addy and Megs both avoid Rosie's mother as much as possible. I haven't seen Megs around her at all and hope I never have to. If Marge is that terrible to Rosie, what would she be like to Megs? Megs is a strong person, but there's a limit to what anyone should have to deal with. At least they all have each other to fall back on. It doesn't seem like Marge comes around too often. That's definitely a good thing.

Megs and Addy start making some breakfast. I ask if Addy actually poisoned Marge's coffee. She says no but still throws out the coffee in the mug. We all chuckle at that. Watching the pair move around the kitchen is like watching a choreographed dance. They both bob and weave, grabbing utensils, cups, plates, whatever they need to create the item they are making. I'm mesmerized watching them. It's not until they are nearly done that I realize I've just been watching.

"Oh, shit. I could've helped. Sorry." I walk into the kitchen, grabbing plates and silverware for all of us. I slide them onto the high top, then grab mugs for the fresh coffee Megs just made. Stepping behind them, I reach around to place the mugs on the counter next to the French press they are working on. I kiss their cheek and thank them. A slight blush appears. Their blush brings a smile to my face. I glide around Addy, kissing her cheek and thanking her too. Taking my seat at the bar, I spread the plates and utensils out as Addy brings over the food and Megs brings the coffee.

As we dig into the food, I ask questions about Rosie's mom.

"Has Marge always been the way she is?" Addy answers me.

"No, she wasn't so bad until we were teens. When we all started discovering our sexual preferences."

That would be a problem for Marge. She mentioned attending church and getting Rosie on the "right path." Rosie hasn't said anything about her parents. She doesn't discuss them much. It's understandable. They aren't a huge part of her life. She talks to her mother regularly. Nothing has ever been said about her father. I don't know much about him. It sounds as though he knows much more about me if Marge is to be believed. I make a mental note to ask Rosie about it later.

We chat about Rosie's parents for a bit longer. We lament their ties to our lives, wishing it weren't the case. It's nice to have someone to talk with about these things. When I was with Whitney, I had no one else to talk to. She constantly berated me when I said anything against her family. None of our friends knew them well enough to commiserate with. All my feelings about my in-laws stayed bottled up inside. Even though Rosie's parents aren't my in-laws, having other people to discuss my feelings with is still nice.

"Megs, you ready to go out with me today?"

Moving my dishes to the sink, I grab theirs too, then Addy's when I realize she is done. I rinse them off and place them in the dishwasher. Megs says they'll get dressed and return in a couple of minutes. I follow suit, changing in my room then moving around to wait on Megs. When they walk out, they wear jean shorts, a band shirt, and low blue Converses. Their hair is wavy and brushed over to the side. I never thought much about an androgynous style, but I find myself enamored with Megs's. A smile forms on my lips as I ask if they're ready.

On the drive, I tell them about this mini-golf course I just learned about and want to take them to. It's not too far, and we arrive after a short drive. As we pay, Megs is looking over the map of the course. I have already seen the map online and am familiar with the different obstacles on the course. I haven't played mini-golf since I was a teen, but I'm sure we will have fun. We grab balls and putters and make our way to the first hole.

The first hole is easy. We both make par, then move on to the second one. The second hole is trickier, with a curve and several small hills. As we play, we both pretend to give each other instructions on how to improve our game. I tell Megs they must bend their knees more, bouncing on my feet to show them. Megs rolls their eyes at me. When it's my turn, they tell me to move my hips more. Megs swings their hips, showing me how. I copy their movement but hit the ball too hard. It goes flying into another area. I yell, "Fore," and we both start laughing.

I was correct about this game being fun for both of us. We enjoy playing and teasing each other. It's so easy to be around Megs. They have a calming presence that allows me to just enjoy being around them. I don't feel the need to impress them or try to be someone I'm not. We play through several holes, laughing, teasing, enjoying each other and the game. Megs is the first to get a hole-in-one.

"Yes! Take that, James!"

"No! You definitely cheated! I saw you! There was...that... illegal move!"

We both laugh at our antics. I bend over, laughing hard. Megs wipes their eyes, trying to declare they didn't cheat. I can't even respond to them. Other people look at us like we're crazy, but we don't care. We're having a great time. We eventually calm down and continue through the course. I don't get a hole-in-one, but the score is close at the end of the game. Our balls are in the final cup, and we collect them. I bend down, grabbing both. I hold my hand out for Megs to take theirs. Instead, they grab my wrist, pulling me close. I'm confused, but don't move. Megs steps up, their chest against mine. Leaning up on their tiptoes, they rise to press their lips against mine. It's a soft kiss, and over before I have time to react.

My eyes are on Megs; realization sets in that they just kissed me. A smile grows across my lips. Megs notices my smirk. They snatch their ball from my hand and step away from me. "Don't make it weird," they declare, walking back towards the hut to return our items. My body begins to function again. I catch up to them, sneaking up on their side. In a sing-song voice, I whisper, "Someone has a crush on me." Megs's eyes go wide as they shove me away. I laugh, stepping back to their side. I nudge them with my shoulder. I whisper in a normal voice. "It's ok. I may have a crush too." I kiss their cheek, then rush ahead, not giving them a chance to respond.

After we return our items, I take Megs's hand as we walk through the parking lot. There is a restaurant that serves healthy food, and Megs will love it. We still need groceries, but that can wait until after lunch. I have no problem spending all day with Megs. While I enjoy running errands with them, it's nice to do fun things that don't involve any chores. We don't speak on the drive to the restaurant, but I keep their hand in mine. They don't pull back.

At the restaurant, they are impressed with the selection of food available. There are wraps and salads and rice bowls with a variety of toppings. Megs looks happy. After we get our food, we pick a table and sit down. I unwrap my food, then notice Megs is just sitting, staring at their food.

"Hey, you okay?"

They look up at me. A smile spreads across their face as they nod.

"Yeah, you just make me really happy." I smile back, not adding anything else. I could tell them how much they mean to me. How happy I am to be here. How welcome they have made me feel. Instead, I eat my food. They start eating too. When we finish, we walk out to the car. I walk them over to the passenger side, opening their door. Before they get in, I grab their wrist. They turn their head towards me. I lean in close.

"You make me really happy too." I press my lips against theirs softly. As much as I want to deepen the kiss, make it more, wrap my arms around them, and claim them, they wouldn't appreciate any of that. I keep the kiss short, like the one earlier. I pull away and walk to the other side of the car. Megs is smiling, staring out the window with a dreamy look on their face. I chuckle silently as I drive to the grocery store.

Rosie returns late in the afternoon after Megs and I finished grocery shopping. The lunch with her parents went much longer than I expected. Megs said it wasn't uncommon for their time together to run long. It is part of the reason Rosie doesn't go very often.

She places some bags on the chair, looking defeated. I close the book I am reading and move towards her. I wrap my arms around her. She leans into my chest but doesn't wrap her arms around me.

"What happened?"

"They gave me a gift."

Confusion darkens my face. Gift-giving shouldn't be a process that leaves a person looking like Rosie does now. I step back from her, looking down at her. Maybe there is a better answer about why she is sad written on her face. She looks up at me. There isn't an answer, but her face confirms my suspicion that she is upset. She motions to the large bag sitting on the chair.

"Mom said I won't fit in her wedding dress until I lose weight, but I can have her veil for now." Tears are forming in her eyes. The words take a few moments for me to process. Her mother called her fat and implied she needed to be married. The anger hits me harder than I anticipate. There is a wild desire rising in me to protect Rosie. To keep her safe. I never want to see her look like this again, especially not due to her own parents.

"Your mom is a bitch and doesn't deserve you. You shouldn't spend time with her."

My comments come out angrier and more demanding than I intend. I don't mean to tell Rosie what to do, but seeing her in this position hurts. She deserves so much better than this. I need to keep her safe. She glares at me, the words hitting her differently than I intended them to. Her face is hardening with anger on top of the hurt. This situation has gone from bad to worse, and it's my fault. This feeling inside me, this desire to protect her, is screaming and thrashing in my body. I need to make this right. I need to fix this.

"You don't get to bad mouth my parents and tell me what to do." She grabs her bag, storming away from me. The bag crashes into my shoulder as she stomps towards her room. She's moving faster than my brain is working. I take a step to follow her, but she's quick.

"No, Rosie, wait...that's not...."

Her bedroom door slams before I finish my thoughts. This is not how I want this to go. I've definitely made things worse for Rosie. It wasn't my intention. I wanted to show her my support, not isolate her more. I take several deep breaths. I can't go storming into her room. That definitely won't help anything. I try to calm my thoughts. Bursting into her room, insisting I'm right, or trying to help isn't the best idea. If my comment upset her, raging in front of her certainly won't help. I need to think through this situation before I try to talk to her. I don't want to ruin what we have before it starts. We just need a minute to cool off. That's all.

Chapter Fifteen

Lunch with my parents did not go well. After my mother insulted my friends and my clothes, they drove me to the restaurant they wanted. Surprise! It was closed today. What restaurant is closed on a Sunday? Instead of letting me pick another restaurant, they said we should just go back to their house. What's the point in allowing me to choose where to eat for my birthday? Why should I pick when they can make all my decisions?

During the meal, they hounded me with questions about James, when we would settle down, when I would move away from my roommates, when I would get a real job. They didn't bother to explain how teaching isn't a real job. The party last night was so wonderful. I was utterly unprepared for a terrible time with my parents. They've never been this insistent before. Even my father was joining in. He usually just sits quietly, nodding along, answering his phone. Today was different, though. My mother insists it's because I'm getting older. I'm wasting my youth, were her exact words.

The wedding dress was just the icing on the cake, which they didn't bother with. I'm not a size 2, but I'm not as large as my mother. I'm perfectly happy with my body and love my little curves and occasional love handles. Addy is always going on about how perfect my body is. James doesn't seem to be upset about it, either. From what I remember from stories, my mother basically starved herself for a month before the wedding to fit in the dress.

Aside from the weight issue, I have no plans to get married, and her dress isn't even one I would choose. It has a very 80's vibe to it. The sleeves have big puffs on the shoulders, then tight lace down to the wrist. The top has a sweetheart cut, a fitted bodice, and a looser skirt. It's covered with lace and beadwork. That was the style when my mother got married, but it is not my style.

The whole day was just awful. They insulted nearly every aspect of my life they could. They were incessant about my relationship with James. They disparaged my relationship with Addy and Megs. Mom insulted my body. Daddy insulted my job. When I finally got home, dropped off by their driver no less, I wanted to be free of insults and demands. While I'm sure James meant well, it really fucking sucked to hear it from him too. It seems everyone has forgotten I'm a grown adult. I can handle myself. I don't need to be married or told what to eat or wear or who to see. I can decide for myself.

I sit on the edge of my bed, ultimately defeated. I want to cry. I want to scream. I want someone to hold me and tell me I'm fine. But my body doesn't want to move. No tears come. My eyes are fixed on the floor, but they aren't seeing anything. I just stare while my brain hurls thoughts of anger, hurt, and indignation at my soul.

There's a slight knock on the door. James asks if he can come in. My gaze shifts towards the door. I try to speak but realize my throat is dry, and no words come out. Instead, I rise and open the door but turn and walk back to my spot on the bed. He comes into the room, closing the door behind him. He just stands there for a moment, taking in my defeated body. My crumpled soul sitting in a crumpled dress on my crisply made bed. At least not everything is crumpled.

He steps closer but pauses near me. Our gazes meet, and he drops down on his knees in front of me. He takes my hands in his, pressing a kiss on both. "I'm sorry." I stare into his eyes, searching, waiting. I want him to tell me what he is sorry for. An apology isn't just those two words. I need more from him. He seems to realize this and begins to speak again.

"I had no right to insult your parents like that. Or tell you what you need to do. Rosie, I..." he squeezes my hands, looking down at them. "I didn't mean to tell you what to do. I wanted it to be a suggestion. Something inside me snapped when you told me what they said. I don't want to see you hurt by anyone, especially not someone who is supposed to protect you. I don't want to hurt you. But I know I did. I'm so sorry, Rosie. I'm going to work on this desire to protect you and make things better, so I don't say asinine shit again."

He is still staring at my hands in his. His thumbs are rubbing over mine. His words settle inside me, smoothing over the ache. It's a situation I would have liked to avoid, but I'm glad he apologized. I take a deep breath. My hand moves to his face, stroking his cheek. My mouth is still dry, and I'm unable to say anything to him. Instead, I lean down and kiss him gently. His hands wrap around my neck, tangling in my hair. His body moves closer to me, deepening our kiss. He's still on his knees, putting his face lower than mine. After a moment, I pull back, pressing my forehead to his.

The apology releases my anger at James but reminds me I won't ever get that from my parents. As much relief as I feel towards James, I'm now burdened by grief from my parents. They'll never give me what I need. My eyes close, holding James close, trying to steal some relief or any other emotion from him. He seems to notice and stands up.

"Do you want to lay down for a bit?"

I nod to him, still unable to form words.

"Want to change into some sweats?"

Another nod. James pulls me up and turns me so my back is to him. He slowly unzips my dress and place a small kiss at the base of my neck. "Put on comfy clothes. I'll be right back." He walks out of the room. I do as I'm told. Despite having a meltdown over being told what to do, I don't mind these instructions. It's what I would have chosen to do on my own anyway. I remove the dress, bra, and panties, then step into a crop top and shorts. James walks back into the room as I hang the dress up to avoid wrinkles. He's carrying my burrito blanket.

"Thanks."

I manage one word before crawling into the bed. He wraps the blanket around, tucking it tightly. He kisses my forehead and moves to leave. I grab his shirt, stopping him. Now isn't the time I want him to go. I needed space earlier, but I don't now. His eyes are searching mine. Without speaking, he settles down next to me. Snuggling into his body, I let him wrap around me, covering me in warmth and safety. Several kisses land across my forehead. Large hands caress my back. The thoughts in my head are dampened. My hands stretch across his chest, feeling his heartbeat through his shirt.

"I've never felt so possessive over another person," he speaks softly. I don't move, rolling his words around in my head. I've never had someone be possessive over me. Addy has her moments but usually lets me make my own decisions. Megs can be possessive but not as aggressive about it as James is. I've read many books about possessive men and have always wondered what it would feel like to have one be that way for me. I never thought it would be so bittersweet.

The demands of not seeing my parents aren't something I want. Though I won't complain about the tenderness that comes with the apology. That's probably what I love most...Woah. Not love. That's not the right word, is it? No. It couldn't be. It's too soon for all that. It's only been like a month and a half. I'm just tired and emotional. I just like that stuff about James. I don't love it. No, certainly not. My brain is just in overdrive. That's ridiculous. I should probably just sleep. Yeah, sleep off the crazy. That's a good plan.

My eyes flutter open, trying to take in my surroundings. I was dreaming because I was talking to a dog walking an octopus. However, I have no idea what time it is, how long I was asleep, or where I am. A warmth under my face rises and falls, and everything comes crashing back. I fell asleep with James, sleeping off the emotions of a difficult afternoon. James is reading a book, and the light is fading outside. I couldn't have been asleep long. Just long enough for the L-word to leave my mind. I'm not thinking about that anymore.

"Sleep well?"

He sits his book down, focusing his attention on me. My mouth is still dry, but I lick my lips, swallowing so I can speak again. "Yeah, what time is it?" One hand rubs my eyes, the other staying on James's chest. He glances at my clock, "You were asleep about an hour." I nod, shifting to sit up. He moves too, grabbing a bottle from the nightstand. He hands the water to me. I feel eternally grateful for the water. After several large gulps, I put the lid on and hand it back to him.

"Thank you," I say softly. My throat feels much better after the water, but I don't feel like speaking in a normal tone. "For the water, the comfort, and the apology. You have a point about my parents, but after having them make so many demands of me, it hurt to hear you make them too."

"I really am sorry, Rosie. I didn't mean to be that possessive of you. You're an adult and can make your own decisions without me." I lean over to him, pressing my lips against his. His hand runs up my back, reminding me I have nothing under my shirt and shorts. His fingers slide across the skin on my back. The touch sends fire through my body, warming me to my core. Instinctually, my lips part against his as my tongue slips inside his mouth. Our tongues meet, swirling and teasing each other. We've had enough teasing lately. I'm ready to pick up where things left off this morning. Both of his hands are on my back, pressing under my shirt.

His fingers glide around to my breast. I move to straddle him, but he notices and pushes me back against the bed. His hands flip up my top, then his lips cover one of my nipples. I moan at the sudden warmth on my breast. My hands go to his back, sliding under his shirt. I tug at the hem, pulling it over his head. He shifts, letting me take it off, then removes mine. Our shirts are tossed aside. The outline of his erect cock is visible through his black lounge pants. The heat rises in my core, and I need to feel him inside me. His mouth covers my other nipple, sucking and biting my hard nipple. My hands roam his back, wanting to touch him more. One of his hands shifts to my shorts, slipping his fingers beneath. They wander as if looking for something.

"Where are your panties, Rosie?"

His eyes meet mine with a devilish grin as his fingers finally reach my core. I moan as he glides over my clit and straight inside me. His finger slides in and out while his palm presses against my clit. My fingers grab his face, pulling him up to mine. Our lips collide in a desperate kiss. We're full of need and desire and so many broken chances. His finger plunges faster, creating more friction, driving me closer to the edge.

"James, I need you."

He pulls back from the kiss, his fingers leaving my body as quickly as they enter. "Do you have condoms?" I nod and tell him they are in the drawer. As he grabs one, I remove my shorts, tossing them to the floor. He notices, bringing his eyes back to my body. One of my hands covers one breast, squeezing and twisting my nipple the way I like. He is mesmerized by my hands on my body. The other hand slips to my core, teasing the outer parts he can see. His gaze burns on my body as his own remains frozen. One finger slips inside my aching pussy. A moan rises from my chest, spurring him to action. In a movement, my brain can barely register; his pants are gone, the condom is in place, and he is between my legs. He pulls my hand away, lining himself up with my entrance.

"I need you now, Rosie."

I thrust my hips, trying to get him closer. I need him, too. This teasing has been going on for too long. If anyone were to disturb us now, they would just get a show. I don't want this to stop for anything. My legs wrap around his back. I grab his face, pulling him close.

"Fuck me."

I press my lips to his. He sinks deep inside me in one motion. I cry out against his mouth. His girth fills me completely, stretching my core to accommodate him. He pauses to give me time to adjust, but this drives me crazy. Using my legs as anchors around his back, I shove my hips against him. He takes the hint and begins thrusting inside me. The friction and the stretch increase my pleasure exponentially. My nails dig into the skin on his back, needing more.

He shifts his body, pulling my legs from around him. He places my legs over his shoulder. My pussy feels tighter in this position. My eyes flutter shut. I grab onto my legs behind my knees as he slams into me. His pounding increases to a relentless pace. I moan loudly, my orgasm rising, nearing its bursting point. I open my eyes, looking at him. He's staring down at my body. His eyes rake from my face to my breast, bouncing beneath my legs to the point where we connect, him slamming deep inside me.

"Fuck, you're gorgeous."

My pussy tightens with an imminent orgasm. "Oh, I...I'm gonna...I'm about to come," I yell out. His hand is between us, finding my clit. He flicks it once, and my orgasm explodes. I yell loudly as my pussy clenches tighter than I have ever felt it squeeze. My legs break past my hands, wrapping around his back. My chest arches towards him as my body is overwhelmed with euphoria. My orgasm seems to trigger his own. His thrusts are erratic as he juts into me. I open my eyes in time to see his face distort with his orgasm. Before he is entirely spent, his lips are on mine, tongue in my mouth, claiming me. My arms wrap around his shoulders, pulling him into me. The need to have him close is overwhelming. I kiss him back deeply, not wanting to separate from him. His body relaxes on top of mine, slightly to the side, to not crush me. At this point, he could crush me, and I wouldn't be that upset. Our breathing settles slowly, both of us lost in orgasmic bliss.

I keep my arms around his body, not wanting him to leave me. He pulls his lips from mine, resting his head next to mine. He presses several kisses along my jaw and neck. "Fuck, Rosie. I knew you would be amazing, but damn, I didn't know it would be that good." I can feel his smile on my cheek. His soft cock is still inside me. I don't want to move at all. I want to stay connected with him like this.

"Ditto," I reply, and we both burst into giggles. He rolls away from me, taking his member to remove the condom. I pull him back once it's in the trash, dragging my blanket over us. He snuggles into me, kissing my cheeks and neck again. This is definitely what heaven should be. It's warm, safe, and snuggly. What more could a girl ask for? I could do without the knocking at the door, though. Always someone to interrupt.

Chapter Sixteen

JAMES

Willow said she would meet me in the office. She is our technical advisor and has been here at least as long as I have. I don't know exactly when she started, but she is good at her job. She's had the thumb drive I got from my source at the bar for a while now. She told me she was finally able to sort through everything and wanted to show it to me. It must be something special. She usually sends emails, occasionally a phone call if it's trickier. She works remotely and only comes in when she must. My curiosity is piqued about what could be on that drive. I hope it's what I need to finish this article.

As I wait, my mind starts to drift. I stare at my desk, the exact spot I had Rosie bent over it. She was absolutely right about making this my new favorite spot. Her smell has faded, and I can sit at my desk without popping a boner. The secretary seems to be happy about this. She even asked me about my upset stomach the other day. That was awkward. Still worth it, though.

My mind drifts to the weekend when I had Rosie in her bed. I never intended to upset her. I am glad I finally got to fuck her, though. Her pussy was so much better than I expected. Rosie is warmer and more inviting than Addy. Addy is fun and exciting and wild. It feels weird to have two different people fill these roles for me. I always thought I needed one person, one woman, to be warm, inviting, fun, exciting, wild, logical, reasonable, accommodating, and everything. One person was supposed to be all of that. I thought it would be Whitney, but she never filled those spots. Rosie, Addy, and Megs, though, do fill all those spots. They serve those spots for each other. I hope when they consider our roles like this, I fill more than just dick. I can be funny sometimes too.

Rosie and I were again interrupted; at least it was after sex this time. Addy gave us a five-minute warning before dinner. Rosie sighed, trying to get out of bed, but I had a better idea. "What's the fastest you've ever orgasmed?"

She looked confused by my question. Normally the goal isn't to orgasm fast, but I had an idea. One hand was on her shoulder, keeping her on the bed, while I leaned on my other arm, hovering over Rosie. She finally shrugged, "I don't know, a few minutes or so?"

"Perfect."

Then I hopped over her body. She squealed at my sudden movement but laid back. Instantly, my mouth was on her, sucking her clit in. I slid two fingers inside her, pumping quickly. I released her clit, wetting a finger on my other hand. I looked up to catch her eyes. I loved when she watched me. Knowing she wanted to see me on her sent chills straight to my dick. I gave her a wicked smile, placing my mouth over her clit. I didn't suck it this time. I flicked my tongue against it, in time with my fingers moving in her pussy. The finger that had just been in my mouth pressed to her back hole, sliding in smoothly. She groaned, shifting her shoulders to prop herself up better. I lifted my head for her, "Come for me, baby." My voice was huskier than I intended, but it worked for her. She bit her lip, eyes staying on me.

It was a bit awkward to support myself while both hands worked her holes, but I wasn't going to let a knock on the door interrupt us again. I sucked her clit between my lips, working it with my tongue as my fingers moved inside her, hitting those spots that I knew would drive her wild. Rosie moaned, her breathing increasing as her pussy clenched around my fingers. She shifted onto her back, eyes closed. One hand went to her breasts, massaging, pulling, twisting. The other hand grabbed the back of my head. She dug her fingers in keeping me in the right position. I slipped a third finger into her cunt, filling her mercilessly. She moaned and cursed, commanding me not to stop, not that I would anyway. I had no intentions of stopping before she was done. She clenched tighter, her breathing quickened. Her body twisted as she yelled out, turning her head into her pillow to silence her cries. Her pussy clenched tightly around my fingers as her hips thrust erratically in my face.

Her fingers softened from a dig to a caress as her body seemed to unwind too. An occasional spasm rolled through as her breathing returned to normal. I slowed my fingers, pausing before I finally removed them. I placed a kiss on her hip. Climbing up over her, I kissed her lips. A soft sensual kiss. She matched the kiss. Pulling away, she giggled and told me that probably was the fastest she had ever come. After we dressed, I ran into the kitchen, proudly announcing I could make her come faster than Addy. Addy wasn't impressed and tried to force Rosie back into the bedroom. Megs stepped in and told us to sit down and behave for dinner. We did, mostly. There was still some taunting and teasing.

During dinner that night, Rosie told us her parents had offered to let us stay in their cabin on a lake over the Fourth of July. Again, they wanted another lunch with Rosie. I tried to argue she didn't need to do that, but all three insisted it was worth it for the cabin. I didn't know if that was true, but I didn't continue arguing. If I got to tag along on vacation to a cabin on a lake, I wouldn't complain too much. The timing worked well for me. The editor said he wanted all stories completed by the Fourth so they could spend time editing and designing before publishing in our August edition. As long as Willow has good information for me today, I can finish this story in time to take a few days off to go to the cabin.

Willow has impeccable timing. My Rosie daydreams are ending as she walks up. Her long black hair falls straight over her shoulders. She is tall and thin with tanned skin. Despite only meeting with her in person a few times, I always love chatting with her. She shares stories from her youth on the reservation. Willow could trace her family back more generations than anyone I know. Her family is from the Dakota tribe, native to the region. She left the reservation as a teen and found a love for technology. She has proficient cyber security skills but knows many other technologies too. It's why she is so valuable to our company. I've asked her to hang out with me several times, but she has social anxiety. I tried accommodating that but could never get her to come out.

She walks into my cubicle, leaning against the desk. "This is some good stuff." She holds the drive out as I take it from her. I look at it as if the answers are written on the outside. She tells me about her process of searching the drive. Nothing she says makes a lot of sense to me. I can work with the basic Microsoft suite and can manage social media, but the technical coding stuff has always been a mystery. Willow explains it in terms I can mostly understand, but it still sounds like gibberish.

"So, I can download this software to your device, then you can access all of their financial documents and most of their emails." I stare at her, stunned for a moment.

"Yeah, whoever gave you that drive is high up in that company and probably hates the boss."

Willow waits for me to move to the side. I stand from my chair, letting her sit while she works on my laptop. She continues talking, walking me through the software. I know many of the employees didn't like the owner, Martin. From what I have gathered, he's not a nice man. Aside from the money laundering, he's been known to be violent with his employees, doesn't follow the labor laws, and treats everyone like he's better than they are. Not one employee had anything nice to say about the man.

Once the software is downloaded, Willow shows me some information I can access. It's an impressive amount of data. It absolutely proves money laundering. Willow suggests it might link to a source if I search enough. Now that she has given me that, it's time to get to work. I thank her, making a mental note to send her lunch or something one day. I would not have found all this information without her. She leaves my cubicle, but I barely notice. This program has captured my attention. I glance at the clock, a few hours until dinner. I'll work, then head back to the apartment. My calendar is sitting just beneath the clock. There are less than two weeks until the fourth. This article needs to be done by then, and I will do everything to make that happen.

ADDY

The past two weeks have been a blur. I've worked more doubles than I ever have in my life. Holidays don't mean much in the bar industry. We'll be closed on the fourth, but the days surrounding it will be open and generally packed. Being on the outskirts of the Cities, we are an ideal stop for bikers passing through, vacationers wanting to get a break from the hustle of the city and a stopping point for other travelers. The area doesn't see many people on vacation, but the locals still swarm us on holidays. I asked Nick for a few days off to go to the cabin with Rosie. He likes her, so I tried to drop her name and how disappointed she would be if I couldn't go. He's still salty about me fucking James in a club. Thankfully Nick realized he was an idiot and hasn't mentioned firing me, but he's still mad for some reason. He agreed to let me go but insisted I needed to pick up extra shifts to make up for my absence.

His logic doesn't make sense, but I don't argue with him. I'm getting a vacation with my three favorite people at the most awesome cabin around. Rosie's dad owns tons of land. He is loaded, despite none of us really knowing what he does. It just means he isn't around much, and nobody complains about that. Not even Rosie's mother, who could complain about anything. We are excited to go to the cabin for a few days. Megs has picked up extra sessions with her clients to compensate for taking a few days off. They've spent extra time coddling their clients to go without them. I can't help rolling my eyes when they say that. A bunch of grown-ass adults needs to be told how to eat for five days so Megs can go on vacation. Ugh.

James has been swamped with his story. He's worked from the apartment for a couple of days. At first, I thought it was so he could spend time with Rosie. She said he doesn't come out of the room, though. She started taking him food and drinks because she didn't think he was eating. He got an excellent lead on his story and has been working through it. Despite working at the apartment, we haven't seen much of him. Maybe getting some space before we are all together for five days on the lake is a good thing. Even Bruiser is tired of me being around. He's not sick enough of me to not come back, though.

It's almost closing time of my last night working before heading to the cabin. Bruiser and another biker are the only people left in the bar. The kitchen closed early, and I've already sent everyone else home. It's just me, Bruiser, and his pal still in the bar. Once they leave, I'm gone. I stand against the wall, staring at them. I've been trying to gain telepathy, but I've been largely unsuccessful so far. The two just continue idly chatting, like I'm not standing here sending death threats mind to mind. I get an idea and move closer, making a drink.

"Here is a blow job for you. This guy loves giving them."

I slide the obscenely named drink in front of the guy I don't know. Bruiser's face goes beet red. He's stunned, speechless. The other man gives me a confused look, then looks at Bruiser. He explodes in laughter, and I follow. Bruiser looks like a tomato. The other man settles down; Bruiser just stares at the bar. He softly asks for his check. The other guy does too. I don't put that drink on either of their bills since it worked, and they are leaving. They pay and walk out together, standing suspiciously close. I shut everything down and make it to the parking lot in record time. Bruiser and his friend are standing near their bikes, intimately speaking to each other. I suspect Bruiser is gay. That may be the push he needs. I wave to them, calling good night. They wave back, and the other guy drops his hand to Bruiser's large shoulder. Yeah, that's going somewhere tonight. I grin at myself, both happy to be going home and glad to see Bruiser with someone. He can be annoying, but he's a good customer.

At the apartment, everyone is in the kitchen. They cheer when I walk in. There are already several drinks around the counter, along with some snacks. I start to grab a beer, but James stops me. "Now that everyone is here, I want to celebrate!" He holds a bottle of champagne, removing the covering around the cap. "I finished my article. It's a huge story, and I want to celebrate that. And all of us going on vacation together."

POP!

The bottle erupts. Rosie squeals; James yells; I start clapping wildly. Megs is just screaming, trying to contain the mess. We should have opened that on the balcony, but it's too late now. James pours a glass for everyone. He pokes Megs a couple of times, trying to get them to stop cleaning and take a drink. They finally do. He raises his glass in a toast.

"To love, life, and the pursuit of sex, or whatever those old guys said."

We all laugh at James's toast but drink anyway. We spend the rest of the night drinking, dancing, and being together. We've been so busy and distant lately; it's nice to reconnect like this. To have an evening to do nothing and just be together. Knowing tomorrow holds nothing essential, and we can let go of our inhibitions and just be.

JAMES

We stayed up drinking and talking for a long time. Rosie and Megs went to bed before Addy and me. She stayed up talking to me while I cleaned up from our evening. The kitchen was sticky when Megs went to bed. It was apparent how much they hated that, but I had promised to clean it. The champagne was my fault anyway. After cleaning, Addy all but jumped on me. We wound up in her bed, having drunk, sloppy sex until we passed out. The evening is exactly how I like celebrating being done with an article and starting a vacation.

After waking up tangled with Addy and her sheets, we all shower, pack, and get on the road. We take two vehicles. Since Rosie needs to have lunch with her family in a couple of days, we don't want to strand the others. The forecast shows a thunderstorm tonight but clear skies the rest of the time. I thought this was terrible, but again, they insist it is perfect. All three refuse to give me more information on what makes this cabin so wonderful that Rosie would suffer through time with her family for it. They just say it is magical and go all starry-eyed, even Megs. I didn't think they would go starry-eyed, but they love the cabin too.

On the drive out, I ride with Addy, Megs insisting they don't want to die. Addy finally shares some stories of their past trips out to the cabin. They don't go every year, but it sounds like they have been many times. She has several stories from their teens of experimenting, relaxing, recovering, celebrating. The magic is beginning to make sense, but it isn't until we turn down a dirt road that it clicks together. We drive two hours away from the city. Then spend another 45 minutes on dirt roads surrounded by trees and brush. We don't see another person on the dirt roads. There are several driveways, but not many.

We finally reach a gate. Rosie goes through first, entering a code to unlock the gate and slide it open. It seems odd that this level of security would be this far out. Addy tells me it is Rosie's father's doing. All kinds of protection are around the property, including a fence around the entire plot of land, which is 40-plus acres. He is a very secretive man and doesn't want anyone on his property. Addy says he tried to install security cameras around this property, but Marge stopped him, insisting they didn't need people watching them on vacation.

As we drive down the long dirt driveway, a sense of seclusion settles over me. Once through the gate, it is several more minutes before the cabin comes into view. The cabin is smaller than I expected. Three stories are built into a hill, with the third floor partially underground. It feels like a typical log cabin, with flowers and rocks decorating the landscape in a way that isn't natural. A lake is visible, shimmering behind the cabin. It isn't a large lake; I can see the entire shoreline. It is a beautiful area. There is a small grassy yard off to the left of the house. This is a perfect area for yard games. A large patio stands between the yard and the side of the house. A door connects to what I assume is the kitchen.

The sky is darkening as we climb out of the cars. It will likely rain at any moment. Not many animals are making sounds around now. The air is clean and has that smell of rain saturating it. I take a deep breath, inhaling nature and the rain. I feel the magic while standing here, breathing this air, and seeing the cabin and lake. I understand why this place is worth a meal with Rosie's family. It's beautiful and peaceful. No other people are around to bother you.

Rosie walks over, wrapping her arms around my stomach, looking up at me. Even she looks more beautiful standing in these woods. The gentle wind lifts a few strands of hair, blowing them behind her. "You get it now, huh?" She says softly. Her body rises on her toes, pressing a small kiss to my lips. As she pulls away, I smile, unable to form words. I nod in response to her statement. She lets me go to move towards the house.

"Good, because you're going to lunch with my parents."

Well, that ripped the magic away. "What?" I yell, following her. She and Addy are already laughing, rushing inside the house. Inside is just as quaint, matching the feel outside. It feels rustic, but there are modern appliances. I was correct that the kitchen leads to the small patio. It isn't a large kitchen but has room for several people to be in and still move around comfortably. Plenty of space and several large windows let in lots of natural light. The room is still bright, despite the storm moving in. Opposite the kitchen is a dining area. This area is large, made almost entirely of windows on the walls. It has a beautiful view of the trees and nature beyond it.

On the other side of the kitchen is a living room. This is a large room with several oversized leather couches. Cute little decorations hang on the walls describing different aspects of "lake life." Several bookshelves containing board games and books. There isn't a tv, which is refreshing. Beyond the living room is a huge deck. It looks like a second living room. More couches and seating. A massive umbrella offers shade for sunny days. A large grill is visible opposite the wall of the cabin. The deck overlooks the lake and the yard leading down to it.

Before I get a chance to explore that more, Addy drags me upstairs, wanting to give me the tour. She tells me there are only two rooms: the master and another room with a twin-queen bunk bed. She says we'll sort out sleeping later. A large bathroom splits the two rooms, with a closet opposite containing more blankets. With everyone's bags deposited upstairs, Addy drags me back towards the basement. Megs insists we hurry up. They didn't mention having other plans, but they didn't tell me much about what they usually do.

The basement is an open space. There are more leather couches down here. A pool table is in the center of the room. Other games line the wall, such as darts, more board games on shelves, and even a pinball machine. A giant tv is mounted on the wall. The space feels lived in and comfortable. Each item was added with thought and intention. Everything is loved, used, and well cared for. I don't know how much time they spend here, but this is a favorite place. I'm glad they welcomed me into this space so willingly. Addy is practically bouncing as she shows me around. Her moods shift a lot between subdued and hyper. She's always fun, though.

Once the tour is over, we head back upstairs. Megs is looking between us and the sky outside. The sky has darkened since we first walked in, but the rain may still be a few minutes away.

"Come on, let's go."

Megs walks out the door, indicating we should follow. Rosie is right behind them, already knowing what they want. Addy goes next, and I follow. We all stand on the deck. I'm still enjoying the lake's fantastic view and surrounding trees when I hear a lighter click. I turn back and see Megs leaning into Rosie. Rosie is trying to spread her body out more. At first, I'm confused, then realize they are trying to light a blunt. I step over, offering my larger body to block the wind that is growing stronger.

They get the blunt lit, take a couple of hits, then pass it to Rosie. Megs is shivering. They are wearing bike shorts and a loose tank top. It would be perfect for this area if it weren't for the storm coming in. I step closer, wrapping my arm around them to offer some comfort. The four of us stand out there, smoking and passing the blunt. We are all silent, looking out over the lake. When we are done, we head inside. The timing is perfect because it starts raining once we shut the door.

In the kitchen, Addy makes drinks while Megs pulls out some snacks. There are a couple of healthy snacks, but I'm surprised by the number of junk food items. There are chips, cookies, brownies, more cookies, more chips, and at least 8 different kinds of candy. Addy and Rosie dig into those. Megs shrugs at me, letting me know this is a vacation. We spend the next few hours snacking, drinking, enjoying the high, and relaxing. The rain pounds on the windows, creating a soothing cadence inside. Eventually, we all drift off to bed. Megs takes the top bunk. I accept the bottom. Rosie and Addy share the master. Despite the bed being uncomfortable, I sleep soundly all night.

Chapter Seventeen

ADDY

After waking next to Rosie, I shower quickly and head down to the kitchen. Megs made coffee and is sitting outside on the deck. I grab a mug and head out to sit with them. They nod at me as I walk out. It's wonderful this morning. The air is crisp but not hot. Birds are chirping. There is a soft breeze blowing. It smells like dirt and rain. Something deep inside me groans to be out there, running in the trees, being free of everything, taking control, hunting. I sip my coffee, staring out past the lake. I've never been a runner, but this place always makes me want to run. To chase and claim. This plot calls to something profound and hidden in my soul.

A heavy body flops down next to me. The sudden appearance shocks me, and I nearly drop my mug, spilling part of it on my legs. "Dammit, James." He chuckles, grabbing a towel Megs brought and wiping my leg.

"What were you thinking about?"

"How I'm going to pound your ass into the dirt," I practically growl at him. I may be hyper and happy sometimes, but never before coffee. Also, never when someone spills my precious life force on me. I scowl, looking down at my now half-full mug. He chuckles again next to me, taking my mug from me, replacing it with his. "You drink that. I'll finish this and then get us both refills. Ok?" I don't smile but sip the drink in acceptance. He's still chuckling as he wraps his arm around me, sipping the mug of half-full coffee. I settle back against him, letting him hold me close.

James and Megs are chit-chatting as my mind wanders back to nature. The song of the trees is calling me again. I don't care for nature the way Megs does. They like to hike and experience the trees and beauty and creatures. That's not what I want. There's a feeling in deep, secluded forests that fuels me. It powers my soul, drives my spirit. The thrill of needing to survive on primal instinct, to hunt or be hunted. An impulse to move, capture, dominate flickers in my chest, urging me to run and claim. I've never acted on it outdoors. Sometimes, I have just run through nature, practicing a hunt. It never quite clenches that feeling.

"Tell me what you are thinking."

James's whisper in my ear brings me back to reality. Megs is looking out at the lake. Their conversation must have ended or stalled. I turn my head slightly closer to James. I sip on my coffee, which is a little cooler than when he handed it to me. A good indicator of how long I had been focused on my feeling.

"I'm thinking about the woods. What it would be like to be a hunter and have to chase my prey. To run after someone with the intent of claiming them for myself." I rest my head against his shoulder, not taking my eyes off the lake and trees beyond.

"Have you ever done that?"

"No. I've chased Rosie around the apartment and once around a hotel. It was fun, but this feels different."

He nods, seeming to let that sink in. I would love to chase him through the trees. Capturing him in a field of grass before claiming him. Sinking low on his dick. I would even be happy chasing Rosie or Megs with a strap-on, but they've never wanted to go by themselves. We haven't been here together, just the three of us, in a long time.

"How would you do it?"

"I would let the other person get a head start. Then chase after them until I caught them. This is actually the perfect place. With the fence all the way around it, we don't have to worry about being on someone else's land or having strangers in our space."

"What if...what if your partner couldn't get it up after running?"

"That wouldn't be an issue. We could find a way to get it up. For some, the chase or hunt drives the pleasure. But if that's not the case, and it's still consensual, we could work something out."

His hand moves to caress my shoulder. It makes me wonder what he is thinking. I'm not going to get my hopes up about him being interested. No one ever has been before.

"I don't think I could get hard right after running."

"I could help with that," Megs adds softly. We both look at them, surprised by their response. I didn't realize they were listening to us. "I could run behind you. Tie him up after you catch him. Then you and I could play until he's ready." I stay silent, processing what Megs has just said. They are willing to give me something I've wanted for a long time. Against my judgment, I let my hope bloom; maybe this is something I could have.

"I could do that," James nods.

"Really?" A huge grin spreads across my face, thrilled by what's happening.

"Yeah, when would you want to go?"

"Tonight? Just before sundown. Then we can still see, but it'll be dark when we're done."

James nods a few times. "I'm in." Megs smiles at me. "Me too." Now, I'm officially hyper. We work out a few more details. Knowing what awaits me, I struggle to find ways to fill the rest of the day.

JAMES

Addy has been extra flirty since I agreed to let her chase me this morning. I'm unsure if she is doing that to stay entertained or trying to get me as excited as she is. Even though we worked out several details, I'm still a bit nervous about the scene. Megs finds a map of the property, letting me get a feel for where we would be. The map gives me some comfort, evening knowing it would look different. There is something familiar about the map, but I push that aside. My mind is probably just confused between arousal and fear and nervousness. Addy tells Rosie about our plans as soon as she wakes up. Rosie wishes us luck but refuses to be part of it. She says she has no desire to "get fucked in the dirt."

The day passes slowly, anticipation building. I debate whether I have made a mistake agreeing to this, but I'm not backing out now. I wait on the deck as the sun begins its final descent. Within an hour, it'll be entirely dark. Bugs are flitting around; birds are chirping. Despite it being July, there is a soft breeze, and it's not terribly hot. The weather seems perfect for this kind of activity. The ground is still soft from the rain from the day before. All in all, it is a good time to do this.

"Ready?"

Megs and Addy walk outside. Both are in running shorts and loose tops. Megs has a crossbody bag over their shoulder. This has the rope and a first aid kit, just in case, along with water and flashlights. Addy reminds me of the fence and places to avoid. She steps close to me, wrapping her arms around me tightly. She whispers in my ear, "Thank you for doing this for me." I hug her back, not trusting my voice, though.

"What's your safe word?" Alpha mode activated.

"Cactus."

A smirk crosses her face. She steps back, but one hand stays on my arm, rubbing it soothingly. My nerves must be evident, but I won't let that stop me.

"Use it if you need it. I won't stop if you say 'no.' Fight back. Don't let me catch you. Push back."

I nod at her, not really sure what else. I say my safe word in my head a few more times. I don't think I will use it, but I don't want to forget it either. She kisses my cheek quickly, then steps back while messing with her smartwatch.

"You get a thirty second head start from the moment you hit the bottom of the stairs." She looks at me, her alpha voice deeper and louder, then gives her command.

"Run."

I make my way down the stairs quickly. Once my feet hit the ground, I run to the left. My heart is already pounding in my chest. I run towards the side of the lake, where the trees grow thicker. I plan to get far enough ahead to stop for a breather. I'm not a runner. Addy isn't either, but I don't know how her body will handle the adrenaline and arousal she's experiencing. I don't want to run out of steam before her.

I burst into the trees, running straight as possible, trying to distance myself from Addy. They insisted I bring sneakers with me. I don't know if Addy was trying to plan this. I'm guessing not since I suggested it. I am glad that I listened and brought my sneakers. I can't help but wonder what will happen when she catches me, but the adrenaline coursing through my body refuses to let me think about that part. The only constant thought in my brain is *Run.*

A faint beeping noise occurs in the direction I just left. My head start must be over. I glance back, wishing I was further away. I race through the trees. Every step crunches dry leaves or branches. Even with the head start, she'll likely be able to hear me moving. Now is a good time to pause and catch my breath. I find a tree large enough to cover me and duck behind it. I bend over, my chest heaving deep breaths as my body tries to recover from the sudden activity. I need to get back to the gym if this will be a regular thing.

Suddenly, a growl reverberates through the area I'm in. My adrenaline-ladled body jumps into action. I sprint at an angle from the direction I came in. My initial response was predator, which is obviously the point. It took a couple of seconds for me to realize that sound came from Addy. I shouldn't be surprised that she could sound like that, but the growl literally spurned me to action. That was unexpected.

"James!"

She sings my name out. She's closer than I anticipated. I dash in the other direction, my primal instincts kicking in, preventing me from running in a straight line. I feel a stitch forming in my side. I need to pause for a breather, but I'm positive she's close enough to catch me now. Maybe I can hide long enough then burst away from her when she gets close. I notice a thick patch of bushes ahead.

I dart towards them, planning to pause. Hopefully, this works, and she doesn't catch me. Or maybe she will, and I'll finally figure out what she has planned.

Addy

This is more invigorating than I have ever imagined. I can see James ahead. He's moving fast, but I'm faster. He starts to run in a zigzag. Good. His instincts are kicking in. His motions send a pulse of heat straight through my core. I didn't wear panties for the sake of access. Now my core is soaked, and I wonder if I should have. He dashes in the other direction. Another growl builds, and I release it from deep in my throat. I've toyed with growling in the past, but it's never felt so deep, so real, so primal as it does now.

I scan the area around us. I'm close enough to catch James with an extra push, but I want to see what he does. I slow my steps just a touch as he changes direction again. A thicket pops up in the direction he is heading. I know this area well from scavenging on previous trips. On the other side of the thicket is a large grassy field. The perfect place for claiming someone. My pussy clenches at the thought. My own fluids are dripping down my leg. I am so desperate and ready to capture him.

As expected, he dives into the bushes, trying to hide. I slow down, creeping quietly. I don't want him to know how close I am. I look back to see where Megs is. They are athletic, so they don't have any issue keeping up. They are a little way back, allowing us to experience the chase. I motion them a little closer so they are ready when I capture James. I stop, looking around the area. I give him the breather he must be after, but not a long one. I circle the bush, hoping I can draw him out.

"Oh, James. Did you really think you could run from me?"

My voice is deeper than usual. There is a hint of the growl under my words. I can hear James breathing deeply in the bush. I step closer, hoping he will run again.

"I know where you are. You can't escape."

I pause, listening for movement. He's surprisingly still. I step closer to the bush, only a few feet away now. I can see his hair behind some of the leaves. The heat in my core is undeniable. My pussy clenches as I growl again. He runs. In the exact direction I want him to.

I take three giant steps, then leap in the air. My body wraps around James, crashing into the ground on top of him.

"Fuck!" He shouts.

Once we hit the ground, he struggles to escape from under me. Because of the advantage when I jumped, I have him in a bear hug, and he can't move. He is struggling, tossing, cursing, and wiggling, trying to break free. I laugh in his ear.

"You're mine now."

I bite down on his neck, not enough to break the skin but enough to cause pain and leave a mark. He yells, bucking against me. His legs are still kicking as Megs comes up. I shift onto my side, dragging him sideways with me. I don't want him on top of me because he would have the advantage of being larger than me. I may be just a couple of inches shorter, but he's wider. I lick his neck, tasting the sweat from his run. My hips grind into his lower back. I'm unable to control the need I have. I want to climb him and fuck him, claim him as mine. Megs ties his hands above his head as I bite his ear, nibbling and kissing it to arouse him. He groans. Once Megs has his hands tied, I shift my position to sit on his stomach. I use my legs to brace his, making it easier for Megs to secure his feet. I lean down in a swift motion. I growl against his neck before claiming his lips in a frantic, desperate kiss.

He's trying to buck me off, but it isn't working. My hands are pressed against his arms, keeping them above his head. Megs now has both of his feet, tying them together. When they're done, I tell them to help me move him over to two trees. We shift him into position, securing the ropes from his hands and feet around the trees so he can't escape. He curses again, stretched out long, unable to escape.

"Pull his shorts down; I need to see his body," I growl as I lift his shirt over his head.

He's lying naked with his clothes wrapped around his hands and feet. Fuck, he's got a great body. My pussy is clenching hard. The adrenaline from the chase, seeing him naked, having him tied between the trees, I need to touch myself, or I'll explode. I quickly rip off my shirt and shorts, leaving me naked. The cool air blows against my skin. The sensation simultaneously cools and heats me. Goosebumps break out against my skin as I stalk towards Megs.

My lips crash into theirs. Their hands are on my body, but I need more. I slide my own hand around, slipping a finger inside my core. I am dripping wet. My finger feels excellent, but it's not what I want. I rip Megs's shirt over their head, leaving their bindings alone. We always leave it up to Megs if they want to remove those or not. I back them against the tree James's feet are tied to. I drop to my knees, feeling sticks and dirt digging into my skin. I pull Megs's shorts and underwear down. They clearly knew underwear would be a good idea. I toss their clothes over with mine. I glance at James to make sure he is watching. His chest is still heaving, but his cock is growing hard.

I hoist one of Megs's legs over my shoulder and dive into their core. My hands stay on their hips as I lick the length of their opening, sucking on the clit. They arch back in a moan, wrapping their hand around my head. I'm a little surprised by how aroused they are. Being asexual, they don't want sex often. I can't help but wonder what got them all worked up. I lick the length of their core again, feeling the wetness building. Their fingers tighten in my hair.

A noise draws my attention to James. He is staring at us, eyes dark with lust. His member is fully erect now, and his hips are bucking. That made the noise, his hips shifting against leaves under him. I pull back from Megs and look up at them. "Seems our prey is ready. Want to move to him, or should I finish you off first?" I leave the decision up to them.

JAMES

Addy's voice has been stuck in alpha mode since she told me to run. Her words stirred something profound in my chest, increasing my arousal. I look to Megs, waiting for a response. I can't wait for Addy to get them off. I need contact now. I knew I was the prey, but I didn't realize torture was on the table. Watching them is fascinating. One of the first things I notice is that Addy doesn't touch Megs the way I would expect. She avoids certain body parts, touching them in more neutral zones. Addy avoided their breasts but gripped their hips tightly. She used more rough touches instead of gentle kisses. Addy is handling Megs the way I would want to be touched. This realization stirs both adoration and desire. I need them to touch me that way too.

"Please, Megs, please come to me," I beg, my voice deep and laced with desire. Megs shifts, whispering to Addy. The words are soft enough that I can't hear them. An ache deepens in my belly at the thought of what they said. A wicked grin grows wildly on Addy's face. She turns to me, lowering Megs's leg. My first thought is, *Thank god, they're coming for me.* Then that grin sinks in, and my second thought is *Oh god, they're coming for me.*

Megs walks over to my head, moving their legs to stand over me. I get a full view of their sex but am distracted by Addy. At the same time, she crawls over and straddles my hips. She holds her hands out to Megs. They take her hands, lowering down over my face, sliding their legs between my outstretched arms. "Lick," Addy commands. She didn't need to tell me. Without hesitation, I begin licking Megs's core. They shift on me, though I can't see what they are doing. I'm savoring the taste of Megs. The feel of their lips on my face, their thighs against my head. My hands yank against the ropes, wishing I could touch them too. I desperately want to feel their skin but settle for tonguing their soaking sex.

Addy shifts on me again. Her hands are on Megs's body, touching them as I want. At least someone is. I suck their clit into my mouth. A muffled moan sounds. They must be kissing Addy. I feel Addy's hand on my cock, pressing it against her ass as she slides up and down. I groan against Megs's core, needing more friction. I buck my hips, feeling grass and dirt clinging to my bare ass as I lift off the ground. Addy moves suddenly. Cool air circles my cock, leaving me with a sense of longing. I moan again, slipping my tongue inside Megs.

Addy moves off me but is back quickly. I can't see anything with Megs on top of me. Addy's warm mouth slides around my cock, swallowing me whole. It takes all my control not to thrust. I try to focus on not humping her face but working Megs over. My tongue stretches to flick against their clit, but they are too far away.

"Sit on my fucking face."

My words are more of a growl than I intended. I am desperate to have them closer, to taste them, to lick them thoroughly. They keep lifting away, and I can't use my hands to pull them back in. Their up and down movements drive me as insane as the chase and capture they just participated in. Addy stops working her mouth against my cock. It feels like she is looking up at Megs. I groan again at this unwanted movement. I just want to thrust inside something with my tongue and my cock. This whole primal thing is really driving me insane. The need to come is more potent than I have ever felt.

With Megs properly sitting against my face, I lick them thoroughly, inserting my tongue as deeply as possible. Pulling their clit into my mouth, I suck viciously, hoping to drive them over the edge. A condom is rolled over my aching dick. My eyes roll back in my head at the touch. Addy sinks her pussy over my dick. It's such a relief and powerful sensation that I open my mouth and cry against Megs's throbbing core. Addy starts bouncing on me. I silently thank every known god and return to my ministrations against Megs's sex. I can feel them clenching over my tongue as I dive as deep as I can into their wet core. Addy rides up and down, swirling her hips against me. I'm already on edge; I know I won't last long. I feel someone's hand against my skin, rubbing Addy's clit. I don't know whose hand it is, but it's not mine. My hands are still struggling against the ropes, wanting to be free, to touch my partners, to explore their bodies.

"Come with me."

Addy's voice is deep and muffled, as if she's kissing Megs. I don't know who she is talking to, but I don't need to be told twice. My balls squeeze tight as my orgasm crashes through. I suck Megs's clit into my mouth harder than I intended, but it seems to drive them over the edge too. My face is soaked with fluids. I release their clit and begin lapping my tongue against their core. The thought crosses my mind that I couldn't use my safe word easily in this position, but it doesn't matter. I was never going to use it anyway.

My hips buck a few more times before settling as my body comes back down from the intense orgasm. Megs lifts off me and shifts away quicker than I would like. But I am left with a view of Addy mid-orgasm. She's so gorgeous. She looks powerful and strong and in her element. The darkening sky casts ethereal shadows across her body. She shivers with the final throws of her orgasm. She crashes down into my chest. Megs releases my hands, and I instantly wrap around Addy's body. My hands stroke her back, keeping her close to me. She is taking deep, heavy breaths, coming back to earth herself. I let the weight of her on top of me soothe me.

Megs moves back to my side after releasing my legs, already dressed. I smile up at them, still rubbing Addy's shoulder. They meet my eyes but glance away quickly. Remembering I have free hands, I reach out and take their hand. I pull it to my mouth, pressing a small kiss to the back of their hand. Addy shifts to the other side of my chest to see Megs too.

"Will you kiss me?" I ask gently, looking at Megs. Addy turns her head, looking up at me. Megs nods, then leans in. Their lips are soft against mine. I open my lips to deepen the kiss, but they pull back. They seem uncomfortable now, so I don't push the issue. I won't release their hand, though. I don't want them to pull away from me yet. I want to stay connected. Addy's breathing is back to normal. We stay like this for another minute before Megs speaks up.

"We should get back. It's almost dark."

Addy rises, grabbing her clothes to dress. I pull my shirt back down, then wipe my ass before pulling my pants up. The three of us walk back to the house, staying close to each other. We don't say much, but I feel content in their presence. Thankfully, Megs knows the way back. I would be lost without them. I was running purely on adrenaline and not taking in my surroundings enough to find my way back. Once at the cabin, Megs claims the first shower. Addy and I wait in the kitchen. Between drinks of water, she kisses me, keeping constant contact with my body. Rosie walks in, asking how our excursion was. Addy and I respond at the same time.

"Amazing."

We burst out laughing. Addy finally steps away from me to refill her drink. Rosie steps up, looking over my exposed skin for any cuts that need care.

"What the fuck?"

She runs her fingers over my neck. The spot hurts, and I flinch. I reach up to touch it, but she swats my hand away. "Addy, are you a vampire or something? That's not going away anytime soon." I look between the two with confusion. Addy turns to look at my neck.

"Oh shit, that does look worse than I thought." She chuckles, walking over to get a better look.

I twist away from the two, walking to a small mirror meant to be decorative but still functional. On the side of my neck is a complete outline of Addy's teeth. It would make any dentist proud. It's on the side of my neck, evident with the collar of my t-shirt.

"Fuck, Addy. He's supposed to go have lunch with my parents tomorrow."

Rosie's claim reminds me of that situation. There is no way a t-shirt will cover this up. Addy cringes, shrugging her shoulders. She apologizes weakly, but we all know she wouldn't change anything. I step over to Rosie, taking her hands.

"It's okay. I can wear a button-up with a collar. That will hide most of it."

I look back in the mirror, touching the marks on my neck. Addy really did a thorough job of claiming me as hers. There is no doubt what that mark is. Maybe Rosie's parents will think it was her's. I don't know if that is any better. Rosie steps to my side, sighing as she looks in the mirror at the mark. She looks dejected. I turn, wrapping my arms around her shoulders, hugging her close. I just want her to not have that look on her face anymore.

"You wanna check my ass for cuts?" I smile at her.

"Addy bit your ass too??"

"No, but I was on the ground."

"Oh," she responds. She's not grasping my suggestions the way I had hoped. She offers to look for me, though. Thankfully, there are no open wounds on my ass, just a few places that will probably bruise. After my shower, I spend the rest of the evening trying to cheer Rosie up. My attention is split between her and Megs. I don't want Megs to think I am avoiding them. Addy is on cloud nine. She zones in and out of a dreamy space with a big goofy grin. Tonight definitely meant more to her than anyone else. I'm glad I was able to give her that experience. Whenever she zones out of the conversation, my chest swells with emotion. I cling tight to Rosie, touching Megs as often as I can. Since they don't stop or respond negatively, I keep physical contact with them as often as possible. When we head to bed, I kick Addy out of Rosie's room and stay with her. I want to soak up as much of her pleasure tonight before we go to lunch with her family tomorrow. I'm nervous about meeting her father, but supporting Rosie is more important than my nerves. Tonight, I'll provide a distraction for her. Tomorrow will be for support.

Chapter Eighteen

As I sit in the ice cream parlor, the dog server brings me a scoop of rainbow-colored ice cream in a bowl shaped like a bear. I lift my chopsticks, ready to dive in, when a delicious sensation sweeps across my pussy. I moan, twisting to get more of that delightful touch. The dog waiter walks over as the warmth spreads through my whole body. "Excuse me, are you okay?" The dog's head tilts sideways in confusion.

"Yes!"

Light suddenly fills my eyes. I'm back in the master bedroom at my parent's cabin. I was dreaming when James started licking me. I groan again, letting the sensation take over my body. He licks expertly, straight through my core, flicking against my clit, then sucking it into his mouth. I enjoyed my time alone yesterday but was glad when they returned. I could have done without Addy marking James so much. We have to see my parents today, and I don't want to answer questions about how he got those marks.

Pleasure fills my body, pushing me closer to the edge. I moan out his name, lacing my fingers through his hair. I push him closer to my core, increasing the pressure. It's just what I need to push me over the edge. My body spasms then calms with the orgasm. In the two months he has been with us, he's learned everything that makes me tick. I love the way he can handle me better than I can myself.

As I settle down, he crawls up, pulling me into his arms. "Good morning," he whispers, pressing his lips to mine in a gentle kiss. I stroke my hands on his sides, snuggling against his chest. "Just another hour or so?" I beg, not wanting to wake up this early.

"I'm down for that, but you said you needed to wake up now to have time to get ready to meet your parents. Think we should just ghost?" He wiggles his eyebrows at me, and I laugh against his chest. I would love to ghost my parents, but I like using the cabin more than I dislike going to lunch with them. With a disappointed groan, I get up to get ready.

"What were you dreaming about?"

"Huh? Oh, I was in an ice cream parlor. Why?"

"Hmm, you were barking."

I burst out laughing as my cheeks burn with embarrassment. I had no idea I talk in my sleep, let alone bark. "Oh god. The server was a dog. I guess I was speaking to him." James laughs with me, shaking his head at the craziness. I blame Addy. She is always coming up with peculiar things like that.

After my shower and getting dressed, I walk out to the kitchen where everyone else is. James is wearing dark jeans that aren't ripped anywhere, along with a collared shirt. The buttons are undone, and the marks Addy left on him are mostly visible. He notices me looking at them.

"I'll button it before we get there."

I nod. Megs has travel mugs of coffee ready. Thank god, because I don't have time to sit and enjoy it. James and I get in my Jeep and head out. Nerves are trickling through my body. James has met my mother before. He isn't fond of her, but he was nice enough when he made dinner for her. He didn't hold back his feelings after my birthday, though. My dad is more stoic. He typically doesn't speak much, but I don't know what he'll be like with James. I've never brought another man home. Not that I'm really bringing James home. That's not what this is. Though, that is what my parents think this is. Oh, I hope this goes well. James seems to pick up on my nerves. He reaches over and takes my hand, gently stroking me. It helps me relax a bit.

As we leave the dirt paths of the forest, my phone rings. It's my mother. This isn't a good sign.

"Hello?" I say, after sending the phone through Bluetooth in my car.

"Oh, hi, baby! Have you left yet?"

"Yes, we're on our way. Should be there in about an hour."

"Perfect. I'm so happy to see you, but your father won't be there. He got called in for something with work. You know how those things are for him. He sends his love, though. Is James still coming?"

Maybe being away from her has made me more sensitive, but she does not stop talking.

"Yes, James is coming. That's fine about Daddy. We'll see you in a bit. Love you."

I disconnect the phone before she says anything else. I don't know what will come out of her mouth anymore. Driving and talking on the phone isn't something I like to do. I prefer to focus on traffic. Or sing. Or just not talk to my mother. Any of those are great options while driving. James doesn't say anything, just stroking my hand. Maybe he is nervous too. I hope his feelings from after my birthday don't cause a problem today.

We arrive at my mother's house. She insists we have lunch there. She wants to cook for James. The plan had been for my father to grill. My mom is pretty good on the grill too. This isn't the first time he's left last minute like that. He doesn't tell us much about what he does. He really focuses on keeping his work life and home life separate. I used to think he had a second family. Honestly, I just can't see my father being willing to entertain more people. He barely tolerates us.

My mom hugs both of us and begins talking about everything and anything that pops into her mind. Her filter is broken. Megs made a dessert for us to bring. Mom didn't ask us to bring anything, but Megs makes delicious food. I won't turn down the chance to eat some of their baking. James forgot to button the collar before walking in. My eyes go wide, and I cough to get his attention. My hands trace around my throat, hoping he'll get the hint. He does, but my mom turns to us to see why I'm coughing.

"Can I get some water?"

My voice sounds scratchy, like I actually need water. Mom turns to get a cup for me. James quickly buttons his shirt, covering the marks on his neck, just in time. My mom hands me the cup, and I take a large gulp. She finally tells us to head into the dining room to eat. We sit down, putting food on our plates. Mom did all the grilling and cooking. There is far too much food for four people to eat. I'm sure she'll be sending us back with plates. We chat idly for a little bit. It's surprisingly pleasant. Mom hasn't said anything terrible, not any more than expected. James is being friendly. My body starts to relax just a little.

"James, how old are you now?"

Oh crap. Here we go.

"Uh, 28."

He sounds unsure of his answer. I am, too, now. Is he unsure of his age or this line of questioning? That's the real concern.

"I see. So when do you plan to settle down and get married?"

There it is. There's that unpleasantness I was expecting. Of course, it comes when I start to relax.

"Well, since I'm not officially divorced yet, I don't see getting married again anytime soon, if ever."

Shit. That's his truth, but a simple 'I don't know' would've been better.

"Divorced?!?" She's practically screeching. "Rosie! You are dating a married man? You ruined a marriage? How could you? I raised you better than that! You need to find this woman and apologize! How dare you!"

"No, Marge! Wait. Rosie is innocent here. I met her after I filed for divorce. My ex-wife is the one that ruined my marriage."

My mother is stunned into silence. I've never seen her at a loss for words. James and I continue eating as my mother processes what James said. My father never speaks back or corrects my mother when her opinions spew like this. I rarely do. I prefer to just let her say her piece and move on. I'm glad James corrected her, but I'm also worried about what will come out of her mouth next. Her body settles, relaxing back into her chair.

"Fair enough. When will your divorce be finalized? Will you marry Rosie after that? She needs a good man to take care of her."

"Mom!"

"I don't know when the divorce will be finalized. Currently, I have no plans to marry Rosie. She's expressed that isn't something she wants."

"Nonsense. Of course that's what she wants. She just doesn't know it yet."

I roll my eyes. I've been through this with her before. She is insistent that I get married. It must be important to her now if she's even lowering her standards to consider a not-yet-divorced man. James takes a deep breath, readying himself to say more. I reach out and take his hand, squeezing it tightly. He looks at me, releasing his breath. I shake my head slowly, encouraging him to keep his mouth shut. He squeezes my hand tightly and goes back to eating. Apparently, Mom was watching all of this and just has to comment.

"See? You two already have that married couple communication down. You're perfect. You should have a fall wedding. That would be beautiful. Rosie looks splendid in fall colors. Not so much the bright colors of spring or summer."

I wore a bright pink dress today. It's one of my favorites. That dig hurts more than I want to admit. James stands up, and his chair hits the ground with a loud bang. Mom looks startled, clutching her chest as if grabbing for pearls.

"Marge, get it through your thick skull that I will not be marrying Rosie. Any person that is worth a damn would not try to marry her either. She is a grown-ass woman and has decided she does not want to get married. You need to shut your fat mouth and let her live her own life."

He grabs my hand, pulling me up from the table. My brain can't process everything he just said. I'm in complete shock.

"And you're wrong about Rosie's colors. She looks beautiful in everything she wears. But she's the most stunning when she's naked and has Addy's mouth on her pussy."

I squeak at his words. My mother literally screams. James drags me towards the door. My mind and body aren't working at all. I can't walk correctly and bump into everything. He stops in the kitchen, grabbing my purse and keys. Then he steps back and takes the dessert Megs made. He shoves me out of the house and slams the door behind me. The loud noise jerks me back to reality. I walk towards the Jeep, but he guides me towards the passenger side. He helps me in, then shuts the door. I buckle as he climbs in the driver's side. He doesn't adjust the seat or mirrors as he starts the engine. As he turns the car around, I see my mother walk out the front door. I know she is screaming, but I can't make out any words. He floors the gas, speeding out of the driveway.

He turns the wrong way but doesn't seem to realize it. He is angry and tense, breathing heavily. His eyes are focused on the road. I'm still stunned. At this point, the entire conversation is turning to mush, despite just having heard it. I've never had anyone stand up to my mother like that. He finally glances over at me.

"I don't actually know where I'm going," he speaks softly. There is a tenderness to his voice that settles my nerves. My phone begins ringing. He pulls out his so I can plug in the directions. I get that set up quickly and answer my phone, raising it to my ear.

"Hi, Daddy."

My father is raging mad. I'm not used to hearing him so angry. I try to explain what happened, but he is just yelling about how upset my mother is. He insists we must turn around, apologize, and make things right with her. I tell him we just need space to cool down. Then he starts yelling about marriage and divorces and all kinds of stuff. I just sit and listen. My body is beginning to ache. The tension of the situation is wearing off. All my emotions are crashing down. My shoulders hurt. My stomach is rolling. Tears are building behind my eyes. I swipe at them, saying, "Yes, Daddy," as he continues.

My father finally stops yelling, telling me to take a breather and call them tomorrow. I agree and hang up the phone. James slides his hand over my thigh. I place my phone into the console. The emotions I had been holding in burst through. I begin sobbing into my hands. I don't understand why this happened. If my mother and James had kept their mouths shut, we could have had a civil lunch and left it at that.

James pulls the Jeep onto the side of the road. He moves quickly out of the car and to my side, pulling the door open. He wraps his arms around me, pulling me close. But I don't want his comfort. I want this to have never happened. I want this to be over with. I want different parents. I want a relationship that doesn't need to be explained to everyone. I just want to be alone. I shove him off me, climbing out of the car for fresh air. He looks stunned that I pushed him away.

"Rosie..."

"No, James," I start, but I don't know how much I want to say. From a healthy aspect, it would be best to calm down and wait for this conversation. However, we're an hour and a half from the cabin with only one car. We aren't getting space apart to process our feelings. That realization drives my anger higher.

"If you would have just kept your mouth shut, none of this would have happened. I know my mother can be terrible, but she's still my mother. She loves me and only wants what she thinks is good for me. She doesn't have bad intentions." I pause, taking a breath. "And how fucking dare you say that shit about Addy and me. What the fuck was that?"

He takes a step towards me, but I back away. We're on a road between neighborhoods, but there aren't many other cars out.

"I couldn't sit there and listen to her spew those things about you, Rosie. Her beliefs are ass-backward. I don't care who she is; I'm not going to let anyone talk about you that way."

"There was no need for you to talk to her that way, though."

The tears stream down my face, and I don't try to stop them. I wrap my arms around myself. James steps towards me, but I turn away from him. I don't want him to touch me now. I didn't think this meal would go perfectly, but I never expected it to go like that. I just want to get back to the cabin. I can just drink my emotions away and deal with the rest tomorrow. A car blows past us, kicking up some dirt.

"Please," a soft sob escapes before I can stop it. "Please just drive back to the cabin."

He sighs, clearly defeated. He moves around to the driver's side. I climb in, staring out the window. My parents have always been a sore spot for me. Addy and Megs learned a long time ago to not push the issue. Some would probably tell me to cut ties with them. Some might try to correct their behavior. My parents are obviously of the mindset that children just respect their elders. Respect means to be quiet and accept what they dish out. I don't have any other relatives. All my grandparents died when I was young. Somehow both of my parents were only children. There are no cousins. There are no big family get-togethers. No one to turn to when things get bad or weird or crazy. It's just the three of us. As hard as it can be to accept their beliefs, I can't turn my back on them either. They've always taken care of me when I needed help. I need therapy to recover from dinner with them, but I still have them.

JAMES

This isn't how these things are supposed to go. Parents love me. I can get along with them well. Even Whitney's parents love me. They may have changed their mind lately. I glance over to Rosie in the passenger seat. She fell asleep shortly after we got back in the car. Her relationship with her parents astounds me. There must be a good reason she continues to see them. I couldn't hear what her father said to her earlier, but it couldn't have been much better than what her mother said.

Thinking back over the conversation, I realize I went too far. I do need to apologize for my last comment about Addy's mouth. That was excessive. True, but excessive. These feelings for Rosie are something I've never dealt with before. I've never been so protective. There hasn't been anything worthy of protecting. No, that's not right. Because Addy and Megs are also worthy of protection. Addy and Megs are strong physically. Rosie is strong too, but she looks like she wouldn't be. I know she is. My brain doesn't want to believe it. My heart tries to stand up for Rosie when she doesn't do it for herself. She likes to placate others, not stand up for herself. My heart won't stand for that. That may be her way of responding, but I simply cannot do that.

I've not always been a stand-up and fight guy. For so long, I let Whitney step on me. She said hurtful things. Not quite as bad as the trash Marge can spew, though. That woman's comments would make the devil cringe. I placated Whitney for years, and it got me nowhere. I was left on the streets, literally, until Addy took me in. I know the situation isn't the same for Rosie, but it strikes a very raw, very painful spot in my chest to see it happening to Rosie. She deserves better; she can have better. She's shown me that. I won't let her settle for less when she has shown and given me so much more.

Once we reach the cabin, I'm more confused than when we drove off from the side of the road. Nothing makes sense. Everything feels wrong. I need to speak to Rosie before we go inside. Addy and Megs will have questions. I don't want to go in on bad terms with Rosie. I park the car and walk around to the passenger side. I need to face her. I need to touch her. This conversation can't happen sitting side by side. There needs to be contact. I open the door slowly. She still jerks awake at the movement. She unbuckles her seat belt. I step up, blocking her in. Maybe not the best start, but I need her to hear me.

"Rosie."

She rubs her eyes then takes in where we are. She doesn't say anything but waits for me to say more. She is so patient and soft. There is an ache in my heart that anyone would ever treat her the way her parents do.

"I'm so sorry for the comment about Addy. That was too far. Even though it's true, I know I shouldn't have said that to your mom. I understand why you are angry at me. I can't apologize for the outburst, though. I'm not the kind of person that can sit by and listen to someone speak the way your mother did. Rosie," I place my hands on her thighs, looking down. I can't meet her gaze right now. Tears creep behind my eyes, threatening to spill free. They are angry, hurt tears. I take a deep breath, calming myself so I don't cry. "I can't be the person that sits by while they treat you that way. I did that with Whitney and literally slept in an alley for it. You mean too much to me. You deserve better. I won't accept you being in that same position."

She sighs, placing her hands on top of mine. "Thank you for the apology." She takes a deep breath, meeting my eyes. There is something hard in them. The pain and heartache are apparent, but there is more too. "I can't forgive you yet."

A breath whooshes out of me. I feel like I've been punched in the gut. The tears break free, streaming down my face. Rosie reaches up to wipe them away, pressing a soft kiss to each of my cheeks. I suck in a breath, trying to gain some composure. She said yet, not never. My eyes close. I should step away from her, but I can't. I don't want her to leave me. I don't want to be away from her until she forgives me. I need to make this right.

"Just give me time."

She pushes my chest, pushing me away from her. I step back, feeling empty. A slight wind could scoop me up and deliver me across the lake with how hollow I feel. I watch her walk inside. This need to protect is strong. She can take care of herself, but I want to do that for her. She means the world to me, even though I've only been with her for a couple of months.

Addy

"Shit, I guess lunch didn't go well."

Megs and I hear them coming down the driveway earlier than expected. We haven't heard anything from them, but surprisingly, they are back soon. Normally, Rosie's parents keep her forever. Lunch turns into chatting that turns into planning a wedding or something ridiculous that completely disregards Rosie's decisions for herself. It's a huge reason I don't meet with her parents anymore. Aside from them not liking me, I don't hold my tongue around them. I've known them most of my life and have learned how to manage to be around them. James doesn't have that. He's met Marge before, and from my understanding, that went fine.

James stops Rosie from leaving the car. We can't hear what he is saying. From their body language, this isn't good. She isn't trying to beat or force him away, but it doesn't look romantic or friendly. Rosie pushes James out of the way and walks towards the house. He turns away from us so we can't see his face, but his hands wiping his cheeks is undeniable. He's upset. The look on Rosie's face is hurt and angry. I glance at Megs, taking in the situation.

"You want to deal with James or Rosie?'

"James, I think."

Before I have time to say anything else, Rosie opens the door. She hands a bag to Megs. "We didn't make it to dessert. So we brought this back." Megs takes the bag from her, and Rosie bursts into tears. Fuck, this is worse than I thought. I rush over to her, wrapping my arms around her body. Her hands are still by her face as I pull her into my chest.

"Rosie, baby. I'm here for you."

Megs walks outside, heading towards James, who is still standing with his back to us, but his hands are in his pocket. We haven't dealt with any fighting between us as a group. Rosie and James had a tiff a while back over her parents if I remember correctly. But they worked that out between themselves before Megs or I made it home. This is different. This feels more like a fight. Megs and I have taken each of them to offer comfort. I hope they don't mistake this for preferences. That isn't our intention.

Rosie's shoulders shake in my arms. I tighten my arms around her, trying to squeeze the pain out. I whisper gentle words in her ears. Rosie is our comforter. This doesn't come naturally to Megs or me. We're trying, though. I coax her to take steps and move her up to the bedroom. The weather is nice for July, but it's still hot as hell out there. Megs and James can come in without running into Rosie, giving them more space to process what is happening.

Once in the bedroom, Rosie has finally calmed down enough to talk. Sitting beside her on the bed, I still have my arm around her. I ask her what happened. She begins to chuckle, and I'm immediately confused. I don't know how to process the sudden shift in her mood. She starts talking before I completely freak out.

"Mom made this comment about me not looking good in bright colors." She waves her hand at the dress she's wearing. Anger rises because that is one of my favorite dresses she wears. "James got really pissed off, and do you know what he said? Oh, you'll love this." She sniffles before carrying on, building the suspense and driving me crazy.

"Addy, he said I'm always beautiful, but I look best naked with your mouth on my pussy." She turns a delicate shade of red. I burst out laughing. It's a loud, enthusiastic laugh. I bend over, grabbing my stomach, trying to catch my breath. My eyes start watering as I try to regain some composure. Rosie is swiping her eyes, still crying but laughing also. Our eyes meet, and we both collapse into a fit of giggles again. This has to be the funniest thing anyone has ever said to Marge. I struggle to catch my breath because I need to know her reaction, but it's too funny, and I continue laughing.

Finally, the laughter calms down enough, and Rosie tells me her reaction. I'm still cracking up over the comment but have calmed down enough to talk. Taking several deep breaths and wiping the tears from my eyes, I take Rosie's hand.

"While that is the best thing I have heard, probably ever, that doesn't explain why you are back so early or why you came in separately from James after he tried to box you in."

She takes a deep breath, acknowledging my statement with a nod. She starts on the drive over and explains the entire afternoon. When she finishes, I am beyond livid at Marge. That woman should not be allowed around people. She is literally the worst. I understand why Rosie is mad at James, but I also see his side. Rosie doesn't deserve to be treated the way her parents do. Megs and I tried to explain that to her when we were younger but have quit trying. We tolerate her parents when we must and commiserate together when we have to deal with them. We've stopped asking Rosie to avoid them, though. She's still impressive, despite her parents' horrible personalities. James hasn't learned any of that yet.

"Rosie, you know how hard it is for Megs and me to be around your parents. We've had a long time to come to terms with it. I don't think James meant any harm. I know you're angry with him, but you have to admit, Marge deserved it."

"Yeah, but it's not about what she deserved. We're adults too. We shouldn't need to turn to mean words to have an impact."

I nod, considering her point. She isn't mad that James is hurt but mad at how he reacted. Is he aware of that? I sigh, not really sure what else to do.

"Wanna get really drunk?"

"Yes, please."

"Can you be around James?"

"Not yet?" She's bashful with her comment. She doesn't want to upset anyone but also doesn't want to be in an awkward position. That's not a problem for me. "I'll make drinks for everyone, then bring yours back here. Why don't you go wash your face and start a movie?" She moves towards the bathroom as I head into the kitchen. There isn't much else I can do for Rosie besides getting her drunk enough she forgets about lunch.

Megs

After Rosie hands the dessert to me, I place it on the table then go outside to James. He is leaning against the Jeep, hands in his pockets, looking down at the ground. He is lost in thought. His cheeks are red from the emotions earlier. He's been around for two months. It seems odd that I have seen him in a very emotional state several times. I'm no dating expert, but I didn't think that was supposed to happen that fast. The fact that he is comfortable showing his emotions is a good thing in my mind. I step up next to him, shoving my hands in my pockets.

"Hi"

That is a weak start. I know it is. But saying, "I noticed you were crying, need some tissue," feels worse. James barely looks up at me. Should I hug him? Addy hugged Rosie, but Rosie sobbed and ran into her arms. I made a mistake coming out here to comfort James. What was I thinking? I don't know how to comfort people. I wouldn't be better with Rosie anyways. Hopefully, I don't make this situation worse.

"So, it didn't go well?"

Still not a good start. Obviously, it didn't go well.

"No. No, it did not."

"Wanna talk about it?"

He runs his hand through his shaggy hair. He hasn't cut it since he's been with us, and it's wild and wavy and gorgeous. He doesn't respond right away. I wait, giving him time to consider his thoughts.

"Is she always like that? Marge?"

His eyes meet mine. Marge clearly had something to do with their early return. I'm not religious, but I have no doubts Marge is the devil incarnate. She's sly and judgmental, just all-around terrible. I nod my head. She is always the same. Never any different. At least she's consistent.

"And Rosie just lets her say those things? Do you stop her? Either of them? Does Addy?"

I take a deep breath, thinking through my answer. I step closer, placing my hand on his arm. His strong, thick arm.

"Rosie is an only child to two terrible people who also have no siblings. She never had cousins or aunts or anyone else. Rosie has this skewed sense of loyalty to her parents because of their lack of family. Addy and I have tried many times to convince her to cut off her parents. She never listens to us, though. She feels too strongly about them for us to get through. We learned a long time ago it isn't worth the battle. Her parents don't come around often and usually don't want us there anyway. We deal with the fallout, then move on." I pause, meeting his gaze to confirm my suspicion. "You said something to Marge and upset both of them at the same time?"

He nods to me.

"Give Rosie some time. Being around her parents always leaves her raw. I'm sure she'll come back around soon." He places his hand over mine, squeezing. "Thanks for explaining that. I didn't know all of that."

I pull his hand with mine, leading him back inside. While I enjoy chatting with him, it's hot as the dickens out here, and the bugs are wild. As we step into the house, I hear Addy roar with laughter. My face squishes, confused about that noise. My body freezes, unsure what to do next. Why are they already laughing like that?

"Oh, I guess Rosie told her about my comment."

I look back at him. The confusion is still written on my face, and I wait for him to explain all this nonsense.

"Marge said Rosie didn't look good in bright colors. I told her Rosie looks good in everything but looks her best when she's naked, and Addy's mouth is on her pussy."

I spit out laughter. I cover my mouth, cursing at my outburst. "What did Marge do?"

"I'm pretty sure she keeled over. I drug Rosie out of the house before anything else could be said."

My hands cover my face, laughing over his comment. I can only imagine Marge hearing about her precious daughter getting face fucked by Addy. I wish I had been there to see it. Or have it on camera. That would be better because then we can rewatch it.

"Please film the next time you blast Rosie's sexual escapades to Marge. Damn, I'm sad I missed it."

We both laugh about the situation. James seems tired but not quite as upset as before. Maybe I'm not terrible at comforting. He doesn't seem any worse, so that's a plus. Addy walks into the kitchen and moves to the liquor.

"I know it's only like 3 pm, but we're getting shit-faced. What about you two?"

"Fuck yes."

He said that really fast. Okay, maybe I'm not the best comforter out there, but he's not crying or lashing out. A little alcohol won't hurt. Addy starts making drinks. Bartending really suits her. She knows what liquors to mix with other liquids to make it delicious. She also adds in the perfect amount of liquor. Mine are always wrong. Too much or too little. Never just the right amount. As she's mixing, she begins to chat with James. I prop against the wall, mentally taking notes of what she says. I'll learn something about this comforting business.

"What possessed you to tell Marge Rosie looks best with me in her pussy?"

Ok, not putting that on my mental list of comfort. I cringe as James laughs.

"I don't know. She just... I can't fathom why Marge doesn't see how stunning Rosie is and constantly needs to put her down. I wasn't even thinking when I said that. It just came out of my mouth."

Marge really does have this strange ability to trigger everyone but Rosie. Maybe Rosie is immune because she grew up with her, but even Addy, having known her most of her life, still gives in to Marge's taunts frequently. She finally hands us a couple of drinks.

"Marge is the fucking worst." She glances back towards the bedrooms to make sure Rosie doesn't hear. "Rosie isn't quite ready to be around you yet. We're gonna curl up and watch a movie for a bit. I've got extra drinks made for you. We'll catch up around dinner. Yeah?"

Addy's drinks are strong but delicious. I grab the pitcher she left and lead James into the basement. I let him pick a movie, insisting it is his choice. I sit on the couch but slide closer to him once he sits. He could use some physical comfort too, and it isn't entirely comfortable for me to cuddle. He does like to cuddle, though, so I hope it helps.

JAMES

Watching the movie with Megs is nice. They let me pick, so I chose Die Hard again. It's a classic; what can I say? They snuggle into my side. They aren't as confident as Addy or snuggly as Rosie, but it's still nice being close. We keep drinking as the movie plays. All I can think about is how I messed up with Rosie. I should be in there making things up to her.

The time passes, only making the distance hurt more. The pain that would come with actually leaving them seems unbearable. I thought leaving Whitney would hurt. There was pain when I left her, but now, living through Rosie not wanting to be around me has made me realize the pain was never due to Whitney. The problems were about lodging and work and travel and just the unknown. I wasn't hurting because Whitney wasn't there. If it hurts this much to be away from Rosie for a few hours, I won't survive being away from all three of them for good. We don't have any long-term goals for our relationship. It's something we should discuss. Being blindsided by the end of this would definitely be the worst thing in my life.

The movie ends, and we move into the kitchen. Addy comes out and offers to cook with Megs. They get started. At first, they tried to keep me involved, but I drank more than I realized. Those drinks were really strong, and I had several. They tell me to go lay down for a little bit. Moving towards the bedrooms, it doesn't even occur to me that I should go to the bunk bedroom. Rosie is lying on the bed with her back to the door. A smile stretches across my face. All memory of the lunch debacle is hidden under the alcohol.

"Hey, baby."

The door frame supports most of my weight. I can't see straight. I'm pretty sure I'm smiling, but my brain is really foggy.

"What are you...are you drunk, James?"

"Sloshed."

My hand raises as if to toast, but I realize there isn't anything in my hand.

"I think I should lay down."

She sighs but slides over. She pats the bed beside her. I collapse in that spot. She adjusts to my position. I don't move any further than the position I landed in. She grabs my pants leg, pulling my dangling leg up onto the mattress.

"Why are you so drunk right now?"

The filter in my brain is entirely dysfunctional. There is no way I could not tell her the truth. No secret is safe at this point.

"Because you're mad at me. And I hurt you. And you don't want me anymore."

My words are slurred but still understandable. Rosie slides down next to me, wrapping her body around my own. I hold her tight, afraid to let go. My eyes close to keep the room from spinning, but my body takes over that feature. I overdid it with the drinks. Definitely had too many.

"I am mad at you, and you did hurt me. But I do still want you here. You're special, and you belong with us."

Her hands on my back are soothing me into a restful place. Her words comfort me more than I expected. I was less concerned about having hurt her than about having ruined everything. It's easy to be convinced I have ruined everything when I am still in the middle of a divorce. I can feel my body drifting off to sleep, but before I do, my brain insists on throwing some words out into the universe. What good would being totally drunk be if I didn't say something truly embarrassing?

"I'm falling in love with you."

Chapter Nineteen

Rosie comes out for dinner but says James is out on the master. I knew he drank a lot, but I didn't realize how much. Looking back, I had one drink from the pitcher, and he drank the rest. I was just trying to give him space. Rosie isn't passed out drunk. She doesn't even have a buzz at this point. I'm not good at this comforting thing. We sit in the kitchen, eating our food. We are unusually quiet. The day has taken a turn for the worse. This isn't how our vacation was supposed to go.

"Wanna go swimming after dinner?"

Addy's suggestion breaks the silence. I would like to go. Rosie agrees. After eating and cleaning up, we all head down to the lake. I check on James. He is passed out on the bed. I carry a bottle of water and leave some ibuprofen on the nightstand. Hopefully, that will help with the hangover he will undoubtedly have. At the lake, Rosie and I ease into the shallow water. Addy zooms past us, diving into deeper water. We laugh at her as she swims around. We make our way out to her.

"He said he is falling in love with me."

The words explode from Rosie's mouth like she couldn't keep them in any longer. The shock of it is overwhelming. He loves her? Does he love Addy and me? This is what I was afraid of. I knew it would come down to this. The anger starts growing inside me. Of course, he loves Rosie. She's kind and beautiful and easy to love.

"What? When did he say that?" Addy asks.

"Just before he passed out before dinner."

"And what did you say?"

"Nothing. I just left."

Addy pauses, unsure what to ask next. My anger simmers, but maybe he was just being emotional. Perhaps it didn't really mean anything to us as a group. Rosie is the most recent person he's spent time alone with, and they're fighting. That never helps anything.

"Do you love him?" I ask meekly.

Rosie looks at me. There is sadness on her face, but also something else. Hope, maybe. "I don't know. Maybe? I haven't really considered it. He's great, but with his divorce and now this shit with my parents, I'm hesitant to consider anything like that." We float silently in the water for a few minutes when Addy speaks up.

"Megs, do you love him?"

"What, no?" Oh, that came out way too fast. Much too fast.

"Oh. Megs is in love," Addy is singing out the words in an annoying way.

"I said no, dork." I splash water at her, trying to drive home my point. She splashes me back, and suddenly a game starts, and we forget our feelings. We are back to enjoying each other as we normally do here. We spend the next few hours playing in the water, splashing, swimming, floating. We avoid the topic of James and just enjoy our time together until the sun starts to go down.

As we walk back towards the house, I speak up. Even though I have mostly been able to avoid thinking about this, it has been a constant thought all afternoon. "I'm going to check on James when we get in. I feel partially responsible for the state he's in."

"It's not your fault, Megs," Rosie assures me.

"I know, but if I had been more comforting or watched his drinking more, he wouldn't be passed out now," I shrug.

They both have more to say, but they don't push it. We rinse off in the outdoor shower before heading inside. I pad to the master bedroom, but he isn't there. The water and ibuprofen are missing too. At least he got those. I find him in the kitchen, sitting at the table. Stepping behind him, my hands rub his shoulders, trying to offer some comfort. He shifts slightly, acknowledging my presence, but doesn't say anything. This is where the comforting words should come out of my mouth. Ask how he feels, if he's hungry, what he needs. Something. As I open my mouth, he jumps up and runs to the trashcan. He really can't handle that liquor.

He starts getting sick. I step behind him, rubbing his back. Reaching into the sink, I grab a washcloth and wet it with cold water. Being a personal trainer, I've seen enough people vomit. They come in thinking they are in great shape and know what to do, then twenty minutes later, they are barfing up that high-protein snack bar they thought was a good idea. The cloth goes on his neck while I continue stroking his back. After a few minutes, he calms down. He pulls the cloth from his neck to wipe his face. I slide a chair closer to him, and he collapses into it.

He offers a small thanks. I hand him a glass of water but stay near the counter. He doesn't need to be crowded right now. We remain quiet as he drinks the water. When that is mostly empty, I grab him a muffin from the counter. Maybe not the best choice, but it should help. After the first few bites stay down, I empty the trash. He tries to stop me, but I make him sit and finish the muffin. When I come back in, he is looking a little better. Refilling his glass, I ask if he wants to rest more. He nods, so I take him to my room. Rosie always stays in the master. I don't imagine she wants to take care of him now.

Once he lays down, I drape a blanket over him. I plan to turn off the lights and leave, but he grabs my hand, stopping me before I can reach the lights.

"Will you stay with me?"

My heart skips a beat at his words. He asked me to stay. Not to go get Rosie or Addy. A smile grows on my face. Maybe I'm not too bad at the comforting thing. I turn off the lights and sit on the bed beside him.

"Want to watch a movie? I think I can get Die Hard on my tablet."

"You can pick. We watched Die Hard earlier."

He rolls over, wrapping his arms around my waist, resting his head on my lap. I grab my tablet from my stuff on the floor next to us, adjusting him a bit to get it. We settle back in together as I open my favorite streaming app. It's not a mainstream one. I've offered to share the password with everyone, but they insist there aren't shows they like. Pfft. They just don't know what's good. I start up my favorite series, letting it play where I stopped. James hasn't watched this with me before, but he's also never been concerned about starting in the middle of a series. He's always been content to just sit with me. I place the tablet on the bed, further away from his face. I don't want the bright lights to affect him.

My hands settle on his head and arm. I run my fingers through his hair absently, absorbed in my show. He groans, and I freeze.

"No, don't stop. That was perfect."

I chuckle at him, then start up my fingers again. Being here with him is cathartic. I've never felt such comfort and peace in a man's presence. Men have always made me uncomfortable. That is the reason I've never actually had sex with a man. I have wondered what it would be like. To have a large body on top of me. I push those thoughts away, not wanting to focus on them now. The show keeps playing. I keep stroking James's hair. Cuddling with him now doesn't feel as awkward as it did before. We are just together. I don't need to worry about comforting him. He's fine at this point. My eyes start drooping, but I don't turn off the show. I don't want to move at all. This is splendid. I don't want to mess that up.

"Megs."

James says my name softly. I blink my eyes, realizing I fell asleep. He's sitting next to me now. A slight loss is floating around my chest without his arms around me.

"You fell asleep. Why don't we just go to bed?"

I nod, but I need to go shower. I never did bathe properly after swimming. A shower won't take too long but is necessary. James says he'll grab a snack while I shower. The warm water is soothing, cleaning off the grime of the lake. The shower is short and fast; I do not want to be in too long. I don't want to lose the little bit of comfort we had going. Back in the room, he is sitting on the bottom bunk.

"Addy and Rosie are already asleep. Looks like I'm in here tonight."

I step in to put my stuff away. I want to ask if I can sleep beside him tonight, but being straightforward isn't my forte. I stall, hoping he will just ask me himself. Of course, he may not even want me to sleep next to him. This thought gets me moving. I step to the opposite end of the bed from him to climb onto the top. He lunges for me, grabbing my foot that is positioned to climb the ladder. My body freezes, and I look down at him.

"Sleep next to me?"

All my might goes into not letting out the grin fighting to escape.

"Okay."

He releases me and slides back on the mattress. I appreciate him letting me take the outside. I haven't spent an entire night in the same bed as someone. I had my own space at sleepovers with friends. I always go back to my own room at some point when I'm with Rosie and Addy. Even when I was with Kendra, one of us went to a different space to get sleep. My nerves ramp up, realizing how big this is. It doesn't mean as much to him. He was married and likely shared a bed. Plus, he's slept with Rosie and Addy overnight. He holds the covers up for me. I slide in, turning my back to him. He shifts his arm so I can rest my head on it. The covers drape over me. He kisses my shoulder, rubbing his hand over my arm. He slides his hand down to rest on top of my hand.

His warmth is almost overwhelming. I never realized cuddling would be so warm. Obviously, I knew there was some warmth, but not this much. Is he hotter than ordinary people? Not hotter. He's undoubtedly attractive. One of the hottest men I have been around. Whew, these thoughts are running wild tonight.

"Can I ask you something?"

His breath is warm against my neck. His fingers are tracing small circles on my arm. I can't recall a time I have ever felt so warm and safe. I nod, not wanting to speak too loudly, which I am positive will happen.

"Do you wear a binder all the time?"

That isn't a question I was expecting. I clear my throat, but my words are still too loud at first.

"No... no. Not all the time. I feel more comfortable in it, but I take breaks from it."

"Oh, like now?"

"Yeah, like for sleep."

"Do you like having your chest touched?"

That is another question I hadn't expected. I haven't thought about it in such a long time. When I first started having sex, I didn't like having my chest touched at all. Addy and Rosie learned quickly and have always left that decision up to me. Before I started wearing binders regularly, there were a lot of awkward moments during play. They would touch me where I didn't want to be touched. It took me a while to get comfortable speaking up before we started. Then I just started leaving my tops on. That worked as a better signal for all of us. Sometimes I'll take the top off, but not always. More often than not, I leave it on.

"I don't always like it, no." I consider turning to see his face, but it's too dark. I wouldn't be able to see it anyway. "Is that a problem for you? Do you need breasts to touch?" I'm trying not to hold my breath for his answer. I'm too close to him. Surely, he can feel my breathing is irregular. He's really considering his response, and it makes me nervous. He seems to snap out of deep thought. He shifts his body, pulling me tighter to his body.

"No, I don't need breasts." He shakes his head against my back. "I didn't mean anything like that. I just... I noticed the other night with Addy that you left the binder on, and she didn't touch you there. No one has ever mentioned it. I...I guess what I'm trying to get at is, are there...do you...."

His stuttering prompts me to turn to face him. I can only see the outline of his face. My body stays close but far enough back to look at him. He takes a deep breath, pushing it away from me.

"Sorry. I'm not used to asking this. Normally, with girls, I just start touching and expect them to tell me what they like or don't like. I...I don't want to do that with you, though. I want you to be comfortable through everything. Not that I want you to do anything. I'm not trying...I mean, I want to have se... Whoa. I'm shutting up now."

His words start flowing out faster the more he says. I giggle at his nervousness, glad I'm not the only one feeling that way. I lean in and kiss him gently on the lips. He returns my kiss, rubbing his fingers around my shoulders. I'm not very upset over this turn of events. It's been a long day. It's better to end on a high note than where we were before dinner.

"I like my breast touched sometimes. I don't want sex as much as Addy or even Rosie. I still play with them mostly to stay involved. We have developed a system for touching. When I leave clothing on, that's my signal that I don't want to be touched. When Addy is leading a scene, she always asks what I want. That works for us."

He pulls me closer to him, his head resting on top of mine. I snuggle up to his chest, wishing he wasn't wearing a shirt. He moves his hand to my exposed bicep. The sleeves of my shirt were ripped off a long time ago. I love this shirt for sleeping but don't wear it anywhere else. My hands are on his back, stroking his muscles.

"You can put your hands under my shirt," I whisper into his neck.

He moves slowly, tentatively, worried I might change my mind. He lifts my shirt then his hand touches my side, resting on the skin. His hand feels like it's burning. His breathing is as shallow as my own. My body is on fire, noticing every little touch, every little movement.

"James," his hand tightens on my back. "Can I kiss you?"

He shifts back to look down at me. Instead of waiting for his answer, I reach up to kiss him. The kiss is gentle and tentative. He is letting me lead. I'm setting the pace. As I realize this, I place my hands under his shirt, wanting to feel his skin. His hand glides further up my back, stroking my spine up and down. His tongue runs between my lips. I part them gently, allowing his tongue into my mouth, his swirls against mine calmly. The taste of his minty toothpaste fills my mouth. I don't do a lot of kissing, but I enjoy this. I match his movements. Desire builds inside me. It's different than I have ever felt before. I need more. I've wanted more in the past, but this differs from those times. All my anxiety and stress are replaced with need and want.

I grab his hand, pulling it around to my front. He breaks our kiss, looking down at his hand draped over my breast. His thumb strokes the top. The touch is gentle, lighting a fire inside me. My breathing is shallow. My chest barely moves against his hand. He scoops my breast into his hand, thumbing my budding nipple. My hands are by my side now, and I'm unsure what to do. I wish Addy were here. She could tell me. She's so good at directing.

"Megs."

Hearing my name draws me back to reality. I open my eyes, looking at James. His gaze is intent.

"Do you want me to stop?"

I bite my lip. Do I want him to stop? Part of me does. Am I really ready for this? My body is screaming for him to continue. My emotions are more jumbled. Before I can sort through them, his hand is gone, leaving me feeling bare. The hem of my shirt is tugged down. He nudges my shoulder, encouraging me to roll on my side with my back to him. He curls back around me, but I don't overlook his hips being pushed away from me.

"Sleep, Megs."

His arm drapes over mine again, but his fingers lace between mine. He presses several kisses to my shoulder before stilling next to me. I immerse myself in his warmth. My mind attempts to decipher my feelings. He didn't push me. He let me lead and set the pace. A swell of warmth consumes me. I would have gone farther, but would I have regretted that later? His breathing becomes deep and slow, indicating he is asleep. Peace and love settle over me as I listen to his breaths. I stop trying to figure out what everything means, what I'm feeling. I can do that later. For now, I will soak up his warmth and sleep wrapped in his arms.

ROSIE

I walk around the kitchen, looking for coffee. It's our final day at the cabin. We're supposed to be leaving in a couple of hours. Megs is nowhere to be found, and there is no coffee! This is vacation. How is anyone supposed to function without coffee? And where is Megs? They are always the first one to wake up. I search the deck and basement, but there would be coffee if they are awake. Megs must still be asleep. This is super weird, though.

I slowly crack open the door, unsure what I will find inside. Thankfully, it's not nearly as bad as I thought. Megs is just still asleep. In the bottom bunk with James. Slowly closing the door, I remember Megs never sleeps with anyone. They always get up and leave before the night is over. Were they there all night? Maybe they got up to go to the bathroom, and he pulled them in, and they fell back asleep? No, that can't be it. In the kitchen, I search again, but this time for coffee. Guess I'm making my own today.

Most of my strong emotions from yesterday have settled. I need to talk to my parents soon, but that is not something I want to do, and will absolutely put it off until the last possible minute. The anger towards James has subsided. His confession last night softened my feelings. I have strong feelings for him too. Falling would be an accurate description. He belongs with us.

Something with my parents must change, though. I don't want to live through situations like this regularly. James has a good point. To sit back and accept what they say isn't an act I should have to deal with. He also went too far in what he said to my mother. He did apologize for that. I plan to talk to him before we leave today. I don't want to get back to the apartment on awkward terms.

Addy walks in wearing shorts and a tank top. She kisses my cheek just as the coffee is made. I hand her a mug as she leans against the counter next to me. I rest my head against her shoulder. I have always loved being close to her. She brings me a certain calmness that I can't get anywhere else. She is wild and exciting, and downright crazy. However, she has this innate ability to bring calm when things get crazy. It's the reason she's my best friend, and I refuse to let her leave my life.

"I'm gonna go in the woods for a bit before we leave. Wanna go?"

Her eyebrows waggle at me suggestively. For the most part, our kinks and sexual escapades line up. We complement each other in what we like and can adapt to. But fucking in the forest will never be something I'm down for. Maybe in a tent, but not in the grass with bugs and leaves. No, thank you.

"I'll pass."

I kiss her quickly, scanning the kitchen to see what food is left. We don't have to take it with us. My parents said they are coming out next weekend. I'm hungry now and don't want to leave anything that will be bad before they get here. I grab some fruit and start eating it straight from the container. No sense in making more dirty dishes. Addy swipes a piece before going outside. I stand, looking around, zoning out. The past few days play through my mind.

Overall, the time away has been great. We've had fun, relaxed, and spent time together. The only thing that would make this trip any better is skipping lunch with my mom. I should have just stayed in bed with James. They can survive without having lunch with me. We could find another cabin to stay in. Though, not for free and not this private. My parents take up too much space with their negativity in my life. We don't have these same issues with Addy's or Megs's parents. They call them occasionally and see them once or twice a year. That is a better approach than what I am doing. This is twice now I've had issues with James because of my parents.

Oh.

This is our first fight. I would have expected the fighting to be worse for a man in the middle of a divorce. He was partially wrong, but so was I. He's right. I shouldn't let my parents affect me the way they do. Addy and Megs refuse to be around them. James has lashed out twice now because of them. I need to set better boundaries with my parents. Let them know what they are saying isn't okay. I need to stop their behavior before it ruins the best parts of my life.

As if on cue, James walks into the kitchen, rubbing his eyes. I smile at him, handing him a mug of coffee. Megs hasn't appeared yet. I wonder what's keeping them.

"Sleep well?" A smirk spreads on my face.

"Yes," he shrugs, missing my expression.

"Where's Megs?"

"They're still asleep."

He sips his coffee, still oblivious to my line of questioning. Maybe he doesn't know why sleeping with them is a big deal. It's possible Megs doesn't think it's a big deal either. It is, though. His confession last night rattled me a bit. Megs's hit harder, though. They may not be willing to admit their feelings for him, but the feelings are there.

"How are you feeling?"

"Better. Megs took care of me. Sorry I got so drunk. I don't do that often."

He rubs his hand behind his head, not making eye contact with me. He's leaning against the counter opposite me, sipping on his coffee. I step up to his side, lacing my arm around his back, leaning against his chest. He drapes his arm around my body.

"Thank you for giving me time yesterday. You are right about my parents. I need to set better boundaries with them. I'm sorry you were put in that position."

He squeezes me tight, pressing a kiss to the top of my head. I settle against his chest. While Addy grounds me with her presence, James offers something different. There is more comfort and security in his space. He will protect me, even when I don't want that protection. It is always there. Addy gives me the freedom to sort through my issues. James tries to save me from them. I'm no damsel in distress. I don't need saving, but I do appreciate the effort.

His fingers lift my chin, pulling my face to his. He presses a small kiss on my lips. I love these tender moments. I love the wild and exciting parts of life, but these tender moments are what I live for. Being held and kissed delicately are my favorite things. I may not be a damsel, but I do love being held like one.

We stay standing together, chatting until Megs walks in. When they come in, we all snap into action. We need to pack and get ready to go. I don't want to return to regular life with everyone working. I don't get much choice, though. Addy returns shortly after. When the cars are loaded, Megs asks if they can ride back with me. I don't mind at all. In fact, it works out better for me. I need to call my parents and plan to do it on the drive. I don't want to subject James to that now.

Once in the car, we ride silently for a bit. Finally, I can't take it anymore.

"Megs!" I burst out. "Oh my god. Tell me what happened with James last night!!"

They laugh at my outburst. They explain how they cared for him, watched shows, then went to sleep. They try to gloss over the nitty-gritty of their cuddling, but I insist on every detail. They groan but tell me a lot. There are obviously things they are leaving out of the conversation. I don't intend to push too hard, but I want details. James is so good with Addy and me. He also needs to be good with Megs for this to work. They're an essential part of our dynamic. He said he wanted to try a relationship with all three of us. So he has to live up to that too. We already have a good relationship between just the three of us.

"So, did you want to have sex with him?"

"Yeah..."

"Then why did you let him stop?"

Megs bites their lip. This is clearly something they are struggling with. This may be why they wanted to ride with me today. Patience is a virtue of mine. The conversation doesn't need to be rushed. It's over two hours until we get back to the apartment. Giving them space to talk out whatever stopped them is one thing I can do.

"I...I... didn't know what to do."

"What do you mean? You don't know how to have sex?"

"No, doofus," they sigh loudly. A small giggle escapes from me. "I didn't know how to push things forward. James is leaving everything up to me, so I'm comfortable. But I didn't know what to do."

Well, that has me stumped. It makes sense that Megs wouldn't really know those details. They aren't typically the leader when it comes to sex. Especially knowing they have only been with three people.

"What did you do with Kendra?"

"Kendra always took the lead with me."

"Do you remember what she did? Could you do that? I don't really know how to explain it. It's something we pick up through trial and error. I can tell you what I do with James. But it was also several weeks before I finally got to have sex with him. I don't normally recommend Addy for advice, but she could probably tell you more."

It's silent for a moment as we think about things. I'm trying to come up with good tips. It's hard to say what would work or what would make them more comfortable. This line of thinking is also making me horny. My core is tightening, a slow heat rising deep inside me.

"So, okay, we were kissing, and he was touching my breast. But I didn't know what to do with my hands."

My eyebrows shoot up. This statement is shocking. They never let anyone touch their breast. I've only seen them once or twice out of the binder.

"Megs! He touched your breast!! You let him?"

They laugh at me. "Yes. I wanted him too."

"Aww, you really do like him." A cheesy grin is plastered on my face. Megs giggles again. "Okay, well, in that case, you could've pulled him tighter. Grab his ass. Your fingers could go in his hair or face. Or if you really want to move things quickly, you could pull him on top of you, or push him back and climb on top if you prefer that. Or just go all out and grab his dick."

Megs chokes at my last statement. I shrug, "I assure you that one will always work." We burst into laughter. When we settle down, they hold their hands up to slow me down.

"Okay, okay. I think I've got it. Thanks, Rosie."

I reach over and squeeze their hand. They turn the radio up, and we drive through the small towns on back roads. Eventually, I stop at a gas station, and Addy pulls in behind us. I was unaware they were so close on the road. We all go inside, grab snacks, go to the bathroom, just take our time. As we walk back to the cars, I hesitate before getting in, and Megs gives me a confused look.

"I need to call my dad. Could you drive?"

They nod and take the keys from me. They squeeze my arm as they move around. As they move away, I take a deep breath to settle the growing nerves. Large arms wrap around my stomach. James presses his lips to my neck. His warmth consumes me, driving away my nerves. He presses several light kisses along my neck and cheek. He whispers, "Let us know how it goes." Then he steps away from me. A small smile spreads as I watch him.

A hard smack lands on my ass, causing me to jump. Addy shoves her face on the other side of my neck, nipping roughly. I laugh, trying to squirm away, but her arm wraps around my waist, holding me close. "Don't take their shit. You're my baby girl, not theirs." She pops my other ass cheek and walks away from me. Great, now my ass is sore for the ride home. At least there were only two pops and not more.

Back on the road, Megs insists I send the call through Bluetooth so they can listen. Even though I'm calling my dad and not my mother, he could still say some insensitive stuff. They are insistent, though, so I connect my phone through Bluetooth. He answers after a couple of rings.

"Hello?"

"Hi, Daddy."

"Rosie. How was your stay at the cabin?"

"It was good. Thank you for letting us use it."

"You're welcome."

"Daddy..." I take a deep breath. I can do this. I can tell him to stop treating me like shit. That mom needs to stop treating me like shit. Megs's hand slides onto my knee, squeezing to show support. I blow out my breath hard. "I'm sorry for the things James said to mom the other day. His comments were uncalled for, and he is sorry for having said them. But I also need you and Mom to understand your actions that led to this. The underhanded insults need to stop. I'm a grown woman and can make my own decisions. The way you treat me is affecting me and my relationships."

He's silent for several moments. I glance at Megs, and they meet my gaze quickly before turning back to the road. Just before I ask if he's still there, he finally speaks.

"I understand, baby. I've long thought that your mother was out of line. You always seem to handle it well. I never felt the need to step in. I will talk to her for you." A breath rushes out of me.

"Thank you, Daddy."

"You should probably call her in a few days to talk with her about this yourself, but I'll tell her for now."

"Thank you. I love you."

"Love you too, baby."

The call disconnects. My father is never one to mince words. I said what I needed to say, and he seemed receptive. It's annoying that he knew what she was doing and never bothered to stop it. Surely, he knows that isn't good for anyone's mental health. Hopefully, things will change now. There will still be reminders and the need to correct them. We have to start somewhere, though.

I shoot off a text to Addy and James, letting them know it went well. They'll probably have questions when we get back to the apartment. We still have a bit of time before we get back, though. Megs rubs my leg. My eyes feel droopy, suddenly exhausted from the stress of this situation. They tell me to sleep. I don't fight them. Leaning back in the seat, I close my eyes. This trip has been good and bad but it ended on a high note. I made up with James. I set new rules with my parents. Things are looking up.

Chapter Twenty

JAMES

I should have never gone to that cabin.

That was definitely a mistake.

We've been back for a week now. I've had to go into the office every day. Even with Rosie making it a favorite spot of mine, it pales in comparison to the cabin. I'm a journalist; shouldn't I be able to work from any location? Why can't I go back to the cabin and just work there all the time? No, I can't afford it. Yeah, I'd probably get frustrated having to drive so far for essentials, but I could learn to live without that stuff. Who needs to eat anyway? I miss the open air and the water and the trees. Stupid cubicle at work. I added some new photos from our trip to my wall, but it isn't enough.

Accepting that I won't ever get to live in that cabin and do nothing with my partners, I get back to work. Since the main articles have all been submitted, we are filling the rest of the space with fluff pieces, editing, and re-editing to prepare for publishing. There is only a month until the article drops. Martin Stewart will not have a good day when this hits the stands. For some reason, that makes me feel uncomfortable. I've written pieces about people doing illegal things before. Many have even been punished. Granted, no one has ever committed a crime of this magnitude. That doesn't explain my unease. It feels like I'm forgetting something. I've double-checked all my sources, all my information. Everything is accurate and fire-proof. This feeling doesn't have any backing. I brush it off and move on.

Things at the apartment have mostly returned to normal. Addy and Megs are back at work. Rosie is trying to turn herself into a burrito. She's been successful so far. Every day this week, I've found her wrapped in the burrito blanket I got her on her birthday. She's either asleep, watching movies, or reading. Once, I found her struggling with knitting, but that didn't last. For all the patience she claims to have, it does not extend to yarn. I'm glad she has the summer off. Insanely jealous but pleased for her. She deserves to turn into a burrito.

I'm ready for the workday to end. When we returned from the cabin, Megs asked if I wanted to go on a date with them. Obviously, I do. They heard about this new pop-up bar/restaurant they want to go to. We're going there tonight. I don't have any expectations of the night ending with sex. Megs hasn't said anything about the night I slept with them at the cabin. I would love to go further but don't intend to push the issue. They said they haven't been with a man before. The last thing I want is for them to feel obligated to do anything with me.

Addy is working late at the bar. Rosie is asleep in her burrito when I get back. I chuckle but head to my room to change for my date with Megs. I take out my favorite jeans. Looking in the mirror, I debate wearing a collared shirt or jacket. The teeth marks Addy left are gone, but there is still a lot of bruising. I never anticipated the bruise to take this long to heal, but it was a big one in a sensitive area. I settle on wearing a t-shirt. It's hot outside, even in the evenings. End of July heat is not forgiving. Plus, Megs took part in the scene that caused the mark. They weren't the one to leave it, but it might be a reminder of fun times. It has been for me. Except at work with the nosey receptionist. I told her I fell in the tub after having stomach problems. She suggested I see a psychiatrist. If she liked me before I started sleeping with Addy, she definitely doesn't now. That poor old woman. She has no clue how to handle this situation. To be fair, neither do I.

Rosie is still asleep on the couch, so I wait in the kitchen for Megs. It's close to the time we agreed to meet. I scroll through my phone, leaning against the counter. Their door opens, and they walk out. They have on dark slacks with a white short-sleeve button-up shirt. The first several buttons are undone, exposing more skin than they normally leave visible. They are wearing dark suspenders with red slip-on shoes. Their hair is curly on top, hanging over one shaved side. I can't stop the grin that breaks across my face. I've always been drawn to women that wear clothes like Addy and Rosie. Rosie is always in a dress, and Addy, when she dresses up, is always in tight-fitting clothes. I've never considered a more androgynous look, something similar to my own. But I absolutely love Megs's style. It fits them so perfectly. It's both sexy and beautiful. Plus, it displays their personality well.

"You look amazing." I kiss their cheek, keeping my voice low to not wake Rosie. "I love this look on you." They smile at me, looking away.

"Would you like it on your floor?"

I laugh at their comment. They don't usually get flirty like that, and it's adorable. I wrap my arms around their body, pulling them in close.

"I would absolutely love to see it on my floor."

Their arms wrap around my waist, giggling. They still have their face away from me, so I press my lips against their neck. I place several kisses, then suck in one spot. Their body pushes into mine like they can't support themselves. I tighten my arms around them. I gently press my teeth against their skin, nipping their neck.

"Whoa."

They pull back from me. I keep my arms around them, not letting them move away. Their hand is on their neck where my mouth just was.

"I was just trying to give us matching marks."

I bring my hand to my neck, showing the bruise still visible. Megs starts laughing at me, swatting me away.

"Ugh, get a room, you two," Rosie calls out from the couch. We clearly aren't as quiet as I meant to be. I offer a small apology, pulling Megs towards the door.

They drive to the restaurant. It's crowded since it's new and a weekend. It isn't terrible, though. We'll still be able to find somewhere to stand. There aren't any seats. Several standing tables fill the space, most only big enough for drinks and one or two dishes. I keep my fingers laced through Megs to keep them close and touch them. I'm glad we are getting some time together without the others. We order some food and beer. I spot a table in the back corner and send Megs to claim it as I wait for our food.

We eat our food, chatting about random things. They tell me about a new book they're reading. I give them an update on the article I'm writing. They always love hearing how it works. Having someone interested and excited about my writing has been almost overwhelming. My parents never really cared. Whitney liked to pretend that wasn't the job I had. She was never satisfied with my job. Rosie and Addy express interest, but not the way Megs does. Megs wants all the details. They want to know my process, how things work, and what the article is about. I've given them a lot of details but tried to keep the key aspects a secret. I want them to enjoy the article release without knowing everything about it.

The food we have is delicious. Megs insisted it would be. I've not always had good experiences with pop-up restaurants, but this is surprisingly good. The beer is from a local brewery that I love. Once we finish eating, Megs clears our table while I get us another drink. When I return, I stand closer to them. My back is towards the main restaurant. They are at an angle and can still see around the room. We lean in together, talking about random things. I drop my hand to their back, pulling them into my side. They step willingly. I decide to push it further. Initially, I wanted Megs to take the lead. They have done enough flirting tonight. I can meet them halfway. I'm also confident they will push me away if I am too aggressive. I lean in to kiss them, closing my eyes as I move in.

Their hand on my chest stops me. Shit.

A wave of instant regret washes over me. Of course, flirting and small touches would differ from kissing in public. I shouldn't have pushed. This is why I want them to take the lead. I don't want to go too far. Especially being in public with an audience. I open my eyes, looking at Megs. Their eyes are off to the side, looking at something behind me. Their hand is still on my chest. They don't look angry or put off.

"You have company," they whisper to me. Their hand drops from my chest down to my arm, and I turn to see what they are looking at. Before I spot anything, I hear it.

"James?"

Whitney. That regret I felt earlier shifts to a more profound ache. A small comfort arises, realizing Megs wasn't rejecting me. But it doesn't even crest the growing frustration, anger, and hurt knowing Whitney is here. I turn, trying to position myself in front of Megs. I don't want them exposed to her again. The last time was frustrating enough. She saunters up to us. Megs's hands are on my back, providing comfort and stability. My feelings towards Whitney have lessened over the summer, but many unresolved issues remain. Finalizing the divorce is the most important.

"Whitney." I seethe, not even trying to be casual. "When are you going to sign the divorce papers?"

She steps in front of me, taking in Megs and me. She gives us both the once over, but I focus on her face. There isn't a need to look her over to know what she is wearing. Short skirt, top pushing her breasts up unnaturally, far too much make-up. When we first started dating, she always wore more conservative clothing. Loose-fitting dresses, pants suits, office attire. After marriage, though, probably around the time she started cheating on me, it all changed. She kept those clothes for work, and anywhere else she wore her new clothes. I never cared for them. They didn't fit her well, but she didn't wear them for me.

"Oh, James, let's not worry about that now." She steps up, placing her hands on my chest. "Come over here, and let's make up. I'm sure this...." Whitney pauses, looking up and down at Megs with absolute contempt. "Man, person, girl? Honestly, James, the people you hang out with. I'm sure she can find her own way home. We can fix this, my love."

Unintentionally, my chest puffs out as anger swirls inside me. I open my mouth to respond, but before I do, Megs steps to my side, reaching up to push Whitney's hands off my chest.

"I have a ride home with James. You need to leave. He is happy and loved, and you can just kindly fuck off."

A look of astonishment grows on my face as I watch Megs respond. My hand wraps around their side, offering a tiny squeeze. They don't need to stand up for me. I'd love to keep them as far away from Whitney as possible. Her closed-mind-edness is more profound than I remember. Whitney slams her hands to her side, huffing out a breath.

"James, you don't need to cause a scene. I just want you to talk to me and come home. All of this ridiculousness about divorce is getting out of hand. Just come home, and we will fix this."

"Whitney, I'm not coming back. You need to get that through your thick skull. Let me go. I can't handle you anymore."

She looks surprised by my claim, as if she didn't realize I didn't want to be with her anymore.

"So, what? I made your life miserable? Was I so mean to you? Did I mistreat you?"

"Yes, Whitney. You did. I want to move on."

"Did I abuse you, James?"

I don't reply to that. While there was plenty of gaslighting and emotional damage, I don't intend to call Whitney an abuser. This just needs to end. The restaurant has grown quiet. Déjà vu crashes over me. It's been weeks since we last saw her in a restaurant when she was escorted out and banned. Does this place even have bodyguards? Megs's hand moves to my arm. Their touch grounds me a bit. My emotions are swirling, and it is hard to stay focused or grounded right now. I turn my head to look away from Whitney, but she talks again.

"Did I hurt you? Did I make you bleed? You have no reason to leave me. I didn't do anything."

She glances down and notices Megs's hand on my arm. Her eyes flare back to mine.

"You want a reason to leave? Fine."

My life begins to move in slow motion. Whitney cocks her elbow back, making a fist. She's threatened to hit me before, even raised her hand once, but has never actually done it. It was always at home after we had been fighting for a while. My disbelief that she will genuinely hit me prevents me from moving. While her hand is pulling back, Megs lets go of my arm. I see them take a step. Then another. My functional brain can't understand what's happening. Megs is moving in front of me to block me. Thankfully, my instincts take over while the rest of my brain just watches. My hands go out, attempting to stop Megs. This isn't their battle.

Megs's second step lands them directly in front of me. Someone in the crowd gasps. Another person is yelling. Someone further back is screaming, possibly at Whitney. Whitney's hand finally surges forward and connects with the side of Megs's face. Whitney was never very strong. However, that punch landed hard. My arms are already around Megs as they drop. I grab their body, spinning around so my back is to Whitney. I cover Megs with my body, glancing back to see what Whitney is doing.

The world crashes down as everything resumes at normal speed. A couple of people are grabbing Whitney, hauling her back. Several people are recording, and some are shouting questions to give feedback to emergency services they've called. Megs's weight brings me back to them. I hoist them up, trying to turn them to look at their face. Both hands cover their face. Their body is still crumpled. My brain goes on the fritz. No logical thoughts are passing through. I grab at Megs's hands, trying to pull them away.

"Megs, let me look. Are you okay? Let me see."

Someone rushes up beside me with a cloth with ice inside. They are wearing one of the shirts with the pop-up's logo. I take the ice pack, trying to pull Megs's hands away again. They notice the pack, taking it to press against their face. It's frustrating that they won't let me look. I glance over my shoulder to see Whitney being held back by a group of people. They aren't letting her leave or get any closer. I wrap my arms tightly around Megs. They won't let me look, but I can at least keep them safe.

"I'm so sorry, Megs. I'm sorry."

I mumble this for several minutes, just holding them tightly. They don't push me away. One hand stays on the ice pack on their face. Eventually, their hand grabs onto the hem of my shirt. People are standing around us, asking if we're okay, if they can help. I nod or shake my head occasionally, just holding Megs tightly against my chest. Sirens are blaring outside. Then a woman walks up, saying she's a paramedic and wants to help us. I release Megs, realizing tears are running down their face. My heart breaks as I look at them.

The paramedic asks what happened. Megs looks at me, so I explain the story to her. The paramedic suggests we go to the ambulance so she can get a better look at Megs's face. Again, they just look at me. I take their hand and lead them out the door. A cop is there, restraining Whitney. I don't look at her as we reach the ambulance. I hold Megs's hand as they climb up, sitting on the stretcher. The paramedic climbs in after. I stand just outside, watching intently. The paramedic finally pulls the ice pack back from her face. The damage Whitney did is present already, even with the ice. Megs's face is swelling and will definitely be bruised. The paramedic suggests going to the hospital to get x-rays. My chest tightens. Everything hurts. My body is tense, and I can barely breathe properly.

Megs is chatting with the paramedic, asking about going to the hospital. I can't hear what they are actually saying. I see their mouth moving, but the sound isn't registering. My ex-wife struck my new partner, and they may have broken bones. My new partner got hit because they were trying to protect me.

"James?"

My eyes dart over to Megs, who has slid closer to me on the stretcher. I look at them, but all I can see is the bruise forming on their face. The paramedic moves, climbing out of the ambulance.

"Here, sit down here, okay?" She looks up to Megs. "Seems like he's in shock."

Shock. My body isn't functioning. My thoughts don't work. The only thing I can see is Megs's swelling face. Their hands are on me, pulling me into the ambulance. They whisper my name again, jolting me back towards reality.

"You should keep the ice on your face."

I'm in the seat the paramedic just left. Megs is sitting directly in front of me. They place the ice back over their face, but their free hand takes mine. They squeeze my hand, allowing my grip on reality to settle. The paramedic is next to me, asking to check my pulse. I let her, even though I'm not the one needing medical attention. One hand with the paramedic, I reach the other out to hold the ice pack on Megs's face. My hand stops on top of theirs. My thumb strokes the back of their hand as my fingertips stroke the side of their head. I keep my touch light, scared of hurting them, but I need contact. I need to know they are okay.

An officer walks to the back of the ambulance, chatting with the paramedic momentarily. He turns his attention to Megs and asks if they want to press charges.

"Yes."

I gasp at their response. I start to tell them it isn't something they need to do. I don't want them to press charges because of me. They hear my gasp and turn to me.

"If I press charges, you can use that against her in court and your divorce."

"You don't have to do that for me."

"Plus, she deserves it."

Pain flares through my heart. This night has gone in a direction I never wanted.

"Hey, it's okay. Let's go talk with the cop, go to the hospital for x-rays, then we'll go home and see if my clothes do look better on your floor."

My mouth pops open. I stutter to tell Megs we can't do that tonight, but they just laugh at me.

"I'm joking with you. Come on. We've got stuff to do, yeah?"

I nod my head, reality seeping in. How is Megs better at handling this situation than I am? I'm not even the one that got punched. They move down to talk with the cop but keep their body close to mine. I keep a hand on them the whole time. My brain slowly returns to normal. As Megs talks with the cops, I pull out my phone to text Rosie and Addy.

> We're okay, but we're going to the hospital for Megs to get x-rays. We'll be home later.

> JAMES!! What the fuck? What happened?

Rosie responded instantly. A few seconds later, a message from Addy pops up.

> I thought you were going on a date.

Sorry, that wasn't clear. We ran into Whitney. It's fine; the paramedics just want to be sure nothing is broken.

My phone starts ringing with a video call from Rosie and Addy. It's not surprising, but it isn't necessary. I answer, shifting to give Megs and the cop some privacy. Rosie starts yelling as soon as it connects.

"What do you mean you ran into her? What is wrong with Megs? What is wrong with you? You know what, no, what hospital are you going to? I'll just meet you there. Go ahead and check yourself in, too, because I'm going to beat you."

Addy laughs through the phone. I glance at the cop, shaking my head, telling him she's not serious. I squeeze Megs's hand and walk away to talk to the girls. I explain what happened at the restaurant and what we are doing next. They ask to see Megs, so I walk back. By then, the cop has left, and Megs is climbing from the ambulance. I hold the phone out so they can see Rosie and Addy. They still have the ice pack against their face but drop it when they are in view of the camera. The lighting isn't great. The full damage isn't visible in the call. My stomach tightens, seeing their eye nearly swollen, already changing colors. They notice my face and step close to me.

"I'm fine. It's not as bad as it looks."

Their body presses against mine, keeping me firmly in reality. I pull them close, holding onto them tightly. Megs speaks up again, pointing at my neck.

"You know I just wanted a mark to match James's. Whitney just has horrible aim," they laugh weakly.

"Fuck, Megs," Rosie says at the same time as Addy says, "Aww, you two are so cute." Rosie flies off the handle, yelling at Addy this time. I don't feel as bad for being unable to say anything. At least I didn't yell obscenities and threaten other people like Rosie is. Megs interrupts and tells them we're heading to the hospital and will be home later. Rosie demands we text her logically throughout the process. We promise to do just that and end the call. Megs hands me the keys, asking me to drive. We make our way to the car, but they stop me.

"Are you okay?"

"Megs, you just got punched in the face. Not me. I'm fine."

"No, I mean, like mentally. How are you doing?"

"I..." I start to answer but realize I don't really know how. No one has ever checked in on me like that. "I mean, not good. I... you..." My hands move up, then down, then between us, trying to help my words but also failing. "I can drive to the hospital and then home." I settle on that and shrug. There isn't much else I can say at this point. They nod, then step up to kiss my cheek, but they wince as they get close.

"Fuck. Let's go," I huff out, frustrated.

I kiss their other cheek, then pull them towards the car. I drive to the hospital and stay with them while they get checked out and have x-rays taken. Thankfully it's still early enough in the evening that the wait isn't terrible. I stay as close to Megs as I can. My mind is functioning normally at this point, but I am still trying to process everything that has happened. The doctors tell Megs nothing is broken. Relief washes through my body. They recommend icing and Tylenol to help with the pain. It would be nice if there was more we could do, but at least it isn't any worse. I shoot off a text, letting Rosie and Addy know the results in a logical manner. Rosie thanks me. We finish up things at the hospital. Finally, heading back for the night.

Megs

Well, tonight has been entirely unexpected. This is not at all how I wanted to spend my evening. Not many people would like to spend it that way. The doctors gave me a strong dose of Tylenol, dulling the ache in my head. I would have never guessed Whitney could hit that hard. I would like to know if she has a personal trainer or is in some martial arts class. I'm almost impressed at the damage she did.

James is more frazzled than I expected. He went into complete shock when the first responders showed up. It's a wonder he didn't pass out. Apparently, my comforting skill is improving because he did not faint. He also regained enough awareness to drive me to the hospital. So there's a silver lining to getting punched in the face. He's still moving in slow motion, but he's almost back to normal.

In the apartment, Addy is already home. That's a good indicator of how long the night has been. Rosie and Addy swarm me, asking questions, looking at my face, assessing the situation. They seem oblivious to James. I position myself in front of him, with Rosie and Addy in front of me. This is the easiest way to keep in contact with him. That is the most helpful in keeping him in the present. Aside from when we had to separate, his hand hasn't left my body. The touch is more welcome than usual. Knowing I'm not alone in this situation is an odd sense of comfort. Rosie smacks James's arm several times for scaring her with his texts. I laugh with Addy. He did deserve that. Those texts were not well thought out.

We finally say goodnight and start to move to our own rooms. James follows behind me, his hand still in mine. We reach my door. He pauses, looking at mine, then at his. He releases my hand. His head and shoulders droop. He kisses my cheek softly then sulks off towards his room. I'm torn at first. I don't want to be alone. I want to be with him. But my room or his?

"Hey," I call out softly. James turns to look back, and I nod towards my room. He lifts up, turning to fully face me. "You're not going to leave me alone now, are you?" His eyes go wide as he starts to walk in my direction. I stretch my arms up and around his shoulders. "I know I promised you could see my clothes on your floor, but would you settle for your clothes on mine?" He huffs out a laugh, pulling me tightly in his arms.

We step into my room. This is the first time he has actually been in here. I usually keep the door shut and go into the other's room. He glances around, taking it in before his eyes are back on me. I pull him to the edge of the bed. Grabbing the hem of his shirt, I lift it over his head. He stretches his arms and pulls it over his arms once it's out of my reach. I reach for his pants, starting to unbuckle them. Both of his hands grab mine, halting the progress.

"Megs."

"Are you really going to sleep in your jeans?"

I speak matter-of-factly. Having sex hasn't crossed my mind. It wasn't what I was thinking when I pulled him in here. He has a normally functioning sexual brain. My asexual brain is just ready to go to sleep. I just want to sleep with him next to me. He's offered so much comfort with his presence tonight; I'm not ready for that to end. He drops his hands. I finish unbuttoning them and step back for him to take them off. I move to the side of my room, taking my clothes off and tossing them on my chair. He's standing next to the bed in black boxer briefs. Even though it has only been a few days since I saw him completely naked, I'm still impressed with his body, broad shoulders, softly defined muscles. He's not as muscular as I am because he isn't in the gym as much. His body is still impressive. I stand in front of him in my binder and boy-cut panties. I take a deep breath and remove my binder, tossing it onto the chair with the rest of my clothes. He bites his lip, clearly fighting some intense feelings. I smirk, moving towards the bed.

Without saying any words, I motion for him to get in. I crawl in with my back to him. He wraps around me, pulling me into the spooning position. I had no idea I liked this position so much, and I probably wouldn't if it were anyone else. But for James, I'll sleep like this forever. His arms wrap around me, avoiding my breasts. We lay snuggled together for a couple of minutes. Then his grip tightens around me.

"Megs."

I rub my hand along his arm. I like the tightness, but I have limits. His grip will need to loosen soon.

"You told Whitney...."

He stops. At this point, I don't even remember what I told Whitney. I was just saying things, hoping she would leave. A lot of the actual conversation became a blur after I was hit. I wrack my brain, trying to remember what I said. Then it hits me.

"He is happy and loved, and you can just kindly fuck off."

Oh. That's what just hit him. I chew the inside of my lip, waiting for his response. I didn't mean to say that. Not that it isn't true, but that isn't really how I want to tell him. It's certainly not what I would have envisioned for first telling that to someone. Maybe he'll think I meant Addy or Rosie. I can't even see his face to know what he is thinking. That may not be the part he's focusing on. I did tell her to kindly fuck off. That's an odd thing to say, right?

He doesn't say anything else. His grip loosens on my body, giving me some breathing room. We both stay quiet. Neither mentioning the thing I sorta kinda accidentally told his ex-wife before him. My body finally relaxes. The stress of the day took over, forcing me to sleep. Just as I lose my grip on reality, I hear James whisper.

"You are loved too."

Chapter Twenty-One

The warmth being emitted next to me is glorious. A soft piece of flesh is pressed against my mouth. I open my mouth in my half-conscious sleep state, tonguing the smooth skin. It's soft, leaving me wanting more. My mouth takes what it wants. A small, hard bud appears in my mouth. My tongue circles it. My arms tighten around a waist. A groan is released from the other person, but it's not one I'm used to hearing. I open my eyes, taking in my surroundings. I'm wrapped around Megs.

They spread out on the bed at some point, and I curled up next to their side. My arms are around their waist, keeping them close. I've never done much cuddling in the traditionally smaller positions. I'm not the little spoon or the one to curl next to someone's body while they assume more space than me. Addy and Megs get me into this position, and I kind of love it. I take the larger positions with Rosie. But these smaller positions, maybe I should've been doing them all along. Realization slaps me in the face that I am sucking on Megs's nipple.

"Shit, Megs. Sorry."

They press their hand to the back of my head and mutter to keep going. I don't need to be told twice. They didn't wear a shirt to sleep, leaving both breasts exposed. I suck it back into my mouth, playing with it. Shifting my weight, I prop myself up more. My hand slides up their chest to play with their other breast. They moan again, clearly enjoying the touch. Their hand is in my hair, caressing me. I slide my free hand down to their hips, resting on their lower abdomen. I lean over, taking the other nipple in my mouth. I tease my fingers over the hem of their panties. I want to go faster and be inside them. My cock is already fully erect. Waking with a nipple in my mouth will have that effect.

Megs's hips lift under my hand, trying to get closer. A smirk spreads across their nipple, still in my mouth. I look up at their face, wanting to gauge their interest before pressing forward. The night before smacks reality back into me. Their face is swollen; they're unable to open their eye. It's heavily bruised, awful shades of black and purple. Their breast drops from my mouth. My hand moves away from their panties to shift my weight higher.

"Fuck, Megs, your face. I'm sorry. I shouldn't have started this."

They groan at me; their body undulating beside mine.

"Shut up, James, and fuck me."

This makes me nervous, but their hands push and pull me to get me on top.

"You sure, Megs? I don't want to hurt you."

"Now, James!"

Well, I guess I can't argue with that. I shift so I am leaning over their body. Usually, I would kiss them, but the bruise covers half their cheek. I'm worried that would hurt more than it would arouse. Instead, I kiss their neck opposite the bruise. I lick and suck the delicate skin. They stretch their neck, extending to allow more space. I slide my hand back down their body, slipping my fingers under the hem of their panties. I pause there, not wanting to go too fast for them. Their hips roll again as they groan.

I leave a trail of kisses from their neck down to their nipple, resuming my toying from earlier. I slide my fingers lower, softly grazing over their clit. They are soaked as my fingers move down. I caress the soft hairs, pressing the skin teasingly. They moan my name; their own pleasure grows. My cock jerks. The memory of their taste consumes me, making me want this more. I slide a finger up the middle of their core, not plunging deep, just lightly skimming. My mind wants to take this slow and make it enjoyable for them, but my cock wants to plunge deep inside their wet core. I'm losing this battle of moving slowly.

I shift my body on top of them. One finger drags their core. My cock drags along their leg, desperate for contact. I watch their face as my finger slides in and out. They are so wet; it's driving me crazy. My member is jerking, hard as a rock, almost unbearable. My brain has difficulty reconciling the bruises on their face, but this doesn't bother my dick. It just wants more motion. I slide my finger out, rising up to circle their clit.

"Can I kiss you?"

I need their lips. I need more contact. Without saying anything, their hands wrap around my head, pulling me in. Despite the force they are using, I still keep the kiss soft. My tongue slides in, swirling with theirs. I shift my hips again, sliding my dick next to my hand, still massaging their clit. They groan against my kiss, working their hips to get more contact.

"Do you have a condom?"

Megs

Shit. I don't keep condoms in here. I don't have sex with men. This is so crazy. My core is literally throbbing to get more contact. I have never been this worked up before. I'm on birth control. Do we need a condom?

"No..." I say, unsure if I should mention the birth control thing. Maybe he prefers a condom. "Shit," he mutters, climbing off me. "Don't move." He turns towards our shared bathroom but looks back. "Or actually, do move. Take those off before I'm back." He's out of the room, shuffling through drawers in the bathroom. I slide my panties off quickly, tossing them to the side. I don't spend a lot of time fully naked. It feels odd to lie on my bed, completely nude and exposed. Despite the awkwardness, I rub my hands over my stomach, my hips, my sides. I need more touch.

What is taking him so long?

I hear him burst out into the living room, cursing. He is moving away from my room. My bedroom door is shut; I can't see what he is doing. I hear a door open, more drawers, then it closes. Then another door opens. Addy is yelling now. He must be having a hard time finding what he needs. Suddenly, my door bursts open. He stops, staring at me. His chest is heaving, cock tenting his boxers, a box of condoms in his hand. His gaze is hungry, taking in all of my body. I don't usually feel sexy or attractive, but the way he looks at me now sends a fire burning through my entire body. He closes the door, locking it behind him. I guess he's worried about Addy storming in.

He stalks towards the bed. His shoulders look more significant as he looms above. He rips a condom from the box, tossing the torn box to the side. He shoves his boxers off, climbing onto the bed. His gaze never leaves me. Hands grab my shins, spreading them apart, giving him access to where I want him most. He tears open the condom package, tossing it aside too. He slides the condom on while maintaining eye contact.

Part of me feels nervous about the brazenness of his actions; a larger part loves it. A much larger part. I watch his fingers slide the condom down the length of his hard cock. I reach out, unable to help myself. My fingers wrap around his massive girth. I knew he was immense, but it feels much bigger now. Worry washes over me about how he will fit inside me.

He leans over me. His lips press against mine. He is gentle with my face. It's probably a good thing. There is a dull ache. I can feel the blood pumping through the injury, but I want him more than the pain is a problem. He slips two fingers inside me, thrusting in and out. My hand is still on his cock, working him up and down. I try to match the pace of his fingers, but his cock is at an odd angle to my hand. I settle for stroking for now. He is working me to make sure I can fit him. I've played with dildos and vibrators before. Not excessively large ones, though. This could hurt a bit.

He pulls his hand back, placing it on the side of my head. His hips shift, leading his dick to my entrance. My fingers are still wrapped around him, so I line him up. I pull my hand back, placing it on his side. This time doesn't feel as awkward as last time. He nudges his member inside me just a little bit. I groan at the stretch but want more. He is watching my face, searching for a reaction. He is satisfied with what he finds because he presses in again, deeper this time. My hands wrap around his back, holding him closer. He settles on his forearms, pressing his lips against mine again. The feel of his penis inside me, combined with the weight of his body, is different than anything I've ever experienced. I open my mouth, pressing my tongue into his.

He slides in again, this time going to the hilt. His hips rub against mine. I scratch my hand down his back, trying to spur him into action. He is in; now he needs to move. He pulls out so slowly. My back arches, pressing my chest against his. I love the sensation of his skin against my hard nipples. He presses back inside just as slowly as he pulls out. I'm pretty sure my soul will leave my body if he keeps moving this slowly. I jerk my hips, trying to get him to move faster. His weight shifts. His hand moves to cup my breast, rolling my nipple between his fingers. This sends a shockwave through my core, causing a loud moan to break through. With his new position, I drag my hand to his hip, digging my fingers in. There is a wicked grin on his face. He knows what he is doing to me. He's teasing me. He is going to be the death of me.

"James, please."

"Please, what, Megs?"

His voice is deep and smooth, causing my core to clench around him. Momentary bliss prevents me from responding. His lips move up my chest to my neck. My head rolls to the side, giving him better access to those tender spots.

"Slower?"

His breath is hot on my neck as he slows his cock to a standstill. I've changed my mind. I'm going to be the death of him if he doesn't stop teasing me.

"Faster, dammit!"

He chuckles but thrusts into me deeply. This isn't his full thrust; he is holding back for my sake. I don't even care at this point; I just need more. My fingers claw at his hips and back. My hips jerk into his as his pace increases. He shifts back on top of me, his weight on his forearms near my head. He gives me several quick kisses. Not the deep passionate ones, but kisses that still claim. My pleasure grows, threatening to burst through. My core starts clenching around him as he thrusts deeper and more sporadically. His weight shifts again, his hand moving between us to where we are joined.

"Come for me, Megs."

His fingers graze my clit, but his words are my undoing. An orgasm crashes over me, more intense than I have ever experienced. My whole body seizes as pleasure washes through me. He thrusts against my clenching core several more times before slowing. My body relaxes against the bed. My eyes close as I glide into the depths of this sex-driven catharsis. He shifts to my side and collapses. I pull him back over me, feeling the chill of the morning air against my now sweaty skin. He obliges, holding me tightly. He presses several kisses to my cheek as our breathing returns to normal.

"How's your face?"

"It hurts, but I'll be okay."

He sighs and rolls away. I feel empty in his absence. He removes the condom, grabs the wrapper from the floor, and tosses them into the trashcan. He moves back towards the bed, pulling my blanket over me.

"Stay here," he starts to walk away but softly adds, "Please."

I wasn't going to wait, but the way he adds please was heart-wrenching. I don't know what he plans, but I will let him do it.

Addy

James woke me up earlier. At first, I was angry that he was disrupting my sleep because he had no condoms. It took me a few minutes to process why he would need them. Clearly, he ran out, and the bathrooms aren't stocked. Rosie always has some, though. Which means he wasn't in Rosie's room. Which means he is with Megs. As far as I know, they don't typically keep condoms in their room. Why would they?

As the realization settles, I jump out of bed and run into Rosie's room. I fill her in on what's happening, then rush back into the kitchen to make coffee. I don't know how long they will be in that room, but I want to be ready when they come out. Rosie slowly moves into the kitchen, sitting on one of the chairs. I slide coffee to her as the door opens. James is standing there in his underwear, hair disheveled, a slight flush on his face. I instantly start clapping. Rosie, bless her soul, copies me.

"Yay! You finally did it!"

"Hooray."

He freezes, seemingly unsure how to handle being applauded for having sex. He quickly shuts the door but turns between his room and the kitchen. He finally huffs and walks over to us.

"You didn't have to clap. I was just coming out for coffee and Tylenol."

About that time, Megs comes out, fully dressed and carrying clothes in their hand. We clap again, causing them to roll their eyes. They hand the clothes to James, taking a mug of coffee off the table. I get a good look at Megs. Their face looks awful. It's still swollen and black and blue. That can't feel good. I'd forgotten about that last night. I grab the bottle of Tylenol left on the counter and pass it to them. They take a couple, drinking their coffee along with it. James wraps an arm around their shoulder, keeping them close. I've never known Megs to be cuddly. They are usually fine just being in the same area without physical contact. This is new.

"How do you feel, Megs?" Rosie looks over them, taking in their face.

"It's sore and swollen, but I'll be fine."

With utter disregard for decency, I spit out, "Megs, she's asking about your face, not your vagina." They choke at my comment, literally spewing coffee across the kitchen. Rosie groans at my statement, but James laughs, keeping his arms around Megs to keep them upright.

"Dammit, Addy."

"Well, keep your boy toy out of my room next time," I smirk at them. James can enter my room anytime, even for condoms with someone else.

Rosie suggests we need to keep more condoms around, especially in Megs's room. They roll their eyes again. They aren't past the awkwardness of fucking yet. It's surprising, given how much we do, but Megs having sex when they want someone else is different.

"I'm on birth control and clean. I went to the doctor a month or so ago. I don't care if we drop the condoms," I toss out. It doesn't bother me either way. I just wanted to throw that out there. Rosie comments next.

"Same for me."

Megs nods, adding, "I have an IUD. I haven't been to the doctor recently, but I've only been with those two in the past few years," they shrug. If we're clean, they're clean. We all look to James at the same time.

"I'll keep that in mind. I haven't been to the doctor recently, though. I'll get an exam scheduled before I go without a condom. I doubt I have anything, but with Whitney sleeping around, I'd rather be safe."

"Cool, then off to the store for condoms!" I cheer, raising my fist in the air. "Ribbed for her pleasure? Ribbed for your pleasure? Ribbed for our pleasure?" I say, pointing at Rosie, Megs, then James. They all chuckle, shaking their heads at my antics. At least they can agree on something.

Rosie speaks in a more serious tone. "Since we are sleeping together now, maybe we should discuss our relationship again?" I shrug. I'm not opposed to having a discussion, but I'm happy with how things are going. It could change and get more complicated now.

"What do you want to discuss?" James asks.

"What about PDA? Anyone have issues? How will we split time?" Rosie suggests. That's a fair point. There is only one James, but I'm not keeping my hands to myself.

Megs speaks up. They are new to receiving so much touching, seeing as how James is still wrapped around them. "I don't mind the PDA between you three. I have different needs than you do. I can communicate, probably non-verbally, when I want touches. Is it a problem for you three?"

"You know I'm going to be touching everyone." I exaggerate the last word. Honestly, I'll never take anything entirely seriously.

Rosie chimes in after a deep eye roll at me, "I think between Addy and James, we should be covered as long as no one gets jealous. Just be sure to say something if you do." She looks at all three of us, but I wonder who that is for. "We should add James to our Google calendar too." Megs and I both nod, but James looks confused. Rosie picks up on that. "We share a calendar so we can know where each other is. It's helpful with Addy and Megs's irregular work schedules. It helps with important events one or more of us need to be at. Plus, now we can schedule dates or alone time with you or each other. That hasn't been a problem with the three of us, but it could get confusing with four."

James looks impressed with her idea. She is the organized one of the bunch. "Oh! Speaking of important dates," James starts, "my boss is hosting a barbecue after the magazine release. He told us to bring friends or family. Would any of you like to go?" He looks around at all of us. Megs seems excited. They have always been interested in his journalism. Rosie looks a bit more nervous, though.

"Do you want to take us all?" Her fingers are fidgeting on her mug. "We look like a standard couple when we are one on one. We just look like a group of friends when we go out to dinner together, but as a whole, at an intimate event, would it be too much?" James thinks for a minute, then shrugs.

"I get what you are saying. And maybe, in general, we need to decide how we approach being in public, but for this specific event, it would mean a lot to me if you all could come. I've never had anyone to take to these parties. Let alone three amazing people who support me."

"Aww, he likes us." I reach up and pinch his cheeks. Nope, never gonna be serious. "I will come if I can get off work. Just add the event to the calendar." Rosie smiles at me, "As long as it's before school starts back, I will be there too." Megs just rests against his shoulder. We know they'll be there.

"What do I call you?" James asks softly. Now there is a good question. It's not something I have considered. Rosie calls him her boyfriend, and I haven't used a term for him. Just sticking to his name or explaining he's our new roommate. I don't know if Megs has said anything. "Well, I still like boyfriend and girlfriend. If you are looking for a collective term, I don't know, partners?"

Megs adds, "I prefer partners, but also like calling you boyfriend."

James presses a kiss on Megs's forehead. They are just too stinking cute. I love watching them together. No, I don't think PDA will be an issue for me. Being serious, though, that is an issue. "I don't care what terms you use. James is sweet cheeks, Megs will be angel face, and Rosie is obviously my foxy little minx." I move over and wrap my arms around Rosie, kissing her cheeks before sitting next to her. If there is a world record for the number of groans and eye rolls in one conversation, I will take the title.

"I swear to god, if you call me a minx anywhere other than the bedroom, I will bite you."

"Promise??" I nudge her shoulder with mine, teasing her. "Okay, okay. I'll stick with partners too."

We all nod in agreement. Megs begins moving around to make some breakfast. James tries to stop them, insisting they shouldn't be doing that much. His guilt over what happened last night is palpable. Rosie calls him to show him how the Google calendar works, leaving Megs to cook. I didn't intend for them to cook for us, but I won't say no. I love their cooking. It is a release for them after particularly emotional days. Or even good days when they just have extra energy. Whatever the case, I will not say no to Megs's food.

Chapter Twenty-Two

The past couple of weeks have been chaotic. The first week, I was busy at work. We were putting the final touches on the magazine before sending it to the press. This issue will be one of the biggest releases we've had. My article is a massive part of the issue. It has the most significant bomb drop for landowners in the region. It's also the most prominent piece I've written for the magazine. I'm ecstatic but also nervous. Those nerves from last month haven't eased, but I can't figure out why I have them.

After finishing up the magazine, I spend a lot of time fretting over Megs. They swear they are fine. They took a few days off work to let their face heal. There is just a small bruise beneath their eye. They followed through with pressing charges. Whitney spent a couple of nights in jail. She'll have to serve community service and has a restraining order from Megs and me. The plus side to all of that is Whitney finally signed the divorce papers. Her parents paid for her lawyer, who insisted she sign. Apparently, they are all very embarrassed about this situation. Her father even called me to try to smooth things over. I suggested they seek mental health treatment for Whitney. I have no hard feelings towards her parents, though.

Things calm down for a minute once the magazine is finalized and sent to production. I am still dealing with the legal stuff from my divorce, but work has calmed down. Megs is back at work. Rosie is still perfecting her burrito. She only has another week or so before going back to school. She says she dreads it, but we all know she's excited. She may love being a burrito, but teaching is her calling. She's been trying to teach me all kinds of things. She taught me how to use Google calendar, which has been more helpful than I thought. I added the event for the barbecue my boss is hosting. I'm excited to show them off finally. A little nervous, especially if the secretary shows up. She will not like this situation at all.

The magazine dropped today. It looks phenomenal. The design, the photos, even all the articles are perfect. I grab a few extra copies to take home with me this time. Usually, I grab one if it's a special edition for me. I've not had anyone that would want a copy in such a long time. Tonight, I want to go celebrate. Since Whitney finalized the divorce, I need to go to the house and get it ready to sell. I've been paying the mortgage these past few months and desperately want to stop paying for a place I'm not using. I'm meeting the locksmith at seven. Despite actually signing the papers, Whitney said she lost the keys. Go figure.

Rosie is sitting at the high top, playing on her phone. Addy is getting ready for work. I'm standing next to the counter, checking my emails. People have been calling in all day with questions and comments. I've taken some but avoided more. I like talking to some people, but I have my limits. My piece covers everything that could be said. Megs finally comes out of their room. I grab one of the magazines from the stack and wave it in front of them. They squeal and rush over to take it from me. Rosie gets a phone call as I hand the magazine to Megs. They sniff it before flipping through it.

"Oh, hi Daddy....What?"

Rosie has the phone up to her ear, speaking into it.

"Yes, he's a journalist."

She glances up at me. I give her a confused look.

"He works for Under."

Why would her father be asking about me?

"Yes. Witler is his last name."

There is a long silence. Her father is going off on some tangent. Megs has started flipping through the magazine slowly, taking it all in. I'm still watching Rosie. Her tone holds more confusion than anything.

"Libel? Daddy, wait, what are you talking about?"

My ears perk up at that. Megs looks up. They glance between Rosie and me. Rosie reaches over to grab one of the magazines. On impulse, I grab it, opening to my article, knowing exactly where it is. Megs starts flipping through their copy faster, first to the table of content, then to my article.

"No, Daddy. That's not what happened. He didn't...."

Her words fade off as he interrupts her. That unease from earlier is growing. Rosie skims the article. It is long, but the first few paragraphs lay out everything. The rest is just the evidence that solidifies my case. Megs gasps beside me. They turn to face Rosie, glancing up at her before turning their attention back to the article.

"Jail, Daddy... The lawyers... No, please don't put Mom on. Oh, hi, Mom."

I can hear her voice from Rosie's phone, but I can't make out the words. Addy walks into the kitchen, ready for work. She doesn't say anything, noticing the tension. Rosie glances at her, seemingly signaling that shit isn't good. Addy just pauses, waiting for more information.

"No, Mom, I didn't know....No, I don't think...Mom."

Megs glances up from the article. They don't make eye contact with me. Instead, they move past me towards Addy. They hand the piece over, not even saying anything. This can't be good. It feels like everyone knows something that I don't.

"I don't think...Well, no, I can't prove.... I didn't say...."

I watch Addy as she skims the article. Her eyes go wide. I knew the report would be shocking, but I didn't expect this reaction from them. This article is about the landowner.

"Okay, Mom. Yes. I'll come out there tonight. Okay. I love you."

Rosie sniffles as she hangs up the phone. Without saying anything else, she walks towards her room. She looks completely defeated. Addy takes off after her.

She gets into her room after Rosie and closes the door behind them. I look over to Megs, hoping they will explain this. They are glaring at me.

"What in the fuck made you think it was a good idea to ruin your girlfriend's father?"

"Ruin?" My brain is misfiring at all the things they just said. "Father?"

"Yes. Rosie Stewart's father, Martin. Landowner." They look down at the article, skimming all the accusations I printed. "Money launderer, abuser, a bad guy. Oh, here it it. Husband and father."

Megs is seething at me. Their breathing is heavy, their body tense. The other shoe has dropped. This is what that nervous feeling was. I hadn't pieced it together, but it had been there. Rosie Stewart. I had intentionally not looked into his personal life. This article was meant to focus on his work. I knew it wouldn't be good for his family, but I didn't think about the full effect of what would happen. I certainly didn't think I would be this involved in it. I'm staring at Megs like a fish out of water. My mouth is opening and closing with thoughts that aren't coming. I need to say something, but what.

Rosie walks out of the room. She's crying and carrying a bag. I say her name, but she doesn't look at me. Instead, Addy addresses Megs.

"Can you give Rosie a ride out to her parents? Don't stay with her, but I need to get to work. Nick is still being a little bitch with me. I'll go pick Rosie up tomorrow."

They don't acknowledge me as they all move towards the door. Megs slams the magazine on the counter and stomps towards Rosie. They shift their demeanor to a calmer one, wrapping their arm around Rosie as they guide her out of the apartment. Addy stops, looking at me. She's upset about this but also seems conflicted.

"Did you know?"

"I had no idea, Addy. I swear. I didn't look into his personal life."

She nods her head, looking back towards the door. "Rosie is going to stay with her parents for now. They believe Martin could be facing jail time, and they're scrambling to get everything in order," she pauses, fumbling with her keys.

Instead of saying anything else, she just walks out of the apartment. This day has gone fucking sideways, and I don't even know what kind of shit I'm in now.

ROSIE

Megs drives to my parents' house. They are fuming about the article. I had no idea James was working on an article about my father. He never said anything. I don't specifically remember him asking any questions about my family, but I can't be certain he didn't. He's been with us for several months now. I don't remember everything. My father suggested James was only with me to get more information about him. I don't want to believe that. Not after everything we've been through. James does get unreasonably upset over my parents, though.

These conflicting thoughts run through my head as Megs drives. They are also raging mad. They haven't said anything this far. I'm not even sure what to say. I'm devastated that this happened. That it came from James. That I wasn't even aware it was happening in my own home. He never said anything specific about the article. Was he hiding this from me?

I clear my throat. The tears are still streaming down my face, and I can't stop them. I glance over to Megs. They are gripping the steering wheel so tight that I'm worried they'll break it in half. "Did you read the whole article?"

They glance at me, then nod.

"How bad is it?"

They take a long breath, trying to settle their body. "It's bad, Rosie. James accused him of laundering millions of dollars. He also accused him of several workplace violations, tax fraud, and being a terrible boss. If the police could confirm any of that stuff, he could easily go to jail."

A sob escapes. I wipe my eyes, unsure what to do. Can the police confirm what is in the article? "Did you know?" My voice is barely above a whisper. They shake their head again, the anger returning to their body. I stay quiet for the rest of the drive. When they stop, they pull me into a tight hug. I try to take comfort in that, but I know I'm entering a volatile situation. I don't expect tonight to end well.

JAMES

I send off several texts to the group chat. I apologize. I swear I didn't know. I promise I would have told them if I did. I promise to make this better. All of my texts go unanswered. I pull up to my house, stuffing my phone in my pocket. I'm a little early, but that will give me time to assess the yard before going inside. I expect to find the house in decent condition. Whitney may have been crazy, but I don't think she would intentionally destroy the whole house.

The flat yard is overgrown with grass and weeds. It hasn't been attended since I moved out. I didn't cut the grass before I left. I left in May. I usually let the grass grow naturally for the early pollinators. The neighbors hated it but never actually did anything. I would be surprised if there aren't citations from the city about the yard now. It's not a big deal. It'll just take an afternoon to clean up. I have that now. I push away thoughts of what will happen to my partners. I can't fix that if they don't talk to me. I can only fix one problem at a time. So, for now, I'll focus on my house.

The traditional suburban home is in a newer development. The blue and grey siding and white accents all look fine from the driveway. I walk towards the front door, stopping when I get there. The large window from the living room has been broken. I step over, seeing glass in the yard, meaning it was broken from the inside. A sense of dread pools inside me. Walking back to the front door, some of window panes have also been knocked out. Were we robbed, or did Whitney become destructive in my absence? I debate calling the locksmith to cancel, but it's probably too late. I take out my phone to check the time. Definitely not to check the messages. There are none. The locksmith should be here any minute. Instead of going inside, I walk around to the garage. From the outside, everything looks fine. At least I won't need to do much work on the exterior.

The locksmith pulls up. I greet him and explain the situation. I planned on replacing the locks, but a broken door must be replaced before the locks can be effective. I offer to compensate him for time and travel, but he waves me off, asking me to call him when I install the new doors. He leaves, and I walk back towards the front of the house. It's time to do this.

Taking a deep, stuttering breath, I try to brace myself for what's inside. I could handle this on a good day, but today is not a good day. My three partners are gone and mad at me. I've possibly ruined the best thing to ever happen to me, and now I'm standing in the midst of another ruined relationship. At this point, I have to consider the common denominator. It's me. Maybe this is what I deserve. This is what I get for not trying harder with Whitney. For thinking I could have three partners. For not researching Martin's private life before I destroyed it. Tears threaten my eyes. I push the thoughts away, opening the front door.

It's so much worse than I expected. There are holes in the walls. Multiple. Large, small, everywhere. Someone was punching and hitting with different objects. The electronics are all gone. That doesn't surprise me, but I assumed Whitney still lived here. I stand in the living room, taking in all the damage. There is glass and dust from the drywall on the floor. It looks like pillows were ripped open and spread around the living room. It's a mess.

It's hard to breathe. My emotions are swirling through my body. I can't force myself to move. A heavy fog is settling in the room. I'm frozen in my spot, unable to function. I was going to ask Megs to come with me tonight. I'm glad I didn't, but then it hits me how angry they are at me. I can see their glare again. I can feel their eyes on me. Only a few months after I first saw that glare, swearing to do anything not to receive it, it's burned in my mind. Their anger will always take up space there. My chest is tightening, my breathing shallows. A breeze blows outside, lifting the curtains away from the broken window. Tears are streaming down my face. It feels like fire.

My body begins functioning again, slightly. I make my way into the kitchen. It's more of the same, but more broken glass. All of our glassware is destroyed. I spot my favorite mug on the floor. A large chunk is still together, showing the image on it. It's an image of Bruce Willis from Die Hard. A buddy from college bought it for me. With the mug still in my hand, I walk through the kitchen to the stairs. The walls are still covered in holes.

Upstairs, my office space is trashed. Papers are everywhere. Ripped and torn and scattered. The frames I had on the walls are shattered on the floors. I don't stay to assess the rest of the damage. I continue moving down the hall. The guest room doesn't look terrible. The bed is in one piece, though the sheets are shredded. I keep moving. There is no feeling in my body. I'm hollow. Moving through the house is the only thing keeping me from falling into the fetal position. My phone hasn't chimed with a new message. The urge to check is overwhelming, but I know what I will, or won't, see.

I take a deep breath standing outside the master bedroom. My nerves are frayed, and my hand shakes as I reach to turn the knob. I push the door open inside. The room is empty. There is nothing. There are no holes, no curtains, no broken glass. All the furniture is gone, all the clothes, the decorations, everything.

The only thing out of place is a photo. An ample space was behind our bed, and Whitney had mounted a canvas print from our wedding. It is black and white. We both look so happy. Staring at each other while we were taking photos. Her arms are around my shoulders, her bouquet beside my head with her wedding ring on display. A slash is cut straight down the middle between us. The words "Fuck you, James" are written across the image. It looks like she used red lipstick.

Megs

Tears are rolling down my face. I can't stop them. My body aches, a physical manifestation of the emotions swirling inside me. I pull my phone out. The screen is blurry behind the tears. I open it, mostly functioning on muscle memory now. I send out one more text before collapsing to the floor, unable to keep my body upright. Sobs wrack my body on the floor of my empty master bedroom.

> I'm sorry.

He's sent several messages tonight. This one comes through a couple of hours after he left. I'm lying in my bed. I toss my phone further away. The apartment feels unusually quiet. I haven't been entirely alone in the apartment in a long time. Rosie has been here all the time. James is always off work when I get home.

I get time alone in the morning, but I know they are just a wall away. This is different. Their presences aren't here. It's just me and my thoughts and this stupid magazine.

I've read it four times since I returned from dropping Rosie off. My anger is mixed with confusion and hurt, and rage. There are so many damning details in this article. I can't understand how he hid it from us. I don't understand why. He says he didn't know, but we stayed in the man's cabin. James is sleeping with his daughter. Why didn't he look into his personal life, at least to know? Why didn't he tell us the name?

Tears stream down my face. I roll over on the bed, noticing something blue on my floor. I wiggle over to grab it. It's a pair of James shorts. He left them in here the last night he spent with me. He's spent several nights with me since his ex hit me. I had so much trust in him. I actually had sex with him. I let him see me in more vulnerable positions than anyone else. I never thought he would turn and do something like this. A fresh wave of despair rolls over my body. I turn into my pillow, pressing my face against it as the tears roll down.

ADDY

Tonight is not a night I want to spend at the bar. Thankfully, it's almost closing time. I haven't heard anything from Rosie. It's hard to tell if that is a good thing or not. I can't fathom what her parent's house is like now, how they treat her. They don't seem to blame her. They think she is a gullible pawn in James's scheme to bring down Martin. I don't believe that's true, but at this point, I don't know what is and isn't true.

Bruiser is at the bar tonight with the man I saw in the parking lot the night before we went to the cabin. They have sat together all night, but there haven't been any signs of PDA. I've been focusing on him and his friend to distract myself. Thankfully, Nick didn't work tonight, so I don't have to deal with him. It is crowded. Weekends always get busy in August. People are trying to soak up the rest of summer and enjoy their downtime.

"What's up with you, Addy?"

I look at Bruiser with confusion. He is definitely one of the most loyal patrons we have. Maybe the most loyal because he always sits at the bar and chats with us. We all know each other pretty well, aside from who his new friend is.

"Just a little distracted."

He nods as if he understands. I pour him another drink. It's almost closing time now, but I'm not in a huge rush to get back to the apartment. James hasn't texted again. Nobody has. I've messaged Rosie several times, but she hasn't responded. Even Megs isn't texting me back. I'm concerned about this radio silence from everyone.

"I haven't seen that tall guy that was staying in the alley around lately."

I swear Bruiser has some weird sixth sense about things. Maybe he is a witch.

"Ah, yeah. He hasn't been around, has he?"

"It's like some beautiful bartender took him in and kept him away from everyone else. Then he hurt her?"

The last part of his statement is more of a question, and I shoot him an unimpressed look.

"It's complicated."

His buddy gets up and heads to the bathroom. I use this time to take a cheap shot.

"Much like the bar patron that orders obscenely named drinks to send to other men."

He shifts uncomfortably. I know it's low. I'm not in a good head space for deep but secretive conversation. I've always been blunt, but especially so when I am angry. Bruiser straightens his back.

"That's not complicated. I just don't want to share my private life."

I glare at him. "Same." His friend comes back, and I walk away. I'm ready to leave now, but there is still half an hour to go. I stand in the office, staring at my phone. No one is communicating. This isn't a good sign. I decide to call Rosie on my way home. I need to check in with her and see how things are going.

The clock finally hits closing time. I shut everything down and go outside. I've calmed down from my interaction with Bruiser. I'm still on edge. This evening has been hell on my nerves. In the parking lot, Bruiser and his buddy are on their bikes again. This time, they share a quick kiss before climbing on and driving off. A swell of happiness crashes through my chest before disappearing. At least someone is happy. I dial Rosie's number once the car is started and pull out of the parking lot. I have my phone mounted on the air vent with the speaker on.

The phone rings several times before Rosie answers. She sounds sleepy.

"Hey, did I wake you?"

"Yeah," she mumbles. Definitely asleep.

"How are things going?"

"Fine. Busy. Daddy has been with lawyers all night. I've mostly been comforting Mom."

"How is she?"

"She's so concerned about Daddy that she hasn't been terrible to me. She hates James, though. That isn't going away anytime soon."

"Yeah, and how about you?"

"I don't know, Addy."

We sit in silence for several minutes. The city lights stream by outside my window. I don't know what to do. I'm not even sure how to feel. I want to believe James didn't know what he was doing, but is that really possible?

"How long will you stay there?"

"I don't know. Probably through the weekend."

"Okay, Rosie. Go back to sleep. I'll check in tomorrow. Love you."

"Love you too."

The call disconnects, and I'm surrounded by silence again. I don't bother to turn the radio on this time. I drive back in silence, letting my thoughts swirl. The quiet is deafening. The apartment is the same way.

Chapter Twenty-Three

JAMES

The sun is shining bright around me. My body hurts. I open my eyes, taking in my surroundings. I'm in my house, on the floor of my empty master bedroom. Sadness swirls around me. My hands rub my face, but I am stabbed with something sharp. I touch the cut, feeling the sting. Blood stains my finger. I look in my hand, finding the remaining shard of my favorite mug. I never let it go last night. I toss it across the room, touching the cut again. It isn't bleeding fast, so I just leave it alone.

I check my phone. No new messages. It is also at 10% battery life. There are no functional chargers in the house. With the remaining battery, I order some food to be delivered, enough for a couple of days. I don't know if they will let me back to the apartment. I'll need to go back eventually, but it won't be now. Lifting my body off the floor takes more effort than I am used to. It feels heavy, like I'm swimming in a thick fog trying to keep me down.

In the kitchen, I sweep most of the glass over to the side of the room. I don't bother with picking it up. The big chunks just need to be out of the way. I'll keep my shoes on while I'm here. I search the cabinet for any remaining dishes. There are none. I find a couple of paper plates left over from some party. That will be fine.

I open the fridge. A putrid smell hits me. Moldy, decaying fruits and vegetables inside release an offensive odor, along with several mystery items. The fridge is unplugged. Everything is wet and moist. I shut the door. A deep sigh leaves my chest. I don't even bother opening the freezer. It was an appliance Whitney insisted on. Large, expensive, a custom color. I bought it for her because she swore it would tie the room together. Now it just stands like an unwavering knight guarding something precious, but nothing is precious here.

The food is finally delivered. I try to eat some but can only manage a few bites. I leave the stuff on the counters. No sense in putting it away. The counters are the safest. I sweep the glass onto the floor. They should be fine for now. I try to make a list of things that need to be done, but every time a new item goes on the list, my mind shuts down and refuses to actually compile a list. There are just things floating around my head. I give up after a couple of minutes. A nap in the bed may help.

I trudge to the guest room with the shredded sheets. I pull them aside, checking the mattress underneath. That was left intact, thankfully. I lay down on the bed, swiftly falling back asleep. My mind and body can't handle this situation.

Megs

I make coffee like always. It's not until after I start everything that I realize there are only two of us instead of four. Maybe Addy will drink a lot of coffee today. She walks in when the coffee is finished, and I hand a mug to her. She nods thanks, taking a sip. She leans against the counter near me. My body aches. I feel like I've run a marathon. Sleep evaded me most of the night, but the tears did not. Nothing makes sense. Nothing feels right.

"Have you heard from either of them?"

"No."

Addy shakes her head, implying she hasn't either. I sigh, sipping my coffee. I don't know what we should do at this point. James didn't come home last night. I assume he is giving us space, but he hasn't texted or called either. We don't know what happened at his house. Rosie is dealing with her parents, a significant feat by itself. Addy and I are along for the ride at this point. Addy breaks the unbearable silence still surrounding the apartment.

"Do you think James knew?"

"I don't know," I shrug. "It's almost hard to believe he didn't, but it's also hard to believe he wouldn't tell us. Either he's a phenomenal actor or at least partially an idiot." The last word comes out with more malice than I intend, and Addy nods.

"I don't think he knew," she pauses, collecting her thoughts. "I think he would've given Rosie a heads up. I think he was so wrapped up in sex and relationship shit that he overlooked that major detail."

"The problem, though, is that it is a major detail."

Addy just nods, not offering any other commentary. We finish our coffee in silence. The silence is becoming overwhelming. When my mug is empty, I turn to put it in the sink but see the container of coffee sitting on the counter. Tears stream down my face as I tell Addy, "I accidentally made too much. I forgot..." A sob gets out before I can stop it. Addy wraps her arms around me tightly, holding me to her chest.

"Why does it hurt so much?"

"Because you love him and Rosie."

ROSIE

Aside from being angry about James, my parents are being surprisingly kind. They are distracted but insist on having meals together. The mood is dark, angry, and anxious. We are all waiting for the fallout of the article. My mother swears the article is pure libel with no basis. My father never comments when she goes off on this tirade. This concerns me, but I haven't confronted him about it. My father can be very intimidating when I feel strong and secure. Now, I feel weak and brittle. I don't think I could handle the force of my father's mood.

I've spoken to Addy and Megs several times over the weekend. I question how much James knew when he published it. When my parents first called, they had me convinced he knew. I was so caught up in the possibility of Daddy going to jail that I couldn't process the other information. Knowing James the way we do, I can't believe this was a malicious attack. He's never met my father, as far as I know. Addy is confident now that he didn't know. Megs is still torn. They aren't handling this well. Addy told me they were upset, crying a lot, and just unhappy. I know the feeling. Megs trusted James so much. They are in love with him. They also loved his writing. This was a hard blow for all of us.

It's been four days since the article was released. We haven't heard from James again. We think he is staying at his house, but we can't be sure. Addy has tried to call him a couple of times. Neither Megs nor I am ready to try to contact him. I only have a few more days before I return to school to set up my class. I'm not ready for the summer to be over now. I want this situation to clear before then, but I don't think it will. I had Addy and Megs bring my Jeep out over the weekend, so I would have a way to travel. I haven't left, though. Daddy has stayed locked in his office. I've been comforting Mom. She plans to stay with her sister in Mississippi for a few days while Daddy sorts everything out. I can't help but wonder if him keeping his work hidden from us has made this situation worse.

I'm sitting in the living room with Mom. I'm reading a magazine while she's playing on her tablet. Daddy has been in his office for several hours now. He has several lawyers and business partners in there too. Suddenly, there is a loud knock on the door.

"Police. Open up."

Mom and I both look at each other. We're both startled by this announcement. We jump into action. She rips the door open, demanding to know what this is about. They ask if Daddy is available. Before Mom can answer, they hand her some papers, saying they have a search warrant for this property and several others. An officer shoves in, corralling my mother and me into the living room. Mom is crying, yelling random thoughts. They don't even make sense. More officers move in, combing through the house.

After several minutes, several cops walk through with Daddy in handcuffs. He is stoic, looking out the door as the cops lead him outside. Mom and I both jump up, following them out. She is in full-blown hysterics now, and her words are unintelligible. Daddy is calm though, angry but calm. He commands her to get ahold of herself and stay with her sister. He looks at me.

The reality of the situation sets in. Daddy is being arrested. He isn't being arrested because of libel. The cops have warrants. Multiple warrants. For arrest and search and seizure. They have probable cause to attain those warrants. Daddy has been holed up with the lawyers trying to prevent this. He wasn't mad that my boyfriend had written the article. He was furious that he was caught. He is mad that he is facing jail time. He's also probably mad that it was my boyfriend that did it.

I stare into his eyes, a calm washing over me. I'm devastated that my father would do something like this, but is that surprising? He never shared any of his work with us. He told us he was a businessman. James's article was about the landowners in the region. Daddy was using the land to launder the money. He's probably been doing it my entire life. This is why there was always so much security. Why the cabin has gates and fences, and he wanted cameras. I wonder what that property is supposed to be, what Daddy has told everyone else it is.

The cops apparently get tired of my stare-off with my father. They shove him towards the car. He moves without saying anything to me. That hurts worse than anything else. He has no words for me, his only daughter. He knows I realize the truth, though. He knows I can see who he is now. The tears stream down my face as I stare at him in the car. His gaze is fixed on the front windshield. My mother is next to the car, crying and screaming for his attention. She couldn't have known what was happening. I doubt he trusted her enough with anything, let alone something of that magnitude.

Eventually, my father's lawyers come out. The oldest, who has been with us the longest, tries to coral my mother. One of the investigators asks me if I could give a statement. I agree, but my father's lawyer says they need to be present. I ask for the man's card and if I could give a statement at another time. He nods, handing me the card. I walk to the living room and wait quietly until the cops finish their search. As I sit, I pull out my phone and open the group messages. I debate which group to text. I finally settle on the one with Addy, Megs, and James.

> He's been arrested.

> I'll be home late.

I shut my phone off. While I grasp the situation, I'm not ready to talk about it.

I get home late in the evening. Even though it is a weeknight, the three of us sit in the living room. I tell them everything that happened. Before I left, I got the investigator away long enough to ask how much evidence they had. He couldn't tell me much but said he wasn't worried about a conviction. Suddenly, it didn't matter if James knew or didn't know who Martin Stewart was. James knew what he had done and was out to expose that story. I still don't know what information the cops have. I don't know what pieces of James's article are authentic or just speculation, but he knew. For now, it's enough that he told the truth in his article.

We stay up late talking, crying, drinking, and crying some more. We eventually all fall asleep on the couch, not wanting to be apart from each other any longer. I am snuggled between Addy and Megs. They call into work the next day, informing their employers they have personal issues to deal with. I'm thankful for that. It means we can deal with this together. At a time that feels really early in the morning, my phone rings. As I pick it up, I realize it is not really early. It is close to lunchtime. I don't recognize the number but decide to answer anyway.

"Hello?"

I sit up, pulling away from Megs and Addy. Both are waking up slowly now.

"Is this Rosie Stewart?"

"Yes, who is calling?"

"Hi, this is kind of awkward, but I'm James's coworker. We ran into each other at the office one time."

My face blushes at that memory. I never did find out how much this man heard when I was with James.

"Oh, right. How can I help you?"

"Right, well, James hasn't been to work. We were wondering if you knew his whereabouts."

I stand up suddenly.

"He hasn't been at work?"

I start pacing around the apartment. We didn't consider that James isn't still doing things he is supposed to do. We just thought he was staying at his house to give us space. We resolved last night to talk with him today.

"No. He skipped the barbecue this weekend. None of us have seen him since Friday."

"Shit."

I look to Addy and Megs, who are more awake now. I wave my hands at them to get them moving. They grasp the severity of the situation. They both jump up and run over to me.

"Do you have the address for his old house?" I ask the man.

"No. He took it off file and changed it to a P. O. box a few months ago. We can't find the address any more."

"Fuck. Okay. Um, sorry. No. I haven't seen him, but I'll let him know to call you if we do."

He says thanks, and we disconnect. I rub my hands over my face. James has been missing since Friday. He texted late Friday night, but we haven't heard anything since then. My mind is racing through all the scenarios. Did he crash? Did his ex get to him? Did my father? Is that something my father would do? Addy's hand squeezes my shoulder. Right, I haven't told them.

"James hasn't been at work since Friday."

I look between the two of them. Shock and fear cover their faces.

"What is the address of his house?"

"He wrote it down and stuffed it in one of these drawers."

Addy rushes into the kitchen, pulling drawers out and digging around. Megs and I follow suit. We get more frantic the more drawers we go through.

"Did he leave it in his room?" I ask quickly, making my way to his room.

"Got it!" Addy yells, holding a yellow piece of paper up. "Get dressed, and let's go. We'll start at his house."

We all rush into our bedrooms to put on clean clothes. I settle for jeans and a tank top today. I'm in no mood to deal with the loose material of a dress. This is serious. As I step back into the living room, my stomach grumbles loudly. I haven't eaten since the cops showed up yesterday. As much as I want to go straight to James's house, I need food. I won't be any help if I'm hangry. I have more than enough emotions swirling inside of me without adding hunger into the mix.

"I'm gonna need food and coffee before we get there. Maybe we can take something for James too? I'll order now, and we can just grab it in the drive-thru. Do you want anything?"

I'm rambling, but Megs and Addy don't say anything about it. They're just as worried as I am. They tell me what they want, and we settle on food for James. Megs drives my Jeep. We want to stay together, but I'm in no shape to drive. My car has the most room, though. We grab our food, then head to James's house. I don't finish the breakfast sandwich I ordered. My stomach will only tolerate half of it. I drink more of the coffee but realize that was a mistake. My nerves were already not good. Now I'm jittery on top of that.

We turn into James's neighborhood. My anxiety kicks up, hoping he is still at his house. It's been five days, though. My stomach is tight with worry. His neighborhood is lovely. It doesn't surprise me that this is the type of home he had with his ex-wife. We turn a corner, and I shout from the backseat, "There's his car!"

Hope floods my system seeing his car still in the driveway. Maybe he has been hiding out for a few days and forgot to tell anyone. He's not great at sharing details. The yard is a mess, like no one has lived here for months. I thought his ex-wife was living here. Was she not maintaining the lawn?

Megs parks next to his car, and I rush out of the vehicle. Addy follows behind with the food. As we get to the door, my heart drops. Broken glass is everywhere, and the entry isn't locked, not that it would matter with broken windows. Addy curses and Megs walks up. Now I'm glad I wore sneakers instead of sandals. Addy pulls me back, not letting me go in first.

We walk inside, taking in the damage to the house. It's completely trashed. My heart speeds up, worried something happened while James was here. Addy calls out to him, but we are met with silence.

"Should we call the cops?" I ask tentatively.

"I'm not waiting," Megs steps around me, running through the house. Addy and I do the same, picking different areas to search. Megs climbs upstairs; I turn down the hall, searching other rooms on the first floor. Addy moves into the kitchen.

"There's food here. He's been here," Addy calls out from the kitchen.

I search through the rooms, not finding anything else. I make it into the kitchen. Bags of chips are open on the counter. A box of James's favorite crackers is spilled on the counter. Several of his other preferred snacks are sitting out, uncovered. I look up to Addy.

"They're stale, but it's recent. There's a receipt from this weekend."

"Up here!"

Megs calls from upstairs. Addy and I rush up there. My heart is pounding. I'm terrified of what we will find. Megs isn't in the hallway. We have to check each room until we find them. In the last room at the end of the hallway, Megs is on the floor, wrapped around James. My heart jerks, a sob bursting out. Addy and I drop to the floor, throwing our arms around any part of James we can. For several minutes, no one says anything. We hold him, crying in a giant pile.

I pull back, needing to look at him. His eyes are glazed over. His skin looks taut, and he has deep purple bags under his eyes. I stroke his cheeks as he sits up. I wrap my arms around him, then the smell hits me. It smells like he hasn't bathed in several days. Probably since the last time we saw him. He looks dehydrated. I sit back again, wiping my eyes. Megs and Addy start fussing over him. I take in the room around us. It's empty and in surprisingly good shape compared to the rest of the house. There is a single item in the room. It's a photo from James's wedding with words written over a slash down the middle. He's been staying in this room since he left. He's been torturing himself.

I turn my attention back to him. He's still watching me. Addy and Megs stop what they are doing and look at me too. I don't actually know what to say, but James speaks first.

"I'm sorry. I didn't know."

His voice is weak and gravelly like he hasn't spoken in several days. He coughs, and his body heaves in deep, dry sobs. I slide in front of him, wrapping my arms around him tightly. He hugs me back, and I don't even care about the odor.

"I know. It's not your fault. He was arrested."

I hold him for a minute before leaning back. I need more answers now.

"James," he shivers as I say his name, "have you been here the whole time?"

He looks at each of us, nodding and dropping his head. Addy and Megs move closer to him, touching him, offering support.

"Have you eaten anything other than the chips and crackers?"

He doesn't even look up this time. He just shakes his head no.

"Have you had anything to drink?"

Again, he shakes his head. He holds out his hand, a broken piece of a mug in his fingers. Addy stands and leaves the room. I don't say anything else to him. I just run my fingers across his cheek, down his neck. He isn't okay, but it's not terrible. He's dehydrated and exhausted but still alive.

"Where is your phone? You need to call work."

"It's dead. Don't have a charger."

I pull mine out as Addy comes back into the room. She brings the food we grabbed for James at the drive-thru. It's not the best for dehydration, but it'll still help. I open my phone app to call James's coworker and realize I don't know his name.

"James, who was that coworker that interrupted us when you were eating me out in your office?"

Megs and Addy are shocked at my question. Addy starts to smirk, but Megs keeps the shocked look on their face. James smiles softly. He gives me a name, then takes the food and drink from Addy, starting to eat. I don't usually like being crass, but it might help break some tension. I call his coworker and let him know James has just been sick and will need a few more days off. The guy says he'll tell their boss. James nibbles on the food, leaning against Megs. Addy is holding his drink, rubbing his leg.

"Can we go home now?"

JAMES

I relish that Rosie asked if we could go home. She called it home. That's what it is. My body hurts. Every inch of it. I've alternated between sleeping on the bed and the floor. I haven't been able to do much more than sleep. My body wouldn't allow me to get further than a different room. I made it to the kitchen a few times but was right back to a room. I've spent the past few days in a fitful sleep or lying on the floor. The weight of my reality was too heavy for me to move through.

I was asleep when they got to the house. I didn't even hear them come in. It wasn't until Megs was wrapped around me that I realized I wasn't alone in the house. The danger that I could have been in was never a concern. It wasn't that I wanted something to happen to me. I just wasn't strong enough to fight back or protect myself from anything.

We all pile in Rosie's Jeep and drive home. They promise we will come back for my car soon, assuring me I won't do it alone. We don't speak much on the way home. Rosie drives, and Megs sits with me, not taking their hand off me. Addy keeps handing me food and drinks. My stomach is full, though. I do try to drink more, knowing I am dehydrated.

At the apartment, relief washes over me. Before I say anything, Rosie pulls me towards my room, then into the bathroom. She drops my hand, steps to the tub, and turns on the water. She checks the temperature, then puts the plugin for a bath. I know I smell bad. I couldn't bring myself to bathe while I was there. The shower curtains were gone, and I couldn't fathom sitting in a bathtub.

Megs and Addy come in and help me remove my clothes. Part of me feels embarrassed, but I want that bath, whatever the cost. Once naked, I step into the tub, sinking in the water. It's not a large tub, but it's enough. Rosie sits on the edge of the tub, splashing water over me. I close my eyes, letting the warmth consume me.

Addy and Megs are standing against the counter, watching Rosie and me. They're scared to let me out of their sight. Something tightens in my chest. I take a deep breath, but Rosie begins to speak before I can say anything.

"My father never told us about his work stuff. It was always separate. Mom always told me he was just a business owner. I had no idea about all of the properties. When the article dropped, my father was angry. It wasn't until last night that I realized he was angry because he was caught. My mom tried blaming you. She insisted it was libel. She swore you had something against our family. That was why you were so rude to her. Why you stayed with me. Why you hid this article from me while obviously stealing information from me." A tear rolls down her cheek. My hand moves to wipe it away, but I remember my hand is wet. That will only make it worse.

"I'm so sorry I believed them. I was so caught up in the thought of my father going to jail that it took me time to stop and realize this wasn't your doing." She struggles when she says, 'my father.' She has always called him Daddy. This must be her way of coming to terms with who her father is, not just who he is to her. "You didn't do anything wrong, and I'm sorry I treated you so terribly." She's sobbing now, and I don't care about my wet hands. I reach up, cupping her face, and bring hers to mine.

Megs walks over, touching my arms. "I'm sorry I didn't give you the benefit of the doubt. I should have known you wouldn't do that intentionally." I move my hand from Rosie's face to Megs's arm, pulling them close. I lean back, looking at both of them and Addy. "I should have researched his personal life more. I knew this would be devastating. I should have known who I was doing this to. I'm so sorry."

Addy steps forward. She places a hand on Rosie's back, the other on my head. "I'm sorry I didn't kick some sense into their asses sooner." We all chuckle softly. Rosie grabs my loofa and soap, washing my body. Addy washes my hair with shampoo. Megs goes into my room and brings clean clothes out. It's odd to be bathed by other people, but I don't fight it. They probably need the closeness as much as I do.

After the bath, we settle in the living room. Addy grabs the remote, starting Die Hard. Rosie adjusts the couch, moving the pieces so it's large enough for all of us to lie together. Megs heads into the kitchen, prepping what I'm sure will be a healthy snack. Rosie pushes me down, grabbing her burrito blanket and wrapping it around us. Addy sits on the other side of Rosie. Megs finally brings the tray of fruits and candy over. I raise my eyebrows at them. They shrug, insisting some comfort foods are necessary. We spend the rest of the afternoon cuddling up, watching my favorite movies. My body is still sore, but my soul is being pieced back together.

Chapter Twenty-Four

Addy and I call into work, taking the rest of the week off. We are all emotionally drained from the events of the last few days. Finding James curled up on the floor of his master bedroom was gut-wrenching. It terrifies me to think what would've happened if we didn't find him when we did. Every time the thought crosses my mind, my breath catches. I have to remind myself that everything is fine.

We spend two days in the living room. We watch movies, sleep, play a few games, read books. We soak up each other's companionship. James tells us about his sources and how he got the information. We order take-out. We also force so much water on James he could fill a swimming pool. By the weekend, he is looking much better. Then Addy tells us we should deal with his house.

That is a bomb no one really wants to deal with, despite it being necessary. We decide to all go out together. We list what needs to be done and start working through it. We take a lot of stuff with us, food, cleaning supplies, a speaker for music, and extra brooms. We probably have too much. Rosie suggests we not leave James alone at all. One of us should stay with him at all times. We don't want him to slip back to where he was. He hasn't returned to his normal personality but isn't curled in the fetal position anymore. We don't want him getting back to that.

At the house, we walk through together. Rosie is making a list of everything that needs to be done. Addy is calling out different things she notices. I stay next to

James, holding his hand. He is silent, taking in the damage caused by his ex-wife. We walk through each room. Some are worse than others. We reach the garage. This room was left alone. Several tools and machines are in good condition. Rosie looks down at her list. "So, this isn't as bad as I thought. Can you call contractors to fix the walls and glass? Or is that something you want to do?"

"I'll call someone. I don't want to deal with it."

"I'll go mow the yard. I haven't done that in years and could use the exercise." Addy steps over to the mower, pulling things out and assessing what remains there. James reaches over and opens the garage door, and it creaks open slowly.

"Good. You start making calls, and Megs and I will start cleaning up the rooms," Rosie instructs.

We all set about our tasks. James goes into the kitchen to make calls, and Rosie starts in there. I head upstairs, working my way through those rooms. They aren't bad and shouldn't take long. I hear the lawn mower start up outside. It takes us several hours, but we eventually get the house in decent shape. James has several people coming out next week, including a realtor. The house should be on the market by the end of the month.

Rosie

Saturday was busy. We spent all day at James's house, preparing it for sale. It still needs work from the contractors, but it's all been scheduled. James handled the whole process better than I hoped. It couldn't have been easy for him. He lived in that house for many years, and it nearly broke him when he returned after finalizing his divorce. He has us now and the apartment. I may be biased, but the apartment is better anyway.

We're relaxing on the couch Sunday morning. I have to go back to the classroom this week. Summer is almost over. I'm excited to meet my new students, but I don't want my time at home to end either. Overall, it's been a great summer.

"Hey," I say to everyone, getting their attention from the cooking show we've been watching for several hours. "Let's go out tonight." They all nod in agreement. We settle on going to a restaurant then to a club for dancing. Nothing wild, but fun nonetheless.

I shower and get dressed. I pull on a silky dress that stops mid-thigh. It has a low neckline and a plunging back. It's sexy and fun. It'll be perfect for dancing. It's a deep blue navy color, almost black in some light. I leave my hair down, letting the curls do what they want. Some days I can control them; some days, I can't. Today falls somewhere in the middle. I apply makeup, choosing bright pink lipstick and natural eye shadows. I slip on a pair of pink pumps. I walk into the living room, where James is already waiting. He has on dark jeans with a grey button-up shirt. He looks fantastic. The color has returned to his face. The dark circles are gone. He doesn't look like the same person we found in his home just a few days ago.

As I walk out, he gives me a two-syllable 'damn.' I swoon at his words. I step up to him, wrapping my arms around his strong shoulders. He places his hands on my hips, and I press my lips against his. He kisses me back, sliding his hands across my skin. I part my lips, letting his tongue slip into my mouth. My hands tighten around his neck, not wanting to let go. We kiss for several moments before he pulls away.

"You're beautiful, Rosie."

"I love you, James."

The words break out faster than I mean for them to. He looks startled at first. I bite my lip, worried he doesn't feel the same way. I'm afraid I messed things up with the article. I knew before the article how I felt about him, and I was just scared to tell him or admit it to myself. I'm not breathing, preparing myself for heartbreak. Just as I am about to tell him he doesn't need to say it back, that I just wanted him to know, a huge grin spreads across his face.

"I love you too, Rosie."

I wrap my arms around him, hugging him tightly. He hugs me back just as tight. We stay pressed together, enjoying the touch of each other. Addy walks into the room, griping about her shoes. James and I pull away from each other, but he presses a quick kiss on my lips. I step over to help her out. I probably should have told Megs and Addy I planned on telling him that, but it wasn't intentional. I'm not trying to hide this from them, but I will keep it between James and me for now. It'll be our little secret. I look back, winking at him before Megs comes out, and we head to the car.

JAMES

Rosie loves me, and I am head over heels in love with her. And Addy. And Megs. It's weird to think about not only being in love but also in a committed relationship with three different people. I would never have considered it if it weren't for them. It's a stark contrast to my supposedly monogamous marriage. It is everything I could ever want and more. I love every minute I get to spend with the three of them.

In the car, Rosie drives. Addy sits in the front passenger seat; I sit in the back with Megs. They have been touching and cuddling more since they brought me back from the house. I don't know if it is something that will last or not, but I plan to soak up every bit I can. I am holding their hand, stroking my thumb against theirs. Rosie and Addy are chatting idly. I'm content to just sit back and listen.

At the restaurant, we are seated and order drinks. Megs sits next to me again, keeping their hand on my leg. They are wearing the outfit I like best on them. Dark jeans, white button-up with sleeves rolled up and top buttons undone. They didn't wear the suspenders today, though. We talk and laugh through dinner. It's a beautiful evening. So much calmer than past restaurant experiences. It's such a cathartic evening; I never want it to end.

After we finish eating, Addy and Rosie go to the bathroom. Megs stays with me. I have noticed they don't like leaving me alone, and I can't say I blame them. I can only imagine the terror of finding me the way they did. When Rosie and Addy are out of sight, I lean over to Megs. I press a small kiss to their neck. Their hand tightens on my leg. I kiss their ear several times before whispering to them.

"I love you, Megs."

They gasp, leaning away to look at me. A big goofy grin is plastered on my face.

"Are you serious?"

I laugh at their question. "Yes, goof wad. I love you." They furrow their eyebrows at me.

"I don't think you're supposed to call someone names when you tell them you love them."

"Well, if that someone would just say it back, I wouldn't have to call them names, dingus."

They laugh at me this time.

"And what makes you so sure I want to say it back?"

I wrap my arms around their waist, pulling them in close. "Because you love me too." I press several kisses against their neck. They stretch their neck, giving me better access. They wrap their arms around my shoulders, keeping me closer. They drop their head so their mouth is next to my ear.

"I love you, too. So much."

I pull back to kiss them. Before we get a chance to deepen the kiss, Addy and Rosie return. "Get a room, you two," Rosie quips. I release Megs, laughing at Rosie. We all leave the restaurant, heading back to the car. I hold Megs's hand. Rosie walks next to me, linking her arm around mine as we walk. Addy follows close behind, messing around on her phone.

Addy suggests we go to her bar when we get in the car. It wasn't the original plan, but I have nothing against it. We all agree, and Rosie begins driving that way. On the way to the restaurant, Megs and I sat in the seats by the door, holding our hands over the middle seat. This time, I pull them into the middle seat, keeping them close to me. They rest their head on my shoulder during the drive. This is the peace I have needed in my life.

Addy

We haven't all been to my bar before. All of them have come separately. Rosie and Megs have visited me before, but we've never been when I wasn't working. I love the bar for its atmosphere, not just because I work there. I can't think of a better way to end a fucking roller coaster of a week.

I held things together on the outside, but I was definitely breaking. Everything was wrong last week. Rosie and James's absence was noticed in the apartment. I hadn't realized how full of life our apartment had been since he moved it. He's made such an impact on our lives; I can't imagine not having him around. All of us were emotional and moody. We need to build our trust and communication. That's really saying something coming from me. No relationship is perfect, and ours isn't any different.

At the bar, it's mostly quiet. There are a few people around. Thankfully Nick isn't in. I messaged the other bartender to be sure he wasn't around. If he watches that closely, he may spot me on the security camera, but I don't think he does. I didn't want to get the third degree over coming to the bar after nearly a week of personal time. I didn't explain the situation to him and don't intend to.

I spot Bruiser at the bar. I step up next to him, being sure my gang is close. They start ordering drinks, but I chat with Bruiser.

"Hey, how's it going, Bruiser?"

"Can't complain, Addy. Can't complain."

"There are some people I want you to meet. This is James, Rosie, and Megs. They're my partners."

Megs and Rosie smile politely at Bruiser. James gives him a wave, wrapping his arm around my waist. Bruiser's eyes raise in shock, but he still acknowledges them all.

"Three partners, huh? That's...."

"A lot," I supply with a laugh.

"I was going to say interesting, but that sounds right too," he gives a loud belly laugh, holding onto his stomach as he does. When he settles down, he leans back, motioning to the man on his side. I instantly recognize him as the guy from the parking lot. He's the one I gave the drink called blow job to rush them out of the bar.

"Addy, this is Gregg, my... boyfriend."

He stumbles over the word but grins wildly when he says it. I match his grin, greeting Gregg. Bruiser looks so happy with him. Gregg wraps his hand over

Bruiser's arm. It fills me with joy to see the two together. I just hope this means Bruiser ordering obscenely named drinks is over. We chat for a couple more minutes while my gang's drinks are made. Once we have them, we walk to a table, waving to Bruiser and his boyfriend.

I fill everyone in at the table on Bruiser's role in my bar and his intuition about James. The energy from the restaurant has carried over here. We are all laughing and talking, and everything feels right and natural. We order more drinks. Rosie orders soda to stay sober to drive. Before too long, one of my favorite songs comes on. Megs is still canoodling with James. So I grab Rosie and drag her to the dance floor. There is no way she got that dressed up to not show it off. We saunter out to the dance floor in front of the jukebox. It's not a large space, but it's enough for several people. Since no one else is here, we have plenty of room.

I hold Rosie close as we move to the beat. We dance in sync. It's been a long time since we have danced together in public. I put my hands on her sides, keeping her close. Her arms stretch around mine. As we move, I kiss her neck several times. No matter who else is in my life, Rosie will always be my first love. I whisper dirty words in her ear, making her blush beautifully. She's always gorgeous, but a blush enhances her features. Megs and James join us on the dance floor when the song changes. We all dance together, moving to the beat, touching each other playfully, and having a great time. Soon, Bruiser and his new boyfriend join us.

The next hour goes by with all of us dancing, switching partners, and dancing some more. I dance with both Bruiser and his new boyfriend. Gregg has been after Bruiser for years but could never get him out of his shell. The drink I delivered was Bruiser's final nudge to accept him. Gregg thanks me several times for that. Bruiser and Gregg head back to the bar and eventually leave together. Rosie and Megs head back to the table, leaving James and me on the dance floor. A slow song comes on. I glance over at the jukebox. I didn't even realize these songs were on there. I thought they were all party songs. James steps towards me, holding his hand out to me.

"May I have this dance?"

I laugh but take his hand. He pulls me in close, wrapping his arms around my back. I settle into his warmth, breathing in his scent. "Thank you for bringing us here tonight. We needed this." I wrap my arms around his neck, resting my head on his shoulder. I sigh happily, content with everything that has happened. We sway together slowly. My gang is the only people left in the bar. The employees are closing everything down, and I know our time is ending.

As the song winds down, I adjust to pull away from James. His grip tightens, holding me in place. "Addy," he whispers. I pause, waiting for him to say more. My arms are loosely draped around his shoulders. His breathing is quick, like he's nervous.

"What, James?"

He blows out a deep breath.

"I love you."

I squeeze him tightly. I'm not one to drop the L-bomb much. I always tell Rosie and Megs, but they are the only people.

"I love you, too."

Guess I have another name to add to the list of people I say the L-word to.

Epilogue

We are going to a Halloween party tonight. We have fallen into a good routine in the apartment. Thanks to Rosie's planning skills, we make events and get time alone in a relationship with four people. It isn't always perfect. We are getting better at it. My house sold shortly after we listed it on the market. A few contractors were able to fix up all the damage Whitney caused. I haven't heard a peep from her since the incident Addy lovingly refers to as "Megs punch bag day." I hate when she calls it that, but everyone else laughs. I'm glad we can laugh about that now.

Rosie's father is in jail, awaiting his court date. He tried to get out on bail, but the court deemed him a flight risk and denied it. I gave all of my information to the cops working the case. They had already built a significant case against him. My article was the final push to arrest him. There were a few bits of information I was able to supply. Rosie was asked to testify against her father. She had witnessed some of the lawyers removing evidence from the house. She agreed to give a statement but refused to appear in court. They told her that was fine. They had enough evidence against Martin that it wouldn't matter either way. Her mother has been in Mississippi. She still calls Rosie frequently, but Rosie always ends the call when her mother makes rude remarks. I'm so proud of her. She's struggled with the idea of who her father is and setting boundaries with her mother. She is working hard, though.

This party is mainly for Rosie, but also for me. I won a couple of local awards for my article. We never did get to celebrate after it was released. I explained to my boss what happened. He was very understanding and didn't hold it against me. He's even given me a few easier articles to write since then. I have been so paranoid about making the same mistake that I haven't been able to properly write articles about people. I've taken on different stories for the time being. I hope to get back to writing normally, but for now, I take it one day at a time. And attend therapy regularly. That helps, too.

This is a dress-up party. I convinced Megs and Addy to help me with this party. It isn't just a regular party. This party is happening in the sex dungeon Addy prefers. That is a secret from Rosie, though. We realized all of our fantasies have been acted out, except for Rosie's. Addy got to chase me. I had sex with Megs. And I have gotten to watch them all several times. I can't prove it, but I am definitely the luckiest man on earth. The idea for the party came to me when Rosie told me she bought a spider costume to wear to school on Halloween. Since spiders spin webs and webs look like rope, I knew I needed to be in rope for her. We told her we all had costumes, but I've managed to keep mine a secret, acting unsure about what I would wear.

Addy is going as a dominatrix. She has a full leather suit, the highest heels I have ever seen, and she's walking around with her flogger and riding crop. It's not her costume so much as a regular Tuesday for her. Though, she does have the excuse to wear the suit. We don't usually go that far on Tuesdays. Megs is dressed up like a skeleton. They have on a black body suit with bones on the front. They painted their face to look like a skull. Overall, the outfit looks great. I have on jeans and a regular shirt. Megs and Addy are tying rope around me to look like a bug caught in a spider web, but less messy and more aesthetically pleasing. I have learned the thing about rope is patience. Rosie has the patience to make the knots beautiful. Megs, Addy, and I have the patience to get the rope on. We all snip at each other several times before they finish tying the rope. The finished effect is perfect. It looks intentional.

Rosie is waiting for us in the kitchen. Addy and Megs walk out first, then I come behind. Rosie looks at me, confused at first. Then the intent dawns on her. She squeals and runs over to me.

"Aww, did you dress up as a bug I caught?"

"Well, I prefer to think of myself as someone you'll suck off later. But sure, we can go with a bug."

She squeals again as Addy and Megs burst into laughter. Addy's brazenness has definitely worn off on me. I've found it's much more fun to say something wild and unexpected. Rosie isn't usually impressed, but she didn't playfully hit me tonight.

We load up the car and drive to the club. Rosie is a little chatterbox tonight. She hasn't stopped talking since we left. She's telling us all about the Halloween party she had in her class. I'm so happy to see her this excited. She deserves to be this happy all the time. They all do. Once we arrive at the club, we climb out of the car. Rosie recognizes the building, asking what we are doing here. I pull her into my arms while Megs and Addy walk ahead.

"Rosie, it's been a wild summer for us. You have dealt with a ridiculous situation and have bounced back so beautifully. You are everything to me, to all of us. I wish I could give you the world. But I can't do that since I don't own it, and I don't think you can technically own the world." She laughs at me, her face softening. "Since I can't give you the world, I will give you something else entirely within my power." I nod my head back towards the club. "There is a party going on in there that we all have tickets to attend, but we also have rented a certain room." Her eyes sparkle with hope and understanding. "Tonight, little minx, you can tie me up and do with me as you please."

"Really?"

I nod, and she bounces up and down in my arms. I laugh at her response. My heart swells with love for her. She really is remarkable. All three of them are. I don't know how I went from sleeping in an alley to dating three of the best people in the world, but I thank Mother Fortune daily for that turn of events. Rosie kisses me quickly, then pulls me towards the door. We catch up with Addy and Megs and make our way inside.

Once inside, we settle at a table to watch other people. Our room rental isn't for another hour. So now we can drink, dance, kiss, and enjoy each other's presence. I stay close to Rosie, feeding off her energy. I'm feeling nervous. Being a bottom in these scenarios is new to me. I trust Rosie completely but still have jitters from a new experience.

Addy has already wandered off to talk to people. Megs is sitting at the table, just watching others. Most people are sitting at tables or walking around the central area. I wrap my arm around Rosie. She's been playing on her phone since we got through the door. I nuzzle into her neck, needing contact to clear my mind. From past experience, my nerves will die down once the scene gets started. I just need to make it until that point. Rosie all but ignores me. Accidentally, I glance down at Rosie's phone. She is looking through photos of Shibari poses.

"Do you have a plan?"

"Not really. I've never topped a suspension. I've always been in the ropes."

She swipes through several more images then taps on one. In the photo, the man is suspended, his stomach down, his arms tied behind his back, and his legs spread far apart. My stomach squeezes tight with nerves. "Is that what you want?" My voice sounds weak, but I don't actually care right now. Rosie finally looks up at me, and she giggles at my face.

"No, love. I won't do that to you. I have no intentions of pegging you tonight. I don't need your asshole exposed."

I give a super awkward laugh that is just puffs of air, leaving my body with a 'ha' sound. She has intentions of pegging me one night? Whew, I think someone just turned on the furnace. It's sweltering in here all of a sudden. I sip my water, trying to remember how to breathe normally. Rosie laughs, seeing my physical reaction.

"Don't worry. It'll be fine."

I nod, not sure anything will be fine. Addy comes running over to us.

"They're doing a costume contest, and I signed you two up as a couple. You have to be over there," Addy points over her shoulder to a corner of the room, then looks at her wrist, where she isn't wearing a watch, "two minutes ago."

Rosie looks excited and hops up, pulling me with her. I didn't know about a costume contest, but I am glad the rope Addy and Megs so exquisitely tied will be appreciated by others. I follow along, lining up with the other couples. An announcer uses a microphone attached to a small speaker on the floor to get everyone's attention.

"Attention, guys, gals, and all other pals!"

A smirk crosses my face at the inclusive greeting. It covers nonbinary people, pets, and anyone else in the room.

"Before we start our demonstrations and room rentals, we're going to have a costume contest!"

People around the room begin cheering.

"Let's start with our couples!!" The announcer really knows how to work the crowd here. "Winners will be chosen based on how much noise the audience makes. First up, a classic. Owner and their kitty."

There are a few cheers around the room. Nothing too crazy. That couple won't win.

"Next, a couple of ponies."

A couple dressed in lingerie with horse masks and hooves steps forward. Again, there is some applause, but not a lot.

"Now we have a nurse and her patient."

There is more cheering, but I think Rosie and I can take them.

"And, last, but certainly not least, this is one I haven't seen before. A spider and a tied-up bug!"

"Um, it's actually a spider and the prey she's going to suck later," Rosie adds into the microphone.

My cheeks flush this time as she smirks at me. She wraps one arm around my back, pulling me close. She rises on her toes, placing her lips against my neck. Her costume has legs off to the side that are flapping against me. The crowd is cheering raucously. We definitely won that.

"Well, folks, you called it. The spider and the prey she will suck off later are our winners! I hope we can watch that!" The announcer waggles his eyebrows at us, but Rosie shakes her head. The announcer hands us a small gift bag, then we return to the table. The announcer is already moving on to the individual contest, but we aren't listening. When we reach the table, Addy takes the bag, asking what's in it. She opens it. There are a couple samples of lube, a small bullet vibrator, and two half-off coupons from a local toy shop. Not a bad prize for a contest I didn't know about or agree to enter.

The demonstrations begin after the individual costume contest, and we can go to the rooms. Addy assures me we will come back sometime to watch the demonstrations. She says she likes watching as much as she enjoys participating. Once we get to the room, Rosie moves around, assessing the space. There isn't a bed. Just a frame with several adjustable loops. There is rope hanging on the walls, along with a dresser that probably has other items. Megs follows along with Rosie, speaking quietly with her. Addy is closing the curtains and locking the door, ensuring we won't be interrupted. Rosie calls out to have Addy remove the ropes I'm currently in. Addy steps up to me but stops.

"Wait, let's take a picture of you together first."

We agreed not to take photos of demonstrations or other people in the room. They didn't want to allow phones in but didn't take them from us. I stand next to Rosie as Addy snaps a few pictures. She slips her phone into a nearly invisible pocket in her leather suit, then waves me over to start removing the rope. She works diligently, having it off in just a few minutes. I turn and walk to Rosie in the middle of the room. She has removed her costume and is standing in her bra and panties. They don't match, and I love it. She likes to have a matching set if she will be showing them off, but she probably wasn't expecting to be a rigger tonight. I start to remove my own clothes, but she stops me.

"I'll do that in a minute. First." She steps up, wrapping her arms around me, pulling me into a long kiss. I return her kiss, feeling more settled than I have since we left the apartment. When she pulls away, she whispers, "Thank you." Then steps back from me. "Tonight, I'm going to do a partial suspension, play with you for a bit, then let you down. Megs will be helping me with rigging. Addy is basically watching, probably touching herself, just generally being a creep."

"Definitely touching herself," Addy interjects.

Rosie rolls her eyes. "I won't be using safe words. 'No' will be fine. I'll check in frequently, making sure you're okay. You have to talk to me. If things do get too intense and you prefer to use your safe word, I'll honor it, but you don't have to. You can just say 'Stop.' Okay?"

"Okay."

She nods, then steps up. She fingers the hem of my shirt, her fingers skimming my skin underneath. The touch sends a jolt down my spine to my balls. I'm so ready to see what she does. "I want you to enjoy this too. Don't let it get uncomfortable, okay?" I nod again, my mouth suddenly dry. She pulls my shirt over my head, pressing her lips against my nipple. I watch. I love seeing her against my chest. Her fingers begin working at the waist of my jeans. She soon has it undone, pushing them down. I step out of the jeans and boxers, and she tosses them into a pile with my shirt and her clothes. Her fingers scrape up and down my body, but she is careful not to touch my cock. I desperately want her to, though.

Rosie

I walk around James, admiring his body. After his breakdown at his house, when he returned to full health, he started working out with Megs. It's been just over two months, but the effort is already showing. His muscles are more defined, and he looks more muscular. I liked the way he looked before. He was fit but not athletic. His muscles were visible but not very defined. I am certainly not complaining about the work he puts in now. Plus, Megs finally has a gym buddy, and they've stopped bugging Addy and me to go. Win-win for everyone.

I drag my fingers over his shoulders, pulling his arms behind his back. "Let's get started, big guy." Megs brings me a length of rope, bight already in place. I've done some bondage on other people. Megs has let me practice on them, but it doesn't lead to sex. Addy doesn't like being tied up and also has zero patience. I can get her in a basic hold, but that's about it. It is fun with Addy because she fights it so much. If she breaks free, the scene takes a turn and gets even more exciting. But tonight, with James, this will be different. This will be sexual and for aesthetics. This will be for me.

The rope wraps around his arms, tying them together first. I slide my fingers between all contact points on his skin, ensuring there is enough space. After securing his arms sufficiently, I move around him, pulling the rope around his chest. I make loops and knots, creating one connection spot at the center of his chest. His eyes are intent on me as I work. Megs hovers to the side, ready to step in if needed. Addy is lurking in the corner somewhere out of my sight. I stay focused on my rope and James. Once I am done with the chest harness, I ask how he is doing. His response is breathy, but that's from his arousal. His cock is hard, sticking out from his body.

I take another length of rope to make a harness around his waist. I don't plan on suspending his lower half, but it looks so sexy. I wrap it around his hips, then separate the two pieces, using each piece to create loops and rings around his legs. I kneel in front of him as I work. I take extra care not to touch his member or get too close. I didn't mean this to be so teasing, but I'm not mad about that either. I tie off the rope around his ankles. His legs are separated, and he can move them as he sees fit. I nod to Megs. They walk over with one of the hooks from the frame.

"We're going to lift you now. You won't be completely off the ground, but you'll be on your toes. The frame will support you. Tell me if it's too much." He nods to me. Megs connects the hook to the harness I created. They double-check my knots, then we lift James up. Just a couple of inches. The harness pulls on his chest, forcing it out. His back arches, creating beautiful lines with his body. His head drops, watching me as he does. I've never seen anything more perfect. My core is flooded. The only reason I am not dripping on the floor is that I still have my panties on. I step up to him, standing in a chair beside him, cradling his head as I kiss him deeply. He returns my kiss. One arm stays wrapped around his head, the other moves to caress his body. I run my fingers along the skin and the taut ropes. It's so delicious. My pussy is clenching around nothing, aroused just by seeing him in the ropes.

I finally break the kiss and climb around to his front. I graze my fingers along his erect cock. A deep groan escapes his lips. I wrap my fingers around his cock, stroking up and down slowly. "Tell us if you need something. Now it's time to play." His hips jerk towards me. I lean down, wrapping my lips around the tip of his cock. He groans again. His body sways, telling me he is lifting off his toes. I wrap my arm around his hips to keep him in place. I continue sucking, taking him in as deep as I can. I press my tongue against the underside of his member as I pull back, swirling around the tip before I plunge down again. His hips thrust harder against my mouth. He is groaning louder than usual. He doesn't normally make a lot of noise during sex. Apparently, being suspended turns him into a moaner.

His hips are moving more erratically. He is getting closer to orgasm. I take all of him in my mouth, my chin pressed against his balls. I look up at Megs, making eye contact. With one hand, I motion for her to raise him up. It would probably be more effective if I took his dick out of my mouth and used my words, but where is the fun in that. His body raises until the tips of his toes are on the floor. I wrap both arms around his waist. I slide my mouth back to the end of his cock, licking the head.

"Fuck Rosie."

I slide him back into my mouth slowly, taking my time on the way down. He jerks again, thrusting himself to the back of my throat. I pull off all the way this time. "Fuck my mouth, James. Thrust your hips until you come down my throat." He groans, tightening his legs around my body to get some stability. I place my lips over the tip of his cock. I feel his ass tighten against my arms as he thrusts. I help him, bobbing up and down but letting him push against me too. His movements become erratic. His breathing is fast and shallow. His body arches more, and his balls tighten. He curses as he explodes down my throat. I hold him tight against my body, bobbing up and down slowly, sucking the last bit of pleasure out of him. My own pussy is soaked, almost unbearable. His body goes slack against mine. I pull back, nodding to Megs to drop him down. They lower him, stepping behind him to support the weight change.

His face is colored with pleasure. I wrap my fingers around his neck, massaging lightly. I kiss him deeply, letting him taste the last remnants of him in my mouth. I pull back, smiling at him. He seems to be able to support his weight now.

"How are you?"

"Perfect." He mumbles, still riding the high of the orgasm.

"Would you like to get down? Or would you like to lick me?"

His eyes go wide. "I want to lick you. Tied up like this?" I nod to him.

"This time, we'll lower you to the ground, stopping about," I hold my hand in front of my core, "here. I'll stand over you while you lick. It won't take me long." I slip a finger through my core, bringing it back to show James. I slip it inside his mouth. "I'm already very worked up from having you tied up." His tongue swirls against my finger in his mouth. When I pull it back, he says, "Yes, please. Yes. Let's do that!" I chuckle at his enthusiasm. It makes me happy.

I call Addy over to help lower him. Megs works the controls while I support his back. Addy holds his feet in the proper position to stretch him out. Once he is at the right height, I ask Addy to bring the chair over for me. I turn it around, propping my arms against the back. I'm not great at supporting my weight during an orgasm, and I plan to have at least one. I suspect it'll be a strong one too. I remove my bra and panties. I take a moment to appreciate James in this position. He is twisting to see what I am doing. I walk along his side, running my fingers over his skin, feeling the rope digging in some places. He is absolutely exquisite tied up like this. Finally, I reach his head. Before I step over him, I speak to him again.

"If this is too much, please stop and tell me. We can let you down quickly."

He almost looks angry at my reminder, like nothing would stop him from eating my pussy. I smile, then step over his head. Before I can fully get into position, his lips are against me. He is kissing and licking. I rest my forehead on my arms against the chair, looking down to watch him. I drop one hand to the top of his head, grabbing his hair. He licks straight through my core, up to my clit, thrusting into it several times. I moan loudly, knowing my orgasm isn't far away. His tongue slides back, pumping in and out of my core. I press against his face, squatting lower to get more contact. He is swaying in the harness. He is getting frustrated at the extra movement. I love the shifts of his head against me. It's an extra tease without the effort.

He slams his legs out, forcing his head tightly against my legs. He's figured out how to use his legs to hold him in place against me. This puts him in the perfect place to suck my clit into his mouth. That is precisely what he does. He covers it and sucks savagely. I release his head, using both hands to grip the chair as my orgasm rips through me. My hips grind against his face. He keeps my clit in his mouth as my pussy clenches and leaks against his chin. My body spasms once, then twice, as it floats back to reality. He releases my clit, swiping his tongue in long, slow movements across my soaking core. It feels euphoric as my orgasm subsides.

I move to step off him, but my legs are wobbly. Megs reaches out, supporting me until I can sit in the chair. I laugh, thanking them. I look down at James, who has a sinister grin. I lean over and kiss him upside down. I can taste myself all over his face. The kiss is awkward in this position, so I keep it short. Addy steps up to help Megs raise him and remove the harness. He steps towards me unhooked, dropping to his knees before me. He crawls between my legs, pressing his lips to mine. I grab onto the side of his head, kissing him deeply. It isn't a kiss meant to arouse or express love. This kiss is a reconnection of two souls shattered with pleasure then put back together.

We finally break the kiss. I rest my forehead against his. We are both breathing deeply.

"Move back so I can untie you."

I start working on his chest harness. Megs comes up behind him, releasing his arms. As we work on the knots, Addy steps up next to us.

"Holy fuck. I don't know that I have ever seen anything that hot. I've seen some crazy shit, but that was, like, next-level porn. And I got some super awesome videos of it too." She holds her phone towards us, showing us several videos and more than twice as many photographs. I roll my eyes at her antics. As we release James from the harness, I rub his arms, letting the feeling return to them. He rubs his wrist in front of his chest, then quickly wraps them around my face, kissing me again.

I laugh into the kiss, pulling back from him. "I take it you really liked that? Stand up so we can get the rest off." He does as he is told. Then answers my question.

"Yeah, I was pretty nervous about it, but that was way better than I expected. I may be a rope bunny." We all laugh at his comment.

Five months ago, when Addy sent us a text telling us she was bringing a guy home, I never expected it would work out like this. We found a member of our group. We added a fourth roommate that is one of us, not just with one of us. James has completed our group in a way we never anticipated. I don't know what the future will bring, but I can handle anything with James, Addy, and Megs.

If you enjoyed Roommates, Please check out my socials and other books.

Go to APRILGAISFORD.COM

PS, Rosie makes an appearance with an update in Corrupt Goddess

Also by

Sweet Briar Series

A why choose fairy tale series about a cursed princess who must find her true love. Spicy, queer, and magical.

Curses and Thunder

Fate and Lightning

Hidden Gods Series

A series of dark romance ranging from sapphic mafia, FFM motorcycle club, MMF mafia, and more.

Corrupt Goddess

Broken Good

Secret God (coming 2025)

About the author

April is a non-binary parent living in Minnesota. They are an avid reader, with a special interest in smut. They love collecting random things, such as coffee mugs, posters, graphic tees, scrunchies, and more. They love long romantic trips around Target and buying new books to add to their emotional support pile.

Acknowledgements

My first acknowledgment has to be my husband. This book wouldn't be complete without your push. Thank you for encouraging and putting up with my crazy ideas. Thank you for being my sounding board and answering all my super random questions. Thanks for keeping the kids away when I was trying to focus!

My bestie from another teste, Stephanie, you my bitch, girl. Thank you for reading and offering your ideas. You're the Addy to my Megs. I love you!

To my actual sister, I apologize for all the unwanted comments and information you received about our sex life. Thank you for being my emotional support ace.

To my brother-in-law, Sam, thanks for recommending a laptop five years ago that got me through a graphic design degree and now a book. I couldn't have done it without that! Be sure to tell all your friends you are acknowledged in a book, and they should buy it!

Last, but not least, my mother. While I hope she never reads this book, I'm glad for the support and help she has offered. I should probably send her some pearls to clutch if she ever does read the book.

And a huge thank you to all my readers. I hope you enjoyed it! Stay spicy, little minxes!